大学英语四级考试阅读
真题多维突破

主　编　杨廷君　李跃平

编写人员　（以拼音为序）

冯彩燕　李跃平　梁　虹　凌　民

裴光兰　单春昕　邬蔚群　熊　艳

杨　国　杨　艳　杨廷君

国防工业出版社

·北京·

内 容 简 介

本书精选大学英语四级考试阅读真题 55 篇，从段落译文、难词释义、写译语块、难句分析、原题再现、单词详解和句子翻译 7 个方面对篇章进行全面、透彻的讲解。

本书可供备考大学英语四级考试的考生使用，也可供英语学习者自学提高选用。

图书在版编目(CIP)数据

大学英语四级考试阅读真题多维突破/杨廷君，李跃平
主编. —北京：国防工业出版社，2011.4
ISBN 978-7-118-07343-0

Ⅰ.①大… Ⅱ.①杨… ②李… Ⅲ.①大学英语
水平考试－阅读教学－自学参考资料 Ⅳ.①H319.4

中国版本图书馆 CIP 数据核字(2011)第 038053 号

※

*国防工业出版社*出版发行
（北京市海淀区紫竹院南路 23 号　邮政编码 100048）
北京嘉恒彩色印刷有限责任公司
新华书店经售
*
开本 710×960　1/16　**印张** 17¼　**字数** 336 千字
2011 年 4 月第 1 版第 1 次印刷　**印数** 1—4000 册　**定价** 29.00 元

(本书如有印装错误，我社负责调换)

国防书店：(010)68428422　　　发行邮购：(010)68414474
发行传真：(010)68411535　　　发行业务：(010)68472764

前　言

评价一个英语学习者的语言应用能力,须从听、说、读、写、译这五个方面进行综合考查。任何英语爱好者都知道,要把自己的英语提升到一个理想的高度,这五个方面应该均衡发展。在具体的学习过程中,我们各个击破,先把这五种能力分为"听、说"和"读、写、译"两大板块,在此基础上分项发展。

由于中国学习者是学习英语,而不是习得英语,所以,要学好英语就必须阅读大量的文献,以确保足够量的语言输入,在此基础上再反复模仿和运用,最终内化这些知识,像母语者那样运用英语。为了帮助中国学习者学好英语,不少英语专业人士编写了针对性强、质量较高的学习辅导用书,但这些用书多是按照专项编写,没有把读、写、译有机地融合在一起;有鉴于此,我们组织了长期从事大学英语教学的一线教师,编写了这本《大学英语四级考试阅读真题多维突破》。

该书从【段落译文】、【难词释义】、【写译语块】、【难句分析】、【原题再现】、【单词详解】、【句子翻译】等方面帮助学生解构大学英语四级考试的阅读文章。这七个方面不但将读、写、译有机地结合在一起,还融入了词汇和语法,因为学习任何语言,词汇量是基础,语法是正确地遣词造句的保证。编者希望将读、写、译、词汇和语法有机融合在一起的这种多维模式能够对英语学习者,特别是对想提高英语阅读能力以及备战大学英语四级考试的人员有所裨益。

本书由杨廷君(宁波大学)和李跃平(西南民族大学)主持编写,并负责全书的策划和编写体例的设计,具体编写分工为:杨廷君(第1—4篇)、梁虹(第5—8篇)、杨国(第9—12篇)、熊艳(第13—17篇)、邬蔚群(第18—22篇)、杨艳(第23—28篇)、单春昕(第29—34篇)、冯彩燕(第35—42篇)、李跃平(第43—46篇)、裴光兰(第47—50篇)、凌民(第51—55篇)。全书由杨廷君统稿,李跃平审校。

由于编者水平有限,难免有错漏和不当之处,热忱欢迎广大专家、学者和读者批评指正。

编　者
2011年1月于宁大花园

目　录

Passage One

You never see them, but they're with you every time you fly. They record where you're going, how fast you're traveling and whether everything on your airplane is functioning normally. *Their ability to withstand almost any disaster* makes them seem like something out of a **comic** book. They're known as the black box.

When planes fall from the sky, as a Yemeni airliner did *on its way to the Comoros Islands* in the Indian Ocean June 30, 2009, the black box is the best bet for identifying what went wrong. So when a French **submarine** detected the device's homing signal five days later, the discovery *marked a huge step toward* determining the cause of a tragedy in which 152 passengers were killed.

In 1958, Australian scientist David Warren developed a flight-memory recorder that would **track** basic information like **altitude** and direction. That was the first model for a black box, which became a requirement on all U. S. commercial flights by 1960. Early models often failed to withstand **crashes**, however, so in 1965 the device was completely redesigned and moved to the **rear** of the plane - *the area least subject to impact*—from its original position in the **landing** wells. That same year, the Federal Aviation Authority required that the boxes, which were never actually black, be painted orange or yellow to aid **visibility**.

Modem airplanes have two black boxes: a voice recorder, which tracks pilots' conversations, and a flight-data recorder, which **monitors** fuel levels, engine noises and other operating functions that help investigators reconstruct the aircraft's final moments. Placed in an **insulated case** and surrounded by quarter-inch-thick panels of stainless steel, the boxes can withstand massive force and temperatures up to 2,000 ℉. When submerged, they're also able to **emit** signals from depths of 20,000 ft. Experts believe the boxes from Air France Flight 447, which crashed near Brazil on June 1, 2009, are *in water nearly that deep*, but **statistics** say they're still likely to turn up. In the **approximately** 20 deep-sea crashes over the past 30 years, only one plane's black boxes were never recovered. (350 words) (2010 年 6 月第 1 篇)

【段落译文】

你从来都看不到它们,但是,你每次飞行它们都与你同行。它们记录你飞往何

1

方,飞行速度是多少,以及飞机上的一切是否正常。它们几乎能抵御任何灾难,这种能力使得它们看起来就像是来自漫画书里的东西一样。人们把它们称为"黑匣子"。

飞机从空中坠毁时,如 2009 年 6 月 30 日也门一架客机在印度洋上非洲科摩罗群岛坠毁,造成 152 名乘客罹难,黑匣子成为帮助确认事故原因的最好工具。五天后,一艘法国潜艇探测到该航班黑匣子导航信号时,灾难原因的确定更为具体。

1958 年,澳大利亚科学家 David Warren 研发出一个飞行记忆记录设备,追踪飞行高度和方向等基本信息,这就是黑匣子的原型。1960 年,美国要求所有商用飞机都必须安装黑匣子。早期型号的黑匣子往往在空难中损毁,因此,1965 年人们对其进行了全新设计。把它移到了机尾,不再放到飞机的起落架舱里,因为机尾受到的影响最小。同一年,美国联邦航空管理局要求所有黑匣子(虽然它们从来都不是黑色的)的颜色统一成橙色或黄色,以便识别。

现代飞机上有两个黑匣子:录音机和飞行信息记录仪。前者记录飞行员的谈话,后者监控油量和发动机的声音,以及其他运作功能,从而帮助调查者重构飞机失事前的情景。黑匣子装在一个密闭的盒子里,周围是厚度为 0.25 英寸的不锈钢板,能承受巨大的冲击力和 2000 华氏度的高温。即使在两万英尺深的水下,它也能发射信号。2009 年 6 月 1 日,法国航空公司 447 次航班在巴西附近坠毁,专家认为黑匣子就处于水下那个深度,不过数据显示,这些黑匣子很可能会最终重现天日。在过去 30 年,近 20 架坠毁于深海的飞机中,只有一架飞机的黑匣子未被找到。

【难词解释】

comic 连环画的	**submarine** 潜水艇
altitude 高度	**track** 跟踪,追踪
crash(飞机)坠毁	**rear** 后部
landing wells 起落架舱	**visibility** 能见度
monitor 监控,监视	**insulated case** 隔绝窗
emit 发出	**statistics** 统计资料,技术资料
approximately 大约	

【写译语块】

1. their ability to withstand almost any disaster 它们能经受几乎任何灾难的能力
2. on its way to the Comoros Islands (飞往)科摩罗群岛途中
3. mark a huge step toward 标志着向……迈出了一大步

4. the area least subject to impact 最不容易受冲击的地方

5. in water nearly that deep 那样深的水中

【难句分析】

1. (第一段第一句)在句子 You never see them，but they're with you every time you fly 中，every time 用作连词，其语法功能相当于 when，as soon as 等引导时间状语从句的连词，具有类似用法的还有 each time，the moment 等。例如：Each time she moves her head she lets out a moan (她每转动一下头，就发出一声呻吟)。

2. (第三段最后一句)句子 That same year，the Federal Aviation Authority required that the boxes，which were never actually black，be painted orange or yellow to aid visibility. 中，动词 required 后面宾语从句的谓语动词使用虚拟语气。该宾语从句内含一个分隔结构，即主语所带的定语从句(which were never actually black，)，orange or yellow 在句中用作主语补足语，不定式 to aid visibility 是目的状语。

3. (第四段第三句)句子 When submerged，they're also able to emit signals from depths of 20,000 ft. 中，when submerged 由从句 when they are submerged 省略而来。在条件、时间、方式等状语从句中，如果主从句主语相同，从句谓语动词是"be＋动词过去分词"形式，可以简化为"连词＋过去分词"结构。例如：If invited (＝ If he is ionvited)，he will come to the party. When locked in prison (＝When he was locked in prison)，he mastered English and German.

【原题再现】

1. What does the author say about the black box?

   A) It ensures the normal functioning of an airplane.

   B) The idea for its design comes from a comic book.

   C) Its ability to ward off disasters is incredible.

   D) It is an indispensable device on an airplane.

2. What information could be found from the black box on the Yemeni airliner?

   A) Data for analyzing the cause of the crash.

   B) The total number of passengers on board.

   C) The scene of the crash and extent of the damage.

   D) Homing signals sent by the pilot before the crash.

3. Why was the black box redesigned in 1965?

A) New materials became available by that time.

B) Too much space was needed for its installation.

C) The early models often got damaged in the crash.

D) The early models didn't provide the needed data.

4. Why did the Federal Aviation Authority require the black boxes be painted orange or yellow?

A) To distinguish them from the color of the plane.

B) To caution people to handle them with care.

C) To make them easily identifiable.

D) To conform to international standards.

5. What do we know about the black boxes from Air France Flight 447?

A) There is still a good chance of their being recovered.

B) There is an urgent need for them to be restructured.

C) They have stopped sending homing signals.

D) They were destroyed somewhere near Brazil.

【单词详解】

【重点单词】**withstand** / wið'stænd / *vt.*

[基本词义] 经受,承受,抵住

[用法导航] The walls can withstand high winds. 这些墙能顶得住强风。// Explorers have to withstand hardships. 探险者得忍受艰苦。

[对比记忆] (1)**sustain** / səs'tein / *vt.* 保持;维持(生命等);支持;经受

(2)**suffer** / 'sʌfə / *vt.* 遭受,蒙受;忍受,承受,容忍

(3)**bear** / bɛə / *vt.* 忍受;负担;承受;怀有;结(果实),生(孩子)

[真题衔接] The region needs housing which is strong enough to _____ severe wind and storms.

A) retain   B) tolerate   C) withstand   D) endure

【重点单词】**subject** / 'sʌbdʒikt / *n.* & *adj.*

[基本词义] 主题,题目;学科,科目;(to)受……支配的,取决于……的;易遭……的

[用法导航] My mother is very subject to headaches. 我母亲动不动就头痛。// At these stages these are proposals and are still subject to change. 在这个阶段,这些只是提议,仍然可以改变。

[对比记忆] (1)**liable** / 'laiəbl / *adj.* (to)可能的,大概的;(for)有法律责任的,有义务的;(to)易于……的,有……倾向的,易患……病的

(2)**prone** / prəun / *adj.* (to)易于……的,很可能……的;俯卧的

(3)**reject** / ri'dʒekt / *vt.* 拒绝;拒纳,退回,摈弃

(4)**project** / 'prɔdʒekt / *n.* 方案,计划,课题,项目;工程

(5)**eject** / i'dʒekt / *vt.* 驱逐,逐出;喷射,排出;弹出

［真题衔接］Care should be taken to decrease the length of time that one is _____ loud continuous noise.（研-1994）

　　A) subjected to 　B) filled with 　　C) associated with 　　D) dropped off

【句子翻译】

6. _____（当被问及经历时）, she told the interviewer she had been a movie star.

7. _____（每次你按下键盘）, you hear a faint but positive sound.

8. We are today in a better position to _____（经经济循环的跌宕起伏）.

9. Most building codes require that glass areas _____（至少应等于每单个房间地板面积的 10%）.

10. Avoidance of the contract releases both parties from their obligations under it, _____（对应负责的任何损害赔偿仍应负责）.

Passage Two

The $11 billion self-help industry is built on the idea that you should *turn negative thoughts* like "I never do anything right" *into* **positive ones** like "I can succeed." But was positive thinking **advocate** Norman Vincent Peale right? Is there power in positive thinking?

Researchers in Canada just published a study in the journal *Psychological Science* that says trying to get people to think more positively can actually have the opposite effect: it can simply **highlight** how unhappy they are.

The study's authors, Joanne Wood and John Lee of the University of Waterloo and Elaine Perunovic of the University of New Brunswick, begin by citing older research showing that when people get feedback which they believe is overly positive, they actually feel worse, not better. If you tell your *dim friend* that he has the potential of an Einstein, you're just **underlining** his faults. In one 1990s experiment, a team including psychologist Joel Cooper of Princeton asked participants to write essays opposing funding for the disabled. When the essayists were later praised for their **sympathy**, they felt even worse about what they had written.

In this experiment, Wood, Lee and Perunovic measured 68 students' **self-esteem.** The participants were then asked to write down their thoughts and feelings for four minutes. Every 15 seconds, one group of the students heard a bell. When it rang, they were supposed to tell themselves, "I am lovable."

Those with low self-esteem didn't feel better after the forced **self-affirmation.** In fact, their moods turned significantly darker than those of the members of the control group, who weren't urged to think positive thoughts.

The paper provides support for newer forms of **psychotherapy** that urge people to accept their negative thoughts and feelings rather than fight them. In the fighting, we not only often fail but can make things worse. **Meditation**（静思）techniques, in contrast, can teach people to put their shortcomings into a larger, more realistic **perspective.** Call it the power of negative thinking. (331 wrods)
(2010 年 6 月第 2 篇)

【段落译文】

110 亿美元的励志产业是基于这样的理念:你把诸如"我从来做不好任何事"这样的消极思维调整为诸如"我会成功"这样的积极思维。但是,推行积极思维的 Norman Vincent Pearl 真的对吗? 积极思维有用吗?

加拿大研究人员在《心理科学》杂志上撰文指出,试图让人们采用积极思维方式实际上会带来反面效果;这反而会突显他们有多么不开心。

此文的作者是来自滑铁卢大学的 Joanne Wood 和 John lee,以及来自 New Brunswick 大学的 Elain Perunovic。他们以引用过去的研究开篇,表明人们收到他们认为是过于积极地反馈时,实际上他们并未因此感觉好些,而是更糟。如果你告诉一个脑子不是很灵活的朋友,他有成为爱因斯坦的潜质,你只是在强调他的缺点。在一个 20 世纪 90 年代的实验中,包括普林斯顿大学心理学家 Joel Cooper 在内的一个小组要求参与者写文章反对设立残疾人基金。当文章作者稍后因为他们的同情心而受到赞许时,他们对当时所写的内容感觉更糟糕了。

在 Wood, lee 和 Perunovic 的实验中,他们测试了 68 名学生的自尊心。参与者被要求写下他们的想法和感受,该过程时长 4 分钟。其中一组每隔 15 秒听到一声铃响。铃响时,他们要对自己说"我很讨人喜欢"。

那些自尊较弱的受试者并不因为强加的自我肯定就会感觉好些。事实上,他们的情绪比那些没有受到积极思维激励的受试者要低落得多。

该论文支持更新形式的心理治疗,即促使他们接受自己的积极想法和感受,而不是一定要和它们抗争。在抗争过程中,我们不仅常常会失败,而且还会使事情变得更糟。相反,静思技巧能够教授人们以更大更实际的角度看待自己的缺点。不妨将其称为消极思考的力量。

【难词解释】

negative 反面的,消极的

positive 积极的,建设性的

advocate 拥护者,提倡者

highlight 强调,突出,使显著

underline 强调,使突出

sympathy 同情,同情心

self-esteem 自尊

self-affirmation 自我肯定

psychotherapy 心理治疗

meditation 静思

perspective 看法,观点

【写译语块】

1. turn negative thoughts into positive ones 把消极想法转变成积极想法
2. dim friend 悲观的朋友
3. those with low self-esteem 自尊心不强的学生
4. accept their negative thoughts and feelings rather than fight them 接受消极想法和感情,而不是排斥它们
5. in contrast 相反,形成对比

【难句分析】

1. (第一段第一句)句子 The $11 billion self-help industry is built on the idea that you should ***turn* negative *thoughts*** like "I never do anything right" ***into positive ones*** like "I can succeed."中,build on 的意思是"建立在……基础上,以……为基础";先行名词 the idea 后面是一个同位语从句;从句中,两个 like 引出的介词词组用作后位修饰语,修饰前面的词组 negative thoughts 和 positive ones,词组 turn ... into ... 的意思是"把……变成……"。

2. (第五段第二句)句子 In fact, their moods turned significantly darker than those of the members of the control group, who weren't urged to think positive thoughts 中,程度副词 significantly 修饰形容词比较级 darker,those 指上文提到的 students,the control group 指实证研究中的"对照组",who weren't urged to think positive thoughts 为非限制性定语从句。

【原题再现】

11. What do we learn from the first paragraph about the self-help industry?

A) It is a highly profitable industry.

B) It is based on the concept of positive thinking.

C) It was established by Norman Vincent Peale.

D) It has yielded positive results.

12. What is the finding of the Canadian researchers?

A) Encouraging positive thinking may do more harm than good.

B) There can be no simple therapy for psychological problems.

C) Unhappy people cannot think positively.

D) The power of positive thinking is limited.

13. What does the author mean by "... you're just underlining his faults" (Sentence 2, Para. 3)?

A) You are not taking his mistakes seriously enough.

B) You are pointing out the errors he has committed.

C) You are emphasizing the fact that he is not intelligent.

D) You are trying to make him feel better about his faults.

14. What do we learn from the experiment of Wood, Lee and Perunovic?

A) It is important for people to continually boost their self-esteem.

B) Self-affirmation can bring a positive change to one's mood.

C) Forcing a person to think positive thoughts may lower their self-esteem.

D) People with low self-esteem seldom write down their true feelings.

15. What do we learn from the last paragraph?

A) The effects of positive thinking vary from person to person.

B) Meditation may prove to be a good form of psychotherapy.

C) Different people tend to have different ways of thinking.

D) People can avoid making mistakes through meditation.

【单词详解】

【重点单词】 **potential** / pə'tenʃəl / *adj.* & *n.*

[基本词义] 潜在的,可能的;潜力,潜能

[用法导航] The dispute has scared away potential investors. 这一争端吓走了潜在的投资者。// She has acting potential, but she needs training. 她有表演潜力,但需要训练。// People under stress tend to express their full range of potential. 处于压力下的人容易发挥自己全部的潜力。

[词性转换] **potentiality** / pəu,tenʃi'æliti / *n.* 潜在性,(发展的)可能性

［对比记忆］(1)**latent** / ˈleitənt / *adj.* 潜在的,隐伏的,不易察觉的

［对比记忆］(2)**underlying** / ˈʌndəˈlaiiŋ / *adj.* 含蓄的,潜在的

［对比记忆］(3)**prospective** /prəsˈpektiv / *adj.* 预期的,未来的,可能的

［对比记忆］(4)**feasible** / ˈfiːzəbl / *adj.* 可行的,可能的,可用的

［真题衔接］There's a(n) _____ danger of being bitten when one plays with a strange dog.

A) potential 　　 B) principal 　　 C) immediate 　　 D) serious

【重点单词】**oppose**/ əˈpəuz / *vt.*

［基本词义］反对,反抗

［用法导航］At first he was opposed to the scheme, but we managed to argue him round. 他起初反对这个计划,可是我们通过辩论最终使他转变了态度。

［词性转换］**opposition** / ˌɔpəˈziʃən / *n.* 反对,反抗,对抗

［对比记忆］(1)**challenge** / ˈtʃælindʒ / *vt.* 反对,公然反抗;向……挑战;对……质疑

(2)**resist** / riˈzist / *vt.* 反抗,抵制;抗(病等),耐(热等);拒受……的影响

(3)**revolt** / riˈvəult / *vi.* 反叛,起义;反抗,违抗

(4)**protest** / ˈprəutest, prəˈtest / *v.* 抗议,反对

［真题衔接］The committee is totally opposed _____ any changes being made in the plans. (CET4-9901)

C) A) of 　　 B) on 　　 C) to 　　 D) against

【重点单词】**suppose** / səˈpəuz / *v.*

［基本词义］料想,猜想,以为;(用于祈使句)让,假定,设;(用于被动语态)期望,认为应该

［用法导航］I suppose (that) he's serious, isn't he? 我猜想他为人严肃,对吗? // Suppose (Supposing) we can't get the necessary equipment, what shall we do? 假设我们弄不到必要的设备,那我们怎么办? // It was supposed to be a surprise, but thanks to your big mouth she knows all about it now. 本来打算来一次惊喜的,但是,就怪你多嘴,她现在什么都知道了。

［对比记忆］(1)**compose** / kəmˈpəuz / *vt.* 组成,构成;创作(乐曲、诗歌等),为……谱曲;使平静,使镇静

(2)**dispose** / disˈpəuz / *vt.* 排列,布置 *vi.* (of)去掉,丢掉,处理,解决

(3)**expose** / iksˈpəuz / *vt.* 暴露;(to)使处于……作用(或影响)下;揭露

(4)**impose** / imˈpəuz / *vt.* (on)强加;征税,处以(罚款、监禁等)

(5)**propose** / prəˈpəuz / *v.* 提议,提出;打算,计划;求婚

9

[真题衔接] He's watching TV? He's _____ to be cleaning his room. (CET4-9706)

  A) known   B) supposed   C) regarded   D) considered

【句子翻译】

16. _____（本以为这种外套能防雨）, but the water has soaked through it.

17. _____（虽然许多人反对他的计划）, he engineered it through to final approval.

18. _____（高利率和潜在的出口市场上的保护主义）worsened the current account balance.

19. Their economy has expanded enormously in the last five years, whereas _____（相比之下，我们反而滑坡了）.

20. Daydreaming alone cannot _____（使你如愿以偿）and you should get down to work.

Passage Three

Throughout this long, *tense election*, everyone has *focused on the presidential candidates* and how they'll change America. Rightly so, but selfishly, *I'm more fascinated by* Michelle Obama and what she might be able to do, not just for this country, but for me as an African-American woman. As the potential First Lady, she would have the world's attention. And that means that for the first time people will have a chance to get up close and personal contact with the type of African-American woman they so rarely see.

Usually, the lives of black women *go largely unexamined*. The prevailing theory seems to be that we're *all hot-tempered* single mothers who can't keep a man. Even *in the world of make-believe*, black women still can't escape the stereotype of being eye-rolling, oversexed females raised by our never-married, alcoholic (酗酒的) mothers.

These images have helped define the way all women are viewed, including Michelle Obama. Before she ever gets the chance to *commit to a cause*, charity or foundation as First Lady, her most urgent and perhaps most complicated duty may be simple to be herself.

It won't be easy. Because few mainstream publications have *done in-depth features* on regular African-American women, little is known about who we are,

10

what we think and what we face *on a regular basis*. *For better or worse*, Michelle will represent us all.

Just as she will have her critics, she will also have millions of fans who usually *have little interest in* the First Lady. Many African-American blogs have written about what they'd like to see Michelle bring to the White House—mainly showing the world that a black woman can support her man and *raise a strong black family*. Michelle will have to work to please everyone—an impossible task. But for many African-American women like me, just a little of her poise, confidence and intelligence will *go a long way in* changing an image that's been around for far too long. (335 words) （2009 年 12 月第 1 篇）

【段落译文】

在持久激烈的总统竞选期间，每个人都把目光聚集在总统候选人身上，并密切关注着他们将如何改变美国。这样无可厚非。但自私点来说，我却对米歇尔·奥巴马更感兴趣，我不但想知道她能为我们国家做些什么，更想了解她能为像我这样的美国黑人做些什么。作为有望成为第一夫人的她，将成为世界的焦点。这意味着人们将第一次有机会近距离接触到他们以前了解甚少的另一类美国黑人妇女。

通常情况下，人们很少会去探究黑人妇女的生活。我们黑人妇女在人们头脑中比较常见的形象似乎是脾气暴躁的单亲妈妈，守不住自己男人的女人。甚至在虚幻世界中，黑人妇女依然摆脱不了固定的形象，通常都是眼球转个不停，纵欲，由她们终身未婚且酗酒成性的母亲抚养长大。

在公众眼里，黑人妇女就是这种形象，米歇尔·奥巴马也不例外。作为第一夫人，她可以有机会致力于自己的事业，资助慈善团体，建立基金会，但在此之前，她最为紧迫的，可能也是最为复杂的职责就是如何做好自己。

这并不是件容易的事，因为很少会有主流刊物去深入细致地报道普通黑人妇女，所以人们不知道我们这些普通黑人妇女到底是些什么样的人，我们在想些什么，我们面临着什么样的问题。现在不管怎样，米歇尔可以代表我们这个群体。

正如她也会有批评者一样，她也会拥有上百万的忠实粉丝，而这些人通常对以前的第一夫人并不感兴趣。很多黑人在博客中写了他们希望看到米歇尔带给白宫的东西——主要是向这个世界展示一个黑人妇女既可以支持她的丈夫也可以支撑一个大家庭。米歇尔必须要努力工作让每个人感到满意——这是件可望不可及的事情。但对像我这样的很多黑人妇女来讲，她沉着、自信、聪慧，仅仅是这些品质中的一小部分就能大大改善长久以来人们心中的黑人妇女形象。

【难词释义】

fascinate 迷住;强烈地吸引

stereotype 刻板模式、

foundation 基金会

poise 沉着

prevailing 占优势的,主要的

charity 慈善事业

mainstream 主流,主要倾向

【写译语块】

1. tense election 激烈的选举
2. focus on the presidential candidate（把目光）集中在总统候选人身上
3. be fascinated by 被……吸引
4. go largely unexamined 没有被探究
5. in the world of make-believe 在虚幻的世界里
6. commit to a cause 致力于一项事业
7. do in-depth features on sth. 对……做深入的报道
8. on a regular basis 定期
9. for better or worse 不管是好是坏
10. have little interest in 对……几乎没有兴趣
11. raise a strong black family 支撑一个大家庭
12. go a long way in changing an image 要走的路还很远;对……有帮助

【难句分析】

1. （第一段第二句）在 Rightly so, but selfishly, I'm more fascinated by Michelle Obama and what she might be able to do, not just for this country, but for me as an African-American woman. 中的 rightly so 和 but selfishly 是句子副词,它们修饰后面的整个句子,体现了作者的态度和看法。not ... but ... 引出平行结构,其前后使用具有相同句法功能的词组。例如 He came not by bus but on foot.（他步行来的,没有坐公交汽车）。

2. （第二段段首）Usually, the lives of black women go largely unexamined. 句中的 go 是连系动词,其用法与 remain 相似,后面接用带有否定前缀 un-的过去分词,该过去分词表示主语所处的状态。

3. （最后一段末尾）在 But for many African-American women like me, just a little of her poise, confidence and intelligence will go a long way in changing an image that's been around for far too long 中,African-American 表示来自非洲的

美国人或非洲裔美国人,就是黑人。poise, confidence and intelligence 三个名词并列,描写第一夫人;go a long way 字面意思是"步行很远的路",此处转义为"对······大有帮助"。

【原题再现】

21. Why does Michelle Obama hold a strong fascination for the author?
    A) She serves as a role model for African women.
    B) She possesses many admirable qualities becoming a First Lady.
    C) She will present to the world a new image of African-American women.
    D) She will pay closer attention to the interests of African-American women.

22. What is the common stereotype of African-American women according to the author?
    A) They are victims of violence.
    B) They are of an inferior violence.
    C) They use quite a lot of body language.
    D) They live on charity and social welfare.

23. What do many African-Americans write about in their blogs?
    A) Whether Michelle can live up to the high expectations of her fans.
    B) How Michelle should behave as a public figure.
    C) How proud they are to have a black woman in the White House.
    D) What Michelle should do as wife and mother in the White House.

24. What does the author say about Michelle Obama as a First Lady?
    A) However many fans she has, she should remain modest.
    B) She shouldn't disappoint the African-American community.
    C) However hard she tries, she can't expect to please everybody.
    D) She will give priority to African-American women's concerns.

25. What do many African-American women hope Michelle Obama will do?
    A) Help change the prevailing view about black women.
    B) Help her husband in the task of changing America.
    C) Outshine previous First Lady.
    D) Fully display her fine qualities.

【单词详解】

【重点单词】 fascinate / ˈfæsineit / vt.

13

［基本词义］迷住,使神魂颠倒;强烈地吸引

［用法导航］I watched her, fascinated. 我瞧着她,完全被她迷住了。// The children are fascinated by the toy in the shop window. 孩子们被商店橱窗里的玩具吸引住了。

［词性转换］(1) **fascination** / ˌfæsiˈneiʃən / n. 魅力,有魅力的东西

(2) **fascinating** / ˈfæsineitiŋ / adj. 迷人的;极美的;极好的

［对比记忆］(1) **capture** / ˈkæptʃə / vt. 俘虏,捕获;夺得,占领 n. 俘获,捕获

(2) **attract** / əˈtrækt / vt. 吸引,引起……的注意

(3) **charm** / tʃɑːm / n. 迷人的特性;魅力;符咒,咒文 vt. 吸引,迷住

(4) **enchant** / inˈtʃɑːnt / vt. 使陶醉,使入迷;使着魔,用妖术迷惑

［真题衔接］The circus has always been very popular because it _____ both the old and the young. (CET6-0309)

A) facilitates B) fascinates C) immerses D) indulges

【句子翻译】

26. I enjoyed spending time with Griz, _____(定期给他特别照料).

27. Because _____(我所有的信都没有得到答复), I gave up the project.

28. I immediately embarked on an experiment which, even though it failed to get rid of the ants, _____(使我整整一天着了迷).

29. _____(不管是好还是坏), there could be no turning back on the high road to international responsibility.

30. If you _____(注重你配偶的良好品质), she'll be more loving.

Passage Four

When next year's crop of high-school graduates arrive at Oxford University in the fall of 2009, they'll be joined by a new face: Andrew Hamilton, the 55-year-old provost of Yale, who'll become Oxford's vice-chancellor—a position equivalent to university president in America.

Hamilton isn't the only educator crossing the Atlantic. Schools in France, Egypt, Singapore, etc, have also recently *made top-level hires from abroad.* Higher education has become a big and competitive business nowadays, and like so many businesses, it's gone global. Yet *the talent flow* isn't universal. High-level personnel tend to head in only one direction: outward from America.

The chief reason is that American schools don't tend to seriously consider looking abroad. For example, when the board of the University of Colorado searched for a new president, it wanted *a leader familiar with the state government*, a major source of the university's budget. "We didn't do any global consideration," says Patricia Hayes, the board's chair. The board ultimately picked Bruce Benson, a 69-year-old Colorado businessman and political activist who is likely to do well in the main task of modern university presidents: fund-raising. Fund-raising is a distinctively American thing, since U. S. schools *rely heavily on donations*. *The fund-raising ability* is largely a product of experience and necessity.

Many European universities, meanwhile, are still mostly dependent on government funding. But government support has failed to *keep pace with rising student number*. *The decline in government support* has made funding-raising an increasing necessary ability among administrators and has hiring committees hungry for Americans.

In the past few years, prominent schools around the world have joined the trend. In 2003, when Cambridge University appointed Alison Richard, another former Yale provost, as its vice-chancellor, the university publicly stressed that in her previous job she had overseen "a major strengthening of Yale's financial position."

Of course, fund-raising isn't the only skill outsiders offer. The globalization of education means more universities will be seeking heads with international experience of some kind to promote international programs and attract a global student body. Foreigners can offer a fresh perspective on established practices.
(2009年12月第2篇)

【段落译文】

2009年秋天毕业的高中生进入牛津大学时,迎接他们的是一个新的面孔:安德鲁·汉密尔顿,55岁的耶鲁大学教务长。他将担任牛津大学副校长,这一职位相当于美国大学的校长。

汉密尔顿并不是第一位跨越大西洋到外国任职的教育家。法国、埃及、新家坡等一些国家的学校近年来纷纷从国外聘请学校的高层管理人员。像其他商业活动一样,如今,高等教育已成为极具竞争力的商业行为,并且日渐全球化。但是人才的流动并不是世界性的。高层的管理人员往往来自一个地方:美国。

其主要原因是美国的学校并不真地想从海外聘请人才。例如,科罗拉多大学董事会在遴选新校长时,想聘用一个与州政府熟悉的领导人,因为州政府是学校的主要资金来源。"我们不会在全球范围内聘用校长"，校董主席帕特里夏·海说。该校最终聘用了布鲁斯·本森，69 岁的科罗拉多州商人、政治活动家。他能够胜任现代大学校长的主要职务：筹措资金。筹措资金颇具美国特色，因为美国大学的运转主要依赖捐款。长期的经验和需求造就了他们募集资金的能力。

与此同时，很多欧洲大学仍然依靠政府投入。而政府的投入却没能跟上不断扩大的学生规模。政府投入的减少，使得筹措资金成为学校管理者的必备能力，于是对美国的人才求贤若渴。

在过去几年里，世界各地的优秀学校都加入了这一行列。2003 年，剑桥大学任命前耶鲁大学教务长艾莉森·理查德为副校长。学校公开强调艾莉森之前的工作确保了"耶鲁大学财政状况良好"。

当然，这些外国管理者不仅只是筹措资金。教育全球化意味着更多的大学将要聘用那些具有国际经验的校长，以促进国际间项目的合作，招收留学生。外国人能够给学校业已成立的体系带来新的活力。

【难词释义】

provost 教务长	**vice-chancellor** 副校长
equivalent 相等的，意义相同的	**budget** 预算
distinctively 特殊地	**prominent** 突出的，杰出的
oversee 强调	**perspective** 视角，观点

【写译语块】

1. make top-level hires from abroad 从国外招聘顶级人才
2. the talent flow 人才流动
3. a leader familiar with the state government 熟悉地方政府的领导
4. rely heavily on donations 严重依赖捐赠
5. the fund-raising ability 筹集资金的能力
6. keep pace with rising student number 与日益增多的学生同步发展
7. the decline in government support 政府资助的下降

【难句分析】

1. (第二段第三句)在 Higher education has become a big and competitive business nowadays, and like so many businesses, it's gone global. Yet the talent flow isn't universal. High-level personnel tend to head in only one direction：outward from America. 中的 gone 在这里是连系动词，gone global 表示"变得全球

化";head 在句中用作动词,表示"向……方向前进"。

2. (第四段第三句)在 The decline in government support has made funding-raising an increasing necessary ability among administrators and has hiring committees hungry for Americans 中的介词词组 in government support 用作状语,限定前面的名词 decline,表示"……方面的下降";increasing 在此处可理解为"越来越……";hungry for 在此处表示"渴求……"。

3. (最后一段第二句)在 The globalization of education means more universities will be seeking heads with international experience of some kind to promote international programs and attract a global student body. Foreigners can offer a fresh perspective on established practices 中的 with 引出的介词词组相当于一个定语从句,可理解为 who have;to promote international programs and attract a global student body 在句中用作目的状语;student body 在此处表示一个学校的全体学生;established practices 中,established 在此处可理解为"现行的,当前的",practice 指"通行的做法,惯例"。

【原题再现】

31. What is the current trend in higher education discussed in the passage?

   A) Institutions worldwide are hiring administrators from the U. S.

   B) A lot of political activists are being recruited as administrators.

   C) American universities are enrolling more international students.

   D) University presidents are paying more attention to funding-raising.

32. What is the chief consideration of American universities when hiring top-level administrators?

   A) The political correctness.

   B) Their ability to raise funds.

   C) Their fame in academic circles.

   D) Their administrative experience.

33. What do we learn about European universities from the passage?

   A) The tuitions they charge have been rising considerably.

   B) Their operation is under strict government supervision.

   C) They are strengthening their position by globalization.

   D) Most of their revenues come from the government.

34. Cambridge University appointed Alison Richard as its vice-chancellor chiefly because _____.

A) she was known to be good at raising money

B) she could help strengthen its ties with Yale

C) she knew how to attract students overseas

D) she had boosted Yale's academic status

35. In what way do top-level administrators from abroad contribute to university development?

A) They can enhance the university's image.

B) They will bring with them more international faculty.

C) They will view a lot of things from a new perspective.

D) They can set up new academic disciplines.

【单词详解】

【重点单词】**equivalent** / iˈkwivələnt / adj & n.

[基本词义] adj. 相等的,等价的,意义相同的; n. 相等物,等价物,意义相同的词

[用法导航] His reply is equivalent to a refusal. 他的回答等于是拒绝。// Some English words have no Chinese equivalents. 有些英文字在中文里没有对应的词。

[词性转换] **equivalence** / iˈkwivələns / n. 相等;等值;等效

[对比记忆] (1) **complement** / ˈkɔmplimənt / n. 补充;补(足)语 vt. 补充,与……相配

(2) **match** / mætʃ / n. 比赛;对手;匹配;火柴 v.(和……)相配

[真题衔接] Physics is _____ to the science which was called material philosophy in history. (CET4-9701)

A) alike   B) equivalent   C) likely   D) uniform

【重点单词】**decline** / diˈklain / n. / vi. & vt.

[基本词义] 下降,减少,衰退;下降,衰退,谢绝,拒绝

[用法导航] As one grows older one's memory declines. 人的记忆力随着年龄增长而衰退。// She declined their invitation. 她婉拒了他们的邀请。// She declined to have lunch with her friend, saying that she wasn't feeling well. 她说她身体不舒服,婉拒了与她的朋友共进午餐。// There is a decline in real wages. 实际工资有所减少。

[对比记忆] (1) **descend** / diˈsend / v. 下来,下降;(from)起源(于),是……的后裔

(2) **diminish** / diˈminiʃ / vi. 变少,变小,降低 vt. 减少,减小,降低

(3) **drop** / drɔp / v.(使)落下;(使)下降,(使)降低;(使)停止,放弃

18

(4) **plunge** / plʌndʒ / *vi.* 纵身投入；猛冲；猛跌 *n.* 投身入水；猛跌，骤降

［真题衔接］Crisis would be the right term to describe the _____ in many animal species.（研-1999）

A）minimization　B）restriction　　C）descent　　D）decline

【句子翻译】

36. We _____（不应该仅仅凭热情）and substitute our personal feelings for policy.

37. Bank loans during the prosperity decade did not _____（随着经济活动水平的提高而增长）.

38. The book I am reading is very interesting, because it describes _____（一个我熟悉的外国的情况）.

39. Notwithstanding _____（学生人数持续减少）, the school has had a very successful year.

40. The new administration would introduce a Bill _____（鼓励扩大私人医疗设施）.

Passage Five

The January fashion show, called FutureFashion，**exemplified** how far green design has come. Organized by the New York-based nonprofit Earth Pledge，the show **inspired** many top designers to work with **sustainable** fabrics *for the first time*. Several have since made **pledges** to include **organic** fabrics in their lines.

The designers who **undertake** green fashion still *face many challenges*. Scott Hahn，cofounder with Gregory of Rogan and Loomstate，which uses all-organic cotton，says high-quality sustain able materials can still be tough to find. "Most designers with existing labels are finding there aren't **comparable** fabrics that can just replace what you're doing and what your customers are used to," he says. For example, organic cotton and non-organic cotton are **virtually indistinguishable** once woven into a dress. But some popular **synthetics**, like stretch nylon, still have few **eco-friendly equivalents**.

Those who do make the switch are finding they have more support. Last year the influential trade show Designers & Agents stopped charging its participation fee for young green **entrepreneurs** who attend its two springtime shows in Los Angeles and New York and gave special recognition to designers whose collections are *at least* 25% sustainable. It now **counts** more than 50 green designers, up from fewer than a dozen two years ago. This week Wal-Mart *is set to announce a major initiative aimed at helping cotton farmers* go organic: it will buy **transitional** cotton at higher prices, thus helping to **expand** the supply of a key sustainable material. "**Mainstream** *is about to occur*," says Hahn.

Some **analysts** are less sure. Among consumers, only 18% are even aware that ecofashion exists, up from 6% four years ago. Natalie Hormilla, a fashion writer, is an example of the **unconverted** consumer. When asked if she owned any sustainable clothes, she replied: "Not that *I'm aware of*." Like most consumers, she *finds little time to shop*, and when she does, she's on the hunt for "cute stuff that isn't too expensive." By her own **admission**, green just isn't yet *on her mind*. But - *thanks to* the **combined** efforts of designers, retailers and suppliers—one day it will be. (367 words) (2009 年 6 月第 1 篇)

【段落译文】

在一月份举行的时装秀,名为"未来时尚",向人们证明了绿色设计已达到何等程度。这次由总部位于纽约的非盈利性机构"地球宣言"组织的时装秀,激发了许多顶级时尚设计师首次使用绿色纤维材料的灵感,其中有几位设计师已经承诺将在他们的设计中使用有机纤维。

从事绿色时尚设计的设计师们仍面临许多挑战。Scott Hahn 与设计师 Gregory 合作,一同创立了时尚品牌 Rogan &. Loomstate 并使用全有机棉材料。他指出,现在很难找到高质量的绿色材料。他说"现有品牌的大部分设计师都发现,几乎很难找到一种替代品可以比得上现在正在使用的而顾客也已经习惯使用的纤维材料"。例如,有机棉和非有机棉材料一旦被织成布料做成服装之后,几乎就没有差别。但是有些很受欢迎的人工合成纤维,如弹性尼龙却仍然很难找到对生态环境有利的替代品。

那些已经做了材料转化的设计师们发现他们正获得越来越多的支持。去年,名为"设计师与代理商"的著名商展机构没有向那些参加了在洛杉矶和纽约两次商展的年轻的绿色企业家们收取参展费用,并且特别赏识那些至少使用了 25% 的绿色材料的设计师们。绿色设计师的人数已由两年前的十人左右增加到了现在的五十多人。沃尔玛将与本周宣布开始一项旨在主动帮助棉农种植有机棉的行动:他们将以高价收购过渡型棉花,从而帮助增加有机棉这种重要的绿色材料的供应。Hahn 说,"这很快就会成为主流了。"

某些分析师对此却不那么确定。顾客群体中,只有 18% 意识到了有利于环保的时尚是真实存在的,四年前则只有16%。时尚作家 Natalie Hormilla 就是尚未转变思想的顾客之一。当被问及她是否拥有绿色材料制成的衣服时,她答道:"据我所知,没有"。像大多数顾客一样,她很少有时间购物,而每次去购物时,她喜欢寻找那些"不算贵但是很可爱的东西"。她自己承认,绿色时尚还没有引起她的关注。但是,由于设计师、零售商和供应商的共同努力,相信绿色时尚总有一天会到来的。

【难词释义】

exemplify 举例说明	**inspire** 赋予某人灵感
sustainable 足以支撑的	**pledge** 保证,承诺
organic 有机的	**undertake** 从事
comparable 比得上的	**virtually** 差不多,几乎
indistinguishable 难区分的	**synthetic** 合成纤维
eco-friendly 不妨害生态环境的	**equivalent** 相等的东西
entrepreneurs 企业家	**count** 计算
initiative 新方案	**transitional** 过渡型的
expand 增强,扩展	**mainstream** 主流
analyst 分析师	**unconverted** 不改的,不变的
admission 承认	**combined** 联合的

【写译语块】

1. for the first time 首次
2. face many challenges 面临许多挑战
3. at least 至少
4. be set to announce a major initiative 宣布开始一项行动
5. aimed at helping cotton farmers 旨在帮助棉农
6. be about to occur 很快就要发生
7. I'm aware of 我意识到,我知道
8. find little time to shop 很少有时间购物
9. on one's mind 挂在心上
10. thanks to 由于

【难句分析】

1. (第二段第三句)在 Most designers with existing labels are finding there aren't

comparable fabrics that can just replace what you're doing and what your customers are used to 中词组 be used to 在句中的意思是"习惯做某事"。existing labels 是动名词短语,表示"已经存在的品牌,即现有品牌"用来限定设计师的范围。finding 后面跟了一个宾语从句,宾语从句中又包含一个 that 引导的定语从句,这个定语从句内再次包含了两个由 what 引导的定语从句,用来形容纤维材料。

2. (第三段第二句)在 Last year the influential trade show Designers & Agents stopped charging its participation fee for young green entrepreneurs who attend its two springtime shows in Los Angeles and New York and gave special recognition to designers whose collections are at least 25% sustainable 中 influential 的意思是"有影响力的,有名气的"。trade show 是指"商展"。stop 后面跟上一个动名词表示停止做某事,句中 stop charging its participation fee 是指"停止收取参展费用"。give special recognition to 的意思是"特别赏识某人或某事"。句中有两个定语从句,who 引导的从句用来修饰那些绿色企业家,whose 引导的从句用来修饰设计师。

【原题再现】

41. What is said about FutureFashion?

　　A) It inspired many leading designers to start going green.

　　B) It showed that designers using organic fabrics would go far.

　　C) It served as an example of how fashion shows should be organized.

　　D) It convinced the public that fashionable clothes should be made durable.

42. According to Scott Hahn, one big challenge to designers who will go organic is that _____.

　　A) a much more time is needed to finish a dress using sustainable materials

　　B) they have to create new brands for clothes made of organic materials

　　C) customers have difficulty telling organic from non-organic materials

　　D) quality organic replacements for synthetics are not readily available

43. We learn from Paragraph 3 that designers who undertake green fashion _____.

　　A) can attend various trade shows free

　　B) are readily recognized by the fashion world

　　C) can buy organic cotton at favorable prices

　　D) are gaining more and more support

44. What is Natalie Hormilla's altitude toward ecofashion?

    A) She doesn't seem to care about it.

    B) She doesn't think it is sustainable.

    C) She is doubtful of its practical value.

    D) She is very much opposed to the idea.

45. What does the author think of green fashion?

    A) Green products will soon go mainstream.

    B) It has a very promising future.

    C) Consumers have the final say.

    D) It will appeal more to young people.

【单词详解】

【重点单词】**inspire** / inˈspaiə / *vt.*

[基本词义] 鼓舞,激励;赋予某人灵感,启迪;感动

[用法导航] His speech inspired the crowd. 他的演说鼓舞了群众。// We were all inspired by their heroic deeds. 我们都被他们的英雄事迹所感动。

[词性转换] **inspiration** / inspəˈreiʃn / *n.* 灵感;鼓舞人心的人(或事物)

[对比记忆](1) **encourage** / inˈkʌridʒ / *vt.* 鼓励,激励;支持;促进;鼓动;劝告;怂恿

(2) **arouse** / əˈrauz / *v.* 唤醒,唤起,引起

(3) **enlighten** / inˈlaitn / *v.* 启发,启蒙,教导

[真题链接] The leader of the expedition _____ everyone to follow his example. (CET4-0206)

    A) sparked   B) inspired   C) promoted   D) reinforced

【重点单词】**recognition** / rekəɡˈniʃən / *n.*

[基本词义] 认识;认出;识别;承认;认可;赞誉;赏识;奖赏

[用法导航] She hoped she would avoid recognition by wearing dark glasses and a hat. 她戴上墨镜和帽子,希望人们认不出来。// The recognition of the new law is unlikely. 这项新法律不大可能获得他们的承认。

[词性转换] **recognize** / ˈrekəɡnaiz / *n.* 认出,识别,承认

[对比记忆](1) **acknowledgement** / əkˈnɔlidʒmənt / *n.* 承认;致谢

(2) **appreciation** / əˌpriːʃiˈeiʃn / *n.* 感激,感谢;欣赏,赏识,理解

(3) **identification** / aidentifiˈkeiʃn / *n.* 鉴定,认出;身份证明;认同;确认

(4) **approval** / əˈpruːvəl / *n.* 赞同,同意;批准,认可;赞许,嘉许

[真题衔接] Ella complained that the company never gave her any _____ for her good work.

    A) sanction   B) approval   C) recognition   D) clap

【句子翻译】

46. _____（多亏了一系列的新发明），doctors can treat this disease successfully.

47. She reached the top of the hill and _____（停下来在一块大石头上休息）by the side of the path.

48. He doesn't seem to _____（意识到）the coldness of their attitude towards his appeal.

49. They will start a project _____（旨在帮助穷苦的孩子得到教育）in the west of china.

50. Although punctual himself, the professor was quite _____（习惯了学生迟到）his lecture.

Passage Six

Scientists have **devised** a way to determine roughly where a person has lived using a **strand** of hair, a **technique** that could help **track** the movements of criminal **suspects** or **unidentified** murder victims.

The method *relies on* measuring how chemical **variations** in drinking water *show up* in people's hair.

"You're what you eat and drink, and that's recorded in your hair," said Thure Cerling, a **geologist** at the University of Utah.

While U. S. diet is **relatively identical**, water supplies **vary**. *The differences result from weather patterns*. The chemical **composition** of rainfall changes slightly as rain clouds move.

Most **hydrogen** and **oxygen** atoms in water are stable, but **traces** of both elements are also present as heavier **isotopes**. The heaviest rain falls first. *As a result*, storms that form over the Pacific **deliver** heavier water to California than to Utah.

Similar patterns exist throughout the U. S.. By measuring the **proportion** of heavier hydrogen and oxygen isotopes along a strand of hair, scientists can **construct** a **geographic** timeline. Each inch of hair *corresponds to* about two months.

Cerling's team collected tap water samples from 600 cities and constructed a map of the **regional** differences. They checked the accuracy of the map by testing 200 hair samples collected from 65 barber shops.

They were able to accurately place the hair samples in broad regions roughly corresponding to the movement of rain systems.

"*It's not good for pinpointing*," Cerling said. "It's good for **eliminating** many possibilities."

Todd Park，a local detective, said the method has helped him learn more about an unidentified woman whose **skeleton** was found near Great Salt Lake.

The woman was 5 feet tall. Police recovered 26 bones，a T-shirt and several strands of hair.

When Park heard about the research，he gave the hair samples to the researchers. Chemical testing showed that over the two years before her death，she *moved about every two months*.

She stayed in the Northwest，although the test could not be more **specific** than somewhere between eastern Oregon and western Wyoming.

"It's still a **substantial** area," Park said. "But it narrows its way down for me." (351words)　（2009 年 6 月第 2 篇）

【段落译文】

科学家们已经找到一种通过一缕头发来大致判断出一个人生活在哪个地方的办法。这种技术有助于追踪犯罪嫌疑人或身份不明的受害者的活动情况。

这种方法依靠测量饮用水体现在人类头发上的化学变化。

犹他大学地质学家 Thure Cerling 说，"你就是你所吃的和所喝的东西，这些都记录在你的头发里。"

虽然美国的饮食习惯相对来说是统一的，但是供水情况却都是不同的。这些不同之处都是源于气候类型的不同。降水中的化学构成会随着雨云的移动而有细微的变化。

水中的大部分氢原子和氧原子是稳定的，但也会出现两种元素都以较重同位素的形式存在的情况。比重最大的雨水最先降落。所以，在太平洋上形成的风暴会给加利福尼亚州带去比犹他州的比重更大一些的雨水。

同样的情况遍布于整个美国。通过测量一缕头发中比重大些的氢和氧同位素的比例，科学家能够构建出一个地理年代表。每一英寸的头发对应的时间大约是两个月。

Cerling 的团队从 600 个城市收集了自来水样本，并且绘制出一张地区差异图。他们通过测试从 65 个理发店收集来的 200 种头发样本检测了这张图的准确性。

大体上根据降雨系统的活动，他们能准确地定位出头发样本所在的区域。Cerling 说："这种方法无法实现精确定位，但对于排除可能性还是有效的。"

Todd Park 是一名当地的侦探，他说这种方法已经帮他掌握了在大盐湖附近发现的不明身份的女性尸骨的许多信息。

这名女性有 5 英尺高。警察找到了 26 块骨头，一件 T 恤衫和几缕头发。

当 Park 听说了这个研究后，他给研究者送去了头发的样本。化学测试显示，死者生前的两年中每两个月就换一次住所。

虽然测试不能给出比在东俄勒冈州和西怀俄明之间的更详细的地点，但是可以知道的是死者生活在西北部。

"虽然区域还是相当大，"Park 说，"但这确实为我缩小了范围。"

【难词释义】

devise 设计，想出	**strand** 一缕
technique 技巧，技术	**track** 追踪，跟踪
suspect 嫌疑犯，嫌疑对象	**unidentified** 不能辨认的，身份不明的
variation 变化，变动	**geologist** 地质学家
relatively 相对地，比较而言	**identical** 完全相同的
vary 呈现不同	**composition** 构成成分
hydrogen 氢（原子）	**oxygen** 氧（原子）
trace 痕迹	**isotope** 同位素
deliver 传送	**proportion** 比例
construct 建构	**geographic** 地理的
regional 区域性的	**pinpointing** 准确定位
eliminating 消除	**skeleton** 骸骨
specific 具体化	**substantial** 大量的

【写译语块】

1. rely on 依赖
2. show up 显现
3. The differences result from weather patterns. 不同之处源于气候类型的不同。
4. as a result 结果是

5. Similar patterns exist throughout the U. S.. 类似的情况遍布真个美国。

6. correspond to 与之相对应的

7. It's not good for pinpointing. 这对于准确定位是没有效果的。

8. move about every two months 每两个月换一个地方

【难句分析】

1. (第八段第一句)在 They were able to accurately place the hair samples in broad regions roughly corresponding to the movement of rain systems 中 be able to 的意思是"有能力做某事"。place 在句中是名词用作动词，表示"找出……的地点"。roughly 在句中表示"大致上，大体上"，用来修饰后面的动名词短语。corresponding to 的意思是"与之相对应的"。

2. (第十三段第一句)She stayed in the Northwest，although the test could not be more specific than somewhere between eastern Oregon and western Wyoming. 该句的难点在于后半句。后半句是个转折句，转折句中包含一个比较句。could not be more specific 的意思是"没有比这更具体的了"。后面 between 引导的介词短语用来修饰 somewhere 进行补充说明。

【原题再现】

51. What is the scientists' new discovery?

   A) One's hair growth has to do with the amount of water they drink.

   B) A person's hair may reveal where they have lived.

   C) Hair analysis accurately identifies criminal suspects.

   D) The chemical composition of hair varies from person to person.

52. What does the author mean by "You're what you eat and drink" (Sentence 1, Para. 3)?

   A) Food and drink affect one's personality development.

   B) Food and drink preferences vary with individuals.

   C) Food and drink leave traces in one's body tissues.

   D) Food and drink are indispensable to one's existence.

53. What is said about the rainfall in America's West?

   A) There is much more rainfall in California than in Utah.

   B) The water it delivers becomes lighter when it moves inland.

   C) Its chemical composition is less stable than in other areas.

   D) It gathers more light isotopes as it moves eastward.

54. What did Cerling's team produce in their research?

A) A map showing the regional differences of tap water.

B) A collection of hair samples from various barber shops.

C) A method to measure the amount of water in human hair.

D) A chart illustrating the movement of the rain system.

55. What is the practical value of Cerling's research?

A) It helps analyze the quality of water in different regions.

B) It helps the police determine where a crime is committed.

C) It helps the police narrow down possibilities in detective work.

D) It helps identify the drinking habits of the person under investigation.

【单词详解】

【重点单词】**roughly** / ˈrʌfli / *adv.*

[基本词义] 大致地,粗略地;粗糙地,粗鲁地

[用法导航] roughly speaking 大致说来 // roughly 20 people attended 大约有 20 人出席 // He was pushed roughly aside. 他被粗鲁地推到了一边。

【词性转换】**rough** / rʌf / *adj.* 毛糙的,粗糙的,不平的 *n.* 毛坯,未加工品

[对比记忆] (1) **approximately** / əˈprɔksimitli / *adv.* 大约,大致,近乎

(2) **exactly** / igˈzæktli / *adv.* 正确地

[真题衔接] In the late seventies, the amount of fixed assets required to produce one vehicle in Japan was _____ equivalent to that in the United States. (CET4-0506)

A) rudely   B) roughly   C) readily   D) coarsely

【重点单词】**correspond** / ˌkɔːriˈspɔnd / *vi.*

[基本词义] (with)相符合,成一致;(to)相当,相类似;通信

[用法导航] The gills of a fish correspond to our lungs. 鱼的腮相当于我们的肺。

[词性转换] **correspondence** / ˌkɔːrisˈpɔndəns / *n.* 通信,信件;记者

[对比记忆] (1) **accord** / əˈkɔːd / *v.* 一致,符合,和谐,协调 *n.* 协议

(2) **conform** / kənˈfɔːm / *vt.* 使一致,使顺从 *vi.* 一致,符合,适应环境

(3) **coincide** / ˈkəuinˈsaid / *v.* 巧合,重合;一致,符合

(4) **disagree** / disəˈgriː / *vi.* 意见不同,不同意;不一致,不符;不适宜

[真题衔接] The power a political party is allowed to exercise should _____ closely to the proportion of votes it receives.

A) submit   B) correspond   C) contribute   D) appeal

【重点单词】**accuracy** / ˈækjurəsi / *n.*

［基本词义］准确,精确度,准确性

［用法导航］Check your work to insure its accuracy. 检查你的工作以确保它精确。

［词性转换］**accurate** / ˈækjurit / *adj.* 准确的;精确的

［对比记忆］(1) **inaccuracy** / inˈækjurəsi / *n.* 错误

(2) **precision** / priˈsiʒən / *n.* 精度,精密,精确,精确度 *adj.* 精密的,精确的

(3) **correctness** / kəˈrektnis / *n.* 正确性

(4) **exact** / igˈzækt / *adj.* 确切的,正确的;精确的

［真题衔接］It is impossible to say with _____ how many are affected.

A) definition　　B) emphasis　　C) accuracy　　D) insurance

【句子翻译】

56. Jane had learned to _____(很小年纪的时候就依靠自己），and she encouraged her daughter to be independent too.

57. There is no doubt that _____(需求的增长导致了价格的上涨).

58. The issue whether it is good or not to education reform _____(已经引起了全国性的热烈讨论).

59. Since my childhood I have found that _____(没有什么比读书对我更有吸引力).

60. _____(随着年龄的增加），it seems she was coming to understand it better.

Passage Seven

If you are a male and you are reading this, congratulations：you are a **survivor**. *According to statistics*, you are more than twice likely to die of skin cancer than a woman, and *nine times more likely to die of AIDS*. **Assuming** you make it to the end of your natural term, about 78 years for men in Australia, you will die on average five years before a woman.

There are many reasons for this—**typically**, men *take more risks than woman and are more likely to drink* and smoke but perhaps more importantly, men don't go to the doctor.

"Men aren't seeing doctors as often as they should," says Dr. Gullotta, "This is particularly so for the over-40s, when diseases tend to strike."

Gullotta says a healthy man should visit the doctor every year or two. For those over 45, it should be *at least once a year*.

Two months ago Gullotta saw a 50-year-old man who had **delayed** doing anything about his smoker's cough for a year.

"When I finally saw him it had already spread and he has since *died from lung cancer*" he says, "Earlier **detection** and treatment may not have **cured** him, but it would have **prolonged** this life. "

According to a recent **survey**, 95% of women aged between 15 and early 40s see a doctor once a year, compared to 70% of men in the same age group.

"A lot of men think they are **invincible**," Gullotta says. "They only come in when a friend drops dead on the golf course and they think, Geez, if it could happen to him. '"

Then there is the **ostrich** approach," some men *are scared of* what might be there and *would rather not know*," says Dr. Ross Cartmill.

"Most men get their cars serviced more regularly than they service their bodies," Cartmill says. He believes most diseases that commonly affect men could be **addressed** by **preventive check-ups.**

Regular check-ups for men would **inevitably** *place strain on the public purse*, Cartmill says. "But prevention is cheaper *in the long run* than having to treat the diseases. Besides, the **ultimate** cost is far greater: it is called **premature** death. "

(369 words) (2008 年 12 月第 1 篇)

【段落译文】

　　如果是位男性并且正在阅读本文的话,那么就要恭喜你啦:你是位幸存者。根据数据显示,男性死于皮肤癌的几率是女性的两倍之多,而死于艾滋病的几率是女性的九倍之多。假如你是按照自然规律走到生命尽头的话,在澳大利亚,男性一般在 78 岁死亡,平均起来会比女性的死亡年龄早五年。

　　有很多原因可以解释这点。主要是因为男性比女性更喜欢冒险,也更喜欢抽烟和喝酒。也许更重要的一点是因为男性不喜欢看医生。

　　"男性看医生的次数达不到他们应该去看的标准,"古罗塔医生说,"那些处于 40 岁以上疾病高发年龄段的男性尤其如此。"

　　古罗塔医生说一个健康的男性每年或每两年去看一次医生。对于 45 岁以上的人,至少要做到一年一次。

　　两个月前,古罗塔认识了一位 50 岁的男性吸烟咳嗽患者,咳嗽一年了却一直耽搁着没有进行任何治疗。

"当我最后见到他的时候，他的癌细胞已经扩散，最终死于肺癌。"他说，"早期的检查和治疗也许治不好他的疾病，但是可以延长他的寿命。"

最近的一次调查显示，处于 15 岁至 40 多岁年龄段的人群中，95％的女性会做到每年看一次医生，而男性却只有 70％会这样做。

"很多男性都认为他们是不可战胜的，"古罗塔说，"他们只有在看到自己的朋友突然病倒在高尔夫球场上才会来看医生并且会担心，'上帝啊，我也许也会有这么一天，……'"

还有些人喜欢使用鸵鸟方式对待此类事情。罗斯·卡米尔说，"有些男性害怕知道自己的身体状况不好，所以他们情愿选择什么都不知道。"

卡米尔说，"许多男性关注自己的车子定期检查要胜过关注自己的身体定期检查。"他认为许多常见的男性疾病是完全可以通过预防性的检查发现的。

男性定期检查肯定是会增加公共开支，卡米尔说，"但是从长远的角度来看，预防性的检查费用要比昂贵的治疗费用低得多。此外，如果不进行早期预防的话，最终代价是高昂的，也就是说会早亡。"

【难词释义】

survivor 幸存者	**statistics** 统计学
assuming 假定	**typically** 代表性的
delayed 耽搁	**detection** 检查，察觉
cure 治疗，治愈	**prolong** 延长
survey 调查	**invincible** 不可战胜的
ostrich 鸵鸟	**address** 对付处理
preventive 预防性的	**check-up** 身体检查
inevitably 不可避免地	**detection** 察觉
ultimate 最终的	**premature** 早熟的

【写译语块】

1. according to statistics 根据数据显示
2. nine times more likely to die of AIDS 死于艾滋病的几率是九倍之多
3. take more risks than woman and are more likely to drink 比女性更喜欢冒险，也更喜欢喝酒
4. at least once a year 至少一年一次
5. die from lung cancer 死于癌症
6. be scared of 害怕

31

7. place strain on the public purse 增加公共开支

8. in the long run 从长远的角度来看

9. would rather not know 宁愿不知道

【难句分析】

1. (第六段末尾) Earlier detection and treatment may not have cured him, but it would have prolonged his life. 该句是虚拟语气的表达方式,具体地说,是由两个虚拟语气的主语从句构成,中间是一层转折关系。当要表示与过去事实相反的情况时,虚拟语气主语从句的构成方式是:主语 + should/would/could/might (或 may, might) (not) + have done。detection 和 treatment 的意思是"检查和治疗";cure 的意思是"治愈";prolong 的意思是"延长"。

2. (第七段第一句) According to a recent survey, 95% of women aged between 15 and early 40s see a doctor once a year, compared to 70% of men in the same age group. 首先要理解该句句首 According to 的意思,表示"根据……所说";其次要理解 compare to 的用法,表示"与……相比",过去分词短语在句中作状语;see a doctor 表示"看医生";the same age group 表示"同个年龄段";once a year 表示"一年一次"。在这个句子中,处于同个年龄段的男性和女性在看医生的人数方面做比较。

3. (第十段第一句) Most men get their cars serviced more regularly than they service their bodies. 这是一个比较句。more regularly than 表示"比……更加经常性的",在句中是比较对身体和对车子的关注程度。

【原题再现】

61. Why does the author congratulate his male readers at the beginning of the passage?

   A) They are more likely to survive serious diseases today.

   B) Their average life span has been considerably extended.

   C) They have lived long enough to read this article.

   D) They are sure to enjoy a longer and happier live.

62. What does the author state is the most important reason men die five years earlier on average than women?

   A) Men drink and smoke much more than women.

   B) Men don't seek medical care as often as women.

   C) Men aren't as cautions as women in face of danger.

D) Men are more likely to suffer from fatal diseases.

63. Which of the following best completes the sentence "Geez, if it could happen to him,' (Sentence2, Para, 8)?

A) It could happen to me, too.

B) I should avoid playing golf.

C) I should consider myself lucky.

D) It would be a big misfortune.

64. What does Dr. Ross Cartmill mean by "the ostrich approach" (Sentence 1, Para. 9)?

A) A casual attitude towards one's health conditions.

B) A new therapy for certain psychological problems.

C) Refusal to get medical treatment for fear of the pain involved.

D) Unwillingness to find out about one's disease because of fear.

65. What does Cartmill say about regular check-ups for men?

A) They may increase public expenses.

B) They will save money in the long run.

C) They may cause psychological strains on men.

D) They will enable men to live as long as women.

【单词详解】

【重点单词】**assume** / əˈsjuːm / vt.

[基本词义] 装出……的样子;假定,认为,猜想;呈现出特点;承担,采取,掌管

[用法导航] He playfully assumed as air of indifference. 他开玩笑地装出一副漠不关心的样子。// I assume that he has gone for a walk. 我猜想他散步去了。// We must assume that he has arrived, but we do not know. 我们必须假定他已经到了,但是我们还不知道。// The problem assumed immense proportions. 此问题事关重大。// The prince assumed power when he was only fifteen. 王子在 15 岁时就开始掌管大权。

[词性转换] **assumption** / əˈsʌmpʃən / n. 假定,假想;臆测,臆断;傲慢,自负

[对比记忆] (1) **presume** / priˈzuːm / v. 推测,假定,(没有证据地)相信;冒昧(做),擅(做);认定,推定 vi. 擅自行为

(2) **resume** / riˈzjuːm / v. (中断后)重新开始,继续,恢复 / ˈrezəmei, ˈrezjuːmei / n. 摘要,概要;简历

(3) **suppose** / səˈpəuz / v. 猜想,料想;认为,以为;假设,假定 conj. 如果

(4) **imagine** / i'mædʒin / *vt.* 想像，幻想；认为，设想；猜想，推测

[真题衔接] I think we can safely _____ that this is legal unless we are told otherwise.

　　A) ascertain　　　B) assume　　　C) generalize　　　D) portray

【重点单词】**preventive** / pri'ventiv / *adj.* &. *n.*

[基本词义] 防止的，预防的；预防手段

[用法导航] preventive measures 预防的措施 // preventive medicine 预防医学 // a preventive drug 预防药物 // preventive detention 预防性拘留

[词性转换] **prevent** / pri'vent / *v.* 防止，阻止，妨碍，使不可能

[对比记忆]　(1) **restraint** / ri'streint / *n.* 抑制，遏制，管制，约束

　　　　　(2) **restrain** / ri'strein / *vt.* 抑制，制止

　　　　　(3) **inhibit** / in'hibit / *vt.* 抑制，约束，制止 *vi.* 使拘束，使尴尬

[真题衔接] We should take _____ measures to guard against possible trouble.

　　A) preventive　　B) practical　　　C) operational　　D) optional

【句子翻译】

66. _____（根据科学研究），listening to music enables us to feel relaxed. Is this really true?

67. This substance _____（反应速度是另外那种物质的三倍）.

68. _____（与西方国家相比），China uses materials very carefully.

69. The victim _____（本来会有机会活下来）if he had been taken to hospital in time.

70. I prefer to live near to my work _____（也不愿意每天花大量的时间在路上）.

Passage Eight

High-quality customer service is **preached** by many, but actually keeping customers happy is *easier said than done*.

Shoppers seldom complain to the manager or owner of a retail store, *but instead will alert their friends*, relatives, co-workers, strangers... and anyone who will listen.

Store managers *are often the last to hear complaints*, and often find out only when their regular customers decide to **frequent** their **competitors**, according to a study jointly **conducted** by Verde group and Wharton school.

"Storytelling hurts retailers and **entertains** consumers," said Paula Courtney,

President of the Verde group. "The store loses the customer, but the shopper must also find a **replacement**."

On average, every unhappy customer will complain to at least four others, *and will no longer visit the specific store*. For every dissatisfied customer, a store *will lose up to three more due to negative reviews*. The resulting "snowball effect" can *be disastrous to retailers*.

According to the research, shoppers who purchased clothing **encountered** the most problems. Ranked second and third were grocery and electronics customers.

The most common complaints include filled parking lots, **cluttered** shelves, overloaded racks, out-of-stock items, long check-out lines, and rude salespeople.

During peak shopping hours, some retailers solved the parking problems by getting **moonlighting** local police to work as parking attendants. Some hired flag wavers to direct customers to empty parking spaces. This guidance eliminated the need for customers to circle the parking lot endlessly, and avoided **confrontation** between those eyeing the same parking space.

Retailers can **relieve** the headaches by redesigning store **layouts**, pre-stocking sales items, hiring **speedy** and experienced cashiers, and *having sales representatives on hand* to answer questions.

Most importantly, salespeople should be **diplomatic** and polite with angry customers.

"Retailers who're responsive and friendly are more likely to smooth over issues than those who aren't so friendly." said Professor Stephen Hoch. "Maybe something as simple as a greeter at the store entrance would help."

Customers can also improve future shopping experiences by *filing complaints to the retailer*, *instead of complaining to* the rest of the world. Retailers *are hard-pressed to improve* when they have no idea what is wrong. (353 words)

（2008 年 12 月第 2 篇）

【段落译文】

许多公司都在大肆鼓吹高质量的客户服务，但是要让顾客满意开心是说起来容易做起来难。

顾客在购物过程中遇到不满很少会直接向商店经理或零售店的老板投诉，取而代之的是他们会把遭遇讲给朋友、亲戚、同事，甚至是愿意倾听的陌生人，并且警告他们不要去那里购物。

维德集团和沃顿商学院的一项联合调查显示,商店经理往往是最后一个了解到顾客不满意状况的人,而这经常是在发现他们的老主顾频繁光顾自己竞争对手的店铺之后,他们才意识到问题的存在。

维德集团的总裁宝拉·科尼特说,"把自己的消费经历当做故事来讲述,伤害了商家的同时却取悦了其他消费者,这样商家就失去了顾客,但是消费者自己同样也得另找卖家。"

平均起来,每一个不满意购物经历的顾客至少会向四个人讲述他们的遭遇,并且再也不会光顾这家商店。只要有一个购物者对某家商店不满意,就意味着这家商店要丧失三个以上对该商店持有看法的消费者。这种"滚雪球效应"对店主们来说会是个灾难。

据这项调查显示,消费者在购买服装类商品时出现的问题最多,其次是杂货和电器商品。

最常见的投诉和抱怨问题包括拥挤的停车场,塞满商品的货架,超载的购物架,缺货的产品,长长的结账队伍,还有态度恶劣的销售人员。

在购物高峰期时段,为了解决停车难问题,有些零售商雇佣当地警察来作他们的兼职停车场管理员。还有些雇来的人员专门挥舞旗子来引导那些需要停车的顾客,指示他们哪里有空闲车位,这样就避免了顾客们在停车场里一直兜圈子的现象以及抢车位的冲突。

零售商可以通过以下方法使问题得到改善,例如重新设计店内布局,提前上架,保证货源充足,雇用效率高有经验的收银员,并且要有销售代表在现场及时地回答顾客问题。

最重要的是,销售人员应该做到一直有策略地并且礼貌友善地面对愤怒的顾客。

史蒂芬·赫哲教授认为,"与态度不友好的商家相比,反应迅速、态度友善的商家更容易解决问题。或许在商店入口处简简单单的一声问候也会起到作用。"

消费者也可以通过直接向商家投诉来改善今后的购物体验,而不是到处和其他人抱怨。如果零售商并不知道哪里出错的话,他们只会费尽力气地盲目改进。

【难词释义】

preach 宣扬	**frequent** 频繁光顾
competitor 竞争对手	**conduct** 实施
entertain 取悦	**replacement** 替代物
encounter 遭遇	**cluttered** 塞满了的
moonlighting 业余兼职的	**confrontation** 冲突
relieve 缓解	**layout** 布局

speedy 快的   **diplomatic** 策略的

【写译语块】

1. easier said than done 说起来容易做起来难

2. but instead will alert their friends 取而代之的是警告朋友

3. are often the last to hear complaints 经常是最后一个听到抱怨的人

4. on average 平均地讲

5. will no longer visit the specific store 再也不会光顾这家商店

6. will lose up to three more due to negative reviews 要丧失三个以上对该商店持有看法的消费者

7. due to 应归于,应归功于;应归咎于

8. be disastrous to retailers 对店主们来说会是个灾难

9. according to the research 据这项调查显示

10. having sales representatives on hand 要有销售代表在现场

11. filing complaints to the retailer 向商家投诉

12. are hard-pressed to improve 费劲力气地改进

13. instead of complaining to 而不是和……抱怨

【难句分析】

1. (第八段最后一句)在 This guidance eliminated the need for customers to circle the parking lot endlessly, and avoided confrontation between those eyeing the same parking space 中 eliminated the need ... 和 avoided confrontation ... 是并列的动宾结构。circle 是动词词性,意思是"环绕行驶";eye 也是动词词性,意思是"盯着"。eyeing the same parking space 是动名词短语作定语,用来修饰those,指那些开车寻找车位的人。

2. (第十一段第一句)在 Retailers who're responsive and friendly are more likely to smooth over issues than those who aren't so friendly 中有两个 who 引导的定语从句,第一个 who 引导的从句是用来修饰句首 retailer 这个主语的,第二个 who 引导的从句是用来修饰后面的 those。句子使用了 more ... than 这个比较级的用法,responsive 的意思是"反应迅速的",are likely to 的意思是"很有可能",smooth over issues 的意思是"解决问题"。

【原题再现】

71. Why are store managers often the last to hear complaints?

A) Most customers won't bother to complain even if they have had unhappy experiences.

B) Customers would rather relate their unhappy experiences to people around them.

C) Few customers believe the service will be improved.

D) Customers have no easy access to store managers.

72. What does Paula Courtney imply by saying "... the shopper must also find a replacement" (Sentence 2, Para. 4)?

A) New customers are bound to replace old ones.

B) It is not likely the shopper can find the same products in other stores.

C) Most stores provide the same.

D) Not complaining to the manager causes the shopper some trouble too.

73. Shop owners often hire moonlighting police as parking attendants so that shoppers _____.

A) can stay longer browsing in the store

B) won't have trouble parking their cars

C) won't have any worries about security

D) can find their cars easily after shopping

74. What contributes most to smoothing over issues with customers?

A) Manners of the salespeople.   B) Hiring of efficient employees.

C) Huge supply of goods for sale.   D) Design of the store layout.

75. To achieve better shopping experiences, customers are advised to _____.

A) exert pressure on stores to improve their service

B) settle their disputes with stores in a diplomatic way

C) voice their dissatisfaction to store managers directly

D) shop around and make comparisons between stores

【单词详解】

【重点单词】complain / kəmˈplein / *vi*. & *vt*.

[基本词义] 抱怨，投诉；申诉，控告

[用法导航] You have no reason to complain. 你没有理由抱怨。// She often complains that he is dishonest. 她常埋怨说他不诚实。// I have to complain to the manager about it. 对这件事我不得不向经理申诉。// He complained to the police that the boys had stolen his apples. 他向警方控告那些男孩偷了他的苹果。

38

［词性转换］**complaint** / kəmˈpleint / *n.* 抱怨，诉苦，怨言；疾病

［对比记忆］（1）**protest** / prəuˈtest / *v.* 提议，反对，申辩 *n.* 抗议，反对

（2）**grumble** / ˈɡrʌmbl / *vi.* 抱怨，发牢骚，咕哝 *n.* 抱怨，牢骚，嘟囔

（3）**object** / ˈɔbdʒikt / *n.* 物体，实物；对象，客体；目的，目标；宾语 *vi.*（to）反对，不赞成

（4）**compliant** / kəmˈplaiənt / *adj.* 遵从的，依从的，顺从的，屈从的，一致的

［真题衔接］Your mother tells me that she _____ continuing pain in her legs for a year, and then the pain stopped.

　　A) complaining of　B) got over　　C) holding out　　D) keeping down

【重点单词】**responsive** / risˈpɔnsiv /*adj.*

［基本词义］反应热烈或良好的；赞同的；支持的；反应灵敏的；易受控制的

［用法导航］a responsive audience 反应热烈的观众 // responsive pupils 积极应答的学生 // She's fairly responsive to new ideas. 她很愿意接受新观念。// The company is highly responsive to changes in demand. 该公司对需求的变化反应特别迅速。

［词性转换］**irresponsive** / irisˈpɔnsiv / *adj.* 无反应的，无答复的，无感应的

［对比记忆］（1）**responsible** / risˈpɔnsəbl / *adj.* 负有责任的；尽责的，可靠的

　　（2）**response** / risˈpɔns / *n.* 回音，回答；反应，相应

　　（3）**sensitive** / ˈsensitiv / *adj.* 有感觉的，敏感的

　　（4）**reactive** / riˈæktiv / *adj.* 反应的，起反应的

［真题衔接］This poem has struck a(n) _____ chord(心弦，感情)in the hearts of its readers.

　　A) influential　　B) responsive　　C) dominant　　D) intensive

【句子翻译】

76. _____（他们没有去游泳），they went to play football that day.

77. Excessive exercise _____（对身体的健康利少弊多）. Therefore we must control the amount of exercise we do.

78. The truck driver is _____（对这起交通事故负全责）.

79. After fruitless negotiation, the innocent patient _____（就服务差的问题向医院负责人提出了投诉）.

80. A lot of people nowadays have muscular problems in the neck, the shoulders and the back _____（主要是由于工作中的压力和紧张造成的）.

Passage Nine

Global warming may or may not be the great environmental crisis of the 21st century, but — *regardless of whether it is or isn't* — we won't do much about it. We will argue over it and may even, as a nation, make some fairly **solemn-sounding commitments** to avoid it. But the more dramatic and meaningful these commitments seem, the less likely they are to be observed.

Al Gore calls global warming an "**inconvenient** truth", as if merely recognizing it could put us on a path to a solution. But the real truth is that we don't know enough to **relieve** global warming, and—without major technological **breakthroughs** we can't do much about it.

From 2003 to 2050, *the world's population is projected to grow from 6.4 billion to 9.1 billion, a 42% increase.* If energy use per person and technology remain the same, total energy use and greenhouse gas **emissions** (mainly CO_2) will be 42% higher in 2050. But that's too low, because societies that grow richer use more energy. We need economic growth unless *we condemn the world's poor to their present poverty* and freeze everyone else's living standards. With modest growth, energy use and greenhouse emissions will more than double by 2050.

No government will *adopt rigid restrictions on* economic growth and personal freedom (limits on electricity usage, driving and travel) that might cut back global warming. Still, politicians want to show they're "doing something". Consider the Kyoto protocol (京都议定书). It allowed countries that joined to punish those that didn't. But it hasn't reduced CO_2 emissions (up about 25% since 1990), and many signatories (签字国) didn't adopt tough enough policies to *hit their 2008 — 2012 targets.*

The **practical** conclusion is that if global warming is a potential **disaster**, the only solution is new technology. Only an **aggressive** research and development program might find ways of breaking our dependence on **fossil** fuels or dealing with it.

The trouble with the global warming debate is that it has become a moral problem when it's really an engineering one. The inconvenient truth is that if we don't solve the engineering problem, we're helpless. (352 words) (2008 年 6 月第 1 篇)

【段落译文】

全球变暖也许会是 21 世纪的环境大危机,也许不会。但是,不管它会不会成为 21 世纪环境大危机，我们为之付诸的行动远远不够。我们对此争论不休，或许会以整个国家的名义作出一些听起来比较庄严的承诺，承诺要避免这一环境大危机。但是这样的承诺越是听起来激动人心、意义深刻，就越是不太可能会被遵守。

阿尔戈尔把全球变暖称作一个"难以忽视的真相"，仿佛单单认识到这一问题就能领我们找到问题解决之路。然而真实的情况是我们对怎样缓解全球变暖知之甚少，而且没有重大技术突破，我们所能做的也是非常有限。

预计从 2003 年到 2050 年间世界人口将从 64 亿增长到 91 亿，增加 42%。如果人均能源使用与技术不变，那么在 2050 年能源使用总量以及温室气体（主要是二氧化碳）的排放量将比现在高出 42%。但是那些日益富裕的社会将使用更多能源，因此到时远远会高出这个预计数。我们需要发展经济，除非我们想让世界上的穷人一直处于目前的贫穷状况，并且固定住其他人的当前生活水平。哪怕是小幅增长，能源使用与温室气体排放量到 2050 年将会是翻一番还不止。

有些限制（如限制用电、驾驶和出行）能缓解全球变暖，但没有政府会对经济增长和个人自由采取严格的限制。尽管如此，政界人士想要表示他们有所作为。拿《京都议定书》来说，它让那些加入其中的成员国来惩罚那些非成员国。但是它未能减少二氧化碳的排放量，从 1990 年以来，增加了约 25%。许多签字国没有采取足够强硬的政策来达到他们 2008 年～2012 年的排放目标。

我们得出的可行结论是如果说全球变暖是一个潜在的灾难，那么唯一的出路在于新技术。或许只有一项变革性的研究和发展项目，才能帮我们找到打破对化石燃料依赖的方法，或者处理这一危机的方法。

这场关于全球变暖争论的麻烦在于全球变暖实际上是一项工程上的问题却已经变成了一个道德上的问题。这个不容忽视的真相就是：如果工程问题不先解决，我们仍将无能为力。

【难词释义】

solemn-sounding 听上去很庄严的

commitments 承诺

inconvenient 不便的

relieve 解除，减轻

breakthroughs 突破

emissions 排放（量）

rigid 严格的，僵硬的，死板的

practical 实用的，可行的

disaster 灾难

aggressive 好斗的，积极的，有闯劲的

fossil 化石

【写译语块】

1. regardless of whether it is or isn't 不管（无论）它是还是不是

2. the world's population is projected to grow from 6. 4 billion to 9. 1 billion, a 42% increase 世界人口预计将从 64 亿增长到 91 亿,增加 42%

3. we condemn the world's poor to their present poverty 我们迫使世界上的穷人一直处于目前的贫穷状况

4. adopt rigid restrictions on 对……采取严格的限制措施

5. hit their 2008-2010 targets 达到了他们所制定的 2008 年~2010 年的目标

【难句分析】

1. (第一段末尾)But the more dramatic and meaningful these commitments seem, the less likely they are to be observed. 该句子结构为"the+比较级……, the+比较级……",意思为"……越……,……越……"有时省略"越……越……"。observe 与 commitments 搭配,意为"遵守承诺";该句后半个分句含句型 be (less) likely to . . . ,意为"(更不)可能……",they 指代 commitments,与 observe 是动宾关系。所以,在 be (less) likely to 结构中要求用不定式的被动形式,即 they are (less likely) to be observed,意为"承诺更不可能被遵守"。

2. (第二段第一句)在 Al Gore calls global warming an "inconvenient truth", as if merely recognizing it could put us on a path to a solution 中 as if 引导带有虚拟语气的方式状语。词组 put somebody on a path to . . . 表示"让人走上一条通往……的道路"。

3. (最后一段第一句)在 The trouble with the global warming debate is that it has become a moral problem when it's really an engineering one 中 that 引导一个表语从句,表示主句主语 the trouble 的具体内容;表语从句中又有 when 引导的时间状语从句。

【原题再现】

81. What is said about global warming in the first paragraph?

    A) It may not prove an environmental crisis at all.

    B) It is an issue requiring worldwide commitments.

    C) Serious steps have been taken to avoid or stop it.

    D) Very little will be done to bring it under control.

82. According to the author's understanding, what is AL Gore's view on global warming?

    A) It is a reality both people and politicians are unaware of.

    B) It is a phenomenon that causes us many inconveniences.

C) It is a problem that can be solved once it is recognized.

D) It is an area we actually have little knowledge about.

83. Greenhouse emissions will more than double by 2050 because of _____.

A) economic growth

B) wasteful use of energy

C) the widening gap between the rich and poor

D) the rapid advances of science and technology

84. The author believes that, since the signing of Kyoto Protocol, _____.

A) politicians have started to do something to better the situation

B) few nation have adopted real tough measures to limit energy use

C) reductions in energy consumption have greatly cut back global warming

D) international cooperation has contributed to solving environmental problems

85. What is the message the author intends to convey?

A) Global warming is more of a moral issue than a practical one.

B) The ultimate solution to global warming lies in new technology.

C) The debate over global warming will lead to technological breakthroughs

D) People have to give up certain material comforts to stop global warming.

【单词详解】

【重点单词】**observe** / əbˈzəːv / *vi*. & *vt*.

［基本词义］说，评述，评论；遵守；注意到，看到，观察

［用法导航］observe the stars 观察星象 // observe the rules and regulations 遵守各项规章制度 Do you also observe the religious festivals? 你们也过这些宗教节日吗？// He observed that it was odd. 他说这件事真奇怪。// I have little to observe on what has been said. 关于刚才所说的这些，我没有什么好评论的。// The police observed him enter the bank with a suspicious box in his arms. 警察看到他抱着一个可疑的盒子进了银行。// The teacher hadn't observed anything unusual in his behavior before he committed suicide. 在他自杀之前，老师没有注意到他的行为有什么反常。

［对比记忆］(1) **remark** / riˈmaːk / *vt*. & *vi*. 谈到，说起；(on / upon) 评论，谈论

(2) **abide** / əˈbaid / *vi*. 容忍，忍受；(by) 遵守

(3) **conform** / kənˈfɔːm / *vi*. (to) 符合，遵照

(4) **behold** / biˈhəuld / *v*. 看到，瞧见，注视

(5) **celebrate** / ˈselibreit / *vi*. & *vt*. 庆祝，祝贺，过节，举行宗教仪式

43

〔真题衔接〕The boy _____ what was going on between Marcel and his sister.

A) estimated   B) observed   C) valued   D) simplified

【重点单词】**relieve** / ri'li:v / *vt.*

〔基本词义〕解除，减轻；给……换班；使……不单调乏味；解围

〔用法导航〕a drug that relieves headaches 缓解头疼的药 // relieve the pressure and stress 减轻压力 // The guard will be relieved at midnight. 卫兵要到午夜才换班。// I went for a walk to relieve the boredom of the day. 一天（工作）下来感到甚是无聊，我去散步调剂了一下。// He was relieved of his duties.（委婉）他被解除了职务。

〔词性转换〕**relief** / ri'li:f / *n.*（痛苦，压力等的）减轻，解除；救济；换班者；浮雕

〔对比记忆〕(1) **relive** / ri:'liv / *vt.* 再体验，重温

(2) **remove** / ri'mu:v / *vt.* 移动；开除；去除

(3) **release** / ri'li:s / *vt.* 释放，发出；发行

(4) **alleviate** / ə'li:vieit / *vt.* 减轻，缓和

(5) **ease** / i:z/ *vt.* 减轻，缓和；使……安心

〔真题衔接〕In order to prevent stress from being set up in the metal, expansion joints are fitted which _____ the stress by allowing the pipe to expand or contract freely.（CET6-0301-64）

A) relieve   B) reconcile   C) reclaim   D) rectify

【重点单词】**adopt** / ə'dɔpt / *vt.*

〔基本词义〕采取，采纳；收养，过继；正式批准，认可，接受

〔用法导航〕adopt a tough approach to the terrorist 对恐怖分子采取强硬的手段 // The family adopted the orphan. 这家人收养了这个孤儿。// We should adopt a precise method to complete the project. 我们应该采用一种精确的方式来完成这个工程。

〔对比记忆〕(1) **adapt** / ə'dæpt / *vt.* (to)改编，使……适应

(2) **adorn** / ə'dɔ:n / *vt.* 装饰，使……生色

(3) **accept** / ək'sept / *vt.* 接受，容纳，承兑

(4) **approve** / ə'pru:v / *vi.* & *vt.* (of)批准

〔真题衔接〕The old couple decided to _____ a boy and a girl though they had three children of their own.（CET4-9706）

A) adapt   B) bring   C) receive   D) adopt

【句子翻译】

86. He says what he thinks, _____（不考虑别人的情绪）.

44

87. His legs were badly injured in the car accident and he _____ (只好整天坐在轮椅上了).

88. If you forecast the market with your gut feelings alone, _____ (你可能永远都达不到目标)

89. The greater the number of bystanders, _____ (他们出手帮忙的可能性就越小).

90. The rate of unemployment in this country _____ (预计下半年会达到25年来的最高点).

Passage Ten

Someday a stranger will read your e-mail *without your permission* or scan the websites you've visited. Or perhaps someone will casually **glance** through your credit card purchases or cell phone bills to find out your shopping **preferences** or calling habits.

In fact, it's likely that some of these things have already happened to you. Who would watch you without your permission? It might be a **spouse**, a girl-friend, a marketing company, a boss, a **cop** or a criminal. Whoever it is, they will see you in a way you never intended to be seen—the 21st century **equivalent** of being caught naked.

Psychologists tell us **boundaries** are healthy, that *it's important to reveal yourself to friends*, family and lovers in stages, *at appropriate times*. But few boundaries remain. The digital bread crumbs (碎屑) you leave everywhere *make it easy for strangers to reconstruct who you are*, where you are and what you like. In some cases, a simple Google search can reveal what you think. *Like it or not*, increasingly we live in a world where you simply cannot *keep a secret*.

The key question is: does that matter?

For many Americans, the answer apparently is "no".

When opinion polls ask Americans about privacy, most say *they are concerned about losing it*. A survey found an overwhelming **pessimism** about privacy, with 60 percent of **respondents** saying they feel their privacy is "slipping away, and that bothers me."

But *people say one thing and do another*. Only *a tiny fraction of* Americans change any behaviors in an effort to **preserve** their privacy. Few people turn down a discount at tollbooths (收费站) to avoid using the EZ-Pass system that can track automobile movements. And few turn down supermarket loyalty cards. Privacy economist Alessandro Acquisti has run a series of tests that reveal people will surrender personal information like Social Security numbers just to **get their hands on** a pitiful 50-cents-off coupon(优惠卷).

But privacy does matter — at least sometimes. It's like health; when you have it, you don't notice it. Only when it's gone do you wish you'd done more to protect it. (353 words) （2008 年 6 月第 2 篇）

【段落译文】

有朝一日，随便一位不认识的人会在未经你许可的情况下，阅读你的电子邮件或者浏览你曾访问的网站。也许有人还会随意翻阅你的信用卡消费记录或手机账单，找出你的购物喜好或你打电话的一些习惯。

事实上，很有可能像这样的一些事情已经发生在你身上。谁会在未经你允许的情况下盯上你？可能会是你配偶、你女朋友、某个销售公司、你老板、一位警察或罪犯。不管是谁，他们都以一种你所不愿意的方式看你，在 21 世纪这样被人观看等于全裸被看见一样。

心理学家告诉我们界限要合理。我们要分阶段地，在合适的时机，向朋友、家人、恋人透露自己的信息，这一点很重要。但是如今界限已经所剩无几。你随处遗留的数字资料碎片很容易使陌生人设想出你是谁，你在哪儿，你喜欢什么。在某些情况下，一个简单的谷歌搜索就能透露你的想法。不管你喜不喜欢，我们正生活在一个越来越难保守秘密的世界里。

关键的问题就是：(你觉得)这要不要紧？

对于许多美国人来说，答案显然是：不要紧。

当就隐私问题进行民意调查询问美国人时，大部分美国人说他们担心会失去它。一项调查发现美国人对隐私持有压倒性的悲观看法，60％的被调查者说他们感到他们的隐私正在悄悄地溜走，这使他们很烦恼。

但是人们说的是一回事，做的却是另一回事。只有极少数的美国人改变他们的行为以求保护隐私。高速公路自动电子收费系统可以追踪汽车动态，但很少有人能拒绝(享用)收费折扣，避而不用这种电子收费卡。另外，很少有人会拒绝超市会员卡。隐私经济学家亚历山德罗·阿奎斯蒂做过一系列测试，这些测试揭示人们会单单为了获取一张 50 美分的折扣优惠券而提供像社会安全号这般重要的个人信息。

但是，隐私确实很重要，起码在某些时候如此。它就像健康，当你拥有它时，你不会注意它；只有当它消失时，你才会后悔你对它保护不够。

【难词释义】

glance 扫视,瞥见

spouse 配偶

equivalent 等价物,相等物

pessimism 悲观

preserve 保存,维持

preference 偏爱,倾向

cop 警察

boundary 边界,范围

respondent 被调查者,应答者

surrender 交出,投降,屈服

【写译语块】

1. without your permission 非经你许可

2. it's important to reveal yourself to your friend . . . at appropriate times 在恰当的时机向你朋友透露你的信息,这一点很重要

3. make it easy for strangers to reconstruct who you are 使陌生人很容易就能设想出你是谁

4. like it or not 不管你喜不喜欢

5. keep a secret 保守秘密

6. they are concerned about losing it 他们担心会失去隐私

7. people say one thing and do another 人们说的是一回事,做的却是另一回事

8. a tiny fraction of 一小部分的

9. get their hands on 得到,获取,攫取

【难句分析】

1. (第二段最后一句)Whoever it is, they will see you in a way you never intended to be seen — the 21st century equivalent of being caught naked. 该句用 whoever 引导一个让步状语从句,表示"不管是谁,(他们都……)";句中的破折号起到总结作用,把前文所叙述的 21 世纪里隐私被随意侵犯的这种情况概括为"相当于以前全裸被人看到那种处境";句中 intend to be seen 表示"有意让自己被看到";equivalent 是名词,后续 of 短语,意为"……的对等物,或与……相当之物"。

2. (倒数第三段最后一句)在 A survey found an overwhelming pessimism about privacy, with 60 percent of respondents saying they feel their privacy is "slipping away, and that bothers me"中 overwhelming 一词常与表示心情或情绪的词连用,表示该心情或感受达到"极度或极致"的程度,这里 overwhelming pessimism 的意思为"极度悲观的思想";句子后半部分是 with 的复合结构,即

"with＋主语＋分词"，分词 saying 后续其宾语从句，宾语从句中又嵌套着宾语从句。

3. (倒数第二段第三句)在 Few people turn down a discount at tollbooths to avoid using the EZ-Pass system that can track automobile movements 中 turn down 是一个常用短语动词，意为"拒绝，驳回"；avoid 一词为动名词作宾语，不定式短语 to avoid ... 表示前面 turn down a discount 可以达成的一个目的。

4. (最后一段最后一句)在 Only when it's gone do you wish you'd done more to protect it 中 gone 一词常用作表语，意为"离去，死去，不见了"；该句子是一个典型部分倒装句，即当"only＋状语"放句首时，助动词或情态动词前置，放到主语之前，形成倒装句。另外，句中"wish＋从句"，用到了虚拟语气，即 wish 引导的宾语从句中用过去完成时形式表示过去的动作。

【原题再现】

91. What does the author mean by saying "the 21st century equivalent of being caught naked" (Sentence 4, Para. 2)?

   A) People's personal information is easily accessed without their knowledge.

   B) In the 21st century people try every means to look into others' secrets.

   C) People tend to be more frank with each other in the information age.

   D) Criminals are easily caught on the spot with advanced technology.

92. What would psychologists advise on the relationships between friends?

   A) Friends should open their hearts to each other.

   B) Friends should always be faithful to each other.

   C) There should be a distance even between friends.

   D) There should be fewer disputes between friends.

93. Why does the author say "we live in a world where you simply cannot keep a secret" (Sentence 5, Para. 3)?

   A) Modern society has finally evolved into an open society.

   B) People leave traces around when using modern technology.

   C) There are always people who are curious about others' affairs.

   D) Many search engines profit by revealing people's identities.

94. What do most Americans do with regard to privacy protection?

   A) They change behaviors that might disclose their identity.

   B) They use various loyalty cards for business transactions.

   C) They rely most and more on electronic devices.

D) They talk a lot but hardly do anything about it.

95. According to the passage, privacy is like health in that _____.

A) people will make every effort to keep it.

B) its importance is rarely understood

C) it is something that can easily be lost

D) people don't cherish it until they lose it

【单词详解】

【重点单词】intend / in'tend / *vt.*

[基本词义] 打算,意旨,想要

[用法导航] primarily intended for... 主要是为……打算的 // as if intended otherwise 似乎另有打算 // as if not so intended 好像不是如此打算的 // intend this article as teaching material 打算把这篇文章作为教材 // She intended to catch the early train, but she didn't get up in time. 她本打算赶早班火车,可是早上起晚了。// It was meant to be a surprise; I didn't intend you to see it so soon. 这本来是一个惊喜,我不想让你这么早就看到。// His remark was obviously intended for me. 他的话显然是说给我听的。

[词性转换] (1)**intention** / in'tenʃən / *n.* 打算,意图,用意

[词性转换] (2)**intentional** / in'tenʃənəl / *adj.* 有意的,故意的

[对比记忆] (1) **intent** / in'tent / *adj.* & *n.* (on / upon)专心于……的,一心想……的

(2) **tend** / tend / *vi* & *vt.* 趋向,倾向;照料,照顾

(3) **extend** / ik'stend / *vt.* & *vi.* 延伸,伸展;给予;推广

[真题衔接] This law _____ the number of accidents caused by children running across the road hen they get off the bus. (CET6-9401)

A) intending to reduce   B) intends reducing

C) intended reducing   D) is intended to reduce

【重点单词】appropriate / ə'prəuprieit / *adj.* &. *vt.*

[基本词义] 恰当的,适当的;拨出(款项);占用,盗用

[用法导航] singularly appropriate 极其适当的 // music appropriate to/for the occasion 适合该场合的音乐 // position appropriate for him 适合他担任的职务 // appropriate public funds for one's own private use 挪用公款 // A sum has been appropriated for local school building reconstruction. 已经拨出一笔款子作当地校舍重建之用了。

49

［对比记忆］(1) **proper** / ˈprɔpə / *adj.* 适合的，恰当的；合乎体统的，正当的

(2) **adequate** / ˈædikwit / *adj.* 充足的，足够的；适当的，胜任的

［真题衔接］For many patients, institutional care is the most _____ and beneficial form of care. (CET6-9806)

A) persistent   B) appropriate   C) thoughtful   D) sufficient

【重点单词】**preserve** / priˈzəːv / *vt.*

［基本词义］保存，保护，维持，腌

［用法导航］permanently preserve 永久保存 // preserve public order 维护公共秩序 // preserve his calmness 保持镇静 // be well preserved 妥善保存的，保养得很好的 // preserve fruit in sugar 把水果做成蜜饯 // Salt preserve food from decay. 盐能防止食物腐烂。

［词性转换］**preservation** / ˌprezəˈveiʃən / *n.* 保持，保养，保存，维护

［对比记忆］(1) **deserve** / diˈzəːv / *vt.* 应受，应得，值得

(2) **reserve** / riˈzəːv / *vt.* 保留，留存，预定

(3) **conserve** / kənˈsəːv / *vt.* 保存，保藏，保护，不浪费

［真题衔接］The ancient Egyptians knew ways to _____ dead bodies from decay.

A) deserve   B) reserve   C) preserve   D) conserve

【句子翻译】

96. Studying abroad can provide a good language environment to students and _____(使学生容易习得一门外语).

97. _____(不管你喜欢不喜欢), advertisements have become a part of our life.

98. _____(只有当我们开始了大学的学习)do we realize the importance of autonomous learning.

99. She was fired because she was reported to her boss for _____(擅离职守).

100. You should make sure that you'll keep the medicine _____(你儿子拿不到的地方).

Passage Eleven

By almost **any measure**, **there is a boom in** Internet-based instruction. In just a few years, 34 percent of American universities have begun offering some form of distance learning (DL), and among the larger schools, **it's close to 90 percent**.

If you doubt the **popularity** of the trend, you probably haven't heard of the University of Phoenix. It **grants** degrees entirely *on the basis of* online instruction. It enrolls 90,000 students, a statistic used to support its claim to be the largest private university in the country.

While the kinds of instruction offered in these programs will differ, DL usually **signifies** a course in which the instructors post syllabi (课程大纲), reading assignment, and schedules on Websites, and students send in their assignments by e-mail. Generally speaking, face-to-face communication with an instructor is **minimized** or **eliminated** altogether.

The attraction for students might at first seem obvious. Primarily, there's the convenience promised by courses on the Net: you can do the work, as they say, in your pajamas (睡衣). But *figures indicate that* the reduced effort results in a reduced commitment to the course. While **dropout** rate for all freshmen at American universities is around 20 percent, the rate for online students is 35 percent. Students themselves seem to understand the weaknesses inherent in the setup. In a survey conducted for eCornell, the DL division of Cornell University, less than a third of the respondents expected the quality of the online course to be as good as the classroom course.

Clearly, *from the schools' perspective*, there's a lot of money to be saved. Although some of the more ambitious programs require new investments in servers and networks to support **collaborative** software, most DL courses can run on existing or minimally upgraded(升级) systems. The more students who enroll in a course but don't come to campus, the more the school saves on keeping the lights on in the classrooms, paying doorkeepers, and maintaining parking lots. And, while *there's evidence that* instructors must work harder to run a DL course *for a variety of reasons*, they won't be paid any more, and might well be paid less. (2007 年 12 月第 1 篇)

【段落译文】

不管怎么说,基于互联网的教学正在兴起。在短短几年间,34%的美国大学开始提供某种形式的网络远程教育,而在较大一点的大学里头,这个数字将近达到90%。如果你还怀疑这一流行趋势,那你也许还未曾听说菲尼克斯大学吧? 这所大学完全基于网络教学来授予学位。招生达 9 万人数,数据可以支持它自称为美国最大的私立大学。

虽然网络远程教学项目所提供教学的种类不同,但是远程教学通常意味着网上开设某一课程,教师网上公布课程大纲、阅读作业以及课程日历,学生以电子邮件形式发回他们的作业。一般说来,学生与教师之间面对面的交流被最小化了,甚至被完全取消了。

网络远程教学对学生的吸引起初是显见的,主要体现在网上这些课程所允诺的种种便利上。正如他们所言,你可以穿着睡衣做你的功课。但是,数据表明付出努力的减少导致了对课程学习投入的减少。美国大学整体新生辍学率为20%左右,而网络学生的辍学率达35%。看起来学生自己也明白远程教学这一项目内在的缺点。在一项为康奈尔大学远程教育部门 eCornell 所做的调查中,只有不到三分之一的调查对象认为在线课程的质量与课堂授课课程的质量相当。

显然,从学校的角度来看,这将省下许多钱。尽管其中有一些更加雄心勃勃的项目要求在服务器和网络上有新的投资来支持协同软件,但是大多数的远程教学课程可以在已有的或只需稍作升级的系统上运行。报了课程却不来校园的学生越多,那么学校在教室照明、教学楼看护、停车场维护等方面所省下的钱就越多。而且,虽然有证据表明教师由于种种原因必须更加卖力地管理远程课程,但是支付给他们的报酬不会增多,反倒很可能会减少。

【难词释义】

boom 繁荣、兴旺,迅速发展	**popularity** 普及,流行
grant 授予,允许	**signify** 表示,意味
minimize 使……最小化	**eliminate** 消除,排除
dropout 辍学学生,中途退学	**collaborative** 合作的,协作的

【写译语块】

1. by any measure 从任何方面来讲,无论按什么标准来衡量
2. there is a boom in ... 在……领域/方面出现了蓬勃发展的势头;出现了高潮
3. it's close to 90 percent 这一数字接近90%
4. on the basis of ... 在……基础之上;基于……
5. figures indicate that ... 数字显示/表明……
6. from the school's perspective 从学校的角度来看
7. there is evidence that ... 有证据可以表明
8. for a variety of reasons 由于种种原因

【难句分析】

1. (第一段最后一句)在 It enrolls 90,000 students, a statistic used to support its

claim to be the largest private university in the country 中 support 与 claim 搭配成词组,表述"支持某一说法/声明/主张";句中 a statistic 是前文数字"90,000"的同位语,用过去分词短语作其后置定语,引出这一数据的分量与意义。

2. (第二段第一句)在 While the kinds of instruction offered in these programs will differ, DL usually signifies a course in which the instructors post syllabi, reading assignment, and schedules on Websites, and students send in their assignments by e-mail 中 while 引导让步状语从句,相当于 although;同时,主句宾语 a course 由 which 引导的定语从句所修饰,介词 in 前置,放到了关系代词 which 的前面;which 引导的定语从句里又是一个并列句,由 and 连接两个分句,分别叙述教师与学生在这样的远程网络课程里做些什么。

3. (最后一段最后一句)在 while there's evidence that instructors must work harder to run a DL course for a variety of reasons, they won't be paid any more, and might well be paid less 中 there's evidence that ... 是一个常用结构,表示"有证据可以说明或支持……";might well 常出现在动词前面表示"很可能……";while 引导的从句包含一个由 that 引导的同位语从句,主句中 and 连接并列谓语 won't be paid 和 might well be paid。

【原题再现】

101. What is the most striking feature of the University of Phoenix?

    A) All its courses are offered online.

    B) Its online courses are of the best quality.

    C) It boasts the largest number of students on campus.

    D) Anyone taking its online courses is sure to get a degree.

102. According to the passage, distance learning is basically characterized by _____.

    A) a considerable flexibility in its academic requirements

    B) the great diversity of students' academic backgrounds

    C) a minimum or total absence of face-to-face instruction

    D) the casual relationship between students and professors

103. Many students take Internet-based courses mainly because they can _____.

    A) earn their academic degrees with much less effort

    B) save a great deal on traveling and boarding expenses

    C) select courses from various colleges and universities

    D) work on the required courses whenever and wherever

104. What accounts for the high drop-out rates for online students?

    A) There is no strict control over the academic standards of the courses.

    B) The evaluation system used by online universities is inherently weak.

    C) There is no mechanism to ensure that they make the required effort.

    D) Lack of classroom interaction reduces the effectiveness of instruction.

105. According to the passage, universities show great enthusiasm for DL programs for the purpose of _____.

    A) building up their reputation

    B) cutting down on their expenses

    C) upgrading their teaching facilities

    D) providing convenience for students

【单词详解】

【重点单词】**boom** / buːm / *vt.* , *vi.* & *n.*

[基本词义] (使)迅速发展,(使)兴旺;繁荣,景气,迅速增长(期)

[用法导航] the post-war baby boom 战后的婴儿出生高峰期 // the "build-it-yourself" boom "自己动手建造"热 // a boom in real estate 房地产生意兴隆 // There's been a boom in exports this year. 今年出口激增。

[词性转换] **booming** / 'buːmiŋ / *adj.* 兴旺的,繁荣的,大受欢迎的

[对比记忆] (1) **boon** / buːn / *n.* 恩惠,有用之物

    (2) **bloom** / bluːm / *v.* & *n.* 使(开花),(使)茂盛;花,青春

    (3) **boost** / buːst / *vt.* & *n.* 促进,增加,支援;推动,帮助,宣扬

    (4) **prosper** / 'prɔspə / *vt.* & *vi.* (使)成功,(使)昌盛,(使)繁荣

    (5) **flourish** / 'flʌriʃ / *vi.* & *n.* 繁荣,兴旺,茂盛,处于旺盛、活跃时期

    (6) **thrive** / θraiv / *vi.* 繁荣,兴旺,茁壮成长

[真题衔接] The post-World War II baby _____ resulted in a 43 percent increase in the number of teenagers in the 1960s and 1970s. (CET6-0406)

    A) boost   B) boom   C) production   D) prosperity

【重点单词】**perspective** / pə'spektiv / *n.* & *adj.*

[基本词义] 透视法;正确判断;合理观察;远景;视角,看法,眼力;透视的

[用法导航] a distorted perspective of the nation's history 对这个国家历史的歪曲看法 // a historical perspective 历史眼光 // in the right perspective 正确地(观察事物)// lack perspective 缺乏眼力 // From the global perspective, it is very important. 从全球的角度来看,这是很重要的。// From which perspective do you want to view the issue? 你想从什么视角来看待这一问题? // The new evidence put an entirely different perspective on the case. 新的证据使我们要从完全不同的角度来看待这一案子。

[对比记忆] (1) **retrospective** / ˌretrəu'spektiv / *adj.* 回顾的,怀旧的,可追溯的

(2) **perceptive** / pə'septiv / *adj.* 感知的,知觉的,有知觉力的

(3) **respective** / ri'spektiv / *adj.* 分别的,各自的

(4) **vision** / 'viʒən / *n.* 视力,眼力,构想,念头,幻想

(5) **angle** / 'æŋgl / *n.* 角度

(6) **viewpoint** / 'vju:pɔint / *n.* 观点,看法,视角

[真题衔接] It is useful occasionally to look at the past to gain a(n) _____ on the present.

A) vision   B) imagination   C) concept   D) perspective

【句子翻译】

106. In all likelihood, and _____(无论按什么标准来衡量), China's economy will be the world's largest 25 years from now.

107. _____(已经迅速发展繁荣起来) in the tourist industry in this area in recent years.

108. We judge a worker _____(根据工作表现).

109. _____(有证据显示) that unemployment is becoming a deeply planted cultural phenomenon, not to say a way of life.

110. Standing on the edge of the worldly society, she concerns every single isolated individual _____(以女性的独特视角).

Passage Twelve

In this age of Internet chat, videogames and reality television, ***there is no shortage of* mindless** activities to ***keep*** a child ***occupied***. Yet, despite the competition, my 8-year-old daughter Rebecca wants to spend her leisure time writing short stories. She wants to enter one of her stories into a writing contest, a competition she won last year.

As a writer I know about winning contests, and about losing them. I know what it is like to work hard on a story only to receive a **rejection slip** from the publisher. I also know the pressure of trying to ***live up to*** a **reputation** created by previous victories. What if she doesn't win the contest again? That's the strange thing about being a parent. So many of our own past **scars** and dashed hopes can surface.

A revelation (启示) came last week when I asked her, "Don't you want to win again?" "No," she replied, "I just want to tell the story of an angel going to first grade."

I had just spent weeks correcting her stories as she spontaneously (自发地) told them. Telling myself that I was merely an experienced writer guiding the young writer across the hall, I offered suggestions for characters, conflicts and endings for her tales. The story about a fearful angel starting first grade was quickly "guided" by me into the tale of a little girl *with a wild imagination* taking her first music lesson. I had turned her contest into my contest *without even realizing it*.

Staying back and giving kids space to grow is *not as easy as it looks*. Because I know very little about farm animals who use tools or angels who go to first grade, I had to accept the fact that I was co-opting (借用) my daughter's experience.

While stepping back was difficult for me, it was certainly a good first step that I will quickly follow with more steps, putting myself far enough away to give her room but close enough to help if asked. All the while I will be reminding myself that children need room to experiment, grow and find their own voices.
(2007 年 12 月第 2 篇)

【段落译文】

在当今这个充斥着网络聊天、视频游戏和真人秀电视节目的时代里，根本不缺供孩子们消遣的无需动脑的活动。不过，我 8 岁的女儿丽贝卡却把空闲时间用来写短篇小说，尽管竞争激烈，她想拿出其中一篇小说去参加一次作文比赛，在去年的比赛中，她获得了优胜奖。

作为作家，我很清楚写作竞赛中胜与负的含义；我也知道辛辛苦苦写出来的一个故事结果却只收到了出版商退稿信时的感受会是怎样；我还知道努力保住先前夺得胜利所创下的荣誉的那份压力有多大。要是女儿未能在这次竞赛中再次胜出该怎么办？这就是为人父母的奇怪感受了，过去自己的种种伤痕和破碎的希望都可能浮现在眼前。

上周同我女儿的一次对话给了我启示。我问女儿："你不想再赢一次吗？""不想了，"她回答说，"我只是想讲一个天使上小学一年级的故事。"

　　过去几周，女儿自发地讲着一个个故事，我帮她修改这些故事。我内心在说："我是一名有经验的作家正引领着一位小作家穿过文学的殿堂。"我针对她所讲的故事，就人物、冲突和结尾等方面向她提供了许多建议。一个关于坏天使开始读一年级的故事马上经过我的"引导"变成了一个有着无限想象的小女孩上第一堂音乐课的故事。在不知不觉中，我把她的竞赛变成了我的竞赛。

　　退回到自己空间，把成长的空间留给孩子并非像看上去那么容易。因为我对能"使用工具的农场动物"和"上一年级的天使"知道得很少，所以我得承认我其实一直在借用女儿的经历。

　　虽说退回自己空间对我来说不容易做到，但是这肯定是好的开始的第一步，而且我很快会跟上更多步伐，把自己放置于某一位置，离她足够远干涉不到她空间，但又足够近随时向她提供所求的帮助。我将一直提醒自己：孩子需要空间去实验、成长和找到自己声音。

【难词释义】

mindless 不小心的，愚蠢的，无需动脑的　　**rejection** 拒收，抛弃

slip 纸片　　**reputation** 声望，名誉

scar 伤痕，伤疤

【写译语块】

1. there is no shortage of ... 根本不缺少
2. keep ... occupied 使……忙于某事
3. live up to 实践，做到，不辜负
4. with a wild imagination 有着无限想象
5. without even realizing it 没有意识到，不知不觉中
6. (be) not as easy as it looks 并不像看起来那么简单

【难句分析】

1. （第二段倒数第三句）What if she doesn't win the contest again? 该句子用 what if 引出一个疑问，表示"假使……那会怎么样?"或者"如果发生……，那该怎么办?"
2. （第四段倒数第二句）在 The story about a fearful angel starting first grade was quickly "guided" by me into the tale of a little girl with a wild imagination taking her first music lesson 中两个现在分词短语都作后置定语，starting first

grade 修饰 angel，taking her first music lesson 修饰 girl；短语动词被动式 be guided into 作为句子的谓语，句子主干为"一个天使的故事被引导转变成了一个小女孩的故事"；句中 wild imagination 搭配使用，意为"充分自由的想象"。

3. （最后一段第一句）在 While stepping back was difficult for me, it was certainly a good first step that I will quickly follow with more steps, putting myself far enough away to give her room but close enough to help if asked 中 step back 一词意为"后退，不插手什么事"；句中 while 引导让步状语从句，that 引导定语从句，putting 现在分词短语作为 I will quickly follow with more steps 的方式状语。

【原题再现】

111. What do we learn from the first paragraph?

   A) Children do find lots of fun in many mindless activities.

   B) Rebecca is much too occupied to enjoy her leisure time.

   C) Rebecca draws on a lot of online materials for her writing.

   D) A lot of distractions compete for children's time nowadays.

112. What did the author say about her own writing experience?

   A) She did not quite live up to her reputation as a writer.

   B) Her way to success was full of pains and frustrations.

   C) She was constantly under pressure of writing more.

   D) Most of her stories had been rejected by publishers.

113. Why did Rebecca want to enter this year's writing contest?

   A) She believed she possessed real talent for writing.

   B) She was sure of winning with her mother's help.

   C) She wanted to share her stories with readers.

   D) She had won a prize in the previous contest.

114. The author took great pains to refine her daughter's stories because _____.

   A) she believed she had the knowledge and experience to offer guidance

   B) she did not want to disappoint Rebecca who needed her help so much

   C) she wanted Rebecca to realize her dream of becoming a writer

   D) she was afraid Rebecca's imagination might run wild while writing

115. What's the author's advice for parents?

   A) A writing career, though attractive, is not for every child to pursue.

   B) Children should be allowed freedom to grow through experience.

C) Parents should keep an eye on the activities their kids engage in.

D) Children should be given every chance to voice their own opinion.

【单词详解】

【重点单词】occupy / ˈɔkjupai / *vt.*

[基本词义] 占据,占有,占用;(in / with)使从事于,忙于

[用法导航] be fully occupied 忙得不可开交 // be occupied in doing sth. 忙于做某事 // occupy oneself with/in 忙于,专心于 // Is that flat occupied? 这套房子有人住吗? // The enemy occupied the town. 敌人占领了这个城镇。// The story occupied most of the front page of the paper. 这篇报道占去了报纸头版的大部分篇幅。// Is that seat occupied? 那个座位有人吗? // This work keeps my mother occupied. 这份活儿我妈妈有的好忙了。

[词性转换] **occupation** / ˌɔkjuˈpeiʃən / *n.* (一国对另一国的)占领(期间)

[对比记忆] (1) **engage** / inˈgeidʒ / *vt.* & *vi.* 吸引;预订;雇佣;(in)从事于

(2) **possess** / pəˈzes / *vt.* & *vi.* 持有,控制

[真题衔接] Her interest in redecorating the big house kept her _____ for a whole week. (CET6-9806)

A) constrained　　B) dominated　　C) restricted　　D) occupied

【重点单词】despite / diˈspait / *prep.* & *n.*

[基本词义] 尽管,不管;轻视,憎恨

[用法导航] Despite his illness, he came to the meeting. 尽管生病,他还是来参加会议。// Demand for housing is high, despite its price is high. 尽管房价很高,对房子的需求还是很高。// The minister survived the press conference despite the fact that the journalists kept asking him loaded questions. 尽管记者们不停地问一些别有用意的问题,部长还是坚持应对完了这场记者招待会。// They won the game despite overwhelming odds. 尽管实力差异悬殊,他们还是赢得了这场比赛。// The old woman died of despite. 那位大娘饮恨死去。

[词性转换] **despiteful** / diˈspaitful / *adj.* 有恶意的,故意为难的

[对比记忆] (1) **despise** / diˈspaiz / *vt.* 轻视

(2) **spite** / spait / *n.* 恶意,怨恨;不顾

(3) **regardless** / riˈgɑːdlis / *adj.* 不顾,不管

[真题衔接] _____ his great wealth, he always remained a man of simple tastes. (CET4-9101)

59

A) Except for   B) With regard to   C) Despite   D) Although

【重点单词】**remind** / ri'maind / *vt.*

［基本词义］提醒，使想起

［用法导航］be constantly reminded of ... 常被提醒想起…… // The film reminded me of what I had seen in Beijing. 这部电影让我想起了在北京所看到的情况。// I must remind you of your promise. 我必须提醒你答应过的事。// Will you remind me about that appointment? 你到时提醒我那次约会好吗？// The sight of the clock reminded me that I was late. 看到时钟时我想我迟到了。

［词性转换］**reminder** / ri'maində / *n.* 提醒人记忆之物，或起到提醒作用的东西

［对比记忆］（1）**evoke** / i'vəuk / *vt.* 唤起，引起，使人才想起

（2）**occur** / ə'kə: / *vi.* 发生，出现，存在；(to)被想起，被想到

（3）**recall** / ri'kɔ:l / *vt.* 回忆起，回想起；召回，叫回 *vi.* 记得，回想

［真题衔接］She, as a golf widow, had to _____ him that he had a wife.

A) remind   B) reassure   C) convince   D) persuade

【句子翻译】

116. The players _____（辜负了教练对他们的期望）.

117. Booking travel can get complicated, and _____（并不像看起来那么简单）.

118. _____（一点也不缺）media coverage about the rich becoming less rich, including today's Times piece.

119. Unfortunately, we may be wasting gallons of water _____（不知不觉中/没有意识到的情况下）.

120. The young mother _____（忙于）taking care of the newly born baby.

Passage Thirteen

I've been writing for most of my life. The book ***Writing Without Teachers*** introduced me to one **distinction** and one practice that has helped my writing processes **tremendously**. The distinction is between the creative mind and the critical mind. While you need to **employ** both to get to a finished result, they cannot work in parallel no matter how much we might like to think so.

Trying to ***criticize writing on the fly*** is possibly the single greatest barrier to writing that most of us encounter. If you are listening to that 5th grade English teacher correct your grammar while you are trying to capture a fleeting（稍纵即逝

的）thought, the thought will die. If you **capture** the fleeting thought and simply share it with the world *in raw form*, no one is likely to understand. You must learn to create first and then criticize if you want to make writing the tool for thinking that it is.

The practice that can help you *past your learned bad habits* of trying to **edit** as you write is what Elbow calls "free writing." In free writing, the **objective** is to *get words down on paper non-stop*, usually for 15-20 minutes. No stopping, no going back, no criticizing. The goal is to get the words flowing. As the words begin to flow, the ideas will come from the shadows and let themselves be captured on your notepad or your screen.

Now you have raw materials that you can begin to work with using the critical mind that you've persuaded to sit on the side and watch quietly. *Most likely*, you will believe that this will take more time than you actually have and you will *end up staring blankly at the pages* as the deadline draws near.

Instead of staring at a blank, start filling it with words no matter how bad. Halfway through you **available** time, stop and rework your raw writing into something closer to finished product. Move back and forth until you run out of time and the final result will most likely be far better than your current practices. (356 words)　（2007 年 6 月第 1 篇）

【段落译文】

我的大半生一直忙于写作。《自学写作》这本书使我认识到一种区别，教会了我一种练习方法，对我的写作帮助颇大。这种区别是创造性思维和批判性思维的区别。当你需要同时使用这两种思维来完成写作时，无论愿望多强，也不可能让它们同时起作用。

一边写一边对作品进行批评可能是我们大多数人在写作中最大的障碍。当你试图想要抓住转瞬即逝的灵感时，如果还去让教五年级的英语老师纠正语法错误，那么你的灵感就会枯竭。但是如果你只是抓住未经雕琢的灵感与世人分享，恐怕无人能够理解。因此如果你要让写作成为表达思想的工具，就必须学会先创造，后批判。

有种被 Elbow 称为"随意写作"的方法可以帮助你克服边写作边修改的坏习惯。随意写作的目的是在 15 到 20 分钟的时间里不停地把想法写在纸上。写作中一刻不停，不要回头检查，也不进行评判。目的就是不停地写。当文字流淌出来，思想随之由暗到明，然后记录到记事本或屏幕上。

此时你拥有了可以开始处理的原始素材，就可以运用刚才被你搁置一边、冷眼旁观的批判思维。很可能你认为这样做会让你的时间不够用，截稿期限逼近，而你却茫然盯着纸张。

你要做的不是盯着空白页面发呆，而是开始用字填满纸张，不管这些文字有多糟糕。截稿期限过半时再停下去修改原始素材，使之成为接近成品的文章。如此这般反复斟酌，直至时间用完，最终的结果很可能比你现在的做法好得多。

【难词释义】

distinction 差异，区别　　　　　**tremendously** 极大地

employ 利用，使用　　　　　　　**capture** 抓住，捕获

edit 改写，编辑　　　　　　　　**objective** 目的

available 可利用的

【写译语块】

1. criticize writing on the fly 批评正在写作中的文章
2. in raw form 粗糙地，未加工地
3. past your learned bad habits 克服你有的坏习惯
4. get words down on paper non-stop 不停地在纸上写字
5. most likely 极有可能的是
6. end up staring blankly at the pages 最终只能盯着纸张发呆

【难句分析】

1. （第一段末尾）在 While you need to employ both to get to a finished result, they cannot work in parallel no matter how much we might like to think so 中的 both 指前句中的 the creative mind 和 the critical mind，get to a finished result 则指"取得最终的结果"，即"完成文章的写作"。They cannot work in parallel 中的 They 也是指 the creative mind 和 the critical mind；work in parallel 指"同时起作用"，该部分的意思是说"两种思维形式不能同时进行"。

2. （第二段倒数第二句）在 If you capture the fleeting thought and simply share it with the world in raw form, no one is likely to understand 中，词组 in raw form 修饰的是 the fleeting thought（转瞬即逝的想法），it 也是指 the fleeting thought。sb/sth is likely to do/be ... 是较为常用的一个结构，指"某人或某事有可能会……"。

3. （第二段末尾）在 You must learn to create first and then criticize if you want to

62

make writing the tool for thinking that it is 中，词组 make writing the tool for thinking 中动词 make 后面的宾语是 writing，the tool 是宾语补足语，意思是"使写作成为思想的工具"。与之类似的词组如 elect him the chairman 选他作主席。句末的 that it is 是 writing 的定语从句，make writing the tool for thinking that it is 的意思是"让写作成为思想的工具，而且本应如此"。

4. （最后一段末尾）在 Move back and forth until you run out of time and the final result will most likely be far better than your current practices 中，词组 back and forth 指"来来回回地"，如 walk back and forth，run back and forth，look back and forth。run out of time 是常用词组，指"时间用完"。句中的 the final result will most likely be far better than your current practices 有一个类似在难句分析 2 中提到的结构 sb/sth is likely to do/be . . . ，在本句中 likely 是副词，其结构为 sth is most likely be，指"某事极有可能是……"。

【原题再现】

121. When the author says the creative mind and the critical mind "cannot work in parallel" (Sentence 4, Para. 1) in the writing process, he means _____.

    A) no one can be both creative and critical

    B) they cannot be regarded as equally important

    C) they are in constant conflict with each other

    D) one cannot use them at the same time

122. What prevents people from writing on is _____.

    A) putting their ideas in raw form

    B) attempting to edit as they write

    C) ignoring grammatical soundness

    D) trying to capture fleeting thoughts

123. What is the chief objective of the first stage of writing?

    A) To organize one's thoughts logically.

    B) To choose an appropriate topic.

    C) To get one's ideas down.

    D) To collect raw materials.

124. One common concern of writers about "free writing" is that _____.

    A) it overstresses the role of the creative mind

    B) it takes too much time to edit afterwards

    C) it may bring about too much criticism

D) it does not help them to think clearly

125. In what way does the critical mind help the writer in the writing process?

A) It refines his writing into better shape.

B) It helps him to come up with new ideas.

C) It saves the writing time available to him.

D) It allows him to sit on the side and observe.

【单词详解】

【重点单词】**distinction** / disˈtiŋkʃən / *n.*

[基本词义] 区别,不同;优秀,杰出;荣誉,优待

[用法导航] a dubious distinction 令人怀疑的区别 // distinctions between sexes 男女有别 // a diplomat of distinction 一位卓越的外交官 // make/draw a distinction 区别开来 // have the distinction of doing sth 获得荣誉做某事 // The distinctions we have been discussing here are semantic rather than grammatical. 我们一直在讨论的区别是语义上的,而不是语法上的。

[对比记忆] (1) **discrimination** / disˌkrimiˈneiʃən / *n.* 歧视;辨别;区别

(2) **contradiction** / ˌkɔntrəˈdikʃən / *n.* 矛盾,不一致;否认

(3) **reputation** / ˌrepju(ː)ˈteiʃən / *n.* 名气,名誉;美名;信誉

(4) **recognition** / ˌrekəgˈniʃən / *n.* 认出;承认,确认;报偿;赞誉;认可

[真题衔接] Being color-blind, Sally can't make a _____ between red and green. (TEM4-2001-56)

A) difference   B) distinction   C) comparison   D) division

【重点单词】**employ** / imˈplɔi / *vt.*

[基本词义] 雇佣;使用,利用;忙于做某事

[用法导航] employ fire 使用火力 // employ a housekeeper 雇保姆 // employ stalling tactics 采取拖延战术 // He is employed in a bank. 他在一家银行任职。// The report examines teaching methods employed in the classroom. 这个报告考查了课堂教学方法。// Her days are employed in gardening and voluntary work. 她的日子全花在搞园艺和做义工上。

[词性转换] **employment** / imˈplɔimənt / *n.* 工作,职业;雇佣,使用

[对比记忆] (1) **employee** / imˈplɔii, ˌemplɔiˈiː / *n.* 受雇者,雇员

(2) **employer** / imˈplɔiə / *n.* 雇佣者,雇主

(3) **employable** / imˈplɔiəbl / *adj.* 称职的,有资格任职的

(4) **unemployment** / ˈʌnimˈplɔimənt / *n.* 失业,失业人数

(5) **hire** / ˈhaiə / *vt.* & *n.* 租用，雇佣

［真题衔接］If you ask me to finish the work in time, I have to _____ an assistant.

A) employ B) cooperate C) enroll D) rent

【句子翻译】

126. No trait is more likely to improve the quality of life _____ （化逆境为充满乐趣的挑战的能力）.

127. What does the data _____ （原始的）mean?

128. Getting the house ready for the visitors _____ （让母亲忙碌了一整天）.

129. Begin with injuring others and _____ （以害己告终）.

130. These findings _____ （使英国成为污染记录最糟糕的国家）.

Passage Fourteen

I don't ever want to talk about being a woman scientist again. There was a time in my life when people asked **constantly** for stories about what it's like to work in a field **dominated** by men. I was never very good at telling those stories because truthfully I never *found them interesting*. What I do find interesting is the origin of the universe, the shape of space-time and the nature of black holes.

At 19, when I began studying **astrophysics**, it did not bother me *in the least* to be the only woman in the classroom. But while earning my Ph. D. at MIT and then as a **post-doctor** doing space research, the **issue** started to bother me. My every **achievement** - jobs, research papers, awards—was viewed through the lens of gender（性别）politics. So were my failures. Sometimes, when I was pushed into an **argument** on *left brain versus*（相对于）*right brain*, or nature versus nurture （培育）, I would instantly fight fiercely *on my behalf* and all womankind.

Then one day a few years ago, *out of my mouth came a sentence* that would eventually become my reply to any and all **provocations**: I don't talk about that anymore. It took me 10 years to *get back the confidence* I had at 19 and to realize that I didn't want to deal with gender issues. Why should **curing sexism** be yet another terrible burden on every female scientist? After all, I don't study **sociology** or political theory.

Today I research and teach at Barnard, a women's college in New York City. Recently, someone asked me how many of the 45 students in my class were women. You cannot imagine my satisfaction at being able to answer, 45. I know some of my students worry how they will manage their scientific research and a desire for children. And I don't *dismiss those concerns*. Still, I don't tell them "war" stories. Instead, I have given them this: the **visual** of their physics professor heavily **pregnant** doing physics experiments. And *in turn* they have given me the image of 45 women driven by a love of science. And that's *a sight worth talking about*. (372 words) (2007 年 6 月第 2 篇)

【段落译文】

　　我再也不想谈论怎样做一名女科学家这样的话题。在我的人生中有段时间人们总是不停地向我打听诸如在男性占支配地位的领域里你如何工作之类的故事。我并不擅长讲述这类故事，因为我从未觉得这些有什么乐趣可言，真正让我感兴趣的是宇宙的起源、时空的形状和黑洞的本质。

　　我 19 岁起开始学习天体物理学，虽然教室里只有我一个女生，但我一点儿也不为此烦恼。但是当我获得麻省理工学院的博士学位，以及随后成为研究太空的博士后时，这个问题开始令我烦恼。人们戴着性别政治的有色眼镜来看待我取得的每项成就，包括我的工作、研究论文以及获得的奖励，还有我的失败。有时当我被迫卷入关于左脑对右脑、天性对培育之类的争论时，我会立刻猛烈反击，为我自己和所有的女同胞辩护。

　　几年前的某一天我说过我再也不愿谈论那些事，以此作为我对所有挑衅的最终回答。我花 10 年时间才找回了 19 岁时就有的自信，也意识到自己不愿再理会性别问题。为什么僵化的性别歧视会成为压迫所有女科学家的一座沉重大山呢？毕竟我不研究社会学或政治理论。

　　现在我在纽约的 Barnard 女子大学从事教学研究工作。近来有人问我班里 45 名学生中有多少女生。你无法想象我在回答 45 名时得意忘形的模样。我知道我的有些学生担心如何平衡研究工作和生儿育女愿望之间的关系，我不会打消这些顾虑，我也没有告诉他们那些我所经历的"战争"故事。相反，我向她们展现了她们的物理教授拖着怀孕时笨重的身体做物理实验的画面。然后她们向我展示了热爱科学的 45 名妇女的形象。这才是值得谈论的事情。

【难词释义】

constantly 持续地，不停地	**dominate** 支配，控制
astrophysics 天体物理学	**post-doctor** 博士后
issue 事情，问题	**achievement** 成就

argument 争论

curing 固化的，僵化的

sociology 社会学

pregnant 怀孕的

provocations 再三的挑衅

sexism 大男子主义，性别歧视

visual 视觉的，看得见的

【写译语块】

1. find them interesting 觉得那些是有趣的

2. in the least 丝毫，一点儿（用于否定句）

3. on my behalf 为我自己，为我的利益

4. out of my mouth came a sentence 我说了一句话

5. get back the confidence 找回信心

6. dismiss those concerns 解除那些担忧

7. in turn 依次，转而，反过来

8. a sight worth talking about 值得谈论的情景

【难句分析】

1.（第一段第二句）There was a time in my life when people asked constantly for stories about what it's like to work in a field dominated by men. 本句是带定语从句的 there be 句型，when 引导的从句是 a time 的定语。词组 ask constantly for 指不停地追问，what it's like to work in a field dominated by men 作介词 about 的宾语，其中 it 是形式主语，真正的主语是 to work in a field dominated by men，而过去分词短语 dominated by men 是定语，修饰 a field。

2.（第一段末尾）在 What I do find interesting is the origin of the universe, the shape of space-time and the nature of black holes 中，主语部分是由 what 引导的主语从句，其中 do find interesting 中 do 是用于强调动词 find，find 后面可以接形名词或代词再加形容词，即 find sb/sth＋形容词，如 find them interesting。

3.（第三段开头）Then one day a few years ago, out of my mouth came a sentence that would eventually become my reply to any and all provocations：I don't talk about that anymore. 这是一句倒装句，主语是 a sentence，谓语部分是 came out of my mouth。这种形式是介词短语用于句首，然后主谓倒装。

4.（第三段第二句）在 It took me 10 years to get back the confidence I had at 19 and to realize that I didn't want to deal with gender issues 中，it 是形式主语，真正的主语是两个不定式短语 to get back confidence that I had at 19 和 to realize that I didn't want to deal with gender issues。其中 that I had at 19 是限

定 confidence 的定语从句,that I didn't want to deal with gender issues 是动词 realize 的宾语从句。词组 deal with gender issues 的意思是"处理性别问题"。

【原题再现】

131. Why doesn't the author want to talk about being a woman scientist again?

A) She feels unhappy working in male-dominated fields.

B) She is fed up with the issue of gender discrimination.

C) She is not good at telling stories of the kind.

D) She finds space research more important.

132. From Paragraph 2, we can infer that people would attribute the author's failures to _____.

A) the very fact that she is a woman

B) her involvement in gender politics

C) her over-confidence as a female astrophysicist

D) the burden she bears in a male-dominated society

133. What did the author constantly fight against while doing her Ph. D. and post-doctoral research?

A) Lack of confidence in succeeding in space science.

B) Unfair accusations from both inside and outside her circle.

C) People's stereotyped attitude toward female scientists.

D) Widespread misconceptions about nature and nurtured.

134. Why does the author feel great satisfaction when talking about her class?

A) Female students no longer have to bother about gender issues.

B) Her students' performance has brought back her confidence.

C) Her female students can do just as well as male students.

D) More female students are pursuing science than before.

135. What does the image the author presents to her students suggest?

A) Women students needn't have the concerns of her generation.

B) Women have more barriers on their way to academic success.

C) Women can balance a career in science and having a family.

D) Women now have fewer problems pursuing a science career.

【单词详解】

【重点单词】**dominate** / ˈdɔmineit / vt. & vi.

68

［基本词义］在……中占首要地位；支配，统治，控制；耸立于，俯视；拥有优势

［用法导航］dominate a factory economically 在经济上控制一个工厂 // dominate the world 控制世界 // a society in which males dominate 一个由男性支配一切的社会 // The strong dominate over the weak. 强者支配弱者。// Education issues dominated the election campaign. 教育问题成为竞选活动中的主题。// The cathedral dominates the city. 大教堂高高耸立，俯瞰整个城市。// Sue's very nice, but she does tend to dominate the conversation. 苏人很好，但喜欢在谈话中占上风。

［词性转换］**dominant** / ˈdɔminənt / *adj.* 占优势的，支配的，统治的；居高临下的

［对比记忆］(1) **govern** / ˈgʌvən / *vt.* 统治，治理，管理；支配，影响

（2）**overlook** / ˌəuvəˈluk / *vt.* 忽视，忽略，宽恕，宽容；俯瞰，俯视

［真题衔接］For many years the Japanese have _____ the car market. (CET6-0406)

　　A) presided　　　B) occupied　　　C) operated　　　D) dominated

【重点单词】**achievement** / əˈtʃiːvmənt / *n.*

［基本词义］成就，成绩；达到，完成，实现

［用法导航］sense of achievement 成就感 // gigantic achievement 巨大的成就 // no mean achievement 了不起的成绩 // heroic achievement 英雄业绩 // praiseworthy achievement 值得称颂的业绩 // artistic achievement 艺术成就

［词性转换］**achieve** / əˈtʃiv / *vt.* 完成，实现，达到

［对比记忆］(1) **merit** / ˈmerit / *n.* 长处，优点，价值；功绩，功劳，成绩

（2）**fulfillment** / fulˈfilmənt / *vt.* 履行，实现，完成；满足，使满意

［真题衔接］According to the psychoanalyst Sigmund Freud, wisdom comes from the _____ of maturity. (研-1993)

　　A) fulfillment　　B) achievement　　C) establishment　D) accomplishment

【句子翻译】

136. _____(对听到的事情感到震惊), he placed both his hands on his mouth.

137. _____(尽管你的观点值得考虑), the committee finds it unwise to place too much importance on them.

138. You shouldn't relax your vigilance _____(丝毫).

139. The president can't be here today, so I'm going to _____(代表他发言).

140. Moreover, they are a direct irritant in _____(一些政治家和学者所认为的那样)as a coming conflict between the generations.

Passage Fifteen

Reading new peaks of popularity in North America is Iceberg Water which is harvested from **icebergs** off the coast of Newfoundland, Canada.

Arthur von Wiesenberger, who *carries the title Water Master*, is one of the few water critics in North America. As a boy, he spent time in the larger cities of Italy, France and Switzerland, Where **bottled** water is **consumed** daily. Even then, he kept a water journal, noting the brands he liked best. "My dog could tell the difference between bottled and tap water." He says.

But is plain tap water all that bad? Not at all. In fact, New York's **municipal** water for more than a century was called the **champagne** of tap water and until recently considered among the best in the world *in terms of both taste and purity*. Similarly, a magazine in England found that tap water from the Thames River tasted better than several **leading** brands of bottled water that were 400 times more expensive.

Nevertheless, soft-drink companies *view bottled water as the next battleground for market share*-this despite the fact that over 25 percent of bottled water comes from tap water: PepsiCo's Aquafina and Coca-Cola's Dasani are both **purified** tap water rather than spring water.

As diners *thirst for leading brands*, bottlers and restaurateurs salivate (垂涎) over the profits. A restaurant's typical mark-up on wine is 100 to 150 percent, whereas on bottled water it's often 300 to 500 percent. But since water is much cheaper than wine, and many of the fancier brands aren't available in stores, most diners don't notice or care.

As a result, some restaurants are *turning up the pressure to sell bottled water*. According to an article in The Wall Street Journal, some of the more shameless **tactics** include placing attractive bottles on the table for a visual sell, listing brands on the menu without prices, and pouring bottled water without even asking the dinners if they want it.

Regardless of how it's sold, the popularity of bottled water taps into our desire for better health, our wish to appear **cultivated**, even a longing for lost purity. （2006 年 12 月第 1 篇）

【段落译文】

目前在北美流行的最新时尚是从加拿大的纽芬兰岛沿岸冰山萃取的冰山水。

人称"饮水大师"的 Arthur von Wiesenberger 是北美屈指可数的饮水批评家之一。他小时候曾在意大利、法国和瑞士的一些大城市生活,那里的人们每天饮用瓶装水。甚至在那时他就记录饮水日志,记下了他最喜欢的品牌。他表示"我的狗都能分辨出瓶装水和自来水的差别"。

不过普通的自来水真的那样糟糕吗?情况并非如此。事实上,一个多世纪以来纽约市区的自来水被称为自来水中的香槟。最近,不管是从口味上还是纯度上,它还被认为是世上最好的饮用水之一。同样,英格兰的一份杂志发现来自泰晤士河的自来水口味比一些知名品牌的瓶装水还好,但是这些瓶装水的价格要比自来水贵 400 倍。

然而,软饮料公司把瓶装水市场作为竞争市场份额的下一个战场,尽管超过 25％的瓶装水取自自来水。比如百事公司的 Aquafina 和可口可乐公司的 Dasani 都是净化的自来水,而不是泉水。

正如食客渴求知名品牌一样,饮料公司和餐馆垂涎于利润。餐馆一般对酒类加价 100％到 150％销售,而瓶装水通常加价 300％到 500％。不过由于水比酒便宜很多,而且很多奢侈品牌不在商店销售,所以大多数的食客没有注意到或不在意这种差异。

因此一些餐馆加大了推销瓶装水的力度。据《华尔街日报》的一篇文章报道,市场上存在一些厚颜无耻的销售技巧,包括在餐桌上放置诱人的瓶子进行视觉销售,或是在菜单上只列出品牌,但不写明价格,还有事先不征求顾客意见就直接把瓶装水倒入他们的杯中。

不论瓶装水是如何销售的,它的流行度表明我们对于健康的更高追求,对自身文明度表现的期望,甚至是对逝去的纯净心灵的渴望。

【难词释义】

icebergs 冰山	**bottled** 瓶装的
consume 消费,消耗	**municipal** 市政的
champagne 香槟酒	**leading** 知名的,重要的
nevertheless 然而	**purified** 净化的
tactics 策略,手段	**cultivated** 有教养的,文雅的

【写译语块】

1. carry the title Water Master 拥有饮水大师的头衔

2. in terms of both taste and purity 从口味和纯度来说

3. view bottled water as the next battle-ground for market share 把瓶装水市场看

作是争夺市场份额的下一个战场

4. thirst for leading brands 渴望知名品牌

5. as a result 因此

6. turning up the pressure to sell bottled water 加大销售瓶装水的力度

7. regardless of how it's sold 不管它是如何销售的

【难句分析】

1. (第三段第二句)在 In fact，New York's municipal water for more than a century was called the champagne of tap water and until recently considered among the best in the world in terms of both taste and purity 中用了一个比喻说明自来水也并非一无是处，纽约市区的自来水被誉为 the champagne of tap water。谓语部分较长，called 和 considered 都是谓语动词，只不过 considered 前面省掉了 was。词组 in terms of 表示从某方面来说。

2. (第三段末尾)在 Similarly, a magazine in England found that tap water from the Thames River tasted better than several leading brands of bottled water that were 400 times more expensive 中，第一个 that 引导的是动词 found 的宾语从句，第二个 that 引导的是限定 bottled water 的定语从句。Tasted better than several leading brands of bottle water 是过去分词结构作定语修饰 tap water。

3. (第四段末尾)在 PepsiCo's Aquafina and Coca-Cola's Dasani are both purified tap water rather than spring water 中词组 rather than 是一个并列连词，其含义是"是……而不是，与其说是……不如说是……"。它连接的两个成分应该对等，即形容词对形容词，名词对名词或代词，副词对副词或介词词组，动词对动词，从句对从句。如 Such glass could bend like metal when dropped, rather than shatter into bits. 这种玻璃摔在地上时，会像金属一样弯曲，而不是破碎。She insisted on having the bed-room papered rather than painted. 她坚持用纸裱糊卧室，而不是用漆来漆。

4. (第五段第二句)在 A restaurant's typical mark-up on wine is 100 to 150 percent, whereas on bottled water it's often 300 to 500 percent 中，词组 mark-up on wine 指对酒类加价销售。whereas 是一个并列连词，意思是"而，却，然而"，它引出的句子常位于主句之后。如 He must be about sixty, whereas his wife looks about thirty. 他一定 60 岁左右，而他的妻子看上去 30 岁左右。You eat a massive plate of food for lunch, whereas I have just a sandwich. 你午饭吃了一大堆食物，而我只吃了一块三明治。

141. What do we know about Iceberg Water from the passage?

    A) It is a kind of iced water.   B) It is just plain tap water.

    C) It is a kind of bottled water.   D) It is a kind of mineral water.

142. By saying "My dog could tell the difference between bottled and tap water" (Sentence 4, Para. 2)_____.

    A) plain tap water is certainly unfit for drinking

    B) bottled water is clearly superior to tap water

    C) bottled water often appeals more to dogs taste

    D) dogs can usually detect a fine difference in taste

143. The "fancier brands" (Sentence 3, Para. 5) refers to _____.

    A) tap water from the Thames River

    B) famous wines not sold in ordinary stores

    C) PepsiCo's Aquafina and Coca-Cola's Dasani

    D) expensive bottled water with impressive names

144. Why are some restaurants turning up the pressure to sell bottled water?

    A) Bottled water brings in huge profits

    B) Competition from the wine industry is intense

    C) Most diners find bottled water affordable

    D) Bottled water satisfied diners' desire to fashionable

145. According to passage, why is bottled water so popular?

    A) It is much cheaper than wine.

    B) It is considered healthier.

    C) It appeals to more cultivated people.

    D) It is more widely promoted in the market.

【单词详解】

【重点单词】**consume** / kən'sjuːm / *vt.*

［基本词义］消耗，花费；吃完，喝光；(with)使着迷，充满；烧毁，毁灭

［用法导航］consume one's energy 消耗精力 // consume manpower and material resources 消耗人力、物力 // a very time-consuming process 非常耗时的过程 // He was consumed with guilt after the accident. 那次事故以后他深感内疚。

［词性转换］**consumption** / kənˈsʌmpʃən / *n.* 消耗量,消费量;消耗,消费,挥霍

［对比记忆］（1）**presume** / priˈzjuːm / *vt.* 推测,假定;冒昧(做),擅(做);认定,推定

（2）**resume** / riˈzjuːm / *v.* (中断后)重新开始,继续,恢复

（3）**assume** / əˈsjuːm / *vt.* 假定,臆断;承担,就职;呈现,具有,采取

［真题衔接］In Britain people _____ four million tons of potatoes every year. (CET4-0001-62)

A) swallow   B) dispose   C) consume   D) exhaust

【重点单词】**cultivate** / ˈkʌltiveit / *vt.*

［基本词义］耕作,栽培,养殖;培养,陶冶,发展;结交(朋友)

［用法导航］cultivate appreciation // cultivate medicinal herbs // cultivate good habits // cultivate a new generation // The company have been successful in cultivating a very professional image. 该公司在打造专业形象方面非常成功。

［词性转换］**cultivated** / ˈkʌltiveitid / *adj.* 有素养的,有教养的,文雅的;用于耕作的,栽培的

［对比记忆］（1）**elevate** / ˈeliveit / *vt.* 提升……的职位,提高,改善;使情绪高昂,使兴高采烈;举起,使上升

（2）**motivate** / ˈməutiveit / *vt.* 作为……的动机,激励,激发

（3）**private** / ˈpraivit / *adj.* 私人的;秘密的,私下的;私立的,私营的

（4）**activate** / ˈæktiveit / *vt.* 使活动起来,使开始起作用

（5）**aggravate** / ˈæɡrəveit / *vt.* 加重,加剧,使恶化;激怒,使恼火

［真题衔接］Olives have been _____ for centuries in some countries in the Middle East.

A) refined   B) molded   C) cultivated   D) surveyed

【句子翻译】

146. As we have seen, the focus of medical care in our society has been shifting from curing disease to preventing disease — especially _____(在改变我们许多不健康的行为方面), such as poor eating habits, smoking, and failure to exercise.

147. You may soon see and possibly feel the difference in your reaction to the term "associate" _____(而不是对手).

148. _____(不管你的年龄多大), you can make a number of important changes in your life style.

149. _____（因此），during his junior year of high school，Walter failed both English and Latin.

150. Raw honey is a natural sweetener，_____（而精制的糖不是甜味剂）.

Passage Sixteen

As we have seen，the focus of medical care in our society has been **shifting** from curing disease to preventing disease—especially in terms of changing our many unhealthy behaviors，such as poor eating habits，smoking，and *failure to exercise*. The line of thought involved in this shift can be **pursued** further. Imagine a person who is about the right weight，but does not eat very nutritious（有营养的）foods，who feels OK but exercises only occasionally，who goes to work every day，but is not an **outstanding** worker，who drinks a few beers at home most nights but does not drive while drunk，and who has no chest pains or **abnormal** blood **counts**，but sleeps a lot and often feels tired. This person is not ill. He may not even *be at risk* for any particular disease. But we can imagine that this person could be a lot healthier.

The field of medicine has not traditionally *distinguished between someone who is merely "not ill" and someone who is in excellent health* and pays attention to the body's special needs. Both types have simply been called "well". In recent years，however，some health **specialists** have begun to apply the terms "well" and "wellness" only to those who are actively **striving** to **maintain** and improve their health. People who are well *are concerned with nutrition and exercise* and they *make a point of monitoring their body's condition*. Most important，perhaps，people who are well *take active responsibility for all matters related to their health*. Even people who have a physical disease or handicap（缺陷）may be "well，" *in this new sense*，if they *make an effort to maintain the best possible health they can* in the face of their physical **limitations**. "Wellness" may perhaps best be viewed not as a state that people can achieve，but as an ideal that people can strive for. People who are well are likely to be better able to resist disease and to fight disease when it **strikes**. And by *focusing attention on healthy ways of living*，the **concept** of wellness can have a beneficial impact on the ways in which people face the challenges of daily life. （2006 年 12 月第 2 篇）

【段落译文】

正如我们所看到的那样，社会对医疗保健的关注重点已经从治疗疾病转到了对疾病的防范,尤其是在改变我们许多不健康的行为方面,如不健康的饮食习惯、抽烟和缺乏运动。围绕这种转变的思路可以再深入地挖掘。试想一个人,体重正常但不吃有营养的食物,感觉正常但很少运动,每天上班但工作表现不突出,大多数晚上在家喝上几杯啤酒但从不酒后驾驶,不感到胸闷,血压也正常,但嗜睡而且经常感到疲倦。此人没有生病,甚至也没有患上任何一种疾病的危险,不过我们可以想象此人可以变得更健康。

传统医学没有区分只是没有生病的人和身体非常健康并且非常注意身体特殊需求的人,然而近年来一些健康专家开始认为只有那些努力维持和改善身体健康状况的人才能称得上健康。健康的人关心营养,注重运动,重视监控自己的身体状况。最重要的恐怕是健康的人主动承担与身体健康有关的一切责任。在这种全新的意义上,即使是有生理疾病或缺陷的人也可以是健康的,只要他们能在身体残疾的情况下努力保持最佳的健康状态。也许最好别把健康看作是人们能够达到的一种状态,而是把它当成追求的理想。健康的人能更好地预防疾病,当疾病来临时,更容易战胜疾病。通过关注健康的生活方式,健康的概念能对人们如何应付日常生活中的挑战产生有益的影响。

【难词释义】

shifting 转变	**pursued** 追寻,探求
outstanding 杰出的	**abnormal** 异常的
count 计数	**specialist** 专家
striving 努力	**maintain** 维护,保持
limitation 局限,缺陷	**strike** 打击,降临
concept 概念	

【写译语块】

1. failure to exercise 缺乏运动
2. be at risk 处于危险中
3. distinguish between someone who is merely "not ill" and someone who is in excellent health 区分只是没有生病的人和完全健康的人
4. be concerned with nutrition and exercise 关注营养和运动
5. make a point of monitoring their body's condition 特别注重监控他们的身体状况
6. take active responsibility for all matters related to their health 主动承担有关身体健康的所有责任
7. in this new sense 在这种全新的意义上

76

8. make an effort to maintain the best possible health they can 努力保持最佳的健康状态

9. focus attention on healthy ways of living 关注健康的生活方式

【难句分析】

1. （第一段开头）在 As we have seen, the focus of medical care in our society has been shifting from curing disease to preventing disease — especially in terms of changing our many unhealthy behaviors, such as poor eating habits, smoking, and failure to exercise 中，As we have seen 是状语从句，指"正如我们看到的那样"，词组 shifting from curing disease to preventing disease 指"从治疗疾病到预防疾病的转变"，其中的 to 是介词，与 from 搭配使用，表示"从……到……"。词组 such as 后面跟的 poor eating habits, smoking 和 failure to exercise 是三个处于平行位置的结构，用于对前文提到的 our many unhealthy behaviors 进行举例说明。

2. （第二段开头）在 The field of medicine has not traditionally distinguished between someone who is merely "not ill" and someone who is in excellent health and pays attention to the body's special needs 中，谓语部分包括两个动词词组，一个是由动词 distinguish 引导的词组，另一个是动词结构 pay attention to the body's special needs。动词 distinguish 后面常常跟 between ... and ... ，或者是 from ... to ... ，表示"区别……和……"或"使……有别于……"。

3. （第二段第 6 句）在 Even people who have a physical disease or handicap（缺陷）may be "well," in this new sense, if they make an effort to maintain the best possible health they can in the face of their physical limitations 中，词组 in ... sense 指"从……意义上讲"，如 in the cultural sense（从文化的意义上讲），in the geographical sense（从地理意义上讲）。词组 in the face of 也是常用词组，表示"面临……"，如 in the face of the challenge（面对挑战），in the face of danger（面对危险）。physical limitation 指"身体的缺陷"或"身体残疾"。

4. （第二段末尾）在 And by focusing attention on healthy ways of living, the concept of wellness can have a beneficial impact on the ways in which people face the challenges of daily life 中，词组 focusing attention on 指"关注，对……集中注意力"，另一个词组是 have a beneficial impact on，表示"对……产生有利的影响"，如 have an impact on the local community（对本地社区产生影响），have a negative impact on people's live（对人们生活产生消极影响）。

【原题再现】

151. Today medical care is placing more stress on _____.

A) keeping people in a healthy physical condition

B) monitoring patients' body functions

C) removing people's bad living habits

D) ensuring people's psychological well-being

152. In the first paragraph, people are reminded that _____ .

A) good health is more than not being ill

B) drinking, even if not to excess, could be harmful

C) regular health checks are essential to keeping fit

D) prevention is more difficult than cure

153. Traditionally, a person is considered "well" if he _____ .

A) does not have any unhealthy living habits

B) does not have any physical handicaps

C) is able to handle his daily routines

D) is free from any kind of disease

154. According to the author, the true meaning of "wellness" is for people _____ .

A) to best satisfy their body's special needs

B) to strive to maintain the best possible health

C) to meet the strictest standards of bodily health

D) to keep a proper balance between work and leisure

155. According to what the author advocates, which of the following groups of people would be considered healthy?

A) People who have strong muscles as well as slim figures.

B) People who are not presently experiencing any symptoms of disease.

C) People who try to be as healthy as possible, regardless of their limitations.

D) People who can recover from illness even without seeking medical care.

【单词详解】

【重点单词】**strike** / straik / *vt.* , *vi.* & *n.*

[基本词义] *vt.* 使突然想到;打,敲;侵袭,折磨;给……以深刻印象;打(火);划(火柴) *vi.* 罢工;打,击,敲;袭击,侵袭;(钟等)敲响,报时 *n.* 罢工;袭击

[用法导航] strike the eye 抢眼,醒目 // strike the table with his fist 用拳头砸桌子 // strike home 击中要害 // strike a match 划火柴 // strike a chord 引起

共鸣 // go on strike 罢工 // It strikes as a great idea. 我觉得这个主意好极了。 // My foot struck a rock. 我的脚碰在一块石头上。 // Police fear that the killer will strike again. 警方担心凶手会再次作案。 // Tragedy struck two days later when she was in a serious car accident. 两天后, 悲剧突然发生, 她遭遇了严重车祸。 // The church clock began to strike twelve. 教堂的钟开始敲 12 点。

[词性转换] **striking** / ˈstraikiŋ / *adj.* 显著的, 突出的; 惹人注目的, 容貌出众的

[对比记忆] **stroke** / strəuk / *n.* 中风; 一举, 一次努力; 划桨, 划水; 击, 敲; 报时的钟声; 抚摸 *vt.* 抚摸

[真题衔接] I was about to _____ a match when I remembered Tom's warning. (CET4-0306)

    A) rub   B) hit   C) scrape   D) strike

【重点单词】**count** / kaunt / *vt.* , *vi.* & *n.*

[基本词义] *vt.* 计数; 把……算入; 认为, 看作 *vi.* 数, 计算; 值得考虑, 有重要意义 *n.* 计算, 总数

[用法导航] count up to 100 数到 100 // count yourself lucky 认为自己是幸运的 // at the last count 据最新消息 // on several counts 在几个方面 // I count you among my closest friends. 我把你算作我最亲密的朋友。 // First impression really counts. 第一印象确实很重要。 // If I get into trouble I could always count on him. 如果我有麻烦, 我总是可以依靠他。 // The vote was so close that we had to have several counts. 选票如此接近, 我们不得不计算了好几次。

[词性转换] **counter** / ˈkauntə / *n.* 柜台, 柜台式长桌; 筹码; 计数器

[对比记忆] (1) **measure** / ˈmeʒə / *vt.* 量, 测量; 度量, 衡量 *vi.* 有……长 (或宽、高等)

(2) **total** / ˈtəutl / *adj.* 总的, 全部的; 完全的, 彻底的 *n.* 总数, 总计 *vi.* 合计, 总数达 *vt.* 计算……的总和

(3) **account** / əˈkaunt / *n.* 记述, 描述, 报告; 账, 账户; 解释, 说明 *vi.* (for) 说明……的原因, 是……的原因; (在数量、比例方面) 占

[真题衔接] Electrons weigh very little, so they aren't even _____ in the atomic weight.

    A) reckoned   B) balanced   C) valued   D) counted

【句子翻译】

156. Career seekers should not _____(只关注眼前的兴趣).

157. _____(在纯粹的生物学意义上)，fear begins with the body's system for reacting to things that can harm us — the so called fight or flight response.

158. More and more people _____(关心环境问题).

159. It's important to _____(区别避税和逃税).

160. I always _____(特意把新成员介绍给主席).

Passage Seventeen

Communications technologies *are far from equal when it comes to conveying the truth*. The first study to cómpare honesty across *a range of communications media* has found that people are twice as likely to tell lies in phone conversations as they are in emails. The fact that emails are automatically recorded—and can come back to haunt (困扰) you — appears to be the key to the findings.

Jeff Hancock of Cornel University in Ithaca, New York, asked 30 students to keep a communications diary for a week. In it they noted the number of conversations or email exchanges they had lasting more than 10 minutes, and **confessed** to how many lies they told. Hancock then *worked out the number of lies per conversation* for each medium. He found that *lies made up to 14 percent of email*, 21 percent of instant message, 27 percent of face-to-face **interactions** and an **astonishing** 37 percent of phone calls.

His results, to be **presented** at the **conference** on human-computer interaction in Vienna, Austria, in April, have surprised **psychologists**. Some expected emailers to be the biggest liars, reasoning that because **deception** makes people uncomfortable, the detachment (非直接接触) of emailing would make it easier to lie. Others expected people to lie more in face-to-face exchanges because we are most practiced at that form of communications.

But Hancock says it is also **crucial** whether a conversation is being recorded and could be reread, and whether it **occurs** in real time. People appear to be afraid to lie when they know the communication could later be **sued** to *hold them to account*, he says. This is why fewer lies appear in email than on the phone.

People are also more likely to lie in real time—in an instant message or phone call, say—than if they have time to think of a response, says Hancock. He found many lies are spontaneous (脱口而出的) responses to an unexpected demand, such as: "Do you like my dress?"

Hancock hopes his research will help companies work out the best ways for their employees to communicate. For instance, the phone might be the best medium for sales where employees are encouraged to *stretch the truth*. But *given his results*, work **assessment**, where honesty is a **priority**, might be best done using email. (392 words)　（2006 年 6 月第 1 篇）

【段落译文】

在传达真实信息时，各种通信技术差别很大。比较各种通信媒介的诚实度的首项研究表明，人们在电话中说谎的频率可能是电子邮件的两倍。电子邮件可以自动保存记录——并且这些记录会反过来找你的麻烦——这似乎是这项研究结果的关键所在。

纽约州伊萨卡市康奈尔大学的杰夫·汉考克教授让 30 名学生用日记记录自己一周内与人交流的情况。在日记中，学生们记录了自己与人交流十分钟以上的谈话和电子邮件的数量，并且坦白自己在此期间撒谎的次数。然后汉考克计算出各种媒介下每次谈话中的说谎数量。他发现电子邮件中谎话的比例占 14％，即时消息中占 21％，面对面交谈时占 27％，令人惊讶的是电话交谈中说谎的比例竟高达 37％。

四月在奥地利维也纳举行的人机互动会议上，他的研究结果令心理学家非常吃惊。一些心理学家认为在电子邮件中人们最容易说谎，因为说谎会令人不舒服，因此以非直接接触的方式发邮件使人说起谎来更容易。另一些心理学家则认为人们在进行面对面的交流时说谎多一些，因为这种交流方式人们使用得最多。

不过，汉考克认为问题的关键还在于谈话是否被记录，是否可以回查，以及是否是实时交流。他说当人们得知交流内容日后可能会被拿来与他们对证时，似乎就害怕说谎了。这正是电子邮件中的谎言比电话中少的原因。

汉考克指出，与有时间考虑如何应对的情况相比，人们实时交流时，比如发送即时消息或打电话时更容易说谎。他发现很多谎话是对出其不意的问询所做的不假思索的回答，比如"你喜欢我的衣服吗？"。

汉考克希望他的研究能帮助公司为员工设计出最理想的交流方式。比如，电话可能是销售的最好媒介，因为打电话时，雇员们有勇气夸大其词。不过考虑到汉考克的研究结果，诚信优先的工作业绩评定最好还是通过电子邮件进行。

【难词释义】

confess 坦白，承认

astonishing 惊讶的

conference 大会，会议

deception 欺骗

interactions 交谈

present 呈现，展现

psychologists 心理学家

crucial 至关重要的，决定性的

occur 发生
assessment 评价

sue 控告，提起诉讼
priority 优先考虑的事

【写译语块】

1. be far from equal when it comes to conveying the truth 当传达真实信息时，差别很大
2. a range of communications media 各种通信媒体
3. lies made up to 14 percent of email 电子邮件中谎话占 14%
4. work out the number of lies per conversation 计算出每次谈话中说谎的次数
5. hold them to account 让他们承担责任
6. stretch the truth 夸大事实
7. given his results 考虑到他的研究结果

【难句分析】

1. (第一段第二句)在 The first study to compare honesty across a range of communications media has found that people are twice as likely to tell lies in phone conversations as they are in emails 中主语 The first study 与谓语 has found that ... 相隔较远。较难的两个部分，一个是 to compare honesty across a range of communications media，是不定式短语作定语来修饰句子主语 The first study；第二是 that people are twice as likely to tell lies in phone conversations as they are in emails 在句中作宾语，从句中包含有 as ... as 比较结构，如 not as exciting as other rides he'd been on(不像其他的旅行那样令他激动)。

2. (第一段末尾)在 The fact that e-mails are automatically recorded — and can come back to haunt (困扰) you—appears to be the key to the finding 中，主语是 The fact，谓语部分是 appears to be the key to the finding。句子的主语 The fact 之后接的 that e-mails are automatically recorded—and can come back to haunt (困扰)是同位语从句，说明 The fact 的具体内容。动词 appear 在本句中相当于 seem，指"似乎，显得"；词组 be the key to ... 指"是……关键"，注意此时一般要用介词 to。

3. (第三段第二句)在 Some expected e-mailers to be the biggest liars, reasoning that because deception makes people uncomfortable, the detachment (非直接接触) of e-mailing would make it easier to lie 中，现在分词 reasoning 和后面接的 that 从句是状语部分。在 that 从句中，because deception makes people uncomfortable 在从句中作原因状语，意为"因为欺骗会使人不舒服"，而 the de-

tachment (非直接接触) of e-mailing would make it easier to lie 是从句的主句。make people uncomfortable 是 make 后面接名词宾语和形容词补语形式,是 make 的常用结构,如 make me happy // make the students excited // make the guests honored。

4. (第五段开头)在 People are also more likely to lie in real time — in an instant message or phone call, say — than if they have time to think of a response 中,主干是由 more… than 句式构成的。动词 say 用于举例说明,相当于 for instance 或 for example,in an instant message or phone call 对 in real time 起补充说明作用。句尾的 if they have time to think of a response 是比较状语从句。

【原题再现】

161. Hancock's study focuses on _____ .

    A) the consequences of lying in various communications media

    B) the success of communications technologies in conveying ideas

    C) people's preferences in selecting communications technologies

    D) people's honesty levels across a range of communications media

162. Hancock's research finding surprised those who believed that _____ .

    A) people are less likely to lie in instant message

    B) people are unlikely to lie in face-to-face interactions

    C) people are most likely to lie in email communication

    D) people are twice as likely to lie in phone conversations

163. According to the passage, why are people more likely to tell the truth through certain media of communications?

    A) They are afraid of leaving behind traces of their lies.

    B) They believe that honesty is the best policy.

    C) They tend to be relaxed when using those media.

    D) They are most practiced at those forms of communication.

164. According to Hancock, the telephone is a preferable medium for promoting sales because _____ .

    A) salesmen can talk directly to their customers

    B) salesmen may feel less restrained to exaggerate

    C) salesmen can impress customers as being trustworthy

    D) salesmen may pass on instant message effectively

165. It can be inferred from the passage that _____ .

A) honesty should be encouraged interpersonal communications

B) more employers will use emails to communicate with their employers

C) suitable media should be chosen for different communication purpose

D) email is now the dominant medium of communication within a company

【单词详解】

【重点单词】**confess** / kənˈfes / *v.*

[基本词义] 坦白,供认;承认

[用法导航] confess to being a spy 承认当间谍 // confess to murder 承认谋杀 // confess to having a secret admiration for his opponent 承认私下里很钦佩他的对手 // They confessed themselves to have made a great mistake. 他们承认自己犯了大错。// Marsha confessed that she didn't really know how to work the computer. 玛莎承认她其实不会使用电脑。

[词性转换] **confession** / kənˈfeʃn / *n.* 表白,承认;自首,供认

[对比记忆] (1) **press** / pres / *v.* 压,按,挤;压榨,压迫;催促,逼迫

(2) **suppress** / səˈpres / *vt.* 压制,镇压;禁止发表,查禁;抑制(感情等)

(3) **process** / prəˈses / *vt.* 加工,处理,办理

(4) **recess** / riˈses / *n.* (工作等)暂停,休息,休庭;课间休息;凹处,凹室,壁龛;(常 pl.)深处,幽深处,隐秘处

[真题衔接] The man in the corner confessed to _____ a lie to the manager of the company. (CET4-9706)

A) have told   B) be told   C) being told   D) having told

【重点单词】**present** / priˈzent / *vt*

[基本词义] 赠(送),呈献;介绍,陈述;提出,呈交 *n.* 礼物,赠品

[用法导航] present him with the award for best sales in the region 向他颁发本地区最佳销售奖 // present his report to the board 向董事会提出报告 // present your passport to the customs officer 向海关官员出示护照 // present your apologies 致歉 // at present 现在,马上 // for the present 暂时,目前 // The queen was presented with a bundle of flowers at the airport. 在机场,人们给女王献了一束鲜花。// Tobacco companies are trying to present a more favorable image. 烟草公司正试图展现出一种更讨人喜欢的形象。

[对比记忆] presentation / ˌprezenˈteiʃən / *n.* 提供,显示;外观,(显示的)图像;授予,赠送(仪式);报告,介绍;表演

[真题衔接] In preparing scientific reports of laboratory experiments, a student should _____ his findings in logical order and clear language. (CET4-9501)

A) furnish   B) propose   C) raise   D) present

【句子翻译】

166. _____(计划未加仔细完整考虑), their plan cannot be put into practice.

167. How can it be so hard for kids to find something to do when there's never been such _____(可供他们享受的各种刺激性的娱乐)?

168. What's more, _____(我们还得制定出一个切实可行的计划).

169. Your answer, I am sorry to say, _____(你的回答远非令人满意).

170. President Bush says he will take all means necessary _____(让朝鲜承担责任)if it attempts to transfer nuclear weapons.

Passage Eighteen

In a country that defines itself by ideals, not by shared blood, who should be allowed to come, work and live here? **In the wake of** the Sept. 11 attacks these questions have never seemed more **pressing**.

On Dec. 11, 2001, as part of the effort to increase homeland security, federal and local authorities in 14 states **staged** "Operation Safe Travel"—**raids** on airports to arrest employees with **false identification**. In Salt Lake City there were 69 arrests. But those captured were anything but terrorists, most of them **illegal immigrants** from Central America. Authorities said *the undocumented workers' illegal status made them open to* **blackmail** by terrorists.

Many immigrants in Salt Lake City were angered by the arrests and said they felt as they were being treated like **disposable goods**.

Mayor Anderson said those feelings were justified *to a certain extent*. "We're saying we want you to work in these places, we're going to look the other way in terms of what our laws are, and then when it's convenient for us, or when we can try to *make a point in terms of national security*, especially after Sept. 11, then you're disposable. There are whole families being **uprooted** for all of the wrong reasons," Anderson said.

If Sept. 11 had never happened, the airport workers would not have been arrested and could have gone on quietly living in America, probably indefinitely. And Castro, a manager at a Ben & Jerry's ice cream shop at the airport, had been working 10 years, with the same false Social Security card when she was arrested in the December airport raid. Now she and her family *are living under the threat of* deportation. *Castro's case is currently waiting to be settled.* While she *awaits the outcome*, the government has *granted her permission to work here* and she has returned to her job at Ben and Jerry's. (330 words)　(2006 年 6 月第 2 篇)

【段落译文】

在一个以理想，而不是共同的血源来界定的国家里，应该允许谁来这里工作和生活呢？在 9·11 袭击之后，这些问题显得更为迫切。

作为巩固国家安全措施的一部分，2001 年 12 月 11 日，联邦当局和 14 个州的有关部门发起了"安全旅行行动计划"——对机场进行突击搜查，逮捕用假身份证的劳工。在盐湖城，有 69 人被捕。但是这些被逮捕的人根本不是恐怖分子，他们中的大多数是从中美洲或南美洲来的非法移民。当局称这些无正式文件的工人的非法身份容易使他们被恐怖分子讹诈。

这次逮捕激起了盐湖城许多移民的愤慨，他们说感觉自己像是一次性商品。

安德森市长说这种感觉在某种程度上是合乎情理的。"我们（一方面）说我们想要你们在这里工作，从法律方面来说，我们可以网开一面；可是当我们觉得不方便的时候，或者当我们特别重视国家安全的时候，尤其是 9·11 以后，你们就要被打发掉了。有的家庭因为这些错误的原因一家人都被驱逐了"，安德森如此说。

如果 9·11 恐怖袭击事件从未发生过，机场工人就不会被逮捕，就可以在美国静静地生活下去，很可能是一直生活下去。卡斯特罗是设在机场的本和杰里冰淇淋店的经理，一直以来都是用假的社会保障卡，已经工作十年了，这次在十二月的机场突击搜查中被逮捕。现在她和家人受到被驱逐的威胁。卡斯特罗的案子正等待了结。在她等待结果的时间里，政府允许她在此工作。目前她已经回到本和杰里冰淇淋店工作了。

【难词释义】

in the wake of 尾随，紧跟	**pressing** 紧迫的，迫切的
stage 举行，上演	**raid** 突然搜查
false identification 假身份证明	**illegal immigrants** 非法移民
blackmail 讹诈	**disposable goods** 一次性商品
uproot 把……连根拔起，(使)离开家园	**deportation** 驱逐出境

【写译语块】

1. the undocumented workers' illegal status made them open to　无正式文件的工

人的非法身份容易使他们……

2. to a certain extent 在某种程度上

3. make a point in terms of national security 特别重视国家安全

4. be living under the threat of 在……的威胁下生活

5. Castro's case is currently waiting to be settled 卡斯特罗的案子正等待了结

6. await the outcome 等待结果

7. grant her permission to work here 允许她在此工作

【难句分析】

1. (第一段第一句)在 In a country that defines itself by ideals, not by shared blood, who should be allowed to come, work and live here? 中，词组 define sth by … 的意思是"界定"。define sth by … not by … 是并列结构，用在 country 后面作定语，整个结构在全句中作状语，后面一个句子是主句。

2. (第三段第一句)在 We're saying we want you to work in these places, we're going to look the other way **in terms of** what our laws are, and then when it's convenient for us, or when we can try to make a point in terms of national security, especially after Sept. 11, then you're **disposable**. 中，and 连接两个并列句。第一个并列句里，saying 后面跟了两个宾语从句，即 we want you to work in these places 和 we're going to look the other way in terms of what our laws are。在第二个宾语从句中，短语 in terms of 后接 what 引导的名词从句。在第二个并列句中，主句是 you are disposable，or 连接了两个并列时间状语。

3. (最后一段中间)在 And Castro, a manager at a Ben & Jerry's ice cream shop at the airport, had been working 10 years, with the same false Social Security card when she was arrested in the December airport raid 中，a manager at a Ben & Jerry's ice cream shop at the airport 是 Castro 的同位语，是对它的补充说明。with the same false Social Security card when she was arrested in the December airport raid 作状语，修饰动词 working，而在这个部分里又有一个时间状语从句。

【原题再现】

171. According to the author, the United States claims to be a nation _____ .

    A) composed of people having different values

    B) encouraging individual pursuits

    C) sharing common interests

D) founded on shared ideals

172. How did the immigrants in Salt Lake City feel about "Operation Safe Travel"?

A) Guilty.   B) Offended.

C) Disappointed.   D) Discouraged.

173. Undocumented workers became the target of "Operation Safe Travel" because _____.

A) evidence was found that they were potential terrorists

B) most of them worked at airports under threat of terrorist attacks

C) terrorists might take advantage of their illegal status

D) they were reportedly helping hide terrorists around the airport

174. By saying "... we're going to look the other way in terms of what our laws are" (Sentence 2, Para. 4), Mayor Anderson means "_____."

A) we will turn a blind eye to your illegal status

B) we will examine the laws in a different way

C) there are other ways of enforcing the law

D) the existing laws must not be ignored

175. What do we learn about Ana Castro from the last paragraph?

A) She will be deported sooner or later.   B) She is allowed to stay permanently.

C) Her case has been dropped.   D) Her fate remains uncertain.

【单词详解】

【重点单词】**increase** / in'kriːs / v.

[基本词义] 增加,增大,增多

[用法导航] make increased efforts to end the dispute 做出更多的努力来结束这场争论 // increase the price by 50％ 把价格提高了 50％ // Disability increases with age. 人年纪越大,就越容易丧失某种能力。// Incidents of armed robbery have increased over the last few years. 近几年持械抢劫的事件增多了。// Do you find that walking increases the swelling in your ankle? 你感到走路让你脚踝肿胀得更厉害了吗?

[词性转换] **increase** / 'inkriːs / n. 增加,增长,增强

[对比记忆] (1) **decline** / di'klain / vi. 下降,减少;衰退,衰落

(2) **decrease** / diː'kriːs / v. 减小,减少

(3) **enhance** / in'hæns, -'hɑːns / vt. 提高,增加,加强

88

(4) **multiply** / ˈmʌltiplai / *v.* (使)增加,(使)繁殖;乘,(使)相乘

[真题衔接] Last year, these ships transported a total of 83.34 million tons of cargo, a 4.4 per cent increase _____ the previous year. (CET6-9401)

A) over   B) than   C) up   D) beyond

【重点单词】**justify** / ˈdʒʌstifai / *vt.*

[基本词义] 证明……有理;为……辩护

[用法导航] be able to justify your faith in me 肯定不会辜负你的期望 // The Prime Minister has been asked to justify the decision to Parliament. 要求首相就这一决定向议会作出解释。// Are you sure that these measures are justified? 你能肯定这些措施是正确的吗? // I can't really justify taking another day off work. 我没有理由再休息一天了。// The results of the study have certainly justified the money that was spent on it. 研究的结果确实证明了投入的钱是有用的。

[词性转换] **justification** / ˌdʒʌstifiˈkeiʃn / *n.* 正当理由

[对比记忆] (1) **horrify** / ˈhɔrifai / *vt.* 使震惊,使毛骨悚然

(2) **identify** / aiˈdentifai / *vt.* 认出,鉴别;(with)把……等同于

(3) **intensify** / inˈtensifai / *v.* (使)增强,(使)加剧

(4) **magnify** / ˈmægnifai / *vt.* 放大,扩大,夸大,夸张

(5) **notify** / ˈnəutifai / *vt.* 通知,告知,报告

[真题衔接] She worked hard at her task before she felt sure that the results would _____ her long effort. (研-1998)

A) justify   B) testify   C) rectify   D) verify

【句子翻译】

176. The difficulty of a problem was defined _____(以解决这个问题所花时间的长短).

177. Even a few strong and mature individuals die from disease or _____(在食肉动物的攻击下).

178. _____(在某种程度上)I am responsible for breaking the glass case. It's not solely Tom's fault.

179. Developments in the last decades of the 20th century seemed to _____(证明那个时期最有影响之一的一本书的书名是有道理的), *The Declining Significance of Race* (1978)by W. J. Wilson.

180. The committee _____(正在等待一个决定)from the head office before it takes any action.

Passage Nineteen

Just five one-hundredths of an inch thick, light golden in color and with a perfect "**saddle** curl," the Lay's potato chip seems *an unlikely weapon for global domination*. But its maker, Frito-Lay, thinks otherwise. "Potato chips are a **snack food** for the world," said Salman Amin, the company's head of **global marketing**. Amin believes there is no corner of the world that can *resist the charms of* a Frito-Lay potato chip.

Frito-Lay is the biggest snack maker in America, owned by PepsiCo, and accounts for over half of the parent company's $3 billion annual profits. But the U.S. *snack food market is largely saturated*, and to grow, the company has to look overseas.

Its **strategy** rests on two beliefs: first, a global product offers economies of scale with which local brands cannot compete, and second, consumers in the 21st century are drawn to "global" as a concept. "Global" does not mean products that are **consciously** identified as American, but ones that consumers—especially young people—see as part of a modem, innovative (创新的) world in which people are linked across cultures by shared beliefs and tastes. Potato chips are an American invention, but most Chinese, for instance, do not know that Frito-Lay is an American company. Instead, Riskey, the company's research and development head, would hope they *associate the brand with the new world of global communications and business*.

With brand **perception** a crucial factor, Riskey ordered a redesign of the Frito-Lay logo (标识). The logo, along with the company's long-held marketing image of the "irresistibility" of its chips, would help **facilitate** the company's global expansion.

The executives **acknowledge** that they try to *swing national eating habits to a food created in America*, but they deny that amounts to **economic imperialism**. Rather, they see Frito-Lay as spreading the benefits of **free enterprise** across the world. "We're making products in those countries, we're *adapting them to the tastes of those countries*, building businesses and employing people and changing lives," said Steve Reinemund, PepsiCo's chief executive. (334 words)　(2005 年

【段落译文】

雷氏薯片只有百分之五英寸厚,颜色淡黄,有着完美的"鞍状弯曲",它似乎并不足以成为全球统治的武器。但是它的生产者——弗里托·雷却不这样认为。公司负责全球营销的阿敏·萨尔曼说:"薯片是世界性的休闲食品"。阿敏认为世界上没有任何角落可以抵挡弗里托·雷薯片的魅力。

弗里托·雷是美国最大的休闲食品生产商,隶属于百事公司,占母公司中每年30亿美元利润中的一半以上。但是美国休闲食品市场在很大程度上已经饱和了,公司如果想发展,就得瞄准海外市场。

公司的战略基于两点考虑:首先,本土品牌无法与全球性产品所带来的规模经济竞争;其次,"全球"概念对 21 世纪的消费者有吸引力。"全球"并不是那些有意表明是美国的产品,而是被消费者,尤其是年轻人,看做现代、创新世界的一部分产品,在这个世界里不同文化的人们通过共同的信念和品味联系在一起。例如,薯片是美国的发明,但大多数的中国人并不知道弗里托·雷是美国的公司。相反,公司负责研究和发展的瑞斯齐希望他们把该品牌与有着全球性的交流和商业的新世界相连。

由于品牌认可是关键的因素,瑞斯齐要求重新设计弗里托·雷公司的标识。新标识以及公司长期形成的"无法抵挡的"薯片的销售概念将有利于公司的全球扩张。

公司执行官们承认他们试图将该国的饮食习惯导向美国生产的食物,但是他们否认那是经济帝国主义的体现。相反,他们认为这是弗里托·雷公司在全世界传播自由企业的好处。百事公司的行政长官史蒂夫·雷蒙德说:"我们在那些国家生产,我们调整食品口味使之适应那些国家,建立商业,雇佣人员并改变他们的生活。"

【难词释义】

saddle 马鞍	**snack food** 点心,小吃
global marketing 全球营销	**strategy** 战略
consciously 有意识地	**perception** 感知,认识
facilitate 使便利	**acknowledge** 承认
economic imperialism 经济帝国主义	**free enterprise** 自由企业

【写译语块】

1. an unlikely weapon for global domination 占领全球市场的不可能的武器

2. resist the charms of 抵挡……的魅力

3. snack food market is largely saturated 休闲食品市场大大饱和了

4. associate the brand with the new world of global communications and business 把该品牌与有着全球性的交流和商业的新世界相连

5. swing national eating habits to a food created in America 将一国的饮食习惯导向美国生产的食物

6. adapting them to the tastes of those countries 适应那些国家的口味

【难句分析】

1. (第二段第一句)在 Frito-Lay is the biggest snack maker in America，owned by PepsiCo，and accounts for over half of the parent company's $3 billion annual profits 中，词组 account for 的意思是"（数量上、比例上）占"；owned by PepsiCo 是分词作定语，修饰 Frito-Lay。

2. (第三段中间)在"Global" does not mean products that are consciously identified as American，but ones that consumers — especially young people — see as part of a modem，innovative world in which people are linked across cultures by shared beliefs and tastes 中，并列连词 but 连接了两个并列句，两个并列句中又分别带了定语从句。第一个句子中 that are consciously identified as American 是定语从句修饰前面的名词 products；词组 be identified as 的意思是"被确认是"，副词 consciously 的意思是"刻意地"，修饰 be identified as；第二个句子中的 ones 代替前面一句里的 products，ones 后面的 that 引导的定语从句中又包含着一个定语从句(in which people are linked across cultures by shared beliefs and tastes)，修饰名词 world；词组 see sb/sth as 意思是"视作"。

3. (第四段第二句)在 The logo，along with the company's long-held marketing image of the "irresistibility" of its chips，would help facilitate the company's global expansion 中，词组 along with 的意思是"与……同样地"，当它连接两个主语时，谓语动词的数应与第一个主语的数相一致。本句中它连接的两个名词词组(the logo 和 the company's long-held marketing image of the "irresistibility" of its chips)在句中作主语。

【原题再现】

181. It is the belief of Frito-Lay's head of global marketing that _____.

A) potato chips can hardly be used as a weapon to dominate the world market

B) their company must find new ways to promote domestic sales

C) the light golden color enhances the charm of their company's potato chips

D) people all over the world enjoy eating their company's potato chips

182. What do we learn about Frito-Lay from Paragraph 2?

A) Its products used to be popular among overseas consumers.

B) Its expansion has caused fierce competition in the snack market.

C) It gives half of its annual profits to its parent company.

D) It needs to turn to the world market for development.

183. One of the assumptions on which Frito-Lay bases its development strategy is that _____.

A) consumers worldwide today are attracted by global brands

B) local brands cannot compete successfully with American brands

C) products suiting Chinese consumers' needs bring more profits

D) products identified as American will have promising market value

184. Why did Riskey have the Frito-Lay logo redesigned?

A) To suit changing tastes of young consumers.

B) To promote the company's strategy of globalization.

C) To change the company's long-held marketing image.

D) To compete with other American chip producers.

185. Frito-Lay's executives claim that the promoting of American food in the international market _____.

A) won't affect the eating habits of the local people

B) will lead to economic imperialism

C) will be in the interest of the local people

D) won't spoil the taste of their chips

【单词详解】

【重点单词】 **resist** / ri¹ zist / *v.*

[基本词义] 抵抗；对抗

[用法导航] be much better at resisting disease 抗病能力要强得多 // resist temptation, chocolate, the urge to go home early 抗拒诱惑、巧克力、早些回家的冲动 // strongly resisted cutting interest rates 强烈反对降低利率 // A healthy diet should help your body resist infection. 健康饮食有助于身体抗感染。// She couldn't resist laughing at him in those clothes. 看到他穿着

那样的衣服,她忍不住笑了起来。// The party leader resisted demands for his resignation. 党派领导人顶住了要他辞职的压力。// He tried to pin me down, but I resisted. 他试图制伏我,但我奋力反抗。

[词性转换] **resistance** / riˈzistəns / *n.* 抵抗,反抗,抵抗能力

[对比记忆] (1) **assist** / əˈsist / *v.* & *n.* 帮助,协助

　　(2) **consist** / kənˈsist / *vi.* (of)组成,构成;(in)在于,存在于

　　(3) **insist** / inˈsist / *vi.* (on, upon)坚持,强调,坚决要求 *vt.* 坚持,坚决主张

　　(4) **persist** / pəˈsist / *vi.* (in)坚持不懈,执意;持续,继续存在

[真题衔接] Although a teenager, Fred could resist _____ what to do and what not to do. (CET4-0206)

　　A) telling　　　　B) being told　　　C) to tell　　　　D) to be told

【重点单词】 **associate** / əˈsəuʃieit / *v.*

[基本词义] (使)发生联系,(使)联合;结交,结伙

[用法导航] associate the smell of baking with my childhood 一闻到烘烤食物的味道就想起了童年 // He is closely associated in the public mind with horror movies. 在公众的心目中,他总是和恐怖电影紧密联系在一起的。// I don't want my children associating with drug-addicts and alcoholics. 我不希望我的孩子与吸毒者和酗酒者有来往。// The terrorists' victim was not associated with any paramilitary group. 受恐怖分子袭击者并不与任何准军事组织有联系。// I'd rather not associate myself with extremist political statements. 我并不想使自己与极端主义的政治言论有何联系。

[词性转换] **association** / əˌsəusiˈeiʃən, əˌsəuʃi- / *n.* 联合,结合,交往;协会,社团

[对比记忆] (1) **bond** / bɔnd / *n.* 联结,联系;粘合剂;公债,债券;契约,合同

　　(2) **connect** / kəˈnekt / *vt.* 连接,连结;联系,结合 *vi.* 连接,衔接

　　(3) **contact** / ˈkɔntækt / *n.* 接触,联系 / ˈkəntækt, ˈkɔn- / *vt.* 与……取得联系

[真题衔接] They are building the dam in _____ with another firm. (CET4-92-01-47)

　　A) comparison　　B) association　　C) touch　　　　D) tune

【句子翻译】

186. A large organization can be slow to _____(适应变化)and you should give them more time.

187. The bodies were _____(被辨认出是)those of two suspected drug deal-

ers.

188. _____(无可否认)we need to devote more resources to this problem.

189. Those shops take various measures to _____(互相竞争)for increased market shares.

190. We should pay attention to the fact that the Japanese market _____(占公司收入的 35%).

Passage Twenty

In communities north of Denver, residents are **pitching in** to help teachers and administrators as the Vrain School District tries to *solve a $ 13. 8 million budget shortage blamed on mismanagement*. "We're worried about our teachers and principals, and we really don't want to lose them because of this," one parent said. "If we can help ease their financial burden, we will."

Teachers are grateful, but know it may be years before the district is solvent (有偿还能力的). They feel really good about the parent support, but they realize it's impossible for them to solve this problem.

The 22,000-student district discovered the shortage last month. "It's extraordinary. Nobody would have imagined something happening like this at this level," said **State Treasurer** Mike Coffman.

Coffman and **district officials** last week agreed on a state emergency plan freeing up a $ 9. 8 million loan that enabled the payroll (工资单) to be met for 2,700 teachers and staff in time for the holidays.

District officials also took $ 1. 7 million from student-activity accounts in its 38 schools.

At Coffman's request, the **District Attorney** has begun investigating the district's finances. Coffman says he wants to know whether district officials hid the budget shortage until after the November election, when voters *approved a $ 212 million bond issue* for schools.

In Frederick, students' parents are buying classroom supplies and *offering to pay for groceries and utilities* to keep first-year teachers and principals in their jobs.

Some $ 36,000 have been raised in donations from Safeway. A Chevrolet **dealership** donated $ 10,000 and *forgave the district's $ 10,750 bill for renting the driver education cars*. IBM contributed 4,500 packs of paper.

"We employ thousands of people in this community," said Mitch Carson, a hospital **chief executive**, who helped *raise funds*. "We have children in the schools, and we see how they could be affected."

At Creek High School, three students started a website that displays newspaper articles, district information and an email forum（论坛）. "Rumors about what's happening to the district are moving *at lighting speed*," said a student. "We wanted to know the truth, and spread that around instead."（346 words）
（2005 年 12 月第 2 篇）

【段落译文】

在丹佛以北的社区,居民们正加入进来帮助教师和管理者们,因为弗雷恩学区试图解决由于管理不善造成的 138 万美元的预算短缺。"我们担心老师们和校长们,我们真的不想因为这个原因而失去他们,"一位家长说道,"如果我们可以帮助减轻他们的经济负担,我们会做的。"

老师们很感激,但也知道要过许多年后这个区才有偿还能力。他们对学生家长的支持感觉真的很好,但他们认识到靠学生家长解决这个问题是不可能的。

这个有着 22,000 名学生的区是上个月发现预算短缺的。"这非常奇怪。没有人会想到这样的事情会发生,而且是到这样的程度,"财政部部长麦克·考夫曼说道。

考夫曼和区行政官员们上周同意了国家紧急计划,该计划调拨了 980 万美元贷款以及时支付 2,700 名教职工的工资使他们安心度假。

区行政官员们也从该区的 38 所学校的学生活动账户中调取了 170 万美元。

应考夫曼的请求,检查官已经开始调查该区的财政情况。考夫曼说他想知道是否区行政官员将预算短缺隐瞒到 11 月的选举后,届时选民会认可 21.2 亿美元的债券发行。

在弗雷德里克,学生家长们购买教室用品并主动提出支付杂物和公用事业的费用,这样能使第一年的教师和负责人可以保有工作。

安全路地区捐赠了 ＄36,000。一个雪弗兰的经销店捐赠了 ＄10,000 并免除了该区 ＄10,750 租用汽车进行汽车培训的费用。IBM 公司捐了 4,500 包纸。

"我们发动了这个社区成千上万的人",一家医院的行政长官米奇卡森说,米奇卡森帮助筹款,"我们都有孩子在这些学校,我们明白他们会受到怎样的影响"。

在克里克高中,三个学生建立了一个网站展现报纸文章,区信息和一个邮件论坛。"关于该区所发生的事情的谣言以极快的速度在传播",一个学生说,"我们想知道真相并将它公之于众"。

【难词释义】

pitch in 加入　　　　　　　　　　　　　　**State Treasurer** 财政部部长

district official 区行政官员　　　　**District** Attorney 检查官

bond issue 债券发行　　　　　　**utility** 公用事业

dealership 专项商品经销店　　　**chief executive** 行政长官

【写译语块】

1. solve a ＄13.8 million budget shortage blamed on mismanagement 解决由于管理不善造成的 1.38 亿美元预算短缺

2. approve a ＄212 million bond issue 认可 21.2 亿美元的债券发行

3. offer to pay for groceries and utilities 主动提出支付杂货和公用事业的费用

4. forgive the district's ＄10,750 bill for renting the driver education cars 免除了该区 10 750 美元租用汽车进行汽车培训的费用

5. raise funds 筹款

6. at lightning speed 以极快的速度

【难句分析】

1. (第一段第一句)在 In communities north of Denver, residents are pitching in to help teachers and administrators as the Vrain School District tries to solve a ＄13.8 million budget shortage blamed on mismanagement 中,词组 pitch in 的意思是"加入,投入";in communities north of Denver 作地点状语,其中 north of Denver 作定语,修饰 communities。连词 as 引导的句子作状语;状语从句中的 blamed on mismanagement 是过去分词作定语,修饰 budget shortage。

2. (第四段第一句)在 Coffman and district officials last week agreed on a state emergency plan freeing up a ＄9.8 million loan that enabled the payroll (工资单) to be met for 2,700 teachers and staff in time for the holidays 中,freeing up a ＄9.8 million loan that enabled the payroll to be met for 2,700 teachers and staff in time for the holidays 是现在分词作定语,修饰 plan,词组 free sb/sth up 的意思是"使可用于某目的";但这部分还包含着一个定语从句,即 loan 后面的那部分内容直至句尾,修饰 loan;in time 作状语,修饰动词 met;for the holiday 作目的状语。

3. (第六段第二句)在 Coffman says he wants to know whether district officials hid the budget shortage until after the November election, when voters approved a ＄212 million bond issue for schools 中,从 whether 起直至句子末尾都是 whether 引导的宾语从句,其中又有 when 引导的时间定语从句,修饰 the November election。

191. What has happened to the Vrain School District?

A) A huge financial problem has arisen.

B) Many schools there are mismanaged.

C) Lots of teachers in the district are planning to quit.

D) Many administrative personnel have been laid off.

192. How did the residents in the Vrain School District respond to the budget shortage?

A) They felt somewhat helpless about it.

B) They accused those responsible for it.

C) They pooled their efforts to help solve it.

D) They demanded a thorough investigation.

193. In the view of State Treasurer Mike Coffman, the educational budget shortage is _____.

A) unavoidable   B) unthinkable

C) insolvable   D) irreversible

194. Why did Coffman request an investigation?

A) To see if there was a deliberate cover-up of the problem.

B) To find out the extent of the consequences of the case.

C) To make sure that the school principals were innocent.

D) To stop the voters approving the $212 million bond issue.

195. Three high school students started a website in order to _____.

A) attract greater public attention to their needs

B) appeal to the public for contributions and donations

C) expose officials who neglected their duties

D) keep people properly informed of the crisis

【单词详解】

【重点单词】**contribute** / kənˈtribjuːt / vt.

[基本词义] 捐献,捐助,贡献出;起促成作用;撰稿,投稿

[用法导航] personally contributed $5,000 to the earthquake fund 亲自捐赠了 5000 美元给地震基金 // a contributing factor 一个起作用的因素 // contribute little to our understanding of the subject 对我们了解这门学科帮助

甚微 // contributed a number of articles to the magazine 给这家杂志撰写了一些稿件 // I'm not going to contribute towards someone's leaving present when I don't even like him! 我不会在我不喜欢的人离开时捐钱为他买礼物！// We hope everyone will contribute to the discussion. 我们希望大家都能参与讨论。

[词性转换] **contribution** / ˌkɔntri'bjuːʃən / *n.* 捐赠物；贡献；捐款

[对比记忆]（1）**distribute** / dis'tribjuːt，'dis- / *vt.* 分发，分送，分配；使分布，散发

（2）**attribute** / ə'tribjuːt / *vt.* (to)把……归因于，把（过错、责任等）归于

（3）**tribute** / 'tribjuːt / *n.* 颂词，称赞，（表示敬意的）礼物

[真题衔接] Eating too much fat can _____ heart disease and cause high blood pressure. (CET4-0106-56)

A) attribute to   B) attend to   C) contribute to   D) devote to

【重点单词】**display** / di'splei / *vt.*

[基本词义] 陈列，展览，显示

[用法导航] display sign of emotion, a definite trend 喜怒行于色、表现出一种明显的趋势 // She displayed her skating skills to the judges during her performance. 她在表演中向裁判展露了自己的滑冰技巧。// The exhibition gives local artists an opportunity to display their work. 这次展览为当地艺术家提供了展示自己作品的机会。// The screen will display the user name in the top right-hand corner. 屏幕将在右上角显示用户名称。

[词性转换] **display** / di'splei / *n.* 陈列，展出

[对比记忆]（1）**dispose** / dis'pəuz / *vi.* (of)去掉，丢掉，除掉

（2）**dispute** / dis'pjuːt / *vt.* 对……表示异议，就……发生争论

（3）**disregard** / ˌdisri'gɑːd / *vt.* 不理会，漠视

（4）**disrupt** / dis'rʌpt / *v.* 使中断，扰乱

（5）**motivate** / 'məutiveit / *vt.* 作为……的动机，激励，激发

[真题衔接] There were beautiful clothes _____ in the shop windows. (CET4-9301)

A) spread   B) displayed   C) exposed   D) located

【句子翻译】

196. The talk was intended to _____（缓解紧张）between the employer and employees, but in the end it made the relationship even worse.

197. You made a good decision, and I _____（完全赞同）.

198. Part of _____（学校运动会基金）will be used to improve the football pitch.

199. She _____（表示愿意开车送我去车站）and I appreciated that very much though I didn't need any help.

200. I lent you that ＄203 a month ago; I'll _____（免于偿还 3 美元）but I want the ＄200 back.

Passage Twenty-one

"Humans should not try to avoid stress any more than they would shun food, love or exercise." said Dr. Hans Selye, the first physician to **document the effects of stress on the body**. While here's no question that continuous stress is harmful, several studies suggest that challenging situations in which you're able to rise to the occasion can be good for you.

In a 2001 study of 158 hospital nurses, those who **faced considerable work demands** but **coped with the challenge** were more likely to say they were in good health than those who felt they couldn't get the job done.

Stress that you can manage may also **boost immune**（免疫的）**function**. In a study at **the Academic Center for Dentistry** in Amsterdam, researchers **put volunteers through two stressful experiences**. In the first, a timed task that required memorizing a list followed by a short test, subjects believed they had control over the outcome. In the second, they weren't in control: They had to **sit through a gory**（血淋淋的）**video** on **surgical procedures**. Those who did go on the memory test had an increase in levels of **immunoglobulin A**, an **antibody** that's the body's first line of defense against **germs**. The video-watchers experienced a **downturn** in the antibody.

Stress prompts the body to produce certain **stress hormones**. In short bursts these hormones have a positive effect, including **improved memory function**. "They can **help nerve cells handle information and put it into storage**," says Dr. Bruce McEwen of Rockefeller University in New York. But **in the long run** these hormones can **have a harmful effect on the body and brain**.

"Sustained stress is not good for you," says Richard Morimoto, a researcher at Northwestern University in Illinois studying the effects of stress on longevity （长寿）, "It's **the occasional burst of stress or brief exposure to stress** that could be **protective**."（309 words）（2005 年 12 月第 3 篇）

【段落译文】

"人类不应该试图避开压力，正如他们不应该避开食物、爱或锻炼一样"，汉斯·塞利医生说道。他是第一个记录压力对人身体影响的内科医生。毫无疑问，持续的压力是有害的，但一些研究表明能够成功应对的富有挑战性的情形会对你有益。

在一个 2001 年做的对 158 名医院护士的研究中，可以说那些面对相当大的工作要求但是能够应对挑战的人要比那些感觉不能够完成工作的人更健康。

适度的压力也可以提高免疫功能。在阿姆斯特丹的一个牙科学术中心曾做过一个研究：研究人员让自愿者经受两个不同的压力体验。第一个体验是一项定时任务，要求（自愿者）记住一个清单后进行简短测试，实验对象们认为他们能控制结果。第二个体验是实验对象无法控制的：他们必须耐着性子看完一个有关手术过程血淋淋的录像。那些在记忆测试中取得好成绩的实验对象免疫球蛋白 A 水平上升。免疫球蛋白 A 是一种抗体，是抵抗病菌的第一道防线。看录像的那组实验对象的抗体有所下降。

压力促使身体产生一定的应激激素。压力产生的瞬间，这些激素有积极的作用，包括增强记忆功能。"他们能帮助神经细胞处理信息并储存起来"，纽约洛克菲勒大学的医生布鲁斯·麦克依文说道。但是从长远来看，这些激素对人身体和大脑有负面影响。"持续的压力对人是不好的"，伊利诺斯州西北大学的研究员理查德·莫里莫托如是说，他研究压力对长寿的影响。"偶尔面对的压力或短期的遭受压力会有保护作用"。

【难词释义】

the Academic Center for Dentistry 牙科学术中心　surgical procedures 手术过程

immunoglobulin A 免疫球蛋白 A　antibody 抗体

germ 病菌　downturn 下降

stress hormone 应激激素　protective 保护的

【写译语块】

1. document the effects of stress on the body 记录压力对人身体的影响

2. face considerable work demands 面对相当大的工作要求

3. cope with the challenge 应对挑战

4. boost immune function 提高免疫功能

5. put volunteers through two stressful experiences 让自愿者经受两次压力体验

6. sit through a gory video 耐着性子看完一个血淋淋的录像

7. improved memory function 增强记忆功能

8. help nerve cells handle information and put it into storage 帮助神经细胞处理信息并储存起来

9. in the long run 从长远来看

10. have a harmful effect on the body and brain 对人身体和大脑有负面影响

11. the occasional burst of stress or brief exposure to stress 偶尔面对压力或短期的遭受压力

【难句分析】

1. （第一段末尾）在 While there's no question that continuous stress is harmful, several studies suggest that challenging situations in which you're able to rise to the occasion can be good for you 中，词组 rise to the occasion 的意思是"成功应对"。连词 while 的意思是"尽管，虽然"，引导的从句表示对比。主句中 suggest 后面是一个宾语从句，从句主语（challenging situations）带了一个定语从句。

2. （第二段第一句）在 In a 2001 study of 158 hospital nurses, those who faced considerable work demands but coped with the challenge were more likely to say they were in good health than those who felt they couldn't get the job done 中，介词短语 In a 2001 study of 158 hospital nurses 作状语，study 后的 of 结构是定语。主句是比较句，"those . . . be more likely to say than those . . ."；并列句的第一个主语 those 后接定语从句，主语 who 后又有两个由 but 连接的并列的动宾结构（faced considerable work demands 和 coped with the challenge）；并列句的第二个主语 those 后也接了一个定语从句。

3. （第三段第三句）在 In the first, a timed task that required memorizing a list followed by a short test, subjects believed they had control over the outcome 中，In the first（experience）与 a timed task that required memorizing a list followed by a short test 是同位成分。task 后是一个定语从句，宾语 a list 后是过去分词作定语。

【原题再现】

201. The passage is mainly about _____.

    A) the benefits of manageable stress

    B) how to avoid stressful situations

C) how to cope with stress effectively

D) the effects of stress hormones on memory

202. The word "shun" (Sentence 1, Para. 1) most probably means _____.

    A) cut down on   B) stay away from

    C) run out of   D) put up with

203. We can conclude from the study of the 158 nurses in 2001 that _____.

    A) people under stress tend to have a poor memory

    B) people who can't get their job done experience more stress

    C) doing challenging work may be good for one's health

    D) stress will weaken the body's defense against germs

204. In the experiment described in Paragraph 3, the video-watchers experienced a downturn in the antibody because _____.

    A) the video was not enjoyable at all

    B) the outcome was beyond their control

    C) they knew little about surgical procedures

    D) they felt no pressure while watching the video

205. Dr. Bruce McEwen of Rockefeller University believes that _____.

    A) a person's memory is determined by the level of hormones in his body

    B) stress hormones have lasting positive effects on the brain

    C) short bursts of stress hormones enhance memory function

    D) a person's memory improves with continued experience of stress

【单词详解】

【重点单词】sustain / səs'tein / vt.

[基本词义] 支撑,撑住;供养,维持;继续加强,进行下去;蒙受,遭受

[用法导航] sustain life 维持生命存在 // have sufficient resources to sustain our campaign for long 有足够的财力可把运动长期维持下去 // be not rich enough to sustain a large population 无法供养大量人口 // a period of sustained economic growth 经济持续增长的时期 // I only had a little chocolate to sustain me on my walk. 我就是靠一点巧克力走完全程的。 // She managed to sustain everyone's interest until the end of her speech. 她使每个人兴趣盎然,一直听她把话讲完。 // The company sustained losses of millions of dollars. 公司遭受了数以百万元计的巨大损失。

[词性转换] sustenance / 'sʌstənəns / n. 食物,营养;维持,保持

[对比记忆] (1) **abstain** / əbˈstein / *vi.* 弃权；(from)戒除

(2) **ascertain** / ˌæsəˈtein / *vt.* 查明，弄清，确定

(3) **attain** / əˈtein / *vt.* 达到，获得

(4) **contain** / kənˈtein / *vt.* 包含，容纳；控制，抑制

[真题衔接] Europe's earlier industrial growth was _____ by the availability of key resources, abundant and cheap labor, coal, iron ore, etc. (CET6-0306)

A) constrained   B) detained   C) remained   D) sustained

【重点单词】**prompt** / prɔmpt / *vt.*

[基本词义] 促使，推动，引起；提词

[用法导航] prompt an increase in security 促使安全工作的加强 // The recent worries over the president's health have prompted speculation over his political future. 最近对总统健康的担忧引发了对他政治前途的推测。// The thought of her daughter's wedding day prompted her to lose some weight. 她因操心女儿的婚期瘦了不少。// The leading actress had to be prompted twice. 这个女主角不得不被提了两次词。

[对比记忆] (1) **propel** / prəˈpel / *vt.* 推进，推动；激励，驱使

(2) **spur** / spə: / *vt.* 激动，鞭策，促进

(3) **boost** / bu:st / *vt.* 提高，使增长；推动，激励；替……作广告，宣扬

(4) **encourage** / inˈkʌridʒ / *vt.* 鼓励，激励，怂恿；促进，助长，激发

[真题衔接] Fuel scarcities and price increases _____ automobile designers to scale down the largest models and to develop completely new lines of small cars and trucks. (研-1999)

A) persuaded   B) prompted   C) imposed   D) enlightened

【句子翻译】

206. Young brains may be especially able to _____（通过锻炼增强大脑能力），suggested another of Greenough's experiments.

207. The woman saw a dentist to help her _____（对付她的牙疼）.

208. _____（从长远来看是值得的）to introduce new techniques.

209. He seems to find it difficult to _____（与女性长期维持关系）.

210. We had to _____（耐着性子听完将近两个小时的讲话）.

Passage Twenty-two

If you want to teach your children how to say sorry, you must be good at saying it yourself, especially to your own children. But how you say it can be quite **tricky**.

If you say to your children "I'm sorry I got angry with you, but..." what follows that "but" can render the apology ineffective: "I had a bad day" or "your noise was giving me a headache" leaves the person who has been injured feeling that he should be apologizing for his bad behavior *in expecting an apology*.

Another method by which people appear to apologize without actually doing so is to say "I'm sorry you're upset"; this suggests that you are somehow **at fault** for allowing yourself to get upset by what the other person has done.

Then there is the general, all covering apology, which *avoids the necessity of identifying a specific act* that was **particularly hurtful** or **insulting**, and which the person who is apologizing should promise never to do again. Saying "I'm useless as a parent" does not *commit a person to any specific improvement*.

These **pseudo-apologies** are used by people who believe saying sorry shows weakness. Parents who wish to teach their children to apologize should *see it as a sign of strength*, and therefore not *resort to these pseudo-apologies*.

But even when presented with examples of **genuine** contrition (痛悔), children still need help to *become aware of the complexities of saying sorry*. A three-year-old might need help in understanding that other children feel pain just as he does, and that hitting a **playmate** over the head with a heavy toy requires an apology. A six-year-old might need reminding that spoiling other children's expectations can require an apology. A 12-year-old might need to be shown that *raiding the biscuit tin without asking permission* is acceptable, but that borrowing a parent's clothes without permission is not. (314 words) （2005 年 12 月第 4 篇）

【段落译文】

如果你想教你的孩子如何说抱歉,你自己得擅长道歉,尤其是对你的孩子。但是如何道歉会是一件很棘手的事。

如果你对孩子说,"抱歉对你生气了,但是……"。"但是"后面的话会让你的道歉无效:"我今天过得很糟"或"你发出的噪声让我头疼"之类的话让本已受伤害的人感到虽然他在指望着你道歉,但他才是应该为他的不良行为向你道歉的人。

另外一种看似道歉实则并非如此的道歉方式是说,"很抱歉你那么难过"。这话表明你也有过错,因为你允许自己因为另一个人的行为而沮丧。

接下来是一种泛泛的、无所不包的道歉。它避免了这样一种必需,即指明一种特别伤感情的、无礼的行为,这种行为道歉的人应承诺永不再发生。"我是个没用的父(母)亲"这样的话不会使道歉的人有任何的进步。

使用这些伪道歉的人常常认为道歉显示出人的软弱。那些希望教会孩子道歉的人应该将它看做是一种力量,因此才不会使用虚伪的道歉。

但是,甚至在孩子表现出真心的悔悟的时候,仍应帮助他们意识到道歉的复杂性。三岁的孩子需要帮助才能意识到别的孩子也会像他一样感到疼痛,才能明白用重的玩具敲打玩伴的头需要道歉。一个六岁的孩子需要提醒才能知道破坏了其他孩子的梦想需要道歉。一个十二岁的孩子需要知道不经过允许就把饼干盒一扫而空是可以的,但是,不经允许就借用父母的衣服是不可以的。

【难词释义】

tricky 棘手
particularly 特别,尤其
insulting 无礼的
genuine 真诚的

at fault 该受责备的
hurtful 伤感情的
pseudo-apologies 虚伪的道歉
playmate 游戏伙伴

【写译语块】

1. in expecting an apology 期待道歉
2. avoid the necessity of identifying a specific act 无需指明一种特别行为
3. commit a person to any specific improvement 使人有任何的进步
4. see it as a sign of strength 将它看做一种力量
5. resort to these pseudo-apologies 使用伪道歉
6. become aware of the complexities of saying sorry 意识到道歉的复杂性
7. raid the biscuit tin without asking permission 不经过允许把饼干盒一扫而空

【难句分析】

1. (第二段第二句)在 What follows that "but" can render the apology ineffective:"I had a bad day" or "your noise was giving me a headache" leaves the person who has been injured feeling that he should be apologizing for his bad behavior in expecting an apology 中,分号前 what 引导的主语从句作主语,动词 render 后接宾语(the apology)和宾语补足语(ineffective),表示"使得……"。分号后的句子里,I had a bad day 和 your noise was giving me a headache 是并列主语,动词 leave 后接宾语 the person,紧跟在后面的是一个修饰它的定语从句;现在

分词 feeling 这部分句子内容表明 the person 的感受;feeling 后接宾语从句。

2. (第三段第一句)在 Another method by which people appear to apologize without actually doing so is to say "I'm sorry you're upset"中,名词 method 后接定语从句;is 后面是不定式作表语。

3. (最后一段第二句)在 A three-year-old might need help in understanding that other children feel pain just as he does, and that hitting a playmate over the head with a heavy toy requires an apology 中,and 连接两个 understanding 的宾语从句,从 in 到句子末尾都是主句的状语。第一个宾语从句中又包含一个 as 引导的方式状语从句,第二个宾语从句中的主语是动名词短语(hitting a playmate over the head with a heavy toy)。

【原题再现】

211. If a mother adds "but" to an apology, _____.

A) she doesn't feel that she should have apologized

B) she does not realize that the child has been hurt

C) the child may find the apology easier to accept

D) the child may feel that he owes her an apology

212. According to the author, saying "I'm sorry you're upset" most probably means "_____".

A) You have good reason to get upset

B) I'm aware you're upset, but I'm not to blame

C) I apologize for hurting your feelings

D) I'm at fault for making you upset

213. It is not advisable to use the general, all-covering apology because _____.

A) it gets one into the habit of making empty promises

B) it may make the other person feel guilty

C) it is vague and ineffective

D) it is hurtful and insulting

214. We learn from the last paragraph that in teaching children to say sorry _____.

A) the complexities involved should be ignored

B) their ages should be taken into account

C) parents need to set them a good example

D) parents should be patient and tolerant

215. It can be inferred from the passage that apologizing properly is _____.

A) a social issue calling for immediate attention

B) not necessary among family members

C) a sign of social progress

D) not as simple as it seems

【单词详解】

【重点单词】 **render** / ˈrendə / *v.*

[基本词义] 致使;回报,给予;提交

[用法导航] to render sth harmless, useless, ineffective 使某事物无害、无用、无效 // render a service to sb 给某人提供服务 // rendered assistance to the disaster victims 给灾民提供了帮助 // be asked to render a report on the housing situation 被要求提交一份有关住房情况的报告 // New technology has rendered my old computer obsolete. 新技术使我的旧电脑过时了。

[词性转换] **rendering** / ˈrendəriŋ / *n.* 扮演,表演;翻译,翻译作品

[对比记忆] (1) **surrender** / səˈrendə / *vi.* 投降;(to)屈服(于),让步

(2) **bewilder** / biˈwildə / *vt.* 使迷惑,使难住

(3) **consider** / kənˈsidə / *vt.* 考虑,细想;认为,把……看作

(4) **wander** / ˈwɔndə / *vi.* 漫游,闲逛,漫步;偏离正道

[真题衔接] The fact that the golden eagle usually builds its nest on some high cliffs _____ it almost impossible to obtain the eggs or the young birds. (研-2000)

A) renders   B) reckons   C) regards   D) relates

【重点单词】 **spoil** / spɔil / *v.*

[基本词义] 毁坏,毁掉;溺爱;(食物)变质

[用法导航] oil companies that spoil beautiful coastlines 毁坏海岸线美丽景色的石油公司 // You will spoil your appetite for dinner if you have a cake now. 如果你现在吃蛋糕的话,等正式开饭时你就没胃口了。// Her parents spoilt and indulged her with toys and treats of every kind. 她父母用各种各样的玩具和享受来宠她、纵容她。// The dessert will spoil if you don't keep it in the fridge. 如果你不把甜食放进冰箱,它就会变质。

[词性转换] **stimulation** / ˌstimjuˈleiʃən / *n.* 激励,鼓舞,刺激

[对比记忆] (1) **ruin** / ˈruin / *v.* (使)毁灭

(2) **destroy** / disˈtrɔi / *vt.* 破坏,毁灭;消灭,杀死

(3) **hurt** / həːt / *vt.* 使受伤,弄痛;伤……的感情 *vi.* 痛,引起疼痛

(4) **injure** / ˈindʒə / *vt.* 伤害,损害,损伤

(5) **harm** / haːm / *vt.* 伤害,损害,危害

[真题衔接] Children who are over-protected by their parents may become _____. (CET4-9001)

    A) hurt   B) damaged   C) spoiled   D) harmed

【句子翻译】

216. It was easy to _____(将这礼物看成是一种贿赂).

217. When she didn't answer the telephone I _____(只得站在她的窗外)and calling up to her.

218. They called on the developed countries to _____(将更多的钱投入到保护环境).

219. The King, _____(意识到史密斯的能力)and growing influence, offered him a position in court.

220. The shock of her aunt's death _____(完全使她无法继续工作).

Passage Twenty-three

    Is there enough oil beneath the Arctic National Wildlife Refuge(保护区)(ANWR) to help **secure** America's energy future ? President Bush certainly thinks so. *He has argued that* tapping ANWR's oil would help ease California's electricity crisis and *provide a major boost to the country's energy independence*. But no one knows for sure how much crude oil lies buried beneath the frozen earth. The last government **survey**, was conducted in 1998, projecting output anywhere from 3 billion to 16 billion barrels.

    The oil industry goes with the high end of the range, which could equal as much as 10% of U. S. **consumption** for as long as six years. By pumping more than 1 million barrels a day from the reserve for the next two three decades, lobbyists claim, the nation could *cut back on* imports **equivalent** to all shipments to the U. S. from Saudi Arabia. *Sounds good*. An oil boom would also mean a multibillion-dollar windfall(意外之财)in tax revenues, royalties(开采权使用费)and **leasing** fees for Alaska and the Federal Government. Best of all, advocates of **drilling** say, damage to the environment would be **insignificant**. "We've never had a document case of oil rig chasing deer out onto *the pack ice*. " says Alaska State

Representative Scott Ogan.

Not so far, say environmentalists. Sticking to the low end of government estimates, the National Resources Defense Council says there may be no more than 3. 2 billion barrels of economically **recoverable** oil in the coastal plain of ANWR, a drop in the bucket that would do virtually nothing to *ease America's energy problems*. And consumers would wait up to a decade to gain any **benefits**, because drilling could begin only after much **bargaining** over leases, environmental permits and **regulatory** review. As for ANWR's impact on the California power crisis, environmentalists point out that oil is responsible for only 1% of the Golden State's electricity output and just 3% of the nation's. (339 words)　(2005 年 6 月第 1 篇)

【段落译文】

　　在北极野生动物自然保护区地底下是否真地储存着足够的石油来帮助保证美国未来的能源供给? 美国前总统布什认为这是肯定的。他认为提取北极野生动物自然保护区地底下的石油能帮助缓解加利福尼亚的电力危机并且促进本国的能源独立。但是没有人能确切地知道在那冰冷的地底下到底储藏着多少原油。根据 1998 年政府部门最新开展的调查,在那里无论从哪里着手开始勘探,出产的石油从 30 亿到 160 亿桶不等。

　　石油业正以前所未有的速度迅猛发展,发展量相当于美国 6 年所消耗石油总量的 10%。议员们声称,在二三十年里,如果每天从石油储备中抽出多于 100 万桶的石油,美国在石油进口上的开支就少了很多,相当于减少了从沙特阿拉伯到美国所有航船所需要燃烧的石油。这个消息听起来似乎不错。石油业的大幅发展也意味着在财政税收上、开采权使用费上和在阿拉斯加和联邦政府的租用收入上发了一笔多达几十亿美金的意外之财。最关键的是,提倡钻井探油的人称,开采石油对环境造成的危害不是那么的严重。阿拉斯加州的政府代表斯加特·奥根表示"我们从来都没有有关油井钻探设备会把野鹿逼到海面上的浮冰去寻找栖身之所的案例。"

　　环境学家这样认为,到达国家能源底线的这一天已经不远了。国家能源保护委员会的官员认为,在北极野生动物自然保护区的海岸线平原上蕴藏着大概仅仅 32 亿桶的可再生原油。减少开采的石油桶数实际上对缓解美国的能源危机意义不大。石油消费者要等上 10 多年才能得到利益,因为在开采石油前需要在开采费用上讨价还价,得到环保局的首肯和法规上的修订等。关于北极的野生动物保护区底下蕴藏的石油对缓解美国利福尼亚的能源危机的影响,环境保护学者指出,石油只是占到了加利福尼亚电力消耗的 1%,即全国电力消耗的 3%。

【难词释义】

secure 保证,保护   survey 调查

consumption 消耗,消费   lease 租得,租出

equivalent 等同于   insignificant 无意义的,不重要的

drilling 钻井探油   bargaining 讨价还价

recoverable 可恢复的   regulatory 规章的,法制的

benefits 利益,好处

【写译语块】

1. provide a major boost to the country's energy independence 很大程度上促进了国家的能源独立

2. cut back on 减少

3. sounds good 听起来不错

4. the pack ice 海上的浮冰

5. ease America's energy problems 缓解美国的能源问题

【难句分析】

1. (第二段第二句) By pumping more than 1 million barrels a day from the reserve for the next two three decades, lobbyists claim, the nation could cut back on imports equivalent to all shipments to the U. S. from Saudi Arabia. 这句话的内容其实都是 lobbyists 的想法。国家能减少石油的进口(import)由 equivalent 来修饰,减少的进口量就相当于所有的 shipment(从美国到沙特阿拉伯的航船)所需要的石油量,也就是说从 equivalent 开始到句末都在修饰 imports。减少的具体方法则是在句首用 by 来引导,时间的长短是 for 引导的 for the next two three decades 时间状语。

2. (第二段第五和第六句) Best of all, advocates of drilling say, damage to the environment would be insignificant. "We've never had a document case of oil rig chasing deer out onto the pack ice." says Alaska State Representative Scott Ogan. 理解该题时,主要抓住这两个句子的联系。第五句中提到了 insignificant 意为"不重要的",刚好与第六句 Scott Ogan 举的例子达成一致。也就是说,从来都没有有关开采石油而把鹿逼到海上浮冰上去求生的案例,刚好印证了开采石油对环境的影响不是那么得严重,这正是 advocates of drilling 一直倡导钻井探油的一个理由。

3. (末段第一句) Sticking to the low end of government estimates, the National Resources Defense Council says there may be no more than 3.2 billion barrels of economically recoverable oil in the coastal plain of ANWR, a drop in the bucket that would do virtually nothing to ease America's energy problems. 理解这个长句时,要抓住几个对应的表达方法,这样就能理解语句的前后呼应的效果了。the low end of,no more than,do virtually nothing,这三个短语分别是"底线","仅仅","无济于事",正是因为本身 in the coastal plain of ANWR 所储备的石油已经不多了,所以减少开采量也无法挽救美国能源危机,其实作者是想提醒人们,要为子孙保护好将来的能源,光靠减少掠夺大自然的财富是没有意义的。

4. (末段第三句) And consumers would wait up to a decade to gain any benefits, because drilling could begin only after much bargaining over leases, environmental permits and regulatory review. 理解本句的关键是对几个词组的把握。gain benefits 是指得到利益;after 后引导了三个短语,分别是 much bargaining over leases,environmental permits,regulatory review 意为"对租金的谈判,环保局的认可和法规上的修订"。

【原题再现】

221. What does President Bush think of tapping oil in ANWR ?

　　A) It will exhaust the nation's oil reserves.

　　B) It will help secure the future of ANWR.

　　C) It will help reduce the nation's oil imports.

　　D) It will increase America's energy consumption.

222. We learn from the second paragraph that the American oil industry _____.

　　A) believes that drilling for oil in ANWR will produce high yields.

　　B) tends to exaggerate America's reliance on foreign oil.

　　C) shows little interest in tapping oil in ANWR.

　　D) expects to stop oil imports from Saudi Arabia.

223. Those against oil drilling in ANWR argue that _____.

　　A) it can cause serious damage to the environment

　　B) it can do little to solve U. S. energy problems

　　C) it will drain the oil reserves in the Alaskan region

　　D) it will not have much commercial value

224. What do the environmentalists mean by saying "Not so fast"(Sentence 1,

Para . 3)?

A) Oil exploitation takes a long time.

B) The oil drilling should be delayed.

C) Don't be too optimistic.

D) Don't expect fast returns.

225. It can be learned from the passage that oil exploitation beneath ANWR's frozen earth _____ .

A) remains a controversial issue

B) is expected to get under way soon

C) involves a lot of technological problems

D) will enable the U. S. to be oil independent

【单词详解】

【重点单词】**secure** / si'kjuə / *adj.* & *v*

[基本词义] 安全的，受保护的；使某事物安全，保护

[用法导航] secure a building (from collapse) 将建筑物加固（以免倒塌）// The strong-room is as secure as we can make it. 我们的保险库建造得十分安全。// Are we secure from the attack here? 我们这里受不到攻击吧？

[词性转换] **security** / si'kjuəriti / *n* . 安全，保护，保障

[对比记忆] **protective** / prə'tektiv / *adj*. 给予保护的

[真题衔接] The capital intended to broaden the export base and _____ efficiency gains from international trade was channeled instead into uneconomic import substitution. （研-2000）

    A) secure   B) extend   C) defend   D) possess

【重点单词】**insignificant** / insig'nifikənt / *adj.*

[基本词义] 不重要的，无意义的

[用法导航] an insignificant-looking little man who turned out to be the managing director 一个其貌不扬的男人居然是总经理 // be fallen by an insignificant amount 下降的量很小

[对比记忆] (1) **minor** / 'mainə / *adj*. 较小的，较少的；次要的

    (2) **trivial** / 'triviəl / *adj*. 琐细的；不重要的；无价值的

[真题衔接] Although it is a small and _____ bank, it represents the trend of the future.

    A) indispensable   B) insignificant   C) inferior   D) passive

【重点单词】**benefit** / ˈbenifit / *n.*

［基本词义］利益，好处，实惠

［用法导航］Because of illness she didn't get much benefit from her stay abroad. 她待在国外，因生病未能有太多收获。// I have had the benefit of a good education. 我得益于良好的教育。// It was achieved with the benefit of modern technology. 借助现代技术，这个目标已经达到。

［词性转换］beneficial / beniˈfiʃəl / *adj.* 有益的，有好处的

［对比记忆］(1) **advantage** / ədˈvæntidʒ, ədˈvɑːn- / *n.* 优点，有利条件；利益，好处

(2) **behalf** / biˈhɑːf / *n.* 利益，方面

［真题衔接］Not only the professionals but also the amateurs will _____ from the new training facilities. (CET4-0306)

    A) derive   B) acquire   C) benefit   D) reward

【句子翻译】

226. The milk _____（闻起来有点不新鲜）; You should have put it in the ice box.

227. In the college, the students are encouraged to _____（独立思考）.

228. When Dad lost his job, we _____（必须减少娱乐开销）.

229. I will keep on reading extensively, for it _____（使我获益匪浅）.

230. In the flea market, you'd better try your best to _____（与老板讨价还价）.

Passage Twenty-four

"Tear'em apart!" "Kill the fool!" " Murder the referee（裁判）!"

These are common remarks one may hear *at various sporting events*. At the time they are made, they may seem **innocent** enough. But let's not *kid ourselves*. They have been known to influence behavior in such a way as to *lead to* real bloodshed. Volumes have been written about the way words affect us. *It has been shown that* words having certain connotations（含义）may cause us to **react** in ways quite foreign to what we consider to be our usual humanistic behavior. I see the term "opponent "as one of those words. Perhaps the time has come to delete it from sports terms.

The dictionary meaning of the term "opponent" is "adversary", "enemy"; "one who opposes your interests." Thus, when a player meets an opponent, he or she may tend to *treat that opponent as an enemy*. At such times, winning may **dominate** one's intellect, and every action, no matter how gross, may be considered justifiable. I **recall** an incident in a handball game when a referee refused a player's request for a time out for a glove change because he did not considered then wet enough. The player proceeded to rub his gloves across his wet T-shirt and then exclaimed. "Are they wet enough now?"

In the heat of battle, players have been observed to throw themselves across the court without considering the **consequences** that such a move might have on anyone in their way. I have also **witnessed** a player reacting to his opponent's international and illegal blocking by deliberately hitting him with the ball as hard as he could during the course of play. *Off the court*, they are good friends. Does that *make any sense*? It certainly gives **proof** of a court attitude which departs from normal behavior.

Therefore, I believe it is time we elevated (提升) the game to the level where it belongs thereby *setting an example to* the rest of the sporting world. Replacing the term "opponent" with "associate" could be an **ideal** way to start.

The dictionary meaning of the term "associate" is "colleague"; "friend"; "companion." Reflect a moment! You may soon see and possibly feel the difference in your reaction to the term "associate" rather than "opponent." (386 words) (2005 年 6 第 2 篇)

【段落译文】

"把他们撕成碎片!""杀了那个白痴!""把裁判给做了!"

以上这些话在各种体育竞技场上经常能听到。当说这些粗鲁的话时,听起来好像没什么大不了。但是请别跟自己开玩笑了。这些过激的语言可能真的会影响到我们的行动,甚至真的会导致血色暴力事件的发生。大量的资料记载了语言是如何影响人类行动的。有些词汇或语句包含了特殊的含义能使我们人类对这些词语的反映相当的异常,往往大大不同与人类平时的文明的行为。我认为,"对手"这个词就属于上述的情况之一。也许是时候在体育竞技赛场上应该把"对手"这个词永远地删除。

在字典里,"对手"这个词的含义有"相对的,相反的","敌人","那个跟你自身的利益有冲突的人"。因此,当一个选手遇上了他的对手,他或她就很有可能把对手当作了自己的敌人。在那个时候,胜利就占据了人的这个思想,每次行动。不管这听起来有多的夸张,但是人们还是认为它是可以理解的。我记得在一次手球比赛中,当裁判拒绝了一个队员换一个手套的请求,因为当时裁判认为他的手套还没完全被汗水湿透到无法正常使用,该球员就马上开始把手套在自己被汗水湿透的 T 恤衫上摩擦了几下,说道:"现在手套够湿了吧?"在比赛进入高潮时,有球员甚至被看到自己在赛场上满地打滚,丝毫没有考虑到这样做会把别人绊倒从而带来的严重后果。我也曾亲眼目睹了一名球员为了对对方球员的违规阻拦做出反击,竟然在赛场上故意使出他全身的力气用球去猛击对方球员。而在场下,他们还是好朋友。这个例子说明了什么?显然这个例子证明了在赛场上人与人的关系和态度与平时是大大不同的。

在字典中,"伙伴"的意思是"同事","朋友","同伴"。在大脑里稍微反应一会儿!你将很快发现并感觉到你对"伙伴"的反映与对"对手"的反映是截然不同的。

因此,我认为应该把上面的这个比赛上升到为其他比赛做出示范的这样一个高度。把"对手"这个词替换成"伙伴"将会是一种比较理想的开端。

【难词释义】

innocent 无辜的,无罪的   react 对……做出的反应

dominate 占领,占据   recall 回忆

consequences 后果   witness 亲眼目睹

proof 证据   ideal 理想的

【写译语块】

1. at various sporting events 在各种体育赛事中
2. lead to 导致
3. It has been shown that … 这就表明……
4. treat that opponent as an enemy 把(在比赛中的)对手当作了敌人
5. off the court 在场下
6. make(any) sense 有意义
7. set an example to … 为……树立榜样

【难句分析】

1. (第一段第四句)It has been shown that words having certain connotations (含义) may cause us to react in ways quite foreign to what we consider to be our usual humanistic behavior. 这句话中对 foreign 的理解是相当重要的,在这里他不是"外国的"意思,而是"奇怪的,怪异的"意思,它与 to 搭配,与 usual"平常的,正常的"构成鲜明对比,那就是参赛者对待某些词语做出的反映可能会跟平时

的行为大不相同。

2.（第四段末尾）Off the court, they are good friends. Does that make any sense? It certainly gives proof of a court attitude which departs from normal behavior. 这个句群要整体理解。On the court, 对手做出了野蛮的行为, 而在 off the court（在场下）他们是好朋友。Does that make any sense?（这表明了什么呢?）make sense 字面意思是"有意义", 最后作者引出这个案例无非是想说明 a court attitude（赛场上人的态度）与 normal behavior（人平时的行为）是会不同的, 因此在赛场上要注意用词, 避免使选手行为过激, 与文章主旨完全符合。

3.（文章结尾）You may soon see and possibly feel the difference in your reaction to the term "associate" rather than "opponent." 把握几个固定短语就能很好地理解该句的逻辑。feel the difference in 指"感受到……的不同"。opponent 前用了 rather than 其实是表示把它跟 associate 做比较, 在赛场上用 associate, 而不是 opponent。reaction to 是一个固定词组, 意为"对……做出反映"。

【原题再现】

231. Which of the following statements best expresses the author's view?

A) Aggressive behavior in sports can have serious consequences

B) The words people use can influence their behavior

C) Unpleasant words in sports are often used by foreign athletes

D) Unfair judgments by referees will lead to violence on the sports field

232. Harsh words are spoken during games because the players _____.

A) are too eager to win

B) are usually short-tempered and easily offended

C) cannot afford to be polite in fierce competition

D) treat their rivals as enemies

233. What did the handball player do when he was not allowed a time out to change his gloves?

A) He refused to continue the game.

B) He angrily hit the referee with a ball.

C) He claimed that the referee was unfair.

D) He wet his gloves by rubbing them across his T-shirt.

234. According to the passage, players, in a game, may _____.

A) deliberately throw the ball at anyone illegally blocking their way

B) keep on screaming and shouting throughout the game

C) lie down on the ground as an act of protest

D) kick the ball across the court with force

235. The author hopes to have the current situation in sports improved by _____.

A) calling on players to use clean language on the court

B) raising the referee's sense of responsibility

C) changing the attitude of players on the sports field

D) regulating the relationship between players and referees

【单词详解】

【重点单词】**react** / ri'ækt / v.

[基本词义] 作出反应，回应

[用法导航] react positively to a suggestion 对建议作出赞成的反应 // react negatively to a suggestion 对建议作出反对的反应 // react strongly against tax increases 强烈反对增税 // Pinch me and I will react. 你掐我，我就有反应。

[词性转换] **reaction** / ri'ækʃən / n. 反应，回应

[对比记忆] **respond** / ris'pɔnd / v. 反应，回应，响应；回答

[真题衔接] Do children _____ to kind treatment by becoming more self-confident?

    A) appeal   B) react   C) contribute   D) consent

【重点单词】**innocent** / 'inəsnt / adj.

[基本词义] 无辜的，无罪的；天真的

[用法导航] an innocent man 一个无罪的男人 // an innocent bystander 一个无辜受害的旁观者// Don't be so innocent as to believe what he tells you. 不要那么天真，相信他所说的话。

[词性转换] innocence / 'inəsns / n. 无辜，清白；天真

[对比记忆] (1) **naive** / nɑ:'i:v / adj. 幼稚的，轻信的；天真的

    (2) **guilty** / 'gilti / adj. 有罪的

[真题衔接] Can you provide any evidence that he was _____ of the crime?

    A) immune   B) innocent   C) exempt   D) contrary

【重点单词】**recall** / ri'kɔ:l / v.

[基本词义] 回忆，记起

[用法导航] I can't recall his name. 我不记得他的名字了。// Try your best to recall what have happened. 努力回忆所发生的事情。

[对比记忆] memory / 'meməri / *n.* 记忆(力)；回忆；纪念；存储(器)

[真题衔接] Dick _____ having been in Paris to study music when he was a child.

    A) demonstrated   B) intended   C) clarified   D) recalled

【句子翻译】

236. The monitor _____(树立了一个好榜样) to the rest of the class.

237. On the formal occasion, please make sure that _____(你所讲的是有意义的).

238. Greater spending on education is expected to _____(多收学生).

239. A man's intrinsic worth, arising from such qualities as honor and courage, _____(不在财富多寡).

240. The two substances are now in contact (with each other), and _____(产生了化学反应).

Passage Twenty-five

Consumers are ***being confused and misled by*** the hodge-podge (大杂烩) of environmental claims made by household products, according to a "green labeling" study published by Consumers International Friday.

Among the report's more outrageous (令人无法容忍的) findings—a German fertilizer described itself as "earthworm friendly"; A brand of flour said it was "non-polluting" and a British toilet paper claimed to be ***"environmentally friendlier"***.

The study was written and researched by Britain's National Consumer Council (NCC) for lobby group Consumer International. It was **funded** by the German and Dutch governments and the European Commission.

"While many good and useful claims are being made, it is clear ***there is a long way to go*** in ensuring shoppers ***are adequately informed about*** the environmental **impact** of products they buy," said Consumers International director Anna Fielder.

The 10-country study surveyed product packaging in Britain, Western Europe, Scandinavia and the United States. It found that products sold in Germany and the United Kingdom made the most environmental claims ***on average***.

The report ***focused on*** claims made by specific products, such as detergent

(洗涤剂) *insect sprays* and by some garden products. It did not test the claims, but compared them to labeling **guidelines** set by the International Standards Organization (ISO) in September, 1999.

Researchers documented claims of environmental friendliness made by about 2,000 products and found many too **vague** or too **misleading** to *meet ISO standards*.

"Many products had specially-designed labels to make them seem environmentally friendly, but in fact many of these symbols mean nothing," said report researcher Philip Page.

"Laundry detergents made the most number of claims with 158. Household cleaners were second with 145 separate claims, while paints were third on our list with 73. The high numbers show how very confusing it must be for consumers to *sort the true from the misleading*." he said.

The ISO labeling standards ban vague or misleading claims on product packaging, because **terms** such as "environmentally friendly" and "non-polluting" cannot be verified. "What we are now *pushing for* is to have **multinational** corporations meet the standards set by the ISO." said Page. (363 words)　(2005 年 6 月第 3 篇)

【段落译文】

根据消费者国际星期五出版的有关对"绿色标签"的研究,消费者正在被大杂烩式的家居用品中的环保性所迷惑或误导。

在各色报道那些令人无法容忍的发现中,有个德国的化肥品牌居然声称自己是"环保的",一个面粉品牌称自己是"完全没有污染的",一种英国的卫生纸品牌称自己是"更利于环保的。"

关于上述的问题由英国国家消费者委员会为国际消费者议员团体着手调查研究,该项研究由德国和荷兰政府以及欧洲委员会资助。

国际消费者负责人安娜·费尔德称:"当许多商品被制造出来,许多功效被传播,很显然,要确保消费者对他们所购买的产品将对环境造成的影响有充分的认识还是有很长一段路要走。"

在英国,有 10 个国家成员组成的团队对所要调查的产品包装做了研究。分别是西欧、斯堪的纳维亚和美国。研究发现,在德国和英国销售的产品平均做了最多的产品环保说明。

报告着重对一些商品做了阐述,例如,洗涤剂、杀虫剂和一些园艺用品。研究中没有对这些说明进行测试,不过在 1999 年 9 月把这些环保说明与国际标准机构的商标指导方针进行了比较。

　　研究者引用了 2000 多种产品的环保说明，发现这些说明不是太模糊就是有误导性，根本不能达到国际标准机构的要求。

　　其中一个研究员菲力浦·佩基说："很多产品的商标是经过特别设计的，就是为了使他们的产品看起来是环保的，但是事实上很多标志其实没什么特别含义。"

　　国际标准机构严格禁止在产品包装上出现模糊或含有误导性的说明。因为这些术语，例如"环保的"，"无污染的"是无法被证实的。佩基指出："我们现在要努力的是，要让那些跨国公司达到国际标准机构的各项标准和要求。"

　　他还说："卫生间的洗涤剂所做的环保标志最多有 158 项。家用洗洁精排第二有 145 种独立的标识，油漆排第三有 73 种。数量之大使消费者很难从大量的误导信息中找到真实可靠的信息。"

【难词释义】

fund 资金，资助　　　　　　　　　**impact** 影响，作用

guidelines 指导方针　　　　　　　**vague** 模糊的

misleading 误导的　　　　　　　　**terms** 术语

【写译语块】

1. being confused and misled by ... 被……所迷惑或误导

2. environmentally friendlier 环保的，对环境更有益的

3. there is a long way to go 还需要继续努力，还有很长的路要走

4. (be)adequately informed about 充分告知某事件

5. on average 平均

6. focus on 关注，注意

7. insect sprays 杀虫剂

8. meet(ISO)standards 达到……的标准

9. sort the true from the misleading 从错误的信息中探索真相

10. pushing for 为……而努力

【难句分析】

1. （第一段开头）Consumers are being confused and misled by the hodge-podge(大杂烩) of environmental claims made by household products, according to a "green labeling" study published by Consumers International Friday. 该句的重点是理解句子结构。made by 引导的短语（家居用品所做的……）其实是对 en-

vironmental claims(环保声明)的修饰,according to 是个状语,表明前文所提到的信息来源,如果按照中文语序,可以在翻译时放在句首,"根据消费者国际星期五出版的有关对"绿色标签"的研究"。

2. (第二段开头)从 Among the report's more outrageous(令人无法容忍的)findings—a German fertilizer described itself as "earthworm friendly"; A brand of flour said it was "non-polluting" and a British toilet paper claimed to be "environmentally friendlier" 句中,可以积累一定的表达方法,如 environmentally friendlier,non-polluting,earthworm friendly 这三个短语的意思都比较雷同,指得是"环保的,无污染物的"。句中的三个有关化肥、面粉还有卫生纸的品牌都一再强调自己的产品是环保的。

3. (第七段开头)理解 Researchers documented claims of environmental friendliness made by about 2,000 products and found many too vague or too misleading to meet ISO standards. 要把握几个短语。environmental friendliness 是个固定搭配,意为"对环境有益的,环保的",meet ... standards 固定搭配,"达到……的标准要求"。

【原题再现】

241. According to the passage, the NCC found it outrageous that _____.

   A) all the products surveyed claim to meet ISO standards

   B) the claims made by products are often unclear or deceiving

   C) consumers would believe many of the manufactures' claim

   D) few products actually prove to be environment friendly

242. As indicated in this passage, with so many good claims, the consumers _____.

   A) are becoming more cautious about the products they are going to buy

   B) are still not willing to pay more for products with green labeling

   C) are becoming more aware of the effects different products have on the environment

   D) still do not know the exact impact of different products on the environment

243. A study was carried out by Britain's NCC to _____.

   A) find out how many claims made by products fail to meet environmental standards

   B) inform the consumers of the environmental impact of the products they buy

C) examine claims made by products against ISO standards

D) revise the guidelines set by the International Standards Organization

244. What is one of the consequences caused by the many claims of household products?

A) They are likely to lead to serious environmental problems.

B) Consumers find it difficult to tell the true from the false.

C) They could arouse widespread anger among consumer.

D) Consumers will be tempted to buy products they don't need.

245. It can be inferred from the passage that the lobby group Consumer International wants to _____.

A) make product labeling satisfy ISO requirements

B) see all household products meet environmental standards

C) warn consumers of the danger of so-called green products

D) verify the efforts of non-polluting products

【单词详解】

【重点单词】**confuse** / kənˈfjuːz / v.

[基本词义] 把某人弄糊涂，使迷惑

[用法导航] They confused me by asking so many questions. 他们问了那么多问题，把我弄糊涂了。// I always confuse the sisters; they look so alike. 我总是把这两姐妹弄糊涂，她们实在长得太像了。

[词性转换] **confusion** / kənˈfjuːʒen / n. 混乱，杂乱

[对比记忆] (1) **puzzle** / ˈpʌzl / v. 迷惑

(2) **bewilder** / biˈwildə / vt. 使迷惑，使难住

[真题衔接] I was so _____ in today's history lesson. I didn't understand a thing. (CET4-0406)

A) amazed   B) neglected   C) confused   D) amused

【句子翻译】

246. Although you have made great progress, you still _____ (还有很长的路要走)in English study.

247. Boys are considered as taller than girls _____ (平均)in the teenage.

248. Scans have shown that patterns of activity in the brain change depending on

_____（对任务的关注程度）.

249. _____（为了适应农业的需求）we must produce more tractors.

250. _____（虽然航海技术的细节会使读者如堕云雾），shipboard life was in other respects sharply defined.

Passage Twenty-six

Two hours from the tall buildings of Manhattan and Philadelphia live some of the world's largest black bears. They are in northern Pennsylvania's Pocono Mountains, a home they *share with* an abundance of other wildlife.

The streams, lakes, meadows (草地), mountain ridges and forests that make the Poconos *an ideal place for* black bears have also *attracted more people to the region*. Open spaces are **threatened** by plans for *housing estates* and important habitats (栖息地) are endangered by highway construction. To protect the Poconos' natural beauty from **irresponsible** development, the Nature Conservancy (大自然保护协会) named the area one of America's "Last Great Places".

Operating out of a century-old schoolhouse in the village of Long Pond, Pennsylvania, the conservancy's bud Cook is working with local people and business leaders to *balance economic growth with environmental protection*. By forging **partnerships** with people like Francis Altemose, the Conservancy has been able to protect more than 14,000 acres of environmentally important land in the area.

Altemose's family has farmed in the Pocono area for generations. Two years ago Francis worked with the Conservancy to include his farm in a county farmland protection program. As a result, his family's land can be protected from development and the Altemoses will be better able to *provide a secure financial future for* their 7-year-old grandson.

Cook *attributes* the Conservancy's success in the Poconos *to* having a local presence and a commitment to working with local **residents**.

"*The key to* protecting these **remarkable** lands is connecting with the local **community**," Cook said. "The people who live there respect the land. They value quite forests, clear streams and **abundant** wildlife. They are eager to help with conservation efforts.

For more information on how you can help The Nature Conservancy protect the Poconos and the world's other "Last Great Places," please call 1-888-564 6864, or visit us on the World Wide Web at www. tnc. org(330 words) （2005 年 6 月第 4 篇）

【段落译文】

在距离高楼耸立的曼哈顿和费城的两小时路程外，居住着世界上最大的黑熊。他们在宾西法尼亚的芭科纳山脉，那里是黑熊和其他很多野生动物的共同家园。

那里的溪流、湖泊、草地和山脊还有原始森林使芭科纳山变成了黑熊最理想的居住地，同时它也吸引了大量的人去那个地区。开阔的空间却受到了来自房地产开发商的觊觎，动物的重要栖息地也受到了来自高速公路建设所带来的危害。为了保护芭科纳山的美丽原始风光免受来自那些不负责任的肆意开发，大自然保护协会命名那里为"美国最后的佳境"。

当地自然资源保护委员会的成员库克和当地居民和商业领导人一起在郎格池塘边有着百年之久的学院建筑里工作着，他们的合作就是为了平衡经济发展和环境保护。受到了例如弗朗西丝·艾特摩丝这些国际友人的协助，自然资源管理委员会能够保护当地非常重要的方圆 14,000 公顷的生态资源。

艾特摩丝这个家族在芭科纳山脉地区世代耕种。两年前，弗朗西丝开始和自然资源保护委员会合作把自己的农场也含盖到了农场保护计划项目中。因此，他自己的农场也受到了保护，免于不合理开发。艾特摩丝这个家族也能更好地为他们只有 7 岁的孙子的将来提供更好的经济支撑。

想要得到更多关于如何去帮助自然资源保护协会保护芭科纳山的美丽风光和世界上其他的"自然佳境"，可以致电 1-888-564 6864，或者浏览 www. tnc. org 这个网页来更好地了解我们的工作。

库克说："要保护当地美好土地的关键就是要与当地的居民社区保持密切的联系，那里的居民非常地尊重土地。他们把原始森林、清澈的溪水和多样的野外生命看得非常得重。他们很渴望能在自然资源保护上能献出自己的一臂之力。"

库克把自己在自然资源保护委员会取得的成功归功为芭科纳山脉地区当地人的不懈努力以及他长年致力于与当地居民间的合作。

【难词释义】

threaten 威胁	**irresponsible** 不负责任的
partnerships 合作者，合作关系	**residents** 居民
remarkable 显著的	**community** 社区
abundant 充足的，丰富的	

【写译语块】

1. share with 与……分享

2. an ideal place for ... 对……来说是个理想之地

3. attracted more people to the region 吸引了越来越多的人来到此地

4. housing estates 房地产

5. balance economic growth with environmental protection 平衡经济发展与环保

6. provide a secure financial future for ... 为……提供一个平稳的经济发展趋势

7. attribute ... to ... 把……归功于……

8. the key to ……的关键

【难句分析】

1. (第二段第一句) The streams, lakes, meadows (草地), mountain ridges and forests that make the Poconos an ideal place for black bears have also attracted more people to the region. 注意句中的连接词 that, 它其实是在修饰 the streams, lakes, meadows (草地), mountain ridges and forests, 在定语从句中作主语, make 在定语从句中作谓语, 这个长句真正的谓语是 have also attracted, 所以主句是 The streams, lakes, meadows (草地), mountain ridges and forests have also attracted more people to the region。

2. (第二段第二句) Open spaces are threatened by plans for housing estates and important habitats (栖息地) are endangered by highway construction. 请注意该句中两个近义词, endanger 和 threaten, 在这里都用到了其被动语态, "受到了威胁"和"受到了危害", 所以这是个并列句, "广阔的空间受到了来自房地产商的威胁"而"动物的栖息地受到了来自高速公路建设的危害"。

3. (第三段第一句) Operating out of a century-old schoolhouse in the village of Long Pond, Pennsylvania, the conservancy's bud Cook is working with local people and business leaders to balance economic growth with environmental protection. 该句中注意由 to 引导的目的状语, to balance economic growth with environmental protection, balance ... with ... 是一个固定搭配, "使……与……获得平衡", 从上下文中, 不难理解 Cook 与当地居民齐心协力是想让经济发展与环境保护不要起矛盾, 重点还是要注重保护家园。

4. (第五段第一句) 在 Cook attributes the Conservancy's success in the Poconos to having a local presence and a commitment to working with local residents 中。attribute ... to ... 是个固定搭配, "把……归功于……", commitment to 由 commit to 演变而来, "致力于……"。整体可理解为库克把自己在自然资源保护委员会取得的成功归功为芭科纳山脉地区当地人的努力以及他长年致力于与当地居民间的合作。

【原题再现】

251. The purpose in naming the Poconos as one of America's "Last Great Places "is to _____.

A) gain support from the local community

B) protect it from irresponsible development

C) make it a better home for black bears

D) provide financial security for future generations

252. We learn from the passage that _____.

A) the population in the Pocono area is growing

B) wildlife in the Pocono area is dying out rapidly

C) the security of the Pocono residents is being threatened

D) farmlands in the Pocono area are shrinking fast

253. What is important in protecting the Poconos according to Cook?

A) The setting up of an environmental protection website.

B) Support from organizations like The Nature Conservancy.

C) Cooperation with the local residents and business leaders.

D) Inclusion of farmlands in the region's protection program.

254. What does Bud Cook mean by "having a local presence "(Sentence 1, Para. 5)?

A) Financial contributions from local business leaders.

B) Consideration of the interests of the local residents.

C) The establishment of a wildlife protection foundation in the area.

D) The setting up of a local Nature Conservancy branch in the Pocono area.

255. The passage most probably is _____.

A) an official document   B) a news story

C) an advertisement   D) a research report

【单词详解】

【重点单词】**attract** / əˈtrækt / *v.*

[基本词义] 吸引,引起某人的注意

[用法导航] The light attracted many insects. 灯光引来了很多的昆虫。// The new book attracted many young readers. 这本书吸引了很多的读者。// Do any of the designs attract you? 这些设计中有使你感兴趣的么?

[词性转换] (1)**attractive** / əˈtræktiv / *adj.* 有魅力的,有吸引力的

(2)**attraction** / əˈtrækʃən / *n.* 魅力,吸引力

[对比记忆] (1) **absorb** / əbˈsɔːb / *vt.* 吸收;吸引……的注意,使全神贯注;把……并入,同化

(2) **arouse** / əˈrauz / *vt.* 引起,激起,唤起;唤醒

[真题衔接] We derive the important law: opposite charges _____, like charges repel.

A) consent　　B) deserve　　C) defend　　D) atrract

【重点单词】**threaten** / ˈθretn / *v.*

[基本词义] 恐吓,威胁某人

[用法导航] threaten the employees with dismissal 威胁员工要开除他们 // threaten to kill all the passengers on the plane 恐吓说要杀了机上所有的人 // He threatened legal action. 他以起诉相要挟。

[词性转换] **threat** / θret / *n.* 威胁,恐吓

[对比记忆] **intimidate** / inˈtimideit / *v.* 恐吓,威胁

[真题衔接] It is predicted that heavy rains are _____ to flood the area in a few days. (CET4-9201)

A) frightening　　B) threatening　　C) scattering　　D) warning

【句子翻译】

256. The traffic accident in the rushing hour _____(吸引了很多人的注意).

257. _____(解决问题的关键)is to do enough investigation.

258. After several months' study, the doctors _____(把这种病的起因归结为一种未知的病毒).

259. It contain natural moisture factor and _____(平衡皮肤的水分).

260. They threatened _____(切断那个国家的供油).

Passage Twenty-seven

Scratchy throats, *stuffy noses* and body aches all **spell** misery, but being able to tell if the cause is a cold or flu may make a difference in how long the misery lasts.

The American Lung Association (ALA) has **issued** new guidelines on **combating** colds and the flu (流感), and one of the keys is being able to quickly *tell the two apart*. That's because the prescription drugs *available for* the flu need to be taken soon after the illness sets in. As for colds, the sooner a person starts taking *over-the-counter* remedy, the sooner relief will come.

The common cold and the flu are both caused by viruses. More than 200 viruses can cause cold **symptoms**, while the flu is caused by three viruses—flu A, B and C. There is no cure for either illness, but the flu can be **prevented** by the flu vaccine (疫苗), which is, for most people, the best way to fight the flu, according to the ALA.

But if the flu does strike, quick action can help. Although the flu and common cold have many **similarities**, there are some **obvious** signs to look for.

Cold symptoms such as stuffy nose, runny nose and scratchy throat typically develop gradually, and adults and teens often do not get a fever. On the other hand, fever is one of the characteristic features of the flu for all ages. And *in general*, flu symptoms including fever and chills, sore throat and body aches come on suddenly and are more severe than cold symptoms.

The ALA notes that it may be particularly difficult to tell when infants and preschool age children have the flu. It advises parents to call the doctor if their small children have flu-like symptoms.

Both cold and flu symptoms can be **eased** with over-the-counter medications as well. However, children and teens with a cold or flu should not take aspirin for pain **relief** because of the risk of Reye syndrome (综合症), a rare but serious condition of the liver and central nervous system.

There is, of course, no vaccine for the common cold. But frequent hand washing and avoiding *close contact* with people who have colds can reduce the **likelihood** of catching one. (380 words) (2005 年 1 月第 1 篇)

【段落译文】

喉咙发痒、鼻子堵塞和全身疼痛都意味着痛苦,但是如果想要分清痛苦的原因是到底是感冒引起的还是流感导致的,那就要看这种痛苦持续多久。

美国肺病研究协会已经提出了对抗感冒和流感的新的指导方针,其中的关键一点就是要尽快地把感冒和流感区别开来。其中的原因在于一旦确诊是流感那么相关的对抗流感的处方药就应该马上服用。对于一般的感冒而言,患者越快服用非处方药,就能越快减轻他的痛苦。

普通感冒和流感其实都是由病毒引起的。有超过 200 多种病毒可以导致感冒的各种症状,但流感只可能有三种病毒引起——分别是流感 A,B,C。感冒和流感都没什么特效药,但是流感是可以通过打疫苗来预防的。据美国肺病研究协会称,对大部分人来说,注射疫苗是最好的对抗流感的方法。

但是如果流感蔓延情况很严峻,那么就要快速行动起来对抗流感才行。尽管流感和一般感冒有很多的相似之处,但是两者还是有一些明显区别的。

感冒的症状是慢慢显现出来的,有鼻塞、流鼻涕和喉咙痛,成年人和青少年一般不怎么会发烧。但是,发烧在任何年龄段都是流感的一种特征。一般来说,流感的主要症状包括发烧和发冷,喉咙发痛和浑身疼痛会立即袭来,并且要比一般的感冒严重很多。

美国肺病研究协会表示特别对于婴儿和学龄前儿童而言,很难准确地判断他们是何时感染上流感的。建议家长们一旦发现孩子有类似流感的症状就应该马上就医。

感冒和流感症状都是可以通过服用非处方药得到缓解的。但是感染感冒或流感的儿童和青少年不应该服用阿斯匹林来缓解疼痛,以防出现瑞依综合征,这种综合征非常罕见但是对肝脏和中枢神经会有很大的伤害。

当然,对于一般感冒而言没有疫苗可以注射。但是如果我们勤洗手,尽量避免和感染感冒病毒的患者密切接触,那么就可以减少被感染的可能性。

【难词释义】

spell 意味着	**issue** 发表
combat 战斗	**symptom** 症状
prevent 避免,预防	**similarity** 相似之处
obvious 明显的	**ease** 减轻,减缓
relief 解脱	**likelihood** 可能性

【写译语块】

1. scratchy throats 喉咙痛
2. stuffy noses 鼻塞
3. tell the two apart 把两者区分开来
4. available for 为……提供
5. over-the-counter 非处方的
6. in general 一般来说
7. close contact 密切接触

【难句分析】

1. (第一段第一句)Scratchy throats, stuffy noses and body aches all spell misery,

but being able to tell if the cause is a cold or flu may make a difference in how long the misery lasts. 注意句中的个别关键词, tell 在这里不是"告诉"的意思, 而是有 differ 的意思, 应该理解为"区别, 区分", 固定短语有 tell A from B, ... make a difference in how long the misery lasts, 上下文中提到的感冒, 流感的主要区别在于痛苦持续的时间有多长, make a difference in 本身就是个固定短语, "在……中的区别"。

2. (第二段第一句) The American Lung Association (ALA) has issued new guidelines on combating colds and the flu (流感), and one of the keys is being able to quickly tell the two apart. 注意句中的几个关键表达方法, issued new guidelines on ... "对……制定的方针政策", 注意 issue 与 guideline 的搭配; 此外, 还应注意与 key 搭配的介词为 to, 后面用动词 ing 形式, tell ... apart 类似与 tell A from B, differ A from B 意为"把……与……区别开来"。

3. (第七段第二句) However, children and teens with a cold or flu should not take aspirin for pain relief because of the risk of Reye syndrome (综合征), a rare but serious condition of the liver and central nervous system. 理清句子结构非常重要, 注意 a rare but serious condition of the liver and central nervous system 其实是个非限制性的定语从句, 它省略了 which is, 其实是前半句的 Reye syndrome (综合征)。该综合征很罕见, 但对肝脏和中枢神经系统有很大的伤害。

4. (最后一段) But frequent hand washing and avoiding close contact with people who have colds can reduce the likelihood of catching one. 该句中 hand washing 和 avoiding close contact 并列做主语, 谓语是 reduce the likelihood of ... "减少了……的可能性"。

【原题再现】

261. According to the author, knowing the cause of the misery will help _____.

    A) shorten the duration of the illness

    B) the patient buy medicine over the counter

    C) the patient obtain cheaper prescription drugs

    D) prevent people from catching colds and the flu

262. We learn from the passage that _____.

    A) one doesn't need to take any medicine if he has a cold or the flu

    B) aspirin should not be included in over-the-counter medicines for the flu

C) delayed treatment of the flu will harm the liver and central nervous system

D) over-the-counter drugs can be taken to ease the misery caused by a cold or the flu

263. According to the passage, to combat the flu effectively, _____ .

A) one should identify the virus which causes it

B) one should consult a doctor as soon as possible

C) one should take medicine upon catching the disease

D) one should remain alert when the disease is spreading

264. Which of the following symptoms will distinguish the flu from a cold?

A) A stuffy nose.   B) A high temperature.

C) A sore throat.   D) A dry cough.

265. If children have flu-like symptoms, their parents _____ .

A) are advised not to give them aspirin

B) should watch out for signs of Reye syndrome

C) are encouraged to take them to hospital for vaccination

D) should prevent them from mixing with people running a fever

【单词详解】

【重点单词】**available** / əˈveiləbl / *adj.*

[基本词义] 可用的,可得到的;有空闲的

[用法导航] Tickets are available at the box office. 票房有票。// You will be informed when the books are available. 这本书一有货就通知你。// I am available in the afternoon. 我下午有空。

[词性转换] **avail** / əˈveil / *n.* (一般用于否定句或疑问句中)效用,利益,帮助

[对比记忆] **vacant** / ˈveikənt / *adj.* 未被占用的,空着的;(职位、工作等)空缺的

[真题衔接] Convenience foods which are already prepared for cooking are _____ in grocery stores. (CET4-9701)

     A) ready   B) approachable   C) probable   D) available

【重点单词】**prevent** / priˈvent / *vt.*

[基本词义] 阻止,妨碍

[用法导航] prevent the disease from spreading 阻止疾病蔓延 // Nobody can prevent us from getting married. 没人能阻止我们结婚。// Your prompt action prevented a serious action. 你的快速行动避免了一场意外事故。

[对比记忆]（1）**prohibit** / prə'hibit / *vt.* 禁止，不准

（2）**hinder** / 'hində / *v.* 阻碍，妨碍

（3）**forbid** / fə'bid / *vt.* 不许，禁止

[真题衔接] Who can _____ us from getting married now that you are of age?

    A) annoy   B) upset   C) interrupt   D) prevent

【重点单词】**similarity** / ˌsimi'læriti / *n.*

[基本词义] 类似，相似，相似之处

[用法导航] points of similarity between the two men 这两个人的相似之处 // similarities in age and the background 年龄与背景相似

[对比记忆]（1）**identical** / ai'dentikəl / *adj.* （to, with）相同的，相等的；同一的

（2）**alike** / ə'laik / *adj.* 同样的，相像的

[真题衔接] One argument stresses the functional _____ between rule-making and legislation.

    A) similarity   B) debate   C) influence   D) connection

【句子翻译】

266. _____（这两兄弟很难区分开）because they are alike not only in appearance but also in behavior.

267. _____（那两个报告极其相似）suggests that they are written by the same person.

268. Shall we _____（保持联系）by emails when you study abroad.

269. We know from observation that the motion is _____（与挂在弹簧上的物体的运动是相似的）.

270. Ignorance and superstition _____（使他们无法得到现代医学的好处）.

Passage Twenty-eight

In a time of low academic achievement by children in the United States, many Americans are ***turning to*** Japan, a country of high academic **achievement** and economic success, for possible answers. However, the answers provided by Japanese preschools are not the ones Americans ***expected to*** find. In most Japanese preschools, surprisingly little ***emphasis is put on academic instruction***. In one **investigation**, 300 Japanese and 210 American preschool teachers, child development **specialists**, and parents were asked about various aspects of early childhood education. Only 2 percent of the Japanese respondents（答问卷者）listed "to give children a good start academically" as one of their top three reasons for a society to have preschools. *In contrast*, over half the American respondents chose this as one of their top three choices. To prepare children for successful careers in first grade and beyond, Japanese schools do not teach reading, writing, and mathematics, but rather skills such as **persistence**, **concentration**, and the ability to function *as a member of a group*. The vast majority of young Japanese children are taught to read at home by their parents.

In the recent **comparison** of Japanese and American preschool education, 91 percent of Japanese respondents chose providing children with a group experience as one of their top three reasons for a society to have preschools. Sixty-two percent of the more individually oriented (强调个性发展的) Americans listed group experience as one of their top three choices. An emphasis on the importance of the group seen in Japanese early childhood education continues into elementary school education.

Like in America, there is **diversity** in Japanese early childhood education. Some Japanese kindergartens have specific aims, such as early musical training or potential development. In large cities, some kindergartens are *attached to universities* that have elementary and secondary schools.

Some Japanese parents believe that if their young children attend a university-based program, it will increase the children's chances of eventually being *admitted to* top-rated schools and universities. Several more progressive programs have **introduced** free play as a way out for the heavy intellectualizing in some Japanese kindergartens. (354 words) (2005 年 1 月第 2 篇)

【段落译文】

　　有某个时期美国的儿童在学业上取得的成绩不是很理想,很多美国人就向日本去求助、寻找他们想得到的答案,因为日本在学术上取得了很好的成绩并且经济发展也相当迅速。但是美国人在日本学前教育中得到的答案并不像美国人预期的那样。令人吃惊的是,在日本的学前教育中,不怎么重视对儿童在学业上的指导。例如,在一项调查中,分别询问了 300 名日本和 210 名美国学前教育老师,儿童成长辅导专家和家长有关儿童早期教育的几个重要方面。只有 2% 的日本答问卷者认为社会开展学前教育的前三个理由中最重要的原因是"给孩子在学业上有个良好的开端"。相反,有超过半数的美国被调查者认为上文提到的原因是社会开展学前教育的三个重要原因之一。为了使孩子能在一年级或以后在学业上取得更大的成就,日本的学校不是教孩子们读、写和数学,而是教他们养成坚持、专注和团队合作的技巧。大部分日本孩子是由父母在家教会读写技巧的。

在最近的一项美国和日本的学前教育比较中,91%的日本答问卷者选择给孩子提供团队合作的学习经历是社会开办学前教育最重要的前三个原因之一。62%强调个性发展的美国人选择了该项为前三原因之一。在日本早期教育中一再强调的团队合作教育一直要延续到小学教育中。

就像在美国,日本的儿童早期教育的形式是多种多样的。一些日本的幼儿园都有特定的学习目标,比如早期的音乐培训或潜力开发。在一些大城市,很多幼儿园还跟那些有附属小学和中学的大学合作办学。

一些日本的家长认为,如果孩子们从小在以大学基础为学习计划的引导下,他们被顶级的学校或大学录取的几率就更大。在一些日本的幼儿园,一些先进的教学计划里甚至引进了自由玩耍,把孩子们从繁重的课业学习中彻底解放了出来。

【难词释义】

achievement 成就

specialists 专家

concentration 专心致志

diversity 多样性

investigation 调查

persistence 持之以恒

comparison 比较

introduce 引进,介绍

【写译语块】

1. turn to 向……求助

2. expect sb. to do sth 期望……做某事

3. emphasis is put on academic instruction 把重点放在了学术指导上

4. in contrast 相反

5. as a member of a group 作为团队中的一员

6. (be) attached to universities 附属于这个大学

7. (be) admitted to 被……录取

【难句分析】

1. (第一段首句)In a time of low academic achievement by children in the United States, many Americans are turning to Japan, a country of high academic achievement and economic success, for possible answers. 首先要把握这个句子的结构,注意 turn to ... for ... 本身就是个固定词组,表示"向……求助去获得……"。但在该句中,插入了 a country of high academic achievement and eco-

135

nomic success 去修饰 Japan，容易使读者思路混乱。读者一定要清楚地认识到修饰 Japan 的定语从句也可以理解为"为什么美国人向日本去寻求帮助"，是因为日本在学术和经济上都取得了巨大的成功。

2. （第一段五、六句）Only 2 percent of the Japanese respondents（答问卷者）listed "to give children a good start academically" as one of their top three reasons for a society to have preschools. In contrast, over half the American respondents chose this as one of their top three choices. 这两个句子应该合起来理解，以便读懂第六句中的 chose this as one of their top three choices。in contrast, 很明显是表示相对的比较，上文中提到了只有 2% 的答问卷者选择……为重要原因之一，那么在下文中提到了超过半数的人选择……为重要原因之一，形成了一个很明显的数值上的比较，用了短语 in contrast 使读者阅读起来逻辑思维更加清晰了。

3. （第二段末尾）An emphasis on the importance of the group seen in Japanese early childhood education continues into elementary school education. 首先要把握句子的结构。emphasis 与 on 搭配是个固定短语，意为"强调……"，seen 过去分词作定语用来修饰 importance of the group，那就是在日本早期的儿童教育中对团队意识的重要性的培养已经有了，已经被人们所看到了。这句话的谓语是 continues into，主语是句首的 an emphasis on . . . ，所以该句的主干其实就是 An emphasis continues into elementary school education。

4. （文章末尾）Several more progressive programs have introduced free play as a way out for the heavy intellectualizing in some Japanese kindergartens. 这句话中有一系列相关的词语或短语在意思上都是互相呼应的，读者如果感受到了这点就能更好地理解该句。Progressive, introduced, as a way out for . . . 分别是"先进的，进步的"，"引进（好的、先进的东西）"和"……的出路，……的突破"，综合理解起来就是在一些日本的幼儿园，一些先进的教学计划里甚至引进了自由玩耍，把孩子们从繁重的课业学习中彻底解放了出来。

【原题再现】

271. We learn from the first paragraph that many Americans believe _____.

A) Japanese parents are more involved in preschool education than American parents

B) Japan's economic success is a result of its scientific achievements

C) Japanese preschool education emphasizes academic instruction

D) Japan's higher education is superior to theirs

136

272. Most Americans surveyed believe that preschools should also attach importance to _____.

A) problem solving   B) group experience

C) parental guidance   D) individually-oriented development

273. In Japan's preschool education, the focus is on _____.

A) preparing children academically

B) developing children's artistic interests

C) tapping children's potential

D) shaping children's character

274. Free play has been introduced in some Japanese kindergartens in order to _____.

A) broaden children's horizon   B) cultivate children's creativity

C) lighten children's study load   D) enrich children's knowledge

275. Why do some Japanese parents send their children to university based kindergartens?

A) They can do better in their future studies.

B) They can accumulate more group experience there.

C) They can be individually oriented when they grow up.

D) They can have better chances of getting a first-rate education.

【单词详解】

【重点单词】**emphasis** / ˈemfəsis / *n.*

［基本词义］强调

［用法导航］Some schools put great emphasis on language study. 有些学校很注重语言的学习。// The emphasis is laid on hard work not enjoyment. 这里强调的是努力工作而不是享乐。

［词性转换］**emphasize** / ˈemfəsaiz / *v.* 强调

［对比记忆］(1) **stress** / stres / *v.* 强调，重读

    (2) **underline** / ˌʌndəˈlain / *v.* 强调，加下划线

［真题衔接］In recent years much more emphasis has been put _____ developing the students productive skills. (CET4-0106)

    A) onto   B) in   C) over   D) on

【重点单词】**contrast** / ˈkɒntræst, -trɑːst/ *n.*

［基本词义］对比；明显的差异

〔用法导航〕In contrast with their systems, ours seems old-fashioned. 和他们的系统相比，我们的明显比较陈旧。// She had failed the exam; in contrast, her sister did quite well. 她考试不及格，可她的妹妹却考得很好。// The work you did today is quite a contrast to what you did yesterday. 今天做的活儿跟昨天相比是截然不同的。

〔对比记忆〕(1) **contrary** / ˈkɔntrəri / n. 反面，对立面

(2) **difference** / ˈdifərəns / n. 差异

(3) **contradiction** / ˌkɔntrəˈdikʃən / n. 反驳，矛盾，对立

〔真题衔接〕Preliminary estimation puts the figure at around $110 billion, _____ the $160 billion the President is struggling to get through the Congress. （研-1998）

A) in proportion to   B) in reply to
C) in relation to   D) in contrast to

【句子翻译】

276. _____（和他兄弟比较而言），he was always considerate in his treatment of others.

277. When she is in trouble, she always _____（向家人寻求安慰）.

278. He is excited to hear the news that he _____（被录取）the top college.

279. _____（要把重点放在）the training of personal characteristics.

280. Hi-tech _____（被引进）to strengthen the research abilities in the lab.

Passage Twenty-nine

Lead deposits, which **accumulated** in soil and snow during the 1960's and 70's, were **primarily** the result of leaded gasoline **emissions** originating in the United States. In the twenty years that the Clean Air Act has mandated unleaded gas use in the United States, the lead accumulation world-wide has decreased **significantly**.

A study published recently in the journal *Nature* shows that air-borne leaded gas emissions from the United States were the leading **contributor** to *the high concentration of lead in the snow in Greenland*. The new study is a result of the continued research led by Dr. Charles Boutron, *an expert on the impact of heavy metals on the environment* at the National Center for Scientific Research in France. A study by Dr. Boutron published in 1991 showed that lead levels in arctic（北极的）snow were **declining**.

138

In his new study, Dr. Boutron found the **ratios** of the different forms of lead in the leaded gasoline used in the United States were different from the ratios of European, Asian and Canadian gasoline and thus enabled scientists to differentiate (分区) the lead sources. The **dominant** lead ratio found in Greenland snow *matched that found in gasoline from the United States*.

In a study published in the journal Ambio, scientists found that lead levels in soil in the North-eastern United States had *decreased markedly* since the introduction of unleaded gasoline.

Many scientists had believed that the lead would stay in soil and snow for a longer period. The authors of the Ambio study examined samples of the upper layers of soil taken from the same sites of 30 forest floors in New England, New York and Pennsylvania in 1980 and in 1990. The forest environment processed and **redistributed** the lead faster than the scientists had expected.

Scientists say both studies **demonstrate** that certain parts of the ecosystem (生态系统) respond rapidly to reductions in atmospheric pollution, but that these findings *should not be used as a license to pollute*. (338 words)　(2005 年 1 月第 3 篇)

【段落译文】

20 世纪六七十年代在美国土壤和雪地的沉积，主要源于含铅汽油的排放。20 年来，在美国清洁空气法案授权的无铅汽油的推广使用后，全球范围内的铅沉积大幅度减少。

《自然》杂志最近出版一份研究报告显示，美国含铅汽油的使用，其排放的气体是格陵兰积雪高含铅量的主要原因。这项新的研究是由 Charles Boutron 博士，在法国国家科学研究中心，就重金属对环境影响方面的专家不断研究之后得出的。Boutron 博士在 1991 年发表一项研究，表明铅含量在北极雪中开始下降了。

在新的研究中，Boutron 博士发现美国所使用的含铅汽油中不同形式的铅的比例，与在欧洲、亚洲和加拿大的比例不同，从而使科学家能够区分铅的来源。在格陵兰积雪中占主要比例的铅与在美国汽油中发现的铅相匹配。

在 Ambio 杂志发表的研究中，科学家发现，自从无铅汽油投入使用，美国东北部地区土壤中的铅含量已经明显减少。

许多科学家相信，铅会在土壤和积雪中沉积很长时间。Ambio 杂志中这篇研究的作者在 1980 年和 1990 年，研究了 30 个相同的来自新英格兰、纽约和宾夕法尼亚州森林土地中所采取的上层土壤样本。研究发现，在森林环境中对铅的处理和重新分配的速度要比科学家预期得快。

　　科学家们说两项研究都表明生态系统的某些部分因大气污染减少而很快恢复了,但是这些发现不能成为允许污染的通行证。

【难词释义】

accumulate 积聚,累加,堆积　　　　primarily 首先,主要地

emission 发射,射出,发行　　　　　significantly 较大地(重要地)

contributor 贡献者,捐助者,赠送者　　decline 降低

ratio 比率,比例　　　　　　　　　dominant 主要的

redistribute 重新分配　　　　　　　demonstrate 证明

【写译语块】

1. the high concentration of lead in the snow in Greenland 在格陵兰积雪中铅高度集中

2. an expert on the impact of heavy metals on the environment 重金属对环境影响研究方面的专家

3. matched that found in gasoline from the United States 与在美国汽油中发现的铅相匹配

4. decrease markedly 急剧下降

5. should not be used as a license to pollute 不能成为允许污染的通行证

【难句分析】

1. (第一段第一句)Lead deposits, which accumulated in soil and snow during the 1960's and 70's, were primarily the result of leaded gasoline emissions originating in the United States. 文章开题的第一句包含了一个定语从句,主句应该是 Lead deposits were the result of leaded gasoline emissions originating in the United States。这里用 which 来引导一个定语从句,在修饰铅沉积的时间和地点。primarily 翻译成"主要的",the result of 是"……的结果",originate 是"开始"的意思,这句话可以说成 Lead deposits resulted from the emissions of leaded gasoline。

2. (第三段第一句)In his new study, Dr. Boutron found the ratios of the different forms of lead in the leaded gasoline used in the United States were different from the ratios of European, Asian and Canadian gasoline and thus enabled scientists to differentiate(分区) the lead sources. 该长句去掉所有修饰的成

140

分,实际上是 ratios were different from the ratios。the different forms of lead in the leaded gasoline 意思是"含铅汽油中不同形式的铅"。enabled scientists to differentiate（分区）the lead sources 中有一个词组,enable sb to do"使得某人能够做某事"。

3. （第五段第二句）The authors of the Ambio study examined samples of the upper layers of soil taken from the same sites of 30 forest floors in New England, New York and Pennsylvania in 1980 and in 1990. 这个句子中包含了一个定语从句,taken from the same sites of 30 forest floors in New England, New York and Pennsylvania in 1980 and in 1990 实际都是来修饰前面的 soil samples 的,省略了关系词 which were taken from....。upper layers of soil 意思为"上层土壤"。

【原题再现】

281. The study published in the journal *Nature* indicates that _____.

   A) the Clean Air Act has not produced the desired results

   B) lead deposits in arctic snow are on the increase

   C) lead will stay in soil and snow longer than expected

   D) the US is the major source of lead pollution in arctic snow

282. Lead accumulation worldwide decreased significantly after the use of unleaded gas in the US _____.

   A) was discouraged   B) was enforced by law

   C) was prohibited by law   D) was introduced

283. How did scientists discover the source of lead pollution in Greenland?

   A) By analyzing the data published in journals like Nature and Ambio.

   B) By observing the lead accumulations in different parts of the arctic area.

   C) By studying the chemical elements of soil and snow in Northeastern America.

   D) By comparing the chemical compositions of leaded gasoline used in various countries.

284. The authors of the Ambio study have found that _____.

   A) forests get rid of lead pollution faster than expected

   B) lead accumulations in forests are more difficult to deal with

   C) lead deposits are widely distributed in the forests of the US

   D) the upper layers of soil in forests are easily polluted by lead emissions

285. It can be inferred from the last paragraph that scientists _____.

A) are puzzled by the mystery of forest pollution

B) feel relieved by the use of unleaded gasoline

C) still consider lead pollution a problem

D) lack sufficient means to combat lead pollution

【单词详解】

【重点单词】**originate**/ əˈridʒineit / *vt.* & *vi.*

[基本词义] 发起,开始

[用法导航] The hot dog did not originate in the United States, but in Germany. 热狗不是起源于美国,而是德国。// The style of architecture originated from the ancient Greeks. 这种建筑风格起源于古希腊。// Who originated the concept of stereo sound? 立体声是谁发明的? // The quarrel originated in rivalry between the two families. 这次争吵是两家不和引起的。

[词性转换] **origin** / ˈɔridʒin / *n.* 起源,出身

[对比记忆] (1) **original** / əˈridʒinəl / *adj.* 起初的;原来的;独创的;新颖的;最早的

(2) **arise** / əˈraiz / *vi.* 上升,引起,出现(多与 from 连用,侧重指从无到有的产生,表因果关系)

[真题衔接] The Olympic Games _____ in 776 B. C. in Olympia, a small town in Greece. (TEM4-1999)

A) originated   B) stemmed   C) derived   D) descended

【重点单词】**differentiate** / ˌdifəˈrenʃieit / *vt.* & *vi.*

[基本词义] 识别,使差异,求导数,区分,区别对待

[用法导航] One character is not clearly differentiated from another. 人物之间的区别没有明显刻划出来。// It is wrong to differentiate between people according to their family background. 根据出身不同而区别待人是不对的。

[词性转换] **differentiation** / ˌdifərenʃiˈeiʃən / *n.* 区别,分化,变异

[对比记忆] (1) **different** / ˈdifərənt / *adj.* 不同的,不一样的

(2) **distinguish** / disˈtiŋgwiʃ / *vt.* 区别,辨认,特别关注

(3) **discriminate** / disˈkrimineit / *vt.* 区分,区别对待

(4) **discern** / diˈsən / *vt.* & *v.* 辨别,看清楚

(5) **differ** / ˈdifə / *vi.* 不一致,不同(意见)

[真题衔接] We don't _____ between our workers on the basis of their background or ethnic origin.

A) classify   B) appraise   C) compliment   D) differentiate

【句子翻译】

286. The coach repeatedly reminded him that a tennis players _____ during play(需要全神贯注).

287. It's difficult to assess the _____ (总统讲话的巨大影响).

288. These problems are _____ (由于多年管理不善而造成的) and it is not easy to solve them in a short time.

289. I gave him full directions to _____ (好让他能找到那房子).

290. He thought he could beat anyone at tennis, _____ (但遇到她却是旗鼓相当).

Passage Thirty

Exercise is one of the few factors with a **positive** role in long-term **maintenance** of body weight. Unfortunately, that message has not gotten through to the average American, who would rather try switching to "light" beer and low-calorie bread than increase physical exertion. The Centers for Disease Control, for example, found that fewer than one-fourth of overweight adults who were trying to shed pounds said they were *combining exercise with their diet*.

In **rejecting** exercise, some people may be *discouraged too much by* caloric-**expenditure** charts; for example, one would have to briskly walk three miles just to work off the 275 calories in one **delicious** Danish pastry (小甜饼). Even exercise professionals concede half a point here. "Exercise by itself is *a very tough way to lose weight*," says York Onnen, program director of the President's Council on Physical **Fitness** and Sports.

Still, *exercise's supporting role in weight reduction is vital*. A study at the Boston University Medical Center of overweight police officers and other public employees **confirmed** that those who dieted without exercise regained almost all their old weight, while those who worked exercise into their daily **routine** maintained their new weight.

If you have been sedentary (极少活动的) and decide to start walking one mile a day, the added exercise could burn an extra 100 calories daily. In a year's time, assuming *no increase in food intake*, you could lose ten pounds. By increasing the distance of your walks **gradually** and making other dietary **adjust-ments**, you may lose even more weight. (261 words) (2005 年 1 月第 4 篇)

【段落译文】

　　运动是少数几项在长期保持体重上扮演着积极角色的因素之一。然而不幸的是,这一理念却未能被普通美国人所了解。这些人宁愿尝试选择清淡啤酒和低热量的面包,也不愿增加体能的消耗。例如,美国疾病控制中心研究发现,在力图减肥的人群中,不到 1/4 的人将运动和节食结合了起来。

　　在拒绝运动的过程中,一些人或许是因为热量消耗图表而被大大地挫伤了信心。例如,一个人必须要轻快地行走 3 英里,仅仅来消耗由一块可口的丹麦小甜饼所产生的 275 卡热量。甚至就连专业的运动人士对此也不得不部分地承认。美国总统身体健康和运动委员会的项目主管,约克·昂尼说,"运动本身就是一种很困难的减肥方法。"

　　然而,运动对减肥的辅助作用仍然是至关重要的。一份由波士顿大学医学中心所做的对过胖的干警和其他的公职人员的研究证实,那些只节食而不运动的人几乎完全恢复了原有的体重,而那些将运动列入了日常工作的人则保持了新的重量。

　　如果你经常坐着缺乏运动,现在决定开始每天步行一英里,这增添的运动量每天可以额外燃烧 100 卡的热量。在一年之内,假如进食量不增加的话,你可以减 10磅。通过逐渐增加步行的距离以及做些饮食方面的调整,你甚至可以减得更多。

【难词释义】

positive 肯定的,积极的,绝对的　　　**maintenance** 维护,保持,维修

reject 拒绝　　　　　　　　　　　　**expenditure**（时间、劳力、金钱等）支出,使用

delicious 美味的　　　　　　　　　　**fitness** 健康

confirm 确定,批准,证实　　　　　　**routine** 路线

gradually 渐渐地,逐渐地　　　　　　**adjustment** 调整

【写译语块】

1. combining exercise with their diet 将运动和节食结合起来

2. (be)discouraged too much by 被大大地挫伤了信心

3. a very tough way to lose weight 一种很困难的减肥方法

4. exercise's supporting role in weight reduction is vital 运动的辅助作用是至关重要的

144

5. no increase in food intake 进食量不增加

【难句分析】

1. (第一段第二句)Unfortunately, that message has not gotten through to the average American, who would rather try switching to "light" beer and low-calorie bread than increase physical exertion. 这句话中有一个定语从句，who 引导的定语从句是来修饰前面的 average American，美国普通民众的。这里 get through 意为"了解，知道"。可以用 understand 代替。后面 would rather do ... than ... 意为"宁愿……而不愿……"。普通民众不了解，所以宁愿食用 light beer and low-calorie bread，light 这里是"清淡"的意思。physical exertion 指的是"体能的消耗"。

2. (第三段第二句)A study at the Boston University Medical Center of overweight police officers and other public employees confirmed that those who dieted without exercise regained almost all their old weight, while those who worked exercise into their daily routine maintained their new weight. 这个句子中 study 有多个定语短语修饰，at the Boston University Medical Center 在波士顿大学医学研究中心，并且是对 overweight police officers and other public employees，过胖的警员和其他公职人员做的研究，指明了研究对象。confirm 后面跟着一个宾语从句。宾语从句又有两个定语从句构成。dieted without exercise 指"节食而不运动"，worked exercise into their daily routine 意为"将运动列入了日常工作"。

3. (最后一段最后一句)在 By increasing the distance of your walks gradually and making other dietary adjustments, you may lose even more weight 中，by 是"通过"的意思。后面用 and 连接跟了两种方式。increasing the distance of your walks 意为"增加走路的距离"。making other dietary adjustments 意为"做些饮食方面的调整"。dietary 是 diet 的形容词。

【原题再现】

291. What is said about the average American in the passage?

A) They tend to exaggerate the healthful effect of "light" beer.

B) They usually ignore the effect of exercise on losing weight.

C) They prefer "light" beer and low-calorie bread to other drinks and food.

D) They know the factors that play a positive role in keeping down body weight.

292. Some people dislike exercise because _____.

A) they think it is physically exhausting

B) they find it hard to exercise while on a diet

C) they don't think it possible to walk 3 miles every day

D) they find consulting caloric-expenditure charts troublesome

293. "Even exercise professionals concede half a point here" (Sentence 2, Para. 2) means "They _____."

A) agree that the calories in a small piece of pastry can be difficult to work off by exercise

B) partially believe diet plays a supporting role in weight reduction

C) are not fully convinced that dieting can help maintain one's new weight

D) are not sufficiently informed of the positive role of exercise in losing weight

294. What was confirmed by the Boston University Medical Center's study?

A) Controlling one's calorie intake is more important than doing exercise.

B) Even occasional exercise can help reduce weight.

C) Weight reduction is impossible without exercise.

D) One could lose ten pounds in a year's time if there's no increase in food intake.

295. What is the author's purpose in writing this article?

A) To justify the study of the Boston University Medical Center.

B) To stress the importance of maintaining proper weight.

C) To support the statement made by York Onnen.

D) To show the most effective way to lose weight.

【单词详解】

【重点单词】**maintain** / mein'tein / *vt.*

[基本词义] 维持；维修，保养；坚持；断言

[用法导航] Mankind have been trying every means to maintain the balance of nature. 人类采用一切手段保持生态平衡。// We must maintain a firm attitude. 我们必须采取坚定的态度。// The government has taken a measure to maintain the stability of prices. 政府已经采取了措施以确保物价稳定。// The car has to be constantly maintained. 汽车必须经常保养。

[词性转换] **maintenance**/ 'meintinəns / *n.* 维护，保持，维修，生活费用

[对比记忆]（1）**conserve** / kən'səːv / *vt.* 保存，与糖放在一起，保持

（2）**preserve** / pri'zəːv / *vt.* 保护，保持，保存

（3）**reserve** / ri'zəːv / *vt.* 保留，预订，延期

（4）**retain** / ri'tein / *vt.* 保持，保留；记住

[真题衔接] Throughout his life, Henry Moore _____ an interest in encouraging are in the city of Leeds. (CET4-9301)

A) contained   B) secured   C) reserved   D) maintained

【重点单词】 **diet** / 'daiət / *vt.*, *n.* & *adj.*

[基本词义] 日常饮食，规定饮食；照规定饮食

[用法导航] You should eat more high-protein diet. 你应该多吃些高蛋白食物。// I'm on a diet. 我正在节食。

[词性转换] **dieter** / 'daijətə / *n.* 节食者

[对比记忆]（1）**dietary** / 'daiətəri / *adj.* 饭食的，饮食的

（2）**die** / dai / *n.* 金属模子，印模，骰子 *vi.* 死

[真题衔接] The doctor advised him that too rich a _____ is not good for him, for he is too fat.

A) scent   B) taste   C) recipe   D) diet

【句子翻译】

296. _____（他容易泄气）by difficulties and obstacles.

297. Whereas we want a flat _____（而他们却想住一所房子）.

298. This point is _____（对我的论据极为重要）and thank you very much.

299. He looked around _____（以确定周围没人）.

300. Now that more visitors are expected to come, I _____（做了小小的调整）to the seating plan.

Passage Thirty-one

A is for always getting to work on time.

B is for being extremely busy.

C is for the conscientious (勤勤恳恳的) way you do your job.

You may be all these things at the office, and more. But when it comes to getting ahead, experts say, the ABCs of business should include a P, for politics, as in office politics.

Dale Carnegie suggested as much more than 50 years ago: Hard work alone doesn't ensure career **advancement**. *You have to be able to sell yourself and your ideas, both publicly and behind the scenes.* Yet, despite the obvious rewards of engaging in office politics—a better job, a raise, praise—many people are still unable—or unwilling—to "play the game."

"People assume that office politics involves some **manipulative**（工于心计的）behavior," says Deborah Comer, an assistant professor of management at Hofstra University. "*But politics derives from the word 'polite'*. It can mean lobbying and forming **associations**. It can mean being kind and helpful, or even trying to please your superior, and then expecting something in return."

In fact, today, experts define office politics as proper behavior used to **pursue** one's own self-interest in the workplace. In many cases, this involves some form of socializing within the office environment—not just in large companies, but in small workplaces as well.

"*The first thing people are usually judged on is their ability to perform well on a consistent basis*," says Neil P. Lewis, a management psychologist. "But if two or three **candidates** are up for a promotion, each of whom has reasonably similar ability, a manager is going to promote the person he or she likes best. It's simple human nature."

Yet, psychologists say, *many employees and employers have trouble with the concept of politics in the office.* Some people, they say, have an **idealistic** vision of work and what it takes to succeed. Still others associate politics with flattery（奉承）, fearful that, if they speak up for themselves, they may appear to be flattering their boss for favors.

Experts suggest altering this negative picture by recognizing the need for some self-promotion. (364 words) （2004 年 6 月第 1 篇）

【段落译文】

A 代表经常准时上班

B 代表非常忙碌

C 代表勤勤恳恳地工作

这些事情你在办公室可能都能做到，或者你可以做得更多。但是如果说到升职，专家认为，职场的入门知识应该把一个以 P 字母开头的字包括进去，即职场策略。

早在 50 多年前，卡内基就说过：单凭努力工作并不能得到升职。你必须学会销售自己和你的想法,无论是在众人面前还是在幕后。但是,尽管职场策略可以带来诸如得到更好的工作、加薪、赞扬这些显而易见的回报,还是有许多人做不到或不情愿去"耍手腕"。

Hofstra 大学管理专业副教授 Deborah Comer 说:人们往往认为职场策略指的是一些工于心计的做法,但是策略原本来自"礼貌"一词。它可以指游说、建立关系,也可以指友好待人、乐于助人,甚至是努力取悦你的上司,并期望有所回报。

事实上,如今专家们把职场策略定义成了在工作场所为了追求个人利益所做的适当行为。在许多情况下,它是指在办公环境下的一种社交——不仅是在大公司,在小型的工作场所也是如此。

管理心理学家 Neil P. Lewis 说:"通常对职员首要的评判标准是他们能否表现一贯出色,但是如果一个升职的机会有三到四个候选人,他们每个的能力都相差无几,那么管理者会提拔他或她个人最喜欢的那个人。这不过是人的本性。"

但是,心理学家们说,许多雇主和雇员都对职场的策略理解不清。他们说有些人对工作怎样才能成功的认识过于理想化。还有些人认为策略就是奉承,因此担心如果他们销售自己,会让人觉得他们在奉承老板以取悦他们。

专家建议,通过承认职场策略是个人提升的需要来转变对它的负面认识。

【难词释义】

advancement(级别的)晋升,提升,提拔   **manipulative** 工于心计的

derive 取得,获得;导出;形成   **association** 协会组织

pursue 追求,追赶   **consistent** 一致的,连续的,持续的

candidate 候选人,申请人,投考者   **idealistic** 理想主义的

【写译语块】

1. You may be all these things at the office, and more. ? 这些事情你在办公室可能都能做到,或者你可以做得更多。

2. You have to be able to sell yourself and your ideas, both publicly and behind the scenes. 你必须学会销售自己和你的想法,无论是在众人面前还是在幕后。

3. But politics derives from the word 'polite'. 但是策略原本来自"礼貌"一词

4. The first thing people are usually judged on is their ability to perform well on a consistent basis, 通常对职员首要的评判标准是他们能否表现一贯出色。

5. Many employees and employers have trouble with the concept of politics in the office. 许多雇主和雇员都对职场的策略理解不清。

【难句分析】

1. （第二段最后一句）在 Yet，despite the obvious rewards of engaging in office politics — a better job, a raise, praise — many people are still unable — or unwilling — to "play the game"中，despite 是"尽管,虽然"的意思,有转折的含义。despite 和 though 一样,都表示转折,但是 despite 后面只能跟短语词组,不能跟句子。和 in spite of 同义。而 though 后面一般跟句子。engage in office politics 表示采用了这样的职场策略。unwilling to do sth 是"不愿意做某事"。

2. （第三段末尾）In fact, today, experts define office politics as proper behavior used to pursue one's own self-interest in the workplace. In many cases, this involves some form of socializing within the office environment — not just in large companies, but in small workplaces as well. Define . . . as . . . 是"把……定义为……"。proper behavior used to pursue one's own self-interest 是一个定语从句,在 behavior 后面省略了 that is。pursue 是"追求"的意思。self-interest 是"个人利益",interest 在这里不是"兴趣",而是"利益"。this 指代的是"职场策略",socialize 由 society 一词变换而来,是"交际,交往"的意思。

3. （第五段末尾）在 Still others associate politics with flattery（奉承）, fearful that, if they speak up for themselves, they may appear to be flattering their boss for favors 中,associate . . . with . . . 是"与……联系起来"。speak up for 是"为……辩护;替……讲好话"。appear to be 意为 seem to be,即"似乎,看起来好像"。

【原题再现】

301. "Office politics" (Sentence 2, Para. 4) is used in the passage to refer to _____.

    A) the code of behavior for company staff

    B) the political views and beliefs of office workers

    C) the interpersonal relationships within a company

    D) the various qualities required for a successful career

302. To get promoted, one must not only be competent but _____.

    A) give his boss a good impression

    B) honest and loyal to his company

    C) get along well with his colleagues

    D) avoid being too outstanding

303. Why are many people unwilling to "play the game" (Sentence 4, Para. 5)?

A) They believe that doing so is impractical.

B) They feel that such behavior is unprincipled.

C) They are not good at manipulating colleagues.

D) They think the effort will get them nowhere.

304. The author considers office politics to be _____.

A) unwelcome at the workplace

B) bad for interpersonal relationships

C) indispensable to the development of company culture

D) an important factor for personal advancement

305. It is the author's view that _____.

A) speaking up for oneself is part of human nature

B) self-promotion does not necessarily mean flattery

C) hard work contributes very little to one's promotion

D) many employees fail to recognize the need of flattery

【单词详解】

【重点单词】**engage** / inˈgeidʒ / *vt.* & *vi.*

[基本词义] 使从事于；使忙着；使订婚；雇用；接合，啮合；参加

[用法导航] He engaged upon a new profession. 他开始从事新的职业。// Our orders are to engage the enemy immediately. 我们的命令是立即与敌军开战。// Both men were busily engaged in sharpening barrel-staves. 两个男人都正忙于削桶板。// There were six engaged couples at the party. 宴会席上有六对订婚夫妇。// The two cog wheels engaged and the machine started. 那两个齿轮啮合后机器就转动了。

[词性转换] **engagement** / inˈgeidʒmənt / *n.* 约会，约定；婚约；雇用，聘用

[对比记忆] **occupy** / ˈɔkjupai / *vt.* 占，占用，占领；使忙碌，使从事

[真题衔接] The spots of blood on the floor _____ the attention of the police.

A) engaged   B) guarded   C) explained   D) imposed

【重点单词】**promote** / prəˈməut / *vt.*

[基本词义] 促进，提升，升迁；发起；促销

[用法导航] The government decided to promote public welfare. 政府决定发展公共福利。// He likes to read biographies of great men to promote himself. 他喜欢读伟人传记来提高自己。// We must promote commerce with neighboring countries. 我们必须促进与邻国的贸易。

[词性转换] **promotion**/ prəuˈməuʃən / *n.* 晋升,促进,提升

[对比记忆] (1) **spur** / spəː / *n.* 刺激(物),激励 *vt.* 激励,鞭策,促进

(2) **encourage** / inˈkʌridʒ / *vt.* 鼓励,激励,怂恿;促进,助长,激发

[真题衔接] Pupils who pass the test will be _____ to the next grade. (CET6-9206)

A) promoted   B) proceeded   C) progressed   D) proposed

【句子翻译】

306. _____(尽管我们尽了全力)we still lost the game.

307. _____(政治家不应该参与那些商业事务)that might affect their political judgment.

308. In children's minds, summers _____(和郊游连在一起).

309. Common sense, or intuition, or self-evident truths _____(来源于人们对周围世界的感觉).

310. Having been working in that branch for nearly 15 years, the man _____(被提升为经理).

Passage Thirty-two

As soon as it was revealed that a reporter for Progressive magazine had discovered how to make a hydrogen bomb, a group of firearm (火器) fans formed the National Hydrogen Bomb Association, and they are now **lobbying** against any **legislation** to stop Americans from owning one.

"The Constitution," said the association's **spokesman**, "*gives everyone the right to own arms. It doesn't spell out what kind of arms.* But since anyone can now make a hydrogen bomb, the public should be able to buy it to protect themselves."

"Don't you think it's dangerous to have one in the house, particularly where there are children around?"

"The National Hydrogen Bomb Association hopes to *educate people in the safe handling of this type of weapon.* We are **instructing** owners to keep the bomb in a locked **cabinet** and the fuse (导火索) separately in a drawer."

"Some people consider the hydrogen bomb a very **fatal** weapon which could kill somebody."

The spokesman said, "Hydrogen bombs don't kill people — people kill people. The bomb is for self-protection and it also has a **deterrent** effect. If somebody

152

knows you have a nuclear weapon in your house, they're going to think twice about breaking in."

"But those who want to ban the bomb for American citizens **claim** that if you have one locked in the cabinet, with the fuse in a drawer, *you would never be able to* **assemble** *it in time to stop an intruder*（侵入者）."

"Another argument against allowing people to own a bomb is that at the moment it is very expensive to build one. So what your association is backing is a program which would allow the middle and upper classes to acquire a bomb *while poor people will be left* **defenseless** *with just handguns*."（303 words） （2004 年 6 月第 2 篇）

【段落译文】

一名《进步》杂志的记者一报道说他已经发现怎么制造氢弹,一群武器爱好者就成立了一个全国氢弹协会,试图反对任何立法机构制止美国人人拥有一枚。

协会发言人说:"宪法赋予每个人都能拥有自己武器的权利,没有具体说明是什么武器,既然现在任何人都能制造氢弹,公众就应该能够购买以保护自己。"

"难道你不认为家里有一枚氢弹是很危险的事情吗? 尤其是当你家里有小孩的时候?"

"全国氢弹协会希望指导人们如何安全使用这类武器。我们提出人们可以把氢弹弹体锁进橱柜,把导火索分开放置在抽屉。"

"一些人认为氢弹是一种非常致命的武器,可以将人杀死。"发言人说:"氢弹本身不杀人——人才会杀人。氢弹是用来自我保护的,它有制止和预防的作用。若家中藏有氢弹,则会吓阻非法闯入者。"

"但是那些反对核武器的美国公民声称,即使你家里真的有氢弹藏在柜中,若有人侵入,也根本来不及把氢弹组装起来以制止入侵者。"

"另外一条反对意见是目前氢弹的价格十分昂贵,所以你们这个组织只是在支持中上层阶级拥有炸弹来保护自己,而穷人就只剩下手枪自卫而无其他防备了。"

【难词释义】

lobby 游说	**legislation** 立法,法律
spokesman 发言人	**instruct** 指导
cabinet 橱柜	**fatal** 致命的
deterrent 制止,防止,挽留	**claim** 声称
assemble 聚集,集合,装配	**defenseless** 无防备的

【写译语块】

1. give everyone the right to own arms 赋予每个人都能拥有自己武器的权利

2. It doesn't spell out what kind of arms. 没有具体说明是什么武器。

3. educate people in the safe handling of this type of weapon 指导人们如何安全使用这类武器

4. You would never be able to assemble it in time to stop an intruder（侵入者）. 根本不能及时把氢弹组装起来以制止入侵者。

5. while poor people will be left defenseless with just handguns 而穷人就只剩下手枪自卫而无其他防备了

【难句分析】

1. （第一段）As soon as it was revealed that a reporter for Progressive magazine had discovered how to make a hydrogen bomb, a group of firearm（火器）fans formed the National Hydrogen Bomb Association, and they are now lobbying against any legislation to stop Americans from owning one. 该长句主要讲该协会成立的缘由。as soon as 是"一……就……"的意思，reveal 这里指"泄露"。National Hydrogen Bomb Association 指的是全国氢弹协会。lobby 是"游说"的意思，lobby against 就是"游说反对某事物"，stop from 是"阻止"的意思，指的是反对任何阻止美国人拥有氢弹的立法。

2. （第五段结尾）在 The bomb is for self-protection and it also has a deterrent effect. If somebody knows you have a nuclear weapon in your house, they're going to think twice about breaking in 中，self-protection 是"自我保护"的意思。think twice"思考两次"，与汉语里的"思考再三"类似，表示人犹豫不决，考虑再三无法下定决心，在这里就是指闯入者犹豫不决，始终不敢进入有核武器的房子。这的确可以说是一种威慑效果。

3. （最后一段第一句）在 Another argument against allowing people to own a bomb is that at the moment it is very expensive to build one 中，... is that ... 是一个同位语从句。against 是"反对"的意思，后面不能直接跟动词，所以 allow 变成 allowing，allow sb to do sth 是"允许某人做某事"。own 这里是动词，"拥有"的意思。at the moment 是"目前"的意思。

【原题再现】

311. According to the passage, some people started a national association so as to

_____.

A) block any legislation to ban the private possession of the bomb

B) coordinate the mass production of the destructive weapon

C) instruct people how to keep the bomb safe at home

D) promote the large-scale sale of this newly invented weapon

312. Some people oppose the ownership of H-bombs by individuals on the grounds that _____.

A) the size of the bomb makes it difficult to keep in a drawer

B) most people don't know how to handle the weapon

C) people's lives will be threatened by the weapon

D) they may fall into the hands of criminals

313. By saying that the bomb also has a deterrent effect the spokesman means that it _____.

A) will frighten away any possible intruders

B) can show the special status of its owners

C) will threaten the safety of the owners as well

D) can kill those entering others' houses by force

314. According to the passage, opponents of the private ownership of H-bombs are very much worried that _____.

A) the influence of the association is too powerful for the less privileged to overcome

B) poorly-educated Americans will find it difficult to make use of the weapon

C) the wide use of the weapon will push up living expenses tremendously

D) the cost of the weapon will put citizens on an unequal basis

315. From the tone of the passage we know that the author is _____.

A) doubtful about the necessity of keeping H-bombs at home for safety

B) unhappy with those who vote against the ownership of H-bombs

C) not serious about the private ownership of H-bombs

D) concerned about the spread of nuclear weapons

【单词详解】

【重点单词】 **reveal** / ri'vi:l / *vt.*

[基本词义] 显示,透露

［用法导航］Government employees swear an oath not to reveal official secrets. 政府雇员宣誓不泄露官方机密。// An intensive search failed to reveal any clues. 经过彻底搜查未发现任何线索。

［词性转换］**revealer** / ri'vi:lə / *n.* 探测器

［对比记忆］（1）**disclose** / dis'kləuz / *vt.* （侧重指）揭露或泄露（鲜为人知或保密的事）

（2）**expose** / ik'spəuz / *vt.* 暴露，揭穿，使遭受（危险或不快）

（3）**uncover**/ ˌʌn'kʌvə / *vt.* 揭开，揭露

［真题衔接］I hate people who _____ the end of film that you haven't seen before. （CET4-9706）

A) reveal   B) rewrite   C) revise   D) reverse

【重点单词】**handle** / 'hændl / *vt.* , *vi.* & *n.*

［基本词义］买卖，处理，操作，驾驭；柄，把手

［用法导航］The speaker was roughly handled by the mob. 演说者受到暴民的粗暴对待。// I was impressed by her handling of the affair. 我觉得她对此事的处理很了不起。

［对比记忆］（1）**manage** / 'mænidʒ / *vt.* 管理，处理，维持，达成，经营

（2）**deal** / di:l / *vi.* 处理，应付，分配

（3）**treat**/ tri:t / *vt.* 对待，治疗，处理，请客，视为

［真题衔接］He _____ the employees' problems with sensitivity and direction.

A) opposed   B) postponed   C) handled   D) dissolved

【句子翻译】

316. It does not pertain to the young _____（对老年人发号施令）.

317. The government would not even consider _____（他的赔款要求）.

318. _____ employing someone you've never met（你应三思而行）.

319. I promise never to _____（泄漏他的秘密）and I will stick to my promise.

320. Your argument has _____（致命的错误）and it is not convincing.

Passage Thirty-three

Sign has become a scientific hot button. Only in the past 20 years have **specialists** in language study realized that signed languages are **unique** — a speech of the hand. They offer a new way to **probe** how the brain generates and understands language, and ***throw new light on an old scientific*** controversy: whether lan-

156

guage, **complete** with grammar, is something that we are born with, or whether it is a learned behavior. The current interest in sign language has roots in the **pioneering** work of one rebel teacher at Gallaudet University in Washington, D. C. , the world's only liberal arts university for deaf people.

When Bill Stokoe went to Gallaudet to teach English, the school **enrolled** him in a course in signing. But Stokoe noticed something **odd**: among themselves, students signed differently from his classroom teacher.

Stokoe had been taught a sort of gestural code, each movement of the hands representing a word in English. At the time, American Sign Language (ASL) was thought to be no more than a form of pidgin English (混杂英语). But Stokoe *believed the "hand talk" his students used looked richer*. He wondered: Might deaf people actually have a genuine language? And could that language be unlike any other on Earth? It was 1955, when even *deaf people dismissed their signing as "substandard"*. Stokoe's idea was academic heresy (异端邪说).

It is 37 years later. Stokoe — now *devoting his time to writing and editing books* and journals and to producing video materials on ASL and the deaf culture — is having lunch at a café near the Gallaudet campus and explaining how he started a **revolution**. For decades educators fought his idea that signed languages are natural languages like English, French and Japanese. They **assumed** language must be based on speech, the modulation (调节) of sound. But *sign language is based on the movement of hands, the modulation of space*. "What I said," Stokoe explains, "is that language is not mouth stuff — it's brain stuff." (339 words) (2004 年 6 月第 3 篇)

【段落译文】

手语成了科学研究的热门内容。从事语言研究的专家们直到 20 年前才开始认识到手语的独特性——它是手的语言。手语为探索大脑如何产生和理解语言提供了新的途径，而且给弄清科学界关于拥有语法的语言是我们与生俱来之物还是后天习得的行为这个长期存在的争议带来启发。人们目前对手语的广泛兴趣根源于华盛顿特区 Gallaudet 大学一名有反叛精神的教师开拓性的工作，这所大学是世界上唯一一所为聋哑人开办的文科大学。

Bill Stokoe 在教授英语时，学校让他教授一口关于手语的课程。但是他注意到一件奇怪事：学生们之间使用的手语和课堂上老师用的手语不一样。

Stokoe 以前学过一种手势符号，即用手的每个动作代表一个英语单词。当时

157

人们认为美国手语不过是一种混杂英语。但是 Stokoe 坚信他的学生们"手的交谈"更丰富。他想：聋哑人会不会有真正的语言？这种语言能否和世界上任何一种语言都不同？那时是 1995 年，当时就连聋哑人自己都认为他们的手语"不够标准"。因此 Stokoe 的想法被看成是异端邪说。

转眼已是 37 年之后了。现在 Stokoe 把他的时间都用在了编写美国手语和聋哑文化方面的书籍和刊物以及制作相关的音像资料上。此时 Stokoe 正在 Gallaudet 大学校园附近的一家餐厅吃午餐，并解释他是怎样发起了一场革命。几十年来，教育者都在批驳他关于手语和英语、语法、日语一样也是自然语言的观点。他们认为语言必须以话语，即声音的调节为基础。但是手语是以手的运动，即空间调节为基础的。Stokoe 解释说："我要说的是语言不是嘴的事——它是大脑的事。"

【难词释义】

specialist 专家   **unique** 独一无二的

probe 用探针测，详细调查   **controversy** （公开的）争论，争议

complete 完成；使圆满，使完美   **pioneer** 先锋，拓荒者

enroll 登记，使加入，卷起   **odd** 奇怪的

revolution 革命   **assume** 假定，设想，承担；（想当然地）认为

【写译语块】

1. throw new light on an old scientific controversy 为这个长期存在的争议带来启发

2. believed the "hand talk" his students used looked richer 坚信他的学生们"手的交谈"更丰富

3. deaf people dismissed their signing as "substandard" 聋哑人自己都认为他们的手语"不够标准"

4. devoting his time to writing and editing books 把他的时间都用在了编写书籍上

5. sign language is based on the movement of hands, the modulation of space 手语是以手的运动，即空间调节为基础的

【难句分析】

1. （第一段第二句）Only in the past 20 years have specialists in language study realized that signed languages are unique—a speech of the hand. 该句以 only 开头，表示一种强调，直到 20 年前才……。句子中以 only 开头，句子后面要部分倒装，所以原本应该是 specialists have realized 中，have 提前。这里 in language

study 是作为定语来修饰 specialists 的,意为"从事语言研究的专家"。unique 意为"独一无二的,独特的"。a speech of the hand,这里 speech 应理解成为一种语言。

2. (第一段第四句)The current interest in sign language has roots in the pioneering work of one rebel teacher at Gallaudet University in Washington, D. C. , the world's only liberal arts university for deaf people. 这句话中有多个定语连环修饰。其中 one rebel teacher at Gallaudet University in Washington, D. C. 是用来修饰前面的 pioneering work,rebel 指的是"具有反叛精神的",pioneering work 是"开拓性工作"的意思。has roots in 意为"根源于,扎根于",该句意为"目前广泛的兴趣根源于这位反叛精神的教师的开拓性工作"。而后面 the world's only liberal arts university for deaf people 是来修饰这位教师所在的大学的。liberal arts university 是"文科大学"的意思。

3. (第三段开头)Stokoe had been taught a sort of gesture code, each movement of the hands representing a word in English. At the time, American Sign Language (ASL) was thought to be no more than a form of pidgin English. 这里有一个被动语态,被教授过,或者说学过一种手势符号。represent 是"代表"的意思。at the time 意为"在当时",no more than 意为"不过,仅仅",It's no more than a misunderstanding 意为"这只是个误会"。这里指当时人们认为美国手语只不过是一种混杂英语。

【原题再现】

321. The study of sign language is thought to be _____.

A) a new way to look at the learning of language

B) a challenge to traditional views on the nature of language

C) an approach to simplifying the grammatical structure of a language

D) an attempt to clarify misunderstanding about the origin of language

322. The present growing interest in sign language was stimulated by _____.

A) a famous scholar in the study of the human brain

B) a leading specialist in the study of liberal arts

C) an English teacher in a university for the deaf

D) some senior experts in American Sign Language

323. According to Stokoe, sign language is _____.

A) a substandard language   B) a genuine language

C) an artificial language   D) an international language

324. Most educators objected to Stokoe's idea because they thought _____.

A) sign language was not extensively used even by deaf people

B) sign language was too artificial to be widely accepted

C) a language should be easy to use and understand

D) a language could only exist in the form of speech sounds

325. Stokoe's argument is based on his belief that _____.

A) sign language is as efficient as any other language

B) sign language is derived from natural language

C) language is a system of meaningful codes

D) language is a product of the brain

【单词详解】

【重点单词】**represent** / ˌrepriˈzent / *vt.* & *vi.*

[基本词义] 表现,表示,描绘,代表,象征,说明,阐明;提出异议

[用法导航] The rose represents England. 玫瑰花是英格兰的象征。// The king is represented as a villain in the play. 在这出剧中把国王刻画成一个反面人物。// The red lines on the map represent railways. 这张地图上的红线代表铁路。

[词性转换] **representation** / ˌreprizenˈteiʃen / *n.* 表示法,表现,陈述,答辩

[对比记忆] (1) **picture** / ˈpiktʃə / *vt.* 画,描写,想象

(2) **describe** / disˈkraib / *vt.* 描述,画(尤指几何图形)

(3) **sketch** / sketʃ / *vt.* 描绘略图

[真题衔接] The accident victims chose a famous barrister (律师) to _____ them in court.

A) interpret   B) substitute   C) display   D) represent

【句子翻译】

326. The journalist _____ (正在调查几起财务丑闻) and the work would soon come to an end.

327. I made a mistake and I will _____ (我愿为此承担责任).

328. He has achieved great success but his whole school education _____ (加在一块只不过一年).

329. He _____ music(将一生奉献给了音乐) and has not offered a hand to his wife in housework.

330. The story emphasized that a good marriage should _____（建立在互相信任的基础上）.

Passage Thirty-four

It came as something of a surprise when Diana, Princess of Wales, made a trip to Angola in 1997, to support the Red Cross's **campaign** for a total ban on all anti-personnel landmines. Within hours of arriving in Angola, television screens around the world were *filled with images of her comforting* victims *injured in explosions caused by* landmines. "I knew the **statistics,**" she said. "But putting a face to those figures *brought the reality home to me*; like when I met Sandra, a 13-year-old girl who had lost her leg, and people like her."

The Princess concluded with a simple message: "We must stop landmines". And she used every opportunity during her visit to repeat this message.

But, back in London, her views were *not shared by some members of the British government*, which refused to support a ban on these weapons. Angry politicians **launched** an attack on the Princess in the press. They described her as "very ill-informed" and a "loose cannon（乱放炮的人）."

The Princess *responded by brushing aside the criticisms*: "This is a distraction（干扰）we do not need. All I'm trying to do is help."

Opposition parties, the media and the public immediately voiced their support for the Princess. To make matters worse for the government, it soon **emerged** that the Princess's trip had been approved by the Foreign Office, and that she was in fact very well-informed about both the situation in Angola and the British government's policy regarding landmines. The result was *a severe embarrassment for the government*.

To try and limit the damage, the Foreign Secretary, Malcolm Rifkidnd, **claimed** that the Princess's views on landmines were not very different from government policy, and that it was "working towards" a worldwide ban. The Defense Secretary, Michael Portillo, claimed the matter was "a misinterpretation or misunderstanding."

For the Princess, the trip to this war-torn country was an excellent opportunity to use her popularity to show the world how much **destruction** and suffering landmines can cause. She said that the experience had also given her the chance to get closer to people and their problems. (358 words) （2004 年 6 月第 4 篇）

戴安娜王妃在 1997 年访问了安哥拉,访问目的是支持红十字会的禁用地雷运动。这件事的发生使人惊诧不已。在她到达安哥拉的数小时后,全世界的电视屏幕都在播放她安抚地雷受害者的镜头。"我看过地雷受害者相关的数据",她说,"但是面对面的接触将现实带到了眼前,亲眼见到受害者后才真正认识到了现实的情形。像我遇到的那个 13 岁的女孩桑德拉,她失去了一条腿,还有别的和她一样的人。"

王妃用简单的话语总结说:"我们必须停止使用地雷。"并利用她每次访问的机会,不断重复这个观点。

但是,在伦敦,她的观点并没有被英国政府的一些成员所认同,他们拒绝支持对这些武器的禁令。愤怒的政客们还在媒体发动了对王妃的攻击,他们把她描述为"所知甚少"和"乱放炮的人"。

王妃对批评采取了漠视态度。"我们并不需要为此分心。我所要做的就是帮助人们。"

反对党、媒体和大众立即表达了对王妃的支持。对政府来说,事情变得更糟的是,有确凿消息说王妃的非洲之行是在得到外事部门的核准,在确知了安哥拉的情况和英国政府的态度后才决定成行的。这样的结果,使政府处于极度尴尬境地。

为了减小影响,外交秘书长 Malcolm Rifkidnd 宣称政府的政策与王妃的观点相差不多,政府甚至在为全球禁用地雷而努力。国防部秘书长 Michael Portillo 也跳出来说此事存在误会。

对于王妃来说,此次到这个饱受战争摧残国家的行程,是利用自己的知名度来告诉世界地雷能够带来多大的破坏和痛苦的一次好机会。她说这次经历也给了她机会接近民众,了解他们的困苦。

【难词释义】

campaign 战役,运动,活动	**landmine** 地雷
victim 受害者,牺牲	**statistics** 数据
launch 发射,开始	**opposition** 反对,敌对,在野党
emerge 浮现,显现	**embarrassment** 困窘,尴尬,困难
claim 主张,声称,断言	**destruction** 破坏,毁灭,破坏者

【写译语块】

1. filled with images of her comforting victims injured in explosions caused by

landmines 充满了她安抚地雷受害者的镜头

2. brought the reality home to me 真正认识到了现实的情形

3. not shared by some members of the British government 不被英国政府的一些成员所认同

4. responded by brushing aside the criticisms 对批评采取了漠视态度

5. a severe embarrassment for the government 使政府处于极度尴尬境地

【难句分析】

1. (第一段第一句)在 It came as something of a surprise when Diana, Princess of Wales, made a trip to Angola in 1997, to support the Red Cross's campaign for a total ban on all anti-personnel landmines. 长句中, it 代指 when 后面所说的事件。It came as something of a surprise 意思是"这件事的发生使人惊诧不已", make a trip to...意为"去哪里旅行"。to support...后面跟的是目的状语。support campaign 后面的 for a total ban on all anti-personnel landmines 都是来修饰这个战斗的。ban 有"禁止, 取缔"的意思。

2. (第五段第二句)To make matters worse for the government, it soon emerged that the Princess's trip had been approved by the Foreign Office, and that she was in fact very well-informed about both the situation in Angola and the British government's policy regarding landmines. 这是一个长句。make matters worse 意为"使事情变得更加糟糕"。it soon emerged 后面实际跟了两个 that 从句, approved by the Foreign Office 和 well-informed about both the situation in Angola and the British government's policy 是并列的两个从句。approved by 是"核准的"意思。well-informed about 是"对……了解很清楚"。

3. (最后一段第一句)For the Princess, the trip to this war-torn country was an excellent opportunity to use her popularity to show the world how much destruction and suffering landmines can cause. 这句话中用多个定语来修饰 trip 一词。to this war-torn country, to use her popularity, to show the world how much destruction and suffering landmines can cause, 第一个 to 表示目的地, 第二个表示手段, 最后一个表示此行的最终目的。war-torn 意为"饱受战争摧残"。

【原题再现】

331. Princess Diana paid a visit to Angola in 1997 _____.

A) to voice her support for a total ban of landmines

B) to clarify the British government's stand on landmines

C) to investigate the sufferings of landmine victims there

D) to establish her image as a friend of landmine victims

332. What did Diana mean when she said "... putting a face to those figures brought the reality home to me" (Sentence 4, Para. 1)?

A) She just couldn't bear to meet the landmine victims face to face.

B) The actual situation in Angola made her feel like going back home.

C) Meeting the landmine victims in person made her believe the statistics.

D) Seeing the pain of the victims made her realize the seriousness of the situation.

333. Some members of the British government criticized Diana because _____.

A) she was ill-informed of the government's policy

B) they were actually opposed to banning landmines

C) she had not consulted the government before the visit

D) they believed that she had misinterpreted the situation in Angola

334. How did Diana respond to the criticisms?

A) She paid no attention to them.

B) She made more appearances on TV.

C) She met the 13-year-old girl as planned.

D) She rose to argue with her opponents.

335. What did Princess Diana think of her visit to Angola?

A) It had caused embarrassment to the British government.

B) It had brought her closer to the ordinary people.

C) It had greatly promoted her popularity.

D) It had affected her relations with the British government.

【单词详解】

【重点单词】 **criticism** / ˈkritiˌsizəm / n.

[基本词义] 批评,评论

[用法导航] His partial attitude called forth a lot of criticism. 他的偏袒态度招致了不少批评。// Such a questionable assertion is sure to provoke criticism. 这种有问题的主张肯定会招致非议。

[词性转换] **criticize** / ˈkritisaiz / vt. 批评,吹毛求疵,非难 vi. 批评

[对比记忆] (1) **remark** / riˈmɑːk / vt. 说,评论说 vi. (on)谈论,评论

164

(2) **review** / ri'vju: / *vt.* 审查,复查,回顾;复习,温习;评论;检阅

(3) **comment** / 'kɔment / *n.* 评论,意见;闲话,议论 *vt.* 评论

［真题衔接］If you've got any constructive _____, I'd be glad to hear it.

    A) stress   B) criticism   C) version   D) introduction

【重点单词】**support** / sə'pɔːt / *vt. & n.*

［基本词义］支援,帮助,支持,援助,供养

［用法导航］Jim was a great support to us when father died. 父亲死后,吉姆给了我们巨大的帮助。// Support your local theatre: buy tickets regularly! 请大力支持本地剧院,欢迎经常光临！// Her father supported her until she got married. 她父亲抚养她直到她结婚。

［对比记忆］(1) **sustain** / sə'stein / *vt.* 承受,支持,经受,维持

(2) **uphold** / ʌp'həuld / *vt.* 支撑,赞成,鼓励

(3) **advocate** / 'ædvəkeit / *n.* 提倡者,拥护者

(4) **back** / bæk / *vt.* 后退,支持

［真题衔接］The directors were trying to get rid of her, but her staff all _____ her.

    A) comforted   B) guarded   C) defended   D) supported

【句子翻译】

336. The moment I entered her room, I found that the room _____（充满了玫瑰花的香味）.

337. He _____（不理会）my objections to his plan and carried it on.

338. The city council _____（批准了这项建筑计划）and two years later there will a book centre near the square.

339. The sun _____（从云层后面露出来了）and we all cheered.

340. The government would not even consider _____（他的赔款要求）.

Passage Thirty-five

    I'm usually fairly **skeptical** about any research that concludes that people are either happier or unhappier or *more or less certain of themselves than they were 50 years ago*. While any of these statements might be true, they are practically impossible to prove **scientifically**. Still, *I was struck by a report* which concluded that today's children are **significantly** more anxious than children in the 1950s. In fact, the analysis showed, *normal children ages 9 to 17 exhibit a higher level of* *anxiety today* than children who were treated for mental illness 50 years ago.

Why are America's kids so **stressed**? The report cites two main causes: increasing physical **isolation**—brought on by high divorce rates and less involvement in community, among other things—and a growing **perception** that the world is a more dangerous place.

Given that we can't turn the clock back, adults can still do plenty to help the next generation cope.

At the top of the list is **nurturing** a better **appreciation** of the limits of **individualism**. No child is an island. Strengthening social ties helps build communities and protect individuals against stress.

To help kids build stronger connections with others, you can pull the **plug** on TVs and computers. Your family will thank you later. They will have more time for face-to-face relationships, and they will get more sleep.

Limit the amount of virtual violence your children are exposed to. It's not just video games and movies; children see a lot of murder and crime on the local news.

Keep your expectations for your children reasonable. Many highly successful people never attended Harvard or Yale.

Make exercise part of your daily routine. It will help you cope with your own anxieties and provide a good model for your kids. Sometimes anxiety is **unavoidable**. But it doesn't have to ruin your life. (361 words)　(2003 年 12 月第 1 篇)

【段落译文】

任何研究下结论说人们比 50 年前要么快乐要么不快乐或或多或少要自信,我通常都持怀疑的态度。尽管任何一种说法都有可能是对的,事实上它们不可能得到科学的证明。有一篇报告给我留下了深刻的印象,这篇报告说如今的孩子比 20 世纪 50 年代的孩子更忧虑。事实上,分析表明,如今年龄在 9 至 17 岁的正常孩子比 50 年前有精神疾病的孩子显现出更高的忧虑程度。

为什么美国的孩子压力这么大? 报告指出了两个主要原因:一是日益增长的身体上的隔离——源于高离婚率以及很少参与社团和其他一些活动;二是越来越强烈的关于世界是一个更危险的地方这种看法。

虽然我们无法让时间倒退,我们仍然可以做很多事情来帮助我们的下一代处理这些问题。

首先是培养他们更好地认识到个人主义的局限性。没有孩子是一个孤岛。加强社会联系有助于建立共同的兴趣爱好，免受压力的侵扰。

你也可以通过播放电视和电脑来帮助孩子与别人建立较强的联系。以后你的家庭会感谢你的。他们将有更多的时间进行面对面的交流，他们也会得到更多的睡眠。

减少你的孩子所面对的那些虚拟的暴力。这些并不只是在电视电影里面出现。在本地新闻中，孩子们也看到了很多谋杀和犯罪事件。

对你的孩子保持合理的期望。许多非常成功的人从来没有去过哈佛或是耶鲁。

让锻炼成为你生活的一部分。这有助于你对付自己的忧虑，给你的孩子树立一个良好的榜样。有时候忧虑是不可避免的，但这不会毁了你的生活。

【难词释义】

skeptical 怀疑的	**scientifically** 科学地
significantly 重要地	**stressed** 有压力的
isolation 隔离	**involvement** 参与
perception 看法	**nurture** 培育
appreciation 判断，鉴定	**individualism** 个人主义
plug 插头	**unavoidable** 不可避免的

【写译语块】

1. more or less certain of themselves than they were 50 years ago 比 50 年前或多或少要自信

2. I was struck by a report 有一篇报告给我留下了深刻的印象

3. normal children ages 9 to 17 exhibit a higher level of anxiety today 如今年龄在 9 至 17 岁的正常孩子显现出更高的忧虑程度

4. limit the amount of virtual violence your children are exposed to 减少你的孩子所面对的那些虚拟的暴力

5. keep your expectations for your children reasonable 对你的孩子保持合理的期望

6. make exercise part of your daily routine 让锻炼成为你生活的一部分

【难句分析】

1. （第一段第一句）在 I'm usually fairly skeptical about any research that concludes that people are either happier or unhappier or more or less certain of

themselves than they were 50 years ago 中，be skeptical about 表示"对……怀疑"，第一个 that 引导的是一个定语从句，修饰前面的 research，第二个 that 引导的是一个宾语从句，作动词 conclude 的宾语，either ... or 的意思是"或者……或者"表示两者选一，more or less 的意思是"几乎，大约，或多或少"，be certain of 的意思是"确信"。

2. （第二段第二句）在 The report cites two main causes：increasing physical isolation — brought on by high divorce rates and less involvement in community，among other things — and a growing perception that the world is a more dangerous place 中，cite 的意思是"引用，举例"，接下来就列举了两个方面的原因，bring on 的意思是"使出现，使发作，使发展"，这里 brought on by 是被动，表示由居高不下的离婚率引起的，involvement 是动词 involve 的名词形式，表示"参与"，后面 that 引导的是一个定语从句，修饰前面的 perception。

3. （第五段第一句）在 To help kids build stronger connections with others，you can pull the plug on TVs and computers 中，to help kids build stronger connections with others 是一个目的状语，放句首是为了起强调作用，help sb do sth 是一个固定短语，表示"帮助某人某事"，pull the plug on 的意思是"插上插头"。

4. （第八段第二句）在 It will help you cope with your own anxieties and provide a good model for your kids 中，cope (with)表示"对付，处理，能应付得来"，anxiety 的意思是"忧虑"，是 anxious 的名词形式，provide sth for sb 是一个固定短语，表示"为某人提供……"，相同意思的另一个用法是 provide sb with sth. .

【原题再现】

341. The author thinks that the conclusions of any research about people's state of mind are _____.

A) surprising   B) confusing

C) illogical   D) questionable

342. What does the author mean when he says, "we can't turn the clock back" (Sentence 1, Para. 3)?

A) It's impossible to slow down the pace of change.

B) The social reality children are facing cannot be changed.

C) Lessons learned from the past should not be forgotten.

D) It's impossible to forget the past.

343. According to an analysis, compared with normal children today, children treated as mentally ill 50 years ago _____.

A) were less isolated physically

B) were probably less self-centered

C) probably suffered less from anxiety

D) were considered less individualistic

344. The first and most important thing parents should do to help their children is _____ .

A) to provide them with a safer environment

B) to lower their expectations for them

C) to get them more involved socially

D) to set a good model for them to follow

345. What conclusion can be drawn from the passage?

A) Anxiety, though unavoidable, can be coped with.

B) Children's anxiety has been enormously exaggerated.

C) Children's anxiety can be eliminated with more parental care.

D) Anxiety, if properly controlled, may help children become mature.

【单词详解】

【重点单词】 conclude / kənˈkluːd / vt. & vi.

[基本词义] 结束；得出结论；断定；决定

[用法导航] conclude a speech 结束演说 // We conclude that ... 我们断定…… // They concluded (a) peace. 他们缔结和约。// We concluded not to wait any more. 我们决定不再等待了。

[词性转换] conclusion / kənˈkluːʒən / n. 结束，结尾；信念，意见，结论

[对比记忆] (1) include / inˈkluːd / vt. 包括，包含

(2) exclude / iksˈkluːd / vt. 排除；不包括在内

(3) preclude / priˈkluːd / vt. 阻止；排除；妨碍；使……行不通

[真题衔接] She _____ the speech by reminding us of our responsibility.

A) concluded   B) paused   C) interrupted   D) challenged

【重点单词】 involvement / inˈvɔlvmənt / n.

[基本词义] 参与；加入；插手；耗费时间；投入；沉迷恋爱、性爱

[用法导航] The government are trying to play down their involvement in the affair. 政府极力淡化与该事的瓜葛。// His involvement in the scandal was a blot on his reputation. 他因卷入丑闻，在名誉上留下污点。// Many people were elected to take part in democratic involvement. 很多人被选举参与民

主管理。// The police are investigating his possible involvement in the crime. 警方正在调查他卷入那桩罪行的可能性。

[对比记忆] (1) **participation** / pɑːtisiˈpeiʃn / *n.* 参与,参加

(2) **input** / ˈinput / *n.* 输入,投入;输入物,输入的数据

[真题衔接] Researchers at the University of Illinois determined that the _____ of a father can help improve a child's grades. (CET4-0309)

A) involvement B) interaction C) association D) communication

【句子翻译】

346. All the passengers _____(或多或少受伤了)in the accident and they were expecting the compensation.

347. She _____(被他的善良打动)and agreed to marry him.

348. Plants and animals that live near nuclear plants _____(受辐射影响)we don't know about.

349. The sudden cold weather _____(使他发起烧来)again and we had to shut the windows and door.

350. He had a lot of work, but he _____(能应付得来)without help from his family.

Passage Thirty-six

It is easier to negotiate **initial** salary requirement because once you are inside, the organizational constraints (约束) influence wage increases. One thing, however, is certain: your *chances of getting the raise* you feel you **deserve** are less if you don't at least ask for it. Men **tend** to ask for more, and they get more, and this *holds true with other resources*, not just pay increases. Consider Beth's story:

I did not get what I wanted when I did not ask for it. We had cubicle (小隔间) offices and window offices. I sat in the cubicles with several male colleagues. One by one they were moved into window offices, while I **remained** in the cubicles, several males who were hired after me also went to offices. One in particular told me he *was next in line for an office* and that it had been part of his negotiations for the job. I guess they thought me **content** to stay in the cubicles since I did not *voice my opinion either way*.

It would be nice if we all received *automatic pay increases equal to our merit*, but "nice" isn't a quality **attributed** to most organizations. If you feel you deserve a **significant** raise in pay, you'll probably have to ask for it.

Performance is your best **bargaining** chip（筹码）when you are seeking a raise. You must be able to **demonstrate** that you deserve a raise. Timing is also a good bargaining chip. If you can give your boss something he or she needs (a new client or a **sizable** contract, for example) just before merit pay decisions are being made, you are more likely to get the raise you want.

Use information as a bargaining chip too. Find out what you are worth on the open market. What will someone else pay for your services?

Go into the negotiations prepared to place your chips on the table at the **appropriate** time and prepared to use communication style to guide the direction of the **interaction.** (345 words) （2003 年 12 月第 2 篇）

【段落译文】

在工作之前商谈工资问题较为容易,工作之后公司内部的种种约束会限制加薪。然而,有一件事情是确定的:如果你不主动提出,即使你认为你应该加薪,加薪的机会也是渺茫的。男性往往要求的更多,因此得到的也更多,这不仅体现在加薪上,在其他资源方面也是同样的道理。让我们来看一下贝斯的故事:

我不提出要求我就不能得到我想要的。我们公司有小隔间办公室和窗户办公室。我和其他几个男同事一起在小隔间办公室办公。他们一个接着一个地搬到窗户办公室去了,而我继续留在小隔间里,几个比我后来的男同事也搬到窗户办公室去了。有一个男同事特别告诉我说他将是下一个有可能搬到窗户办公室去的,这是他商谈工作时的部分内容。我猜测他们可能认为我很满足于待在小隔间里,因为我从来没有通过任何方式表达过我的看法。

如果我们所有的人都能得到与我们的功劳相当的自动加薪,那将是很好的。然而,"好"并不是大多数公司所拥有的品质。如果你觉得你应得一个明显的加薪,你将不得不提出来。

工作表现将是你要求加薪的最好筹码。你必须能够证明你应该得到加薪。时机也是一个良好的筹码。如果你能给你的老板他(或她)所需要的东西(如一个新客户,或一份大订单),恰好在他决定按功劳付薪水的时候,你更有可能得到你想要的加薪。

也要把信息用作一个加薪的筹码。找出你在这个开放的市场上的价值。别人愿意为你的服务付出多少钱呢?

谈判要不失时机地将反映自己能力的筹码摆到桌面,并巧妙地利用交谈技巧来主导谈话方向。

【难词释义】

initial 最初的,开头的	**deserve** 应得
tend 易于,倾向	**remain** 留下,逗留
content 满足的,满意的	**attribute** 归因于
significant 重要的	**bargain** 讨价还价,商谈
demonstrate 证明,说明	**sizable** 相当大的
appropriate 适当的	**interaction** 合作,配合

【写译语块】

1. chances of getting the raise 加薪的机会
2. hold true with other resources 在其他资源方面也适用
3. be next in line for an office 下一个有可能搬到窗户办公室去的
4. voice my opinion either way 通过任何方式发表过我的看法
5. automatic pay increases equal to our merit 与我们的功劳相当的自动加薪

【难句分析】

1. (第一段第三句)在 Men tend to ask for more, and they get more, and this holds true with other resources, not just pay increases 中,词组 tend to do 的意思是"倾向于,常常",ask for 的意思是"请求,要求",hold true 是一个固定短语,表示"适用,有效",pay increases 是一个名词短语,表示"加薪,工资增长",作介词 with 的宾语。

2. (第二段第三句)在 One by one they were moved into window offices, while I remained in the cubicles, several males who were hired after me also went to offices 中,词组 one by one 的意思是"一个接一个",be moved into 的意思是"搬进",说明一种状态,while 表示转折,引出对比,males 在这里指贝斯的几个男同事,be hired after me 表示"在我之后被雇佣进来"。

3. (第四段第三句)在 If you can give your boss something he or she needs (a new client or a sizable contract, for example) just before merit pay decisions are being made, you are more likely to get the raise you want 中,if 引导一个条件状语从句,he or she needs 是一个定语从句,修饰前面的不定代词 something,merit pay decisions 整体在 before 引导的时间状语从句中作主语,表示"按功劳付薪水的决定",make decisions 表示"做决定",这里把宾语 decisions 提前了,

172

用了被动语态,be likely to do 表示"有可能",you want 仍然是一个定语从句,修饰前面的 raise。

4. (第六段)Go into the negotiations prepared to place your chips on the table at the appropriate time and prepared to use communication style to guide the direction of the interaction. 这是一个祈使句,句中 prepared to do 是分词作状语,省略了主语 you 和谓语动词 are,place your chips on the table 意思是"将(反映自己能力的)筹码摆到桌面",guide the direction of the interaction 的意思是"引导谈话的方向"。

【原题再现】

351. According to the passage, before taking a job, a person should _____.

  A) demonstrate his capability

  B) give his boss a good impression

  C) ask for as much money as he can

  D) ask for the salary he hopes to get

352. What can be inferred from Beth's story?

  A) Prejudice against women still exists in some organizations.

  B) If people want what they deserve, they have to ask for it.

  C) People should not be content with what they have got.

  D) People should be careful when negotiating for a job.

353. We can learn from the passage that _____.

  A) unfairness exists in salary increases

  B) most people are overworked and underpaid

  C) one should avoid overstating one's performance

  D) most organizations give their staff automatic pay raises

354. To get a pay raise, a person should _____.

  A) advertise himself on the job market

  B) persuade his boss to sign a long-term contract

  C) try to get inside information about the organization

  D) do something to impress his boss just before merit pay decisions

355. To be successful in negotiations, one must _____.

  A) meet his boss at the appropriate time

  B) arrive at the negotiation table punctually

  C) be good at influencing the outcome of the interaction

D) be familiar with what the boss likes and dislikes

【单词详解】

【重点单词】**demonstrate** / ˈdemənstreit / vt. & vi.

[基本词义] 说明，演示；论证，证明；显示，表露；举行示威游行(或集会)

[用法导航] Recent events demonstrate the need of change in policy. 最近的事态表明政策需要改变。// All of those demonstrated the correctness of his analysis. 这一切都证明了他分析的正确性。

[词性转换] **demonstration** / ˌdemənsˈtreiʃən / n. 表明；证明；示范；〈非正式〉游行示威

[对比记忆] **display** / disˈplei / vt. 陈列，展览；显示，显露

[真题衔接] The geography teacher used a set of apparatus to _____ that the world is round.

　　A) reveal　　　B) exhibit　　　C) display　　　D) demonstrate

【重点单词】**interaction** / ˌintərˈækʃən / n.

[基本词义] 相互作用，相互影响

[用法导航] The interaction of the two groups produced many good ideas. 两个组的相互交流产生了许多好主意。

[词性转换] **interact** / ˌintərˈækt / vi. 相互作用/影响，互相配合

[对比记忆] (1) **interrelation** / ˌintəriˈleiʃən / n. 相互关系，相互联系

　　(2) **intersection** / ˌintəˈsekʃən / n. 横断；交叉；交叉点，十字路口

[真题衔接] There is not enough _____ between the management and the workers.

　　A) transaction　　B) interaction　　C) expectation　　D) administration

【句子翻译】

356. We have a good _____ (有机会赢得这场比赛) for we are well prepared for it.

357. I believe those principles _____ (在任何地方、对任何人都是至理名言).

358. He has devoted himself to study ever since he came back to school this term and _____ (有可能获得奖学金).

359. Twenty shillings _____ (等于1英镑) before 1971, so his income amounted to 100 pounds.

360. _____ (律师证明) that the witness was lying and she lost the case.

Passage Thirty-seven

When families gather for Christmas dinner, some will *stick to formal traditions dating back to Grandma's generation*. Their tables will be set with the good dishes and silver, and the dress code will be Sunday-best.

But in many other homes, this china-and-silver **elegance** has given way to a stoneware (粗陶)-and-stainless informality, with dresses assuming an equally casual-Friday look. For hosts and guests, the change means greater **simplicity** and comfort. For makers of fine china in Britain, *it spells economic hard times*.

Last week Royal Doulton, the largest employer in Stoke-on-Trent, announced that it is **eliminating** 1,000 jobs—one-fifth of its total **workforce**. That brings to more than 4,000 the number of positions lost in 18 months in the pottery (陶瓷) region. *Wedgwood and other pottery factories made cuts earlier*.

Although a strong **pound** and weak markets in Asia play a role in the downsizing, the layoffs in Stoke have their roots in **earthshaking** social shifts. A spokesman for Royal Doulton admitted that the company *"has been somewhat slow in catching up with the trend"* toward casual dining. Families eat together less often, he explained, and more people eat alone, *either because they are single or they eat in front of television*.

Even dinner parties, if they happen at all, have gone casual. In a time of long work hours and demanding family **schedules**, busy hosts insist, rightly, that it's better to share a takeout pizza on paper plates in the family room than to wait for the perfect moment or a "real" dinner party. Too often, the perfect moment never comes. Iron a fine-patterned tablecloth? Forget it. **Polish** the silver? Who has time?

Yet the loss of formality has its down side. The fine points of etiquette that children might once have learned at the table by **observation** or **instruction** from parents and grandparents ("Chew with your mouth closed." "Keep your elbows off the table.") must be picked up elsewhere. Some companies now offer etiquette **seminars** for employees who may *be competent professionally but clueless socially*. (346 words) (2003 年 12 月第 3 篇)

【段落译文】

当人们聚在一起吃圣诞大餐时,有些人会坚守正式的传统,这些传统可以追溯到祖母一代。他们会在桌上摆上丰盛的菜肴和银器皿，并穿上他们最好的衣服。

但在许多其他家庭，这些瓷器和银器的高雅已经让位给非正式的粗陶和不锈钢，衣服也只是穿着随意的休闲服。对客人和主人来说，这些变化意味着更多的简单和舒适。对英国那些优良瓷器的制造商来说，这却招来了经济的困难时期。

上个星期皇家道尔顿，特伦特河畔斯托克最大的陶瓷公司，宣布将淘汰 1000 名员工——总工人的五分之一。这也导致了陶瓷王国 18 个月内 4000 名员工失去工作。韦奇伍德和其他厂家在更早些时候就裁员了。

虽然这种强烈的冲击和亚洲微弱的市场在陶瓷业的萎缩上产生了一定影响，斯托克的临时解雇在翻天覆地的社会变化中有着自己的根源。皇家道尔顿的一位发言人承认公司在休闲餐上"多少有点落伍了，已无法跟上流行趋势"。他解释到，家人在一起聚餐的机会少多了，更多的人单独吃饭，要么由于他们是单身，要么由于他们在电视机前就餐。

即使有晚宴聚会，也变得随意了。由于工作时间延长，家庭日程排满，繁忙的主人肯定也会坚持认为在家分享可外带的比萨比等待完美时刻或是真正的大餐要好得多。往往，这完美的时候从未出现过。熨烫一块花式漂亮的桌布？忘了它吧。把银器擦擦亮？谁有时间？

然而这种礼节的缺失也有让人沮丧的一面。这些孩子们本来在餐桌上通过观察或是父母、祖父母的教导可能已经掌握的高雅的就餐礼仪（譬如"咀嚼的时候闭上嘴"，"别把你的肘关节放在桌子上"）现在必须通过其他方式习得。有些公司现在为那些工作能力强却缺乏社交技能的员工提供礼仪研讨班。

【难词释义】

elegance 高雅

eliminate 削减，排除

pound 重击

schedule 日程安排表

observation 注意，观察

seminar 研讨班，研讨小组

simplicity 简单，朴素

workforce 劳动力

earthshaking 极为重大的，翻天覆地的

polish 擦亮

instruction 指导，教学

【写译语块】

1. stick to formal traditions dating back to Grandma's generation 坚守可以追溯到祖母一代的正式传统

2. it spells economic hard times 这招来了经济的困难时期

3. Wedgwood and other pottery factories made cuts earlier 韦奇伍德和其他厂家

在更早些时候就裁员了

4. has been somewhat slow in catching up with the trend 在跟上流行趋势方面多少有点落伍了

5. either because they are single or they eat in front of television 要么由于他们是单身，要么由于他们在电视机前就餐

6. be competent professionally but clueless socially 工作能力强却缺乏社交技能

【难句分析】

1. （第二段第一句）在 But in many other homes, this china-and-silver elegance has given way to a stoneware（粗陶）-and-stainless informality, with dresses assuming an equally casual-Friday look 中，give way to 的意思是"给……让路，被……代替"，with dresses assuming an equally casual-Friday look 是伴随状语，assume 的意思是"呈现"，跟在介词 with 后面，所以要用动名词形式，casual-Friday 指周五人们可以穿非常随意的衣服。

2. （第四段第一句）在 Although a strong pound and weak markets in Asia play a role in the downsizing, the layoffs in Stoke have their roots in earthshaking social shifts 中，a strong pound 的意思是"强烈的冲击"，即指如今人们就餐越来越随意，play a role 的意思是"扮演角色，发挥作用"，downsizing 的意思是"减小规模，缩小化"，layoff 的意思是"临时解雇"，shift 的意思是"变化，转变"。

3. （第五段第二句）在 In a time of long work hours and demanding family schedules, busy hosts insist, rightly, that it's better to share a takeout pizza on paper plates in the family room than to wait for the perfect moment or a "real" dinner party 中，in a time of 的意思是"在……时期"，insist 的意思是"坚持认为"，it's better to do . . . than to do . . . 这里将比萨外带到家里吃与等待完美大餐作比较，得出还是前者更好，the perfect moment 与 a "real" dinner party 其实指的是同一回事。

4. （第六段第二句）在 The fine points of etiquette（礼节）that children might once have learned at the table by observation or instruction from parents and grandparents （"Chew with your mouth closed." "Keep your elbows off the table."）must be picked up elsewhere 中，that 引导的是一个定语从句，修饰前面的 fine points of etiquette，这句话的主语是 The fine points of etiquette must be picked up elsewhere，keep . . . off 的意思是"使……不接近"，pick up 的意思是"学会，获得"。

【原题再现】

361. The trend toward casual dining has resulted in _____.

A) bankruptcy of fine china manufacturers

B) shrinking of the pottery industry

C) restructuring of large enterprises

D) economic recession in Great Britain

362. Which of the following may be the best reason for casual dining?

A) Family members need more time to relax.

B) Busy schedules leave people no time for formality.

C) People want to practice economy in times of scarcity.

D) Young people won't follow the etiquette of the older generation.

363. It can be learned from the passage that Royal Doulton is _____.

A) a retailer of stainless steel tableware

B) a dealer in stoneware

C) a pottery chain store

D) a producer of fine china

364. The main cause of the layoffs in the pottery industry is _____.

A) the increased value of the pound

B) the economic recession in Asia

C) the change in people's way of life

D) the fierce competition at home and abroad

365. Refined table manners, though less popular than before in current social life, _____.

A) are still a must on certain occasions

B) are bound to return sooner or later

C) are still being taught by parents at home

D) can help improve personal relationships

【单词详解】

【重点单词】**eliminate** / i'limineit / vt.

［基本词义］消除，排除；忽略；淘汰

［用法导航］You must eliminate an unknown quantity. 你必须消去一个未知数。// Our team was eliminated in the first round. 我们队在第一轮中被淘汰。// The dictator had eliminated all his political opponents. 独裁者干掉了他所有的政敌。

［词性转换］**elimination** / iˌlimi'neiʃən / n. 排除，除去，消除，消灭

[对比记忆] (1) **abolish** / əˈbɔliʃ / *vt.* 废除，废止

(2) **banish** / ˈbæniʃ / *vt.* 放逐，驱逐

(3) **eradicate** / iˈrædikeit / *vt.* 摧毁，完全根除

(4) **erase** / iˈreiz / *vt.* 擦掉，抹去，清除

(5) **remove** / riˈmuːv / *vt.* 移走；排除；开除 *vi.* 迁移；移居

[真题衔接] She once again went through her composition carefully to _____ all spelling mistakes from it. (CET6-9106)

A) withdraw　　B) diminish　　C) abandon　　D) eliminate

【句子翻译】

366. _____(坚守你的岗位)and make sure everything is Ok.

367. We refused to _____(对他的要求做出让步)，which irritated him.

368. The problem has _____(以新的形式出现)and let's find time for the discussion.

369. Our goal is to _____(消除贫困)and ensure everyone can lead a somewhat good life.

370. At the moment our technology is more advanced, but other countries _____(正在赶超我们).

Passage Thirty-eight

Some houses are designed to be smart. Others have smart designs. An example of the second type of house won an Award of Excellence from the American Institute of Architects.

Located on the shore of Sullivan's Island off the coast of South Carolina, the award-winning cube-shaped beach house was built to replace one **smashed** to pieces by Hurricane (飓风) Hugo 10 years ago. In September 1989, Hugo struck South Carolina, killing 18 people and damaging or destroying 36,000 homes in the state.

Before Hugo, many new houses built along South Carolina's **shoreline** were poorly constructed, and **enforcement** of building codes wasn't strict, according to architect Ray Huff, who created the cleverly-designed beach house. *In Hugo's wake*, all new shoreline houses are required to meet stricter, better-enforced codes. The new beach house on Sullivan's Island should be able to **withstand** a Category 3 hurricane *with peak winds of 179 to 209 kilometers per hour*.

At first sight, the house on Sullivan's Island *looks anything but hurricane-proof*. Its redwood shell makes it **resemble** "a large party lantern（灯笼）" at night, according to one observer. But looks can be **deceiving**. The house's wooden frame is **reinforced** with long steel **rods** to give it extra strength.

To further protect the house from hurricane damage, Huff raised it 2.7 meters off the ground on timber pilings—long, slender columns of wood **anchored** deep in the sand. Pilings might appear **insecure**, but they *are strong enough to support the weight of the house*. They also elevate the house above storm surges. The pilings allow the surges to run under the house instead of running into it. "These **swells** of water come ashore at **tremendous** speeds and cause most of the damage done to beach-front buildings," said Huff.

Huff designed the timber pilings to be partially **concealed** by the house's ground-to-roof shell. "The shell masks the pilings so that the house doesn't look like it's standing with its pant legs pulled up," said Huff. In the event of a storm surge, the shell should break apart and let the waves rush under the house, the architect explained. (356 words)　（2003 年 12 月第 4 篇）

【段落译文】

有些房子设计时是为了漂亮，另一些房子的设计却能显现智慧。第二种类型的房子中有个实例获得了美国建筑师协会的优胜奖。

这栋聪明的房屋位于南卡罗来纳的沙利文岛屿海岸，建造目的是为了代替十年前被飓风摧毁的屋子。十年前的那场飓风造成了 18 人死亡，破坏或摧毁 36000 座房屋。

根据建筑师 Ray Huff 的说法，这里以前的房子都是简简单单建造起来的，房子建造要求方面的法律也很松散。Huff 正是聪明屋的设计者。飓风给人们提了个醒，新的法规更为严格了，所有新建房屋必须能够抵御一定量级飓风的冲击，比如 Huff 设计的这所房子就能抵御时速 179 到 209 千米的飓风。

第一眼看去，沙利文海岛上的房子根本不像是能抵御飓风的。根据一个观察者所说，它的红杉外壳使它在晚上就像一个大灯笼，而实际上，房屋的红杉木质结构已经被长长的钢管加强了。

为了进一步使房子不受飓风破坏，设计者还用木桩——细长的圆柱，深深地固定在沙地里，把房子支起，使其离地 2.7 米。木桩看起来不太安全，但其实木桩都非常坚固，足以支持房屋重量；木桩也使得房子免受暴风雨的侵袭。木桩提供的空间可以使海水从屋底流过，避免流入屋内。Huff 说，这些汹涌的海水以巨大的速度冲到海岸上,给海滩房造成许多破坏。

　　Huff 在木桩外面设计了一圈护板,从而部分地隐藏了这些木桩。他说,护板隐藏了木桩以至房子看起来并不像由许多柱子堆砌而成。他又解释道,在遇到海水冲击时,围板会很容易破碎,从而让海水从屋底流过。

【难词释义】

smash 打碎	**shoreline** 海岸线
enforcement 实施,执行	**withstand** 经受
resemble 像	**deceiving** 欺骗的
reinforce 增强	**rod** 棒
anchor (把)系住,(使)固定	**insecure** 不安全的
swell 汹涌	**tremendous** 巨大的
conceal 隐藏	

【写译语块】

1. in Hugo's wake 飓风给人们提了个醒

2. with peak winds of 179 to 209 kilometers per hour 时速 179 到 209 千米的飓风

3. looks anything but hurricane-proof 看上去根本不像是能抵御飓风的

4. to further protect the house from hurricane damage 为了进一步使房子不受飓风破坏

5. be strong enough to support the weight of the house 足以支持房屋重量

【难句分析】

1. (第二段第一句)在 Located on the shore of Sullivan's Island off the coast of South Carolina, the award-winning cube-shaped beach house was built to replace one smashed to pieces by Hurricane (飓风) Hugo 10 years ago 中, locate 的意思是"坐落于", be located in / on / to / at 是固定短语,介词视具体情况不同, in 是在范围之内, on 是接壤, to 是有一定距离 at 也是在范围之内,不过一般指很小的地区。句中 one 指的是 a house, smashed to pieces 是过去分词作定语,修饰前面的 one,意思是"被击成碎片"。

2. (第二段第二句)在 In September 1989, Hugo struck South Carolina, killing 18 people and damaging or destroying 36,000 homes in the state 中, strike 的意思是"攻击,袭击", killing 18 people and damaging or destroying 36,000 homes in the state 是现在分词作伴随状语,它的主语也是 Hugo,是 Hugo 袭击南卡罗来

181

纳的后果。

3. (第五段第一句)在 To further protect the house from hurricane damage, Huff raised it 2. 7 meters off the ground on timber pilings — long, slender columns of wood anchored deep in the sand 中，To further protect the house from hurricane damage 放在句首，作目的状语，protect from 是固定短语，表示"保护，保卫"，介词 off 表示"离开"，anchored deep in the sand 是过去分词作定语，修饰前面的 wood，表示"深深地固定在沙地中"。

4. (第六段第三句)在 In the event of a storm surge, the shell should break apart and let the waves rush under the house, the architect explained 中，短语 in the event of 的意思是"万一，倘若"，此句用了虚拟语气，后面的主句要 should，词组 break apart 的意思是"破碎"，let 是使役动词，因此后面直接跟动词原形，不需要加 to，即 let . . . do。

【原题再现】

371. After the tragedy caused by Hurricane Hugo, new houses built along South Carolina's shore line are required _____ .

    A) to be easily reinforced

    B) to look smarter in design

    C) to meet stricter building standards

    D) to be designed in the shape of cubes

372. The award-winning beach house is quite strong because _____ .

    A) it is strengthened by steel rods   B) it is made of redwood

    C) it is in the shape of a shell   D) it is built with timber and concrete

373. Huff raised the house 2. 7 meters off the ground on timber pilings in order to _____ .

    A) withstand peak winds of about 200 km/hr

    B) anchor stronger pilings deep in the sand

    C) break huge sea waves into smaller ones

    D) prevent water from rushing into the house

374. The main function of the shell is _____ .

    A) to strengthen the pilings of the house

    B) to give the house a better appearance

    C) to protect the wooden frame of the house

    D) to slow down the speed of the swelling water

375. It can be inferred from the passage that the shell should be _____ .

A) fancy-looking   B) waterproof

C) easily breakable   D) extremely strong

【单词详解】

【重点单词】 **reinforce** / ˌriːinˈfɔːs / vt.

[基本词义] 加强,加固;补充;增援,支援

[用法导航] reinforce a wall 给墙加固 // reinforced concrete 钢筋混凝土 // reinforce provisions 补充粮食 // reinforce a fleet 增援一个舰队

[词性转换] **reinforcement** / ˌriːinˈfɔːsmənt / n. 增援,加强,加固,援军

[对比记忆] (1) **aggravate** / ˈincreseæɡrəveit / vt. 使恶化,使更严重;激怒,使恼火

(2) **increase** / inˈkriːs / vt. & vi. 增加,增大,增多

(3) **strengthen** / ˈstreŋθn / vt. & vi. 加强,巩固

(4) **intensify** / inˈtensifai / vt. & vi. (使)增强,(使)加剧

[真题衔接] Susan has _____ the elbows of her son's jacket with leather patches to make it more durable. (CET6-0506)

A) reinforced   B) sustained   C) steadied   D) confirmed

【重点单词】 **elevate** / ˈeliveit / vt.

[基本词义] 举起,提高,提升;鼓舞,使更有修养

[用法导航] He elevated the blinds. 他拉起了百叶窗。// He was elevated. 他受到提拔。// The good news elevated everyone's spirits. 这个好消息鼓舞了每个人的情绪。

[对比记忆] (1) **boost** / buːst / vt. 提升;增加;促进,改善,激励;吹捧,大肆宣传

(2) **lift** / lift / vt. & vi. 举起,抬起 vt. 终止;解除 vi. 消散

(3) **raise** / reiz / vt. 提起;举起;竖起;增加;提升;抚养,饲养

(4) **rear** / riə / vt. 饲养;养育 vt. & vi. 抬起

(5) **hoist** / hɔist / vt. 把……吊起,升起

[真题衔接] These factors helped to _____ the town into the list of the elegant, then most attractive in the country.

A) evaluate   B) initiate   C) elevate   D) cultivate

【句子翻译】

376. After much investigation he _____ (将新店开设在) on Main Street.

377. His visit to Paris was _____ (根本不成功) and that's why he is depressed.

378. Any good speaker should be able to _____（用事实来加强论点）.

379. Citrus growers were cautioned to _____（防霜）.

380. _____（一旦他故去）, his daughter will inherit the money.

Passage Thirty-nine

On **average**, American kids ages 3 to 12 spent 29 hours a week in school, eight hours more that they did in 1981. They also did more household work and **participated** in more of such organized activities as **soccer** and ballet（芭蕾舞）. **Involvement** in sports, in particular, rose almost 50% from 1981 to 1997: boys now *spend an average of four hours a week playing sports*; girls log hall that time. All in all, however, children's leisure time dropped from 40% of the day in 1981 to 25%.

"Children are **affected** by the same time crunch（危机）that affects their parents," says Sandra Hofferth, who headed the recent study of children's timetable. A chief reason, she says, is that more mothers are working outside the home. (Nevertheless, children in both double-income and "male breadwinner" households spent comparable amounts of time interacting with their parents. 19 hours and 22 hours **respectively**. In contrast, children spent only 9 hours with their single mothers.)

All work and no play could make for some very messed-up kids. "Play is the most powerful way a child **explores** the world and learns about himself," says T. Berry Brazelton, professor at Harvard Medical School Unstructured play encourages **independent** thinking and allows the young to **negotiate** their relationships with their **peers**, but kids ages 3 to 12 spent only 12 hours a week **engaged** in it.

The children **sampled** *spent a quarter of their rapidly decreasing "free time" watching television*. But that, believe it or not, was one of the findings parents might regard as good news. If they're spending less time in front of the TV set, however, *kids aren't replacing it with reading. Despite efforts to get kids more interested in books*, the children spent just over an hour a week reading. Let's face it, who's got the time? (309 words) （2003 年 6 月第 1 篇）

【段落译文】

美国 3 岁～12 岁的孩子平均每星期的在校时间为 29 小时，比 1981 年多了 8 小时。同时，他们做家务活多了，并且参加更多诸如足球、芭蕾舞等有组织的活动。

特别是参与体育活动的时间,从 1981 年到 1997 年增长了 50％;现在男孩子平均每周花 4 小时运动,女孩的运动时间是男孩的一半。但是,总的说来,孩子们的空闲时间从 1981 年的 40％降到 25％。

"影响父母的时间危机同样也影响着孩子们,"最近对儿童作息时间表做调研的项目负责人 Sandra Hofferth 这样说。她说一个最主要的原因是更多的母亲外出工作。当然,生活在双收家庭或"父亲挣钱养家型"家庭的孩子有较多的时间与他们的父母沟通,分别是每周 19 或 22 个小时。相反,生活在单身母亲家庭的孩子每周与母亲在一起的时间只有 9 小时。

如果一味地学习,而没有玩耍会使孩子们的生活变得一团糟。哈佛学院的教授 T. Berry Brazelton 说:"玩耍是孩子们探索世界和认识自我的最有效的途径"。自由的玩耍促使孩子们独立地思考,并使他们与同伴协调地相处,然而,3 岁～12 岁的孩子花在玩耍的时间每周只有 12 个小时。

抽样的调查显示,孩子们把已经快速减少的"自由时间"的四分之一用于看电视。但是,不管你相信不相信,家长们对这样的结果还是庆幸的。即使孩子们不花更多的时间看电视,他们也不会把时间用在读书上。尽管家长们费尽心思让孩子们对书本感兴趣,但是,他们每周花在阅读上的时间也只有一个多小时。让我们面对现实吧,谁有时间呢?

【难词释义】

average 平均	participate 参加,参与
soccer(美)足球	involvement 参与,投入
affect 影响,感动	respectively 各自地,分别地
explore 探索,勘查	independent 独立的,自主的
negotiate 谈判,协商	peers 同龄人
engage(使)从事于,(使)忙于	sample 抽样调查

【写译语块】

1. spend an average of four hours a week playing sports 平均每周花 4 小时运动
2. All work and no play could make for some very messed-up kids. 如果一味地学习,而没有玩耍会使孩子们的生活变得一团糟。
3. spend a quarter of their rapidly decreasing "free time" watching television 把已经快速减少的"自由时间"的四分之一用于看电视
4. kids aren't replacing it with reading 孩子们也不会把时间用在读书上
5. despite efforts to get kids more interested in books 尽管家长们费尽心思让孩

子们对书本感兴趣

【难句分析】

1. (第二段第一句)在"Children are affected by the same time crunch (危机) that affects their parents," says Sandra Hofferth, who headed the recent study of children's timetable 中,be affected by 表示被动关系,意思是"被影响",英语中有较多被动,翻译成中文时往往翻成主动关系;引号内的句子中 that 引导的是一个定语从句,that 指代的是前面的 the same time crunch;head 原意是"使……前进",此句中引申为"执行,调查"。

2. (第二段第三句)在 Nevertheless, children in both double-income and "male breadwinner" households spent comparable amounts of time interacting with their parents 中,double-income 表示"双份收入",male breadwinner 意思是"男性赚钱养家"即"父亲赚钱养家",comparable 表示"相当的,可比较的",interacting with 意思是"相互作用,相互影响",在此句中表示"相互交流,相互沟通",与 spend 在一起构成固定语法:spend time ... doing,表示"花费时间做……"。

3. (第三段第二句)在"Play is the most powerful way a child explores the world and learns about himself," says T. Berry Brazelton, professor at Harvard Medical School Unstructured play encourages independent thinking and allows the young to negotiate their relationships with their peers, but kids ages 3 to 12 spent only 12 hours a week engaged in it 中,引号内的句子 a child explores the world and learns about himself 是一个省略了 that 的定语从句,修饰前面的 way, play 在句中作名词,意思是"玩耍"。allow sb to do 是一个固定用法,意思是"允许某人做……",ages 3 to 12 表示"3 岁~12 岁的孩子",age 在句子中作动词,engaged in 在句中是过去分词作定语,修饰前面的 hours。

【原题再现】

381. By mentioning "the same time crunch" (Sentence 1, Para. 2) Sandra Hofferth means _____.

   A) children have little time to play with their parent

   B) children are not taken good care of by their working parents

   C) both parents and children suffer from lack of leisure time

   D) both parents and children have trouble managing their time

382. According to the author, the reason given by Sandra Hofferth for the time crunch is _____.

A) quite convincing   B) partially true

C) totally groundless   D) rather confusing

383. According to the author a child develops better if _____.

    A) he has plenty of time reading and studying

    B) he is left to play with his peers in his own way

    C) he has more time participating in school activities

    D) he is free to interact with his working parents

384. The author is concerned about the fact that American kids _____.

    A) are engaged in more and more structured activities

    B) are increasingly neglected by their working mothers

    C) are spending more and more time watching TV

    D) are involved less and less in household work

385. We can infer from the passage that _____.

    A) extracurricular activities promote children's intelligence

    B) most children will turn to reading with TV sets switched off

    C) efforts to get kids interested in reading have been fruitful

    D) most parents believe reading to be beneficial to children

【单词详解】

【重点单词】**affect** / ə'fekt / *vt.*

[基本词义] 影响；感动；假装；患(病)，中(暑)

[用法导航] The tax increases have affected us all. 加税已经影响了我们所有的人。// The audience was deeply affected. 听众被深深地打动了。// He affected not to see me. 他假装没看见我。

[词性转换] **affection** / ə'fekʃən / *n.* 喜爱，爱；(心)感情

[对比记忆] (1) **influence** / 'influəns / *vt.* 影响；感化；促使采取行动

    (2) **impress** / im'pres / *vt.* 给...以深刻印象，使铭记；印，压印

[真题衔接] Once out of the earth's gravity, the astronaut is _____ by the problem of weightlessness. (CET4-9401)

    A) affected   B) effected   C) inclined   D) related

【重点单词】**comparable** / 'kɔmpərəbl / *adj.*

[基本词义] 类似的，同类的，相当的；可比较的，比得上的

[用法导航] A comparable car would cost far more abroad. 类似的车子在国外要贵得多。// The achievements of an athlete and a writer are not comparable. 运动员的成就与作家的成就不能相提并论。// His handwriting is not bad, but it's hardly comparable with yours. 他的书法不错,但是很难和你的相比。

[对比记忆] **comparative** / kəmˈpærətiv / *adj.* 比较的,相对的

[真题衔接] It was a pleasant beach resort but it wasn't _____ with the one we stayed at in the Bahamas.

    A) superior   B) identical   C) comparable   D) attractive

【句子翻译】

386. I take it for granted that I _____(永远和家人一块过圣诞节).

387. Medical knowledge alone _____(并不能成为好医生) and what you need now is practice.

388. Many chemical substances are now applied _____(影响植物的生长).

389. No horse has a speed _____(能比得上他的马).

390. _____(尽管天气恶劣) we enjoyed our holiday.

Passage Forty

Henry Ford, the famous U. S. inventor and car manufacturer, once said, "The business of America is business." By this he meant that the U. S. way of life *is based on the values of the business world.*

Few would argue with Ford's statement. A brief **glimpse** at a daily newspaper vividly shows how much people in the United States think about business. For example, nearly every newspaper has a business **section**, in which the deals and projects, finances and management, stock prices and labor problems of corporations are reported daily. In addition, business news can appear in every other section. Most national news has an important financial aspect to it. **Welfare**, foreign aid, the federal **budget**, and the policies of the Federal Reserve Bank are all heavily affected by business. Moreover, business news appears in some of the unlikeliest places. The world of arts and entertainment *is often referred to as "the entertainment industry" or "show business."*

The **positive** side of Henry Ford's statement can be seen in the **prosperity** that business has brought to U. S. life. One of the most important reasons so many people from all over the world *come to live in the United States* is the dream of a better job. Jobs are produced in **abundance** because the U. S. economic system *is* *driven by competition*. People believe that this system creates more wealth, more jobs, and a **materially** better way of life.

The **negative** side of Henry Ford's statement, however, can be seen when the word business is taken to mean big business. And the term big business—referring to the biggest companies, is seen *in opposition to labor*. Throughout U. S. history working people have had to fight hard for higher wages, better working conditions, and the fight to form unions. Today, many of the old labor **disputes** are over, but there is still some employee anxiety. Downsizing—the laying off of thousands of workers to keep expenses low and profits high—creates feelings of **insecurity** for many. （334 words） （2003 年 6 月第 2 篇）

【段落译文】

美国最著名的发明家和汽车制造商亨利·福特曾经说:"美国的一切都是商业"。此话的意思是说,美国人的生活方式建立在商品社会的价值观上。

很少有人对福特的说法提出疑义。只要在一张日报上瞥一眼,就不难发现有多少美国人在关心商业。比如,几乎每家报纸都有商业版,对各种工程项目、资金和管理、股票价格和公司的劳动问题都是每日一报。此外,商业信息还在其他版面中出现。大多数国内新闻都反映重要的金融信息。福利、援外、联邦财政预算以及联邦储备银行的政策都极大地受到商业的影响。而且,商业信息还会在一些最不可能的地方出现。艺术和娱乐界经常被称为"娱乐业"或"演艺业"。

福特说法积极的一面可以从商业给美国生活带来的繁荣中看到。之所以有如此众多的人从世界各地蜂拥而至美国,其最重要的原因之一就是实现找到一份更好的工作梦想。工作的机会很多,因为美国的经济制度是由竞争驱动的。人们相信这样的制度能创造更多的财富,提供更好的工作和更好的物质生活。

但是,福特的说法中消极的一面也显而易见,即当商业这个词用来指代大财团的时候。"大财团"这个词——指代与工人相对的最大的商业集团或公司。在美国的历史上,工人们曾经为争取更高的工资、更好的工作环境以及组织工会的权利而艰苦地斗争。今天,许多旧的劳资纠纷已经消失,但是,雇员们仍然存在着忧虑。裁员——解雇成千上万的工人以保证成本和高效益——使很多人产生不安全感。

【难词释义】

glimpse 一瞥,一看

welfare 福利

positive 积极的

section 章节,部分

budget 预算

prosperity 兴旺,繁荣

abundance 大量，充足　　　　　　**materially** 物质地

negative 消极的　　　　　　　　　**dispute** 辩论，争执

insecurity 不安全

【写译语块】

1. be based on the values of the business world 建立在商品社会的价值观上

2. be often referred to as "the entertainment industry" or "show business 经常被称为"娱乐业"或"演艺业"

3. come to live in the United States 蜂拥而至美国

4. be driven by competition 由竞争驱动的

5. in opposition to labor 与工人相对的

【难句分析】

1. (第一段第一句)在 Henry Ford, the famous U. S. inventor and car manufacturer, once said, "The business of America is business. "中，inventor 的意思是"发明家"，manufacturer 的意思是"制造商"。The business of America is business. 这句话中第一个 business 是指"事务"，第二个 business 是指"商业，生意"。

2. (第二段开头)在 Few would argue with Ford's statement. A brief glimpse at a daily newspaper vividly shows how much people in the United States think about business 中，few 的意思是"很少，几乎没有"，argue with 表示"与……争论"，brief 表示"短暂的"，glimpse 后面的介词要用 at，vividly 的意思是"鲜明地，生动地"，how much 在这里表示美国人关心的程度。

3. (第二段第三句)在 For example, nearly every newspaper has a business section, in which the deals and projects, finances and management, stock prices and labor problems of corporations are reported daily 中，in which 等于 where，用在定语从句中作状语，这里指的就是前面的 business section。

4. (第四段最后一句)在 Downsizing — the laying off of thousands of workers to keep expenses low and profits high — creates feelings of insecurity for many 中，downsizing 指"裁减员工"，与 laying off"暂时解雇"意思相同，在句中是动名词作主语，keep＋名词＋形容词结构表示"使……保持……状态"，feelings of insecurity 意思是"不安全感"。

【原题再现】

391. The United States is a typical country _____.

190

A) which encourages free trade at home and abroad

B) where people's chief concern is how to make money

C) where all businesses are managed scientifically

D) which normally works according to the federal budget

392. The influence of business in the U. S. is evidenced by the fact that _____.

A) most newspapers are run by big businesses

B) even public organizations concentrate on working for profits

C) Americans of all professions know how to do business

D) even arts and entertainment are regarded as business

393. According to the passage, immigrants choose to settle in the U. S., dreaming that _____.

A) they can start profitable businesses there

B) they can be more competitive in business

C) they will make a fortune overnight there

D) they will find better chances of employment

394. Henry Ford's statement can be taken negatively because _____.

A) working people are discouraged to fight for their fights

B) there are many industries controlled by a few big capitalists

C) there is a conflicting relationship between big corporations and labor

D) public services are not run by the federal government

395. A company's efforts to keep expenses low and profits high may result in _____.

A) reduction in the number of employees

B) improvement of working conditions

C) fewer disputes between labor and management

D) a rise in workers' wages

【单词详解】

【重点单词】**refer** / ri'fə: / *vt.* & *vi.*

[基本词义] 提到;针对;关系到;送交,提交;归于;参考;查阅

[用法导航] Don't refer to the matter again. 不要再提这件事了。// He referred the case to the High Court. 他把案子提交给高级法庭处理。// Some people refer all the troubles to bad luck instead of lack of ability. 有些人把自己

所有的苦恼都归咎于运气不佳,而不认为是缺乏能力。// Refer to the dictionary when you don't know how to spell a word. 当你不知道怎么拼写一个词时,查阅一下词典。

[对比记忆] (1) **defer** / di'fə: / *vt.* 拖延,延缓,推迟 *vi.* 服从某人的意愿,遵从

(2) **infer** / in'fə: / *vt.* 推断,推知

(3) **offer** / 'ɔfə / *vt.* 主动提供;主动提出;出价 *vi.* 出现,显现

(4) **suffer** / 'sʌfə / *vi.* 受痛苦;受损害 *vt.* 忍受;容许,允许;遭受,蒙受

[真题衔接] Migration is a generic term used to _____ both to immigration and to emigration.

A) apply   B) balance   C) guide   D) refer

【重点单词】**aspect** / 'æspekt / *n.*

[基本词义] 方面;方位,朝向;面貌,模样,神态

[用法导航] The training program covers every aspect of the job. 训练计划的范围包括了这种工作的各个方面。// The house has a north-facing aspect. 这栋房子朝北。// He is a man of enormous size and terrifying aspect. 他是一个面目狰狞的彪形大汉。

[对比记忆] (1) **expect** / iks'pekt / *vt.* 期待,盼望,预料;指望,希望,要求

(2) **prospect** / 'prɔspekt / *n.* 景象;前景;有希望的候选人

(3) **respect** / ris'pekt / *vt.* 尊重,敬佩 *n.* 尊敬;考虑;方面;敬意,问候

(4) **suspect** / sə'spekt / *vt.* 猜疑,怀疑;怀疑……有罪 *n.* 嫌疑犯

[真题衔接] The most significant _____ of the election was not the victory of the opposition but the defeat of the ruling party.

A) indication   B) proof   C) aspect   D) purpose

【句子翻译】

396. We should always bear in mind that a theory should _____(以事实为基础的).

397. It can also _____(指冲突或不和), often involving violence.

398. The machine is _____(用电力驱动)and is perfectly environment-friendly.

399. We found ourselves _____(同我们的朋友意见相反)on this question.

400. The boss of the factory decided to _____(解雇工人)because of the drop in sales.

Passage Forty-one

Professor Smith recently persuaded 35 people, 23 of them women, to keep a diary of all their **absent-minded** actions for a **fortnight**. When he came to analyse their **embarrassing** lapses (差错) in a scientific report, he was surprised to find that nearly all of them *fell into a few groupings*, Nor did the lapses appear to be entirely random (随机的).

One of the women, for instance, on leaving her house for work one morning threw her dog her **earrings** and tried to *fix a dog biscuit on her ear*. "The explanation for this is that the brain is like a computer," explains the professor. "People programme themselves to do certain activities regularly. It was the woman's custom every morning to throw her dog two biscuits and then put on her earrings. But somehow *the action got reversed in the programme*." About one in twenty of the incidents the **volunteers** reported were these "programme assembly failures."

Altogether the volunteers **logged** 433 unintentional actions that they found themselves doing — an average of twelve each. There appear to be peak periods in the day when we are at our zaniest (荒谬可笑的). These are two hours some time between eight a. m. and noon, between four and six p. m. with a smaller peak between eight and ten p. m. "Among men the peak seems to be when a **changeover** in brain 'programmes' occurs, as for instance *between going to and from work*." Women on average reported **slightly** more lapses — 12.5 compared with 10.9 for men m probably because they were more **reliable** reporters.

A startling finding of the research is that the absent-minded activity is a hazard of doing things in which we are skilled. Normally, you would *expect that skill reduces the number of errors we make*. But trying to avoid silly **slips** by concentrating more could make things a lot worse m even dangerous. (325 words)
(2003 年 6 月第 3 篇)

【段落译文】

史密斯教授最近说服了 35 个人,其中有 23 位妇女,坚持记两周日记,把他们所有心不在焉的行为都记下来。当他在一份科研报告中分析这些令人尴尬的差错时,他惊奇地发现几乎所有的差错都可以归入几类。这些差错并不是毫无规律的。例如,其中的一位妇女,早晨离家上班的时候,把她的耳环扔给了她的狗,却试图把宠物饼干戴在耳朵上。"对这种行为的解释是,大脑就像是计算机",教授说,"人们为自己设定好了程序去做一些经常性的事务。对这位妇女来说,扔给她的狗两块饼干,然后戴上耳环是每天早晨的习惯。但是,有时候程序中的步骤颠倒了"。报告中受试者的差错约有二十分之一属于"此类程序排列错误"。

受试者共记录了 433 件他们自己认为是无意识的而做的事情——平均每人十二件。研究发现人们在一天中的高峰时段经常会做出荒谬可笑的事情。一天中共有两个这样的时间段,分别出现在早晨 8 点到中午,下午 4 点到 6 点之间,晚上 8 点到 10 点之间有个小高峰。"对男人来说,高峰时段出现在大脑'程序'需要切换的时候,比如,上下班的时候"。报告还称,平均而言,妇女的差错更高一些——男女之比为 12.5:10.9——这也许是因为女性是更可靠记录者。

此项研究一个惊人的发现是心不在焉的行为原来是我们在做熟练之事时所犯的。一般来说,人们希望熟练能减少我们所犯的错误。但是,通过集中注意力避免愚蠢的失误会使事情更糟——甚至更危险。

【难词释义】

absent-minded 心不在焉的   **fortnight** 两星期

embarrassing 令人尴尬的   **earrings** 耳环

volunteers 志愿者,自愿者   **log** 把……记入日志

changeover 完全改变,转变   **slightly** 轻微地,稍稍

reliable 可靠的   **slip** 小过失,失误

【写译语块】

1. fall into a few groupings 可以归入几类
2. fix a dog biscuit on her ear 把宠物饼干戴在耳朵上
3. the action got reversed in the programme 程序中的步骤颠倒了
4. between going to and from work 上下班的时候
5. expect that skill reduces the number of errors we make 希望熟练能减少我们所犯的错误

【难句分析】

1. (第二段第一句)在 One of the women, for instance, on leaving her house for work one morning threw her dog her earrings and tried to fix a dog biscuit on her ear 中,词组 for instance 意思是"比如,例如",on + doing 结构表示"在……的时候",此处的 on 相当于 as soon as,词组 throw sb sth 意思是"把……扔给……",try to do 意思是"努力做……",fix ... on ... 意思是"把……固定在……"。

2. (第三段第一句)在 Altogether the volunteers logged 433 unintentional actions that they found themselves doing — an average of twelve each 中,unintentional 的意思是"无意识的",后面 that 引导的是一个定语从句,修饰前面的 unin-

194

tentional actions,find sb doing 的意思是"发现……正在做",an average of 意思是"平均",each 指的是前面的每一个 volunteer,强调"单个的"。

3. (第三段第三句)在 These are two hours some time between eight a. m. and noon, between four and six p. m. with a smaller peak between eight and ten p. m 中,some time 指的是"一段时间",between ... and 是指"在两者之间",between eight a. m. and noon 指"上午8点到中午",between four and six p. m. 指"下午4点到6点之间",with + sth 意思是"有,带着"表示一种伴随状态,peak 在这里指的是"时间的高峰"。

4. (第四段第一句)A startling finding of the research is that the absent-minded activity is a hazard of doing things in which we are skilled. 这是一个包含了表语从句和定语从句的复杂的复合句。句中 startling 的意思是"令人震惊的",finding 作名词,表示"调查或研究的结果",sth is that ... 是一个表语从句,hazard 的意思是"危险,公害",be skilled in 表示"擅长",这里把介词 in 放到了 which 前面。

【原题再现】

401. In his study Professor Smith asked the subjects _____.

A) to keep track of people who tend to forget things

B) to report their embarrassing lapses at random

C) to analyse their awkward experiences scientifically

D) to keep a record of what they did unintentionally

402. Professor Smith discovered that _____.

A) certain patterns can be identified in the recorded incidents

B) many people were too embarrassed to admit their absent-mindedness

C) men tend to be more absent-minded than women

D) absent-mindedness is an excusable human weakness

403. "Programme assembly failures" (Sentence 6, Para. 2) refers to the phenomenon that people _____.

A) often fail to programme their routines beforehand

B) tend to make mistakes when they are in a hurry

C) unconsciously change the sequence of doing things

D) are likely to mess things up if they are too tired

404. We learn from the third paragraph that _____.

A) absent-mindedness tends to occur during certain hours of the day

B) women are very careful to perform actions during peak periods

C) women experience more peak periods of absent-mindedness

D) men's absent-mindedness often results in funny situations

405. It can be concluded from the passage that _____.

A) people should avoid doing important things during peak periods of lapses

B) hazards can be avoided when people do things they are good at

C) people should be careful when programming their actions

D) lapses cannot always be attributed to lack of concentration

【单词详解】

【重点单词】**reverse** / riˈvəːs / *vt.* & *vi.*

[基本词义]（使）反转；（使）颠倒；（使）翻转；推翻，取消；使倒退，逆转

[用法导航] Please reverse the positions of two pictures. 请把两张图片的位置倒转过来。// The appeal court reversed the original verdict and set the prisoner free. 上诉法庭撤销了原判，把那个犯人释放了。// The car reversed out. 汽车倒退出去。

[对比记忆]（1）**invert** / inˈvəːt / *vt.* 使倒转，使倒置，使颠倒

（2）**overthrow** / ˌəuvəˈθrəu / *vt.* 推翻，打倒；使终止 *n.* 推翻，终止，结束

[真题衔接] Several international events in the early 1990s seem likely to _____, or at least weaken, the trends that emerged in the 1980s. （研-1998）

A) revolt　　B) revolve　　C) reverse　　D) revive

【重点单词】**occur** / əˈkəː / *vi.*

[基本词义] 发生；举行；存在；被发现；想到[起]

[用法导航] I hope this won't occur again. 我希望不要再发生这种事情。// The word "gratitude" did not occur in his words. "感激"两字在他的话中是听不到的。

[对比记忆]（1）**chance** / tʃɑːns / *vi.* 偶然发生；冒险

（2）**happen** / ˈhæpən / *vi.* 发生；产生结果，发生作用；碰巧，恰巧

[真题衔接] Most hurricanes _____ before leaf drop and during or following heavy rains.

A) sweep　　B) occur　　C) affect　　D) damage

【句子翻译】

406. Don't let it _____（落入敌人的手中）or we'll suffer a great loss.

407. His coat _____ (能翻过来穿) when it begins to rain and he finds it saves space.

408. _____ (刚一看到飞机向我飞来)，I dashed for cover.

409. Chinese? rural? residents? have _____ (平均 6.9 年) of schooling and there is room for improvement.

410. _____ (空难发生了) only minutes after take-off and it was lucky that his brother missed the plane.

Passage Forty-two

It's no secret that many children would be healthier and happier with **adoptive** parents than with the parents that nature dealt them. *That's especially true of children who remain in abusive homes* because the law **blindly** favors biological parents. It's also true of children who suffer for years in foster homes (收养孩子的家庭) because of parents who can't or won't care for them but *refuse to give up custody* (监护) *rights.*

Fourteen-year-old Kimberly Mays fits neither description, but her recent court victory could eventually help children who do. Kimberly has been the object of an angry custody baffle between the man who raised her and her biological parents, with whom she has never lived. A Florida judge ruled that the teenager can *remain with the only father she's ever known* and that her biological parents have "no legal claim" on her.

The ruling, though it may yet be reversed, sets aside the principle that biology is the primary **determinant** of parentage. That's an important development, one that's long **overdue**.

Shortly after birth in December 1978, Kimberly Mays and another **infant** were mistakenly **switched** and sent home with the wrong parents. Kimberly's biological parents, Ernest and Regina Twigg, received a child who *died of a heart disease* in 1988. Medical tests showed that the child wasn't the Twiggs' own daughter, but Kimt only was, thus **sparking** a custody battle with Robert Mays. In 1989, the two families agreed that Mr. Mays would maintain custody with the Twiggs getting visiting rights. Those rights were ended when Mr. Mays decided that Kimberly was being harmed.

The decision to leave Kimberly with Mr. Mays **rendered** her suit debated. But the judge made clear that Kimberly did *have standing to sue* (起诉) *on her* *own behalf*. Thus he made clear that she was more than just property to be handled as adults saw fit.

Certainly, *the biological link between parent and child* is **fundamental**. But biological parents aren't always **preferable** to adoptive ones, and biological parentage does not convey an absolute ownership that cancels all the rights of children. (357 words) （2003 年 6 月第 4 篇）

【段落译文】

很多孩子在养父母家比在亲生父母家过得更健康、更快乐，这已经不是秘密了。对于那些由于法律盲目偏袒生物学意义上的父母而留在那些受虐待的家庭的孩子来说尤其如此。同时，对那些由于父母没有能力或不愿意照顾他们，但又不肯放弃监护权而痛苦地生活在收养家庭的孩子来说也是如此。

14 岁的 Kimberly Mays 不属于上述情况，但是，她最近的一场官司的打赢最终可以帮助那些有相同情况的孩子。Kimberly 一直是一场愤怒的监护权争夺战中的争夺对象，一方是他的养父，另一方是她从来没有一起生活过的亲生父母。佛罗里达州的法官作出裁定，该少年应继续与她唯一熟悉的养父生活在一起，她的亲生父母"在法律上没有权利主张"得到她。

这个裁定尽管有可能是本末倒置，但它驳回了血缘是决定父母身份的这一准则。这是一个重要进步，是一个人们期待已久的进步。

1978 年 12 月，Kimberly Mays 刚出生就与另一个孩子被弄混而被错抱到了不是亲生的父母家中。Kimberly 的亲生父母 Ernest and Regina Twigg 收养的孩子于 1988 年死于心脏病。医学检查显示孩子不是 Twigg 家的女儿，而 Kimberly 却是，于是引发了 Twigg 家与 Robert Mays 争夺监护权的官司。1989 年，两家同意 Mays 先生保留监护权，Twigg 夫妇有权探望。后来 Mays 先生认为 Kimberly 受到了伤害，探视权被终止。

把 Kimberly 判给 Mays 先生使此案引起了争议。但是，法官表示 Kimberly 有权以自己的名义起诉。于是，他表明了她并不是一件可以由成年人认为合适的方式被处理的商品。

当然，父母与孩子的血缘关系是基本的。但是，亲生父母并非一定比养父母好，同时，血缘上的父母身份不能拥有取消孩子一切权利的绝对所有权。

【难词释义】

adoptive 收养的　　　　　　　　　　**blindly** 盲目地

determinant 决定因素　　　　　　　**overdue** 迟到的，延误的

infant 婴儿 　　　　　　　　　　**switch** 转变,改变

spark 导致 　　　　　　　　　　**render** 使,致使

fundamental 基本的 　　　　　　**preferable** 更好的,更可取的

【写译语块】

1. That's especially true of children who remain in abusive homes 对于留在那些受虐待的家庭的孩子来说尤其如此

2. refuse to give up custody（监护）rights 不肯放弃监护权

3. remain with the only father she's ever known 继续与她唯一熟悉的养父生活在一起

4. die of a heart disease 死于心脏病

5. have standing to sue（起诉）on her own behalf 有权以自己的名义起诉

6. the biological link between parent and child 父母与孩子的血缘关系

【难句分析】

1. （第二段第一句）在 Fourteen-year-old Kimberly Mays fits neither description, but her recent court victory could eventually help children who do 中,fit 在这里作动词,意思是"适合",description 指的是上文提到的两种情况,即 remain in abusive homes 和 suffer for years in foster homes。who do 是一个定语从句,who 指代 children,do 指 fit either description,即指适合任何一种上述提到的情况。

2. （第二段第二句）在 Kimberly has been the object of an angry custody baffle between the man who raised her and her biological parents, with whom she has never lived 中,object 的意思是"对象",custody baffle 指的是"监护权争夺战",who raised her 是一个定语从句,修饰前面的 man,raise 表示"抚养",biological parents 的意思是"亲生父母",whom 即指代前面提到的 biological parents。

3. （第五段第三句）在 Thus he made clear that she was more than just property to be handled as adults saw fit 中,词组 made clear 的意思是"表明,讲清楚",more than 的意思是"不只是,不仅仅",property 的意思是"财产,资产",to be handled 作后置定语,修饰 property,表示"被处理",as 引导一个时间状语从句。fit 在这里是形容词,意思是"合适的"。

4. （第六段第二句）在 But biological parents aren't always preferable to adoptive ones, and biological parentage does not convey an absolute ownership that cancels all the rights of children 中,preferable 的意思是"更好的,更可取的",a-

doptive ones 对应前面的 biological parents,是"养父母"的意思,parentage 的意思是"父母亲的身份",ownership 的意思是"所有权",that cancels all the rights of children 是一个定语从句,修饰前面的 ownership,cancel 的意思是"取消"。

【原题再现】

411. What was the primary consideration in the Florida judge's ruling?

    A) The biological link.   B) The child's benefits.

    C) The traditional practice.   D) The parents' feelings.

412. We can learn from the Kimberly case that _____.

    A) children are more than just personal possessions of their parents

    B) the biological link between parent and child should be emphasized

    C) foster homes bring children more pain and suffering than care

    D) biological parents shouldn't claim custody rights after their child is adopted

413. The Twiggs claimed custody rights to Kimberly because _____.

    A) they found her unhappy in Mr. Mays' custody

    B) they regarded her as their property

    C) they were her biological parents

    D) they felt guilty about their past mistake

414. Kimberly had been given to Mr. Mays _____.

    A) by sheer accident   B) out of charity

    C) at his request   D) for better care

415. The author's attitude towards the judge's ruling could be described as _____.

    A) doubtful   B) critical

    C) cautious   D) supportive

【单词详解】

【重点单词】**victory** / ˈviktəri / *n.*

[基本词义] 胜利,成功,赢

[用法导航] a major victory 大捷 // narrow victory 很勉强的胜利,险胜 // Pyrrhic victory 极大的牺牲换来的胜利 // Winged Victory 胜利女神 // At last they experienced the joy of victory. 最终他们尝到了胜利的欢乐。

[词性转换] **victorious** / vikˈtɔːriəs / *adj.* 胜利的

200

[对比记忆] (1) **conquest** / ˈkɔŋkwest / *n.* 攻取，征服，克服

(2) **success** / səkˈses / *n.* 成功；成就；成功者，成功的事迹

(3) **triumph** / ˈtraiəmf / *n.* 胜利，成功；巨大的成就[成功]

(4) **winning** / ˈwiniŋ / *n.* 缴获；占领；胜利，成功

[真题衔接] People were shooting off pistols in the streets to celebrate the _____.

A) victory   B) occasion   C) instance   D) reception

【句子翻译】

416. We are satisfied for the food is good and _____(服务质量也不错).

417. She _____(没有离开办公室)all afternoon and was utterly exhausted.

418. Don't trouble to do it _____(为了我)，for I could go without it.

419. The boss needed to _____(说明这些指令)to the workers before they could operate the machines.

420. Ann and Mary _____(保持着她们之间的友谊)for the next thirty years ever since they met in London.

Passage Forty-three

Like many of my generation, I *have a weakness for hero worship*. *At some point*, however, we all begin to question our heroes and our need for them. This leads us to ask: What is a hero?

Despite **immense** differences in cultures, heroes around the world generally *share a number of characteristics* that **instruct** and **inspire** people.

A hero *does something worth talking about*. A hero has a story of adventure to tell and a community who will listen. But *a hero goes beyond mere fame*.

Heroes serve powers or principles larger than themselves. Like high-voltage **transformers**, heroes take the energy of higher powers and step it down so that it can be used by ordinary people.

The hero lives a life worthy of **imitation**. Those who imitate a **genuine** hero experience life with new depth, **enthusiasm**, and meaning. A sure test for would-be heroes is what or whom do they serve? What are they willing to live and die for? If the answer or evidence suggests they serve only their own fame, they may be famous persons but not heroes. Madonna and Michael Jackson are famous, but who would claim that their fans find life more **abundant**?

201

Heroes are catalysts（催化剂）for change. They have a vision from the mountaintop. They have the skill and the charm to move the masses. They create new possibilities. Without Gandhi, India might still be part of the British Empire. Without Rosa Parks and Martin Luther King, Jr., we might still have segregated（隔离的）buses, restaurants, and parks. It may be possible for large-scale change to occur without leaders with **magnetic** personalities, but the pace of change would be slow, the vision uncertain, and the committee meeting endless.
(293 words)（2002 年 12 月第 1 篇）

【段落译文】

　　像许多同龄人一样,我也喜欢崇拜英雄人物。然而,在某个时候我们又都开始怀疑我们所崇拜的英雄人物,怀疑我们是否需要他们。我们不禁产生疑问:什么是英雄人物?

　　尽管各种文化间存在着巨大的差异,但世界各地的英雄人物有着引导、鼓舞民众的共性。

　　英雄人物会做出一些值得称赞的事情。英雄人物有一段值得一讲的传奇经历,人们愿意倾听。但英雄人物不仅仅是名声。

　　英雄人物发挥的力量和榜样作用远远大于他们自己。像变压器能够变压一样,英雄人物能够吸收力量,将崇高的理想转化以便为普通人能够仿效。

　　英雄人物的生活值得世人仿效。那些效仿真正的英雄人物的人将能体验到一种从未有过的深刻、充满激情和更富意义的生活。要检验谁将成为未来的英雄人物,标准是看他们是为谁或为什么而尽心尽力? 看他们愿意过什么样的生活、愿意为什么而献身? 如果答案或事实表明他们仅仅是为了自己的名誉而努力,那他们可能是名人,但不是英雄。麦当娜和迈克尔·杰克逊很有名气,但谁能说他们的歌迷因为模仿他们而使自己的生活变得更充实了?

　　英雄是促进变革的催化剂。他们高瞻远瞩,具有感动民众的技巧和个人魅力,能够创造新的可能性。如果没有甘地,印度可能还是大英帝国的殖民地。如果没有帕克斯·罗莎和马丁·路德·金,在美国,种族隔离可能依然存在于公共汽车、餐馆和公园里。即使没有才能卓越的领导,巨大的变革也可能会发生,但是变革的步伐将会是迟缓的,前景将会是不明朗的,争论将会是无休止的。

【难词解释】

worship 崇拜	**immense** 巨大的
instruct 引导,教育	**inspire** 鼓励,鼓舞

transformers 变压器
genuine 真正的,真实的
abundant 丰富,充裕

imitation 模仿,仿效
enthusiasm 热情,激情
magnetic 有吸引力的,有魅力的

【写译语块】

1. have a weakness for hero worship 喜欢崇拜英雄人物
2. at some point 在某些时候,在某个阶段
3. share a number of characteristics 具有一些共同特征
4. do something worth talking about 做了一些值得称赞的事情
5. a hero goes beyond mere fame 英雄人物不仅仅是名声

【难句分析】

1. (第二段第一句)在 Despite immense differences in cultures, heroes around the world generally share a number of characteristics that instruct and inspire people 中,介词 despite 引导一个介词短语可置于句首,作让步状语,表示"尽管"之意,短语 in spite of 与之同义,但不能置于句首;句中的 share a number of characteristics 意为"拥有许多共同的特征",与 have sth in common 同义;a number of 意为"许多",可修饰可数名词复数,也可以修饰不可数名词;宾语 characteristics 后是一个由连接代词 that 引导的定语从句,that 在从句中作主语。

2. (第三段)A hero does something worth talking about. A hero has a story of adventure to tell and a community who will listen. But a hero goes beyond mere fame. 在 does something worth talking about 表达中 something 是一个兼语式成分,既作 does 的宾语,又作 talking about 的宾语,worth talking about 含义为"值得谈论";a hero goes beyond mere fame 与前两句构成一种因果关系,正因为有前面讲述的"他们做了一些值得称赞的事"、"有一段值得讲述的传奇经历",所以"英雄绝非仅仅是名声",即是说,英雄必须有英雄的言行和壮举!go beyond 意为"超过,远非,决不是"。

3. (第四段第二句)Like high-voltage transformers, heroes take the energy of higher powers and step it down so that it can be used by ordinary people. 该句使用明喻修饰手法,把英雄的作用比作变压器,能够做到"吸收高能"(take energy of higher powers),并将其"转换,降低"step it down,以便普通人物能够学习、仿效(use)。

4. (第六段第五、六句)Without Gandhi, India might still be part of the British Empire. Without Rosa Parks and Martin Luther King, Jr., we might still

have segregated buses, restaurants, and parks. 这两句都是由介词 without 引出的一种假设，因都与现在的事实相反，所以主句的谓语都用的虚拟结构：might still be part of the British Empire 和 might still have segregated。

5. （第六段第七句）It may be possible for large-scale change to occur without leaders with magnetic personalities, but the pace of change would be slow, the vision uncertain, and the committee meeting endless. 该句也是一个由介词 without 引导的虚拟假设，主句是四个并列句，第一个分句中是由 it 引导的一个形式主语结构，真正的主语是不定式 to occur；第三、四个分句都是省略句，都省略了谓语动词 would be。

【原题再现】

421. Although heroes may come from different cultures, they _____.

   A) generally possess certain inspiring characteristics

   B) probably share some weaknesses of ordinary people

   C) are often influenced by previous generations

   D) all unknowingly attract a large number of fans

422. According to the passage, heroes are compared to high-voltage transformers in that _____.

   A) they have a vision from the mountaintop

   B) they have warm feelings and emotions

   C) they can serve as concrete examples of noble principles

   D) they can make people feel stronger and more confident

423. Madonna and Michael Jackson are not considered heroes because _____.

   A) they are popular only among certain groups of people

   B) their performances do not improve their fans morally

   C) their primary concern is their own financial interests

   D) they are not clear about the principles they should follow

424. Gandhi and Martin Luther King are typical examples of outstanding leaders who _____.

   A) are good at demonstrating their charming characters

   B) can move the masses with their forceful speeches

   C) are capable of meeting all challenges and hardships

   D) can provide an answer to the problems of their people

425. The author concludes that historical changes would _____.

A) be delayed without leaders with inspiring personal qualities

B) not happen without heroes making the necessary sacrifices

C) take place if there were heroes to lead the people

D) produce leaders with attractive personalities

【单词详解】

【重点单词】 **imitation** / imiˈteiʃən / *n.*

[基本词义] 模仿；仿制，仿制品；赝品

[用法导航] a blind imitation of 对……的盲目模仿 // spontaneous imitation 无意识模仿 // voluntary imitation 有意识模仿 // an imitation of leather 皮革仿制品 // She bought an imitation of a famous painting when she was on her business trip to New York. 她因公出差去纽约时买了一幅名画的仿制品。

[词性转换] **imitate** / ˈimiteit / *vt.* 模仿，模效；仿制，仿造

[对比记忆] **limitation** / ˌlimiˈteiʃən / *n.* 限制，局限性

[真题衔接] These drawings are poor _____ of the original ones.

　　A) imitations　　B) editions　　C) tracts　　D) versions

【重点单词】 **abundant** / əˈbʌndənt / *adj.*

[基本词义] 大量的，充足的；(in)丰富的，富裕的

[用法导航] be abundant in 丰富 // abundant proof of one's guilt 充分的证据证明某人有罪 // be abundant in petroleum deposits 石油储量丰富

[词性转换] **abundance** / əˈbʌndəns / *n.* 大量，多，充足；丰富，富有，富裕

[对比记忆] (1) **fertile** / ˈfəːtil, ˈfəːtail / *adj.* 肥沃的，富饶的；多产的，丰产的；(想象力或创造力)丰富的

　　(2) **plentiful** / ˈplentiful / *adj.* 丰富的，充足的，大量的

　　(3) **rich** / ritʃ / *adj.* 富的，有钱的；富饶的，丰富的；盛产的，肥沃的

[真题衔接] There is _____ evidence that cars have a harmful effect on the environment.

　　A) abundant　　B) fertile　　C) infinite　　D) overall

【句子翻译】

426. An increasing number of young people _____（喜欢崇拜体育和电影明星）.

427. No matter who are heroes or heroines _____（都具有一些共同特征）.

428. Countless unknown heroes _____（做了一些值得称赞的事情）.

429. True art has a universal value that _____（超越国界）, ethnic groups and cultures.

430. _____（在某种程度上）during *The Sound of Music*, I realized I was actually watching *Snow White & the Seven Dwarfs*.

Passage Forty-four

According to a survey, which *was based on the responses of* over 188,000 students, today's traditional-age college freshmen are "more **materialistic** and less altruistic（利他主义的）" than at any time in the 17 years of the poll.

Not surprising in these hard times, the students' major objective *"is to be financially well off*. Less important than ever is developing a meaningful philosophy of life."* It follows then that today the most popular course is not literature or history but accounting.

Interest in teaching, social service and the **"altruistic"** fields is at a low. On the other hand, **enrollment** in business programs, engineering and computer science is way up.

That's no surprise, either. A friend of mine (a sales **representative** for a chemical company) was making twice the salary of her college instructors her first year on the job—even before she completed her two-year associate degree.

While it's true that we all need a career, it is equally true that our civilization has **accumulated** an **incredible** amount of knowledge in fields far removed from our own and that we are better for our understanding of these other contributions—be they scientific or artistic. It is equally true that, in studying the **diverse** wisdom of others, we learn how to think. More important, perhaps, education teaches us to see the connection between things, as well as to see beyond our immediate needs.

Weekly we read of unions who went on strike for higher wages, *only to drive their employer out of business*. No company; no job. *How shortsighted in the long run*!

But the most important argument for a broad education is that in studying the accumulated wisdom of the ages, we improve our moral sense. I saw a cartoon recently which shows a group of businessmen looking puzzled as they sit around a conference table; one of them is talking on the intercom（对讲机）"Miss Baxter," he says, "could you please send in someone who can **distinguish** right from wrong?"

From the long-term point of view, that's what education really ought to be about. (353 words)　(2002 年 12 月第 2 篇)

【段落译文】

从 188000 多名大学新生的问卷调查反馈结果显示,他们比开展这项调查 17 年以来的任何一届大学新生都"更追求物质主义,少了点利他主义"。

一点也不让人感到意外,在现在严峻的形势下,学生们的主要目标"将是经济上富足。与过去相比,培养一种有意义的人生观已显得无足轻重了。"由此产生的后果是:现今最实用的课程不是文学或历史,而是会计学。

他们对当教师、社会服务和其他需要奉献精神领域的兴趣都降到最低点,另一方面,攻读商业科目、工程学及计算机科学的学生人数却一路攀升。

这种现象也不令人诧异。我的一位朋友(一个化工公司的销售代表)在工作的第一年所挣的钱就已是大学教师薪水的两倍了——这还是她获得两年制大专文凭之前的事。

尽管我们每个人都需要一份职业,这是事实,但在与我们自己从事的业务领域相去甚远的其他领域里,我们的文明已积累了数量惊人的知识;对这些领域知识的理解有助于我们更好地了解其他领域的知识——无论是科学领域的,还是艺术领域的。这也是事实。在研究这些领域的各种各样知识过程中,我们学会如何去思考,这同样是事实。也许更重要的是,教育不仅使我们视野开阔,超越了眼前的需求,而且引导我们去发现事物间的联系。

我们每周都在报纸上读到这样的新闻:为了涨工资,工会组织工人罢工,其结果只是促使了他们的老板破产。公司没有了,工人失业了。从长远的观点来看,他们的目光是多么的短浅啊!

赞成通才教育最重要的理由是:在学习世世代代积累下来的知识的过程中,我们提高了我们的道德观念。最近,我看了一部动画片,片中描述了一群围坐在圆会议桌旁的商人,个个看上去都很迷茫;其中一个商人对着对讲机说:"巴克斯特小姐,能否能派个能分清是非的人进来?"

从长远的观点来看,这就是教育真正应该要做的。

【难词解释】

materialistic 物质主义的,唯物主义的　　**financially** 经济上的,财政上的

altruistic 利他的,无私心的　　**enrollment** 招收,招入,登记

representative 代理人,代表　　**incredible** 难以置信的,惊人的

accumulate 积累,累积　　**diverse** 多样的,各种各样的

shortsighted 目光短浅的，近视的   **distinguish** 辨别，区分，分辨

【写译语块】

1. be based on the responses of 建立在对……问题回答的基础上
2. to be financially well off 将是经济上富足
3. that's no surprise 毫不令人感到奇怪
4. only to drive their employer out of business 只是促使了他们的老板破产
5. How shortsighted in the long run! 从长远的观点来看，他们的目光是多么的短浅啊！

【难句分析】

1. (第二段第二句) Less important than ever is developing a meaningful philosophy of life. 该句是一个倒装句，正常语序应该是 Developing a meaningful philosophy of life is less important than ever。倒装语序是英语句子结构中的一个重要的表达结构，比如：Only by shouting at the top of his voice was he able to make himself heard. 又如：Not until eleven o'clock did he stop working last night。

2. (第五段第一句) 在 While it's true that we all need a career, it is equally true that our civilization has accumulated an incredible amount of knowledge in fields far removed from our own and that we are better for our understanding of these other contributions — be they scientific or artistic 中，连接词 while 引导一个让步状语从句。该从句是一个由 that 引导的主语从句的结构，it 是形式主语；主句是由 and 连接的两个并列句，两个并列句的主语也是由 that 引导的主语从句的结构，it 是形式主语；be they scientific or artistic 是一个省略形式的让步状语从句的倒装句，原句是 no matter what they would be scientific or artistic。

3. (第六段第二句) How shortsighted in the long run! 该句是一个省略形式的感叹句，句中的 in the long run 意为"从长远的观点来看"，比如：In the long run, the best is unquestionably the cheapest. 从长远来看，最好的毫无疑问是最便宜的。

【原题再现】

431. According to the author's observation, college students _____.

    A) have never been so materialistic as today

B) have never been so interested in the arts

C) have never been so financially well off as today

D) have never attached so much importance to moral sense

432. The students' criteria for selecting majors today have much to do with _____.

A) the influences of their instructors

B) the financial goals they seek in life

C) their own interpretations of the courses

D) their understanding of the contributions of others

433. By saying "While it's true that... be they scientific or artistic" (Sentence 1, Para. 5), the author means that _____.

A) business management should be included in educational programs

B) human wisdom has accumulated at an extraordinarily high speed

C) human intellectual development has reached new heights

D) the importance of a broad education should not be overlooked

434. Studying the diverse wisdom of others can _____.

A) create varying artistic interests

B) help people see things in their right perspective

C) help improve connections among people

D) regulate the behavior of modern people

435. Which of the following statements is true according to the passage?

A) Businessmen absorbed in their career are narrow-minded.

B) Managers often find it hard to tell right from wrong.

C) People engaged in technical jobs lead a more rewarding life.

D) Career seekers should not focus on immediate interests only.

【单词详解】

【重点单词】 **incredible** / inˈkredəbl / *adj.*

[基本词义] 不能相信的，不可信的；难以置信的，不可思议的，惊人的

[用法导航] give an incredible explanation of the cause of the accident 对事故发生的原因作了令人难以置信的解释 // earn an incredible amount of money 挣的钱多得惊人

[词性转换] **incredibility** / inˌkrediˈbiliti / *n.* 不能相信，不可信的事物

[对比记忆] (1) **absurd** / əbˈsəːd / *adj.* 荒谬的，荒唐的

(2) **ridiculous** / ri'dikjuləs / *adj.* 可笑的，荒唐的

(3) **credible** / 'kredəbl, 'kredibl / *adj.* 可信的，可靠的

［真题衔接］He is only 12 years old? I find that completely _____.

    A) curious   B) incredible   C) casual   D) imaginary

【重点单词】**distinguish** / dis'tiŋgwiʃ / *vt.*

［基本词义］区分，辨别；看清，听出；(oneself)使杰出，使扬名

［用法导航］distinguish good from evil 分辨善恶 // distinguish distant objects 辨别出远处的物体// The monitor distinguished himself by his performance in the examination. 班长在考试中成绩优异，因而显得突出。

［对比记忆］(1) **discern** / di'səːn / *v.* 看出，觉察出；识别，认出

    (2) **detect** / di'tekt / *vt.* 察觉，发现；查明，侦察出

    (3) **dignify** / 'dignifai / *vt.* 使有威严，使高贵；授以荣誉，加以尊称

［真题衔接］It's not the beauty so much as the range of his voice that _____ him from other tenors.

    A) benefits   B) advances   C) distinguishes D) demonstrates

【句子翻译】

436. _____(理论的基础是实践)and in turn serves practice.

437. The greatest happiness _____(是为教育事业而工作).

438. _____(只有这样我们才能)quickly adapt the society after graduation.

439. If you work hard and do your best，_____(最后一定会成功的).

440. _____(尽管我承认困难很大)，I don't agree that they cannot be solved.

Passage Forty-five

New technology links the world as never before. Our planet has **shrunk**. It's now a "global village" where countries are only seconds away *by fax or phone or satellite link*. And, of course, our ability to benefit from this high-tech **communications** equipment is greatly **enhanced** by foreign language skills.

Deeply involved in this new technology is a **breed** of modern businesspeople who have a growing respect for the economic value of doing business abroad. In modern markets，success **overseas** often helps support **domestic** business efforts.

Overseas **assignments** are becoming increasingly important to advancement within **executive** ranks. The executive stationed in another country *no longer need fear being* "out of sight and out of mind." He or she can be sure that the overseas effort is central to the company's plan for success, and that **promotions** often follow or accompany an assignment abroad. If an employee can succeed in a difficult assignment overseas, **superiors** will *have greater confidence in his or her ability* to cope back in the United States where cross-cultural considerations and foreign languages issues are becoming more and more prevalent (普遍的).

Thanks to a variety of relatively inexpensive communications devices with business applications, even small businesses in the United States are able to get into international markets.

English is still the international language of business. But there is an ever-growing need for people who can speak another language. A second language isn't generally required to get a job in business, but having language skills gives a candidate the edge when other qualifications appear to be equal.

The employee posted abroad who speaks the country's principal language has an opportunity to fast-forward certain negotiations, and can have the cultural insight to know when it is better to move more slowly. The employee at the home office who can communicate well with foreign clients over the telephone or by fax machine is an obvious **asset** to the firm. (322 words) （2002 年 12 月第 3 篇）

【段落译文】

新技术以前所未有的程度联系着世界。地球变小了，变成了一个"地球村"，通过传真、电话或卫星网络联系，国与国之间仅有数秒之遥。当然，我们的能力受益于这种高科技通信设备，若再懂外语就更是如虎添翼了。

对新技术依赖最大的是现代商人，他们越来越重视海外贸易的经济价值。在现代市场经济中，海外贸易的成功常常有助于国内生意的发展。

被派驻海外工作对于管理人员今后的职位升迁越来越重要。派驻海外的行政主管人员不必担心"未被看到而不被考虑"。他或她相信：他们在海外的业务成就对于公司计划的成功是至关重要的，被派往国外往往伴随着提升。如果一位雇员能够出色地完成海外的艰巨的任务，上司将对其回国后处理事情的能力更有信心，因为在美国，工作中考虑跨文化因素和外语的问题变得越来越普遍。

由于有了各种多样的、相对便宜的、配有商业应用软件的通信设备，即便是美国的一些小公司也能够开拓国际市场。

尽管英语已经成为国际通用商业语言。但是对会讲其他语言的人才的需求仍在不断增长。第二语言不再只是商界求职时的必要条件，但在相同条件下，具备语言技能的求职者将更具优势。

派往海外并能够讲该国官方语言的员工在商务谈判时就能有机会加快谈判进程,具有对当地文化方面的洞察力,就知道何时该放慢判断速度。公司总部的员工如果能通过电话、传真与外国客户很好地进行交流,这无疑是公司一笔显而易见的财富。

【难词解释】

shrink 收缩,缩短,变小　　　　　　communications 通信,通信系统

enhance 提高,增强　　　　　　　　breed 品种,种类,类型

domestic 国内的,家庭的　　　　　　assignments 任务,作业

executive 行政的,管理的　　　　　　promotions 提拔,晋升,升迁

superiors 上级,长官;长者　　　　　　asset 资产,有用的东西

【写译语块】

1. by fax or phone or satellite link 通过传真、电话或卫星系统联系

2. be deeply involved in this new technology 与新技术紧密相连

3. no longer need fear being 不用再担心被(遗忘)

4. have greater confidence in his or her ability to do sth. 对他们做某事的能力有极大的信心

5. thanks to a variety of... 由于各种各样的……

【难句分析】

1. (第二段第一句)Deeply involved in this new technology is a breed of modern businesspeople who have a growing respect for the economic value of doing business abroad. 该句是一个倒装句,主语是一个短语,而主词又受到定语从句的修饰,使主语结构增加了长度,为避免头重脚轻而使用倒装结构,正常的语序是 A breed of modern businesspeople who have a growing respect ... is deeply involved in this new technology.

2. (第三段第四句)If an employee can succeed in a difficult assignment overseas, superiors will have greater confidence in his or her ability to cope back in the United States where cross-cultural considerations and foreign languages issues are becoming more and more prevalent. 该句是一个真实条件句,主句中包含一个由关系副词 where 引导的定语从句修饰地点状语 in the United States;句中的短语 succeed in(doing sth.)意为"成功做了某事",have confidence in sb. to do sth. 意为"对某人做某事有信心"。

3. (第二段第一句) The employee posted abroad who speaks the country's principal language has an opportunity to fast-forward certain negotiations, and can have the cultural insight to know when it is better to move more slowly. 该句是一个由 and 连接的并列句,但第一个分句是一个主从复合句,主语 The employee 分别受到动词过去分词短语 posted abroad 和 who 引导的定语从句的修饰;第二个分句则是带有一个由 when 引导的时间状语从句。

【原题再现】

441. What is the author's attitude toward high-tech communications equipment?

    A) Critical.   B) Prejudiced.

    C) Indifferent.   D) Positive.

442. With the increased use of high-tech communications equipment, businesspeople _____.

    A) have to get familiar with modern technology

    B) are gaining more economic benefits from domestic operations

    C) are attaching more importance to their overseas business

    D) are eager to work overseas

443. In the passage, "out of sight and out of mind" (Sentence 2, Para. 3) probably means _____.

    A) being unable to think properly for lack of insight

    B) being totally out of touch with business at home

    C) missing opportunities for promotion when abroad

    D) leaving all care and worry behind

444. According to the passage, what is an important consideration of international corporations in employing people today?

    A) Connections with businesses overseas.

    B) Ability to speak the client's language.

    C) Technical know-how.

    D) Business experience.

445. The advantage of employees having foreign language skills is that they can _____.

    A) better control the whole negotiation process

    B) easily find new approaches to meet market needs

    C) fast-forward their proposals to headquarters

D) easily make friends with businesspeople abroad

【单词详解】

【重点单词】**enhance** / inˈhæns, inˈhɑːns / *vt.*

[基本词义] 提高,增加,加强

[用法导航] enhance the status of sb. 提高某人的身份 // enhance the reputation of sb. 提高某人的声望 // enhance the position of sb. 提高某人的地位 // enhance one's political consciousness 提高政治觉悟 // Passing the English examination should enhance your chances of getting the post. 通过了英语考试会增加你获得这个职位的机会。

[词性转换] **enhancement** / inˈhɑːnsmənt / *n.* 提高,增加,加强

[对比记忆] (1) **enrich** / inˈritʃ / *vt.* 充实,使丰富;使富裕,使富有

(2) **improve** / imˈpruːv / *vt.* 改建,改善 *vi.* 改善,变得更好

(3) **boost** / buːst / *vt.* 提高,使增涨;推动,激烈;替……作广告,宣扬

[真题衔接] The reviews of the poet's most recent book _____ his reputation.

A) measured   B) enhanced   C) prevailed   D) pronounced

【重点单词】**executive** / igˈzekjutiv / *adj.*

[基本词义] 执行的,行政的

[词性转换] **executive** / igˈzekjutiv / *n.* 主管,高级行政人员,行政官;行政部门

[用法导航] an advisory body lacking executive powers 缺乏执行权力的顾问团 // executive experience and skills 经营管理的经验和技能 // the executive committee of a political party 一个政党的执行委员会 // She says executive function skills can be improved. 她说执行功能技能是可以改善的。

[对比记忆] (1) **administrative** / ədˈministrətiv / *adj.* 管理的;行政的

(2) **supportive** / səˈpɔːtiv / *adj.* 支持的,有支持/作用力的

[真题衔接] She is now a senior _____ having worked her way up through the company.

A) council   B) assistant   C) agent   D) executive

【句子翻译】

446. If, however, the plants are not begun now, you will _____(便不再有选择的余地了).

447. If _____(你对自己失去信心) that makes the vote unanimous.

448. _____(由于这段经历),we find ourselves better positioned to be in the

career that is right for us.

449. You must believe in what you do and who you are, if you _____ (想在这个世界上取得成功).

450. Emergency measures are being taken to save _____ (中国特有的珍稀动物).

Passage Forty-six

In recent years, Israeli consumers have grown more demanding as they've become wealthier and more worldly-wise. Foreign travel is a national **passion**; this summer alone, *one in* 10 *citizens* will go abroad. *Exposed to higher standards of service* elsewhere, Israelis are returning home expecting the same. American firms have also *begun arriving in large numbers*. Chains such as KFC, McDonald's and Pizza Hut are setting a new standard of customer service, using strict employee training and **constant** monitoring to ensure the friendliness of frontline staff. Even the American habit of telling departing customers to "Have a nice day" has caught on all over Israel. "Nobody wakes up in the morning and says, Let's be nicer,'" says Itsik Cohen, director of a consulting firm. "Nothing happens without competition."

Privatization, or the threat of it, is a **motivation** as well. Monopolies (垄断者) that until recently have *been free to take their customers for granted* now fear what Michael Perry, a marketing professor, calls "the revengeful (报复的) consumer." When the government opened up competition with Bezaq, the phone company, its international branch lost 40% of its market share, even while offering competitive rates. Perry says, "People wanted revenge for all the years of bad service." The electric company, whose **monopoly** may be short-lived, has suddenly stopped requiring users to wait half a day for a repairman. Now, *appointments are scheduled to the half-hour*. The **graceless** EI AI Airlines, which is already at auction (拍卖), has **retrained** its employees to emphasize service and is **boasting** about the results in an ad campaign with the slogan, "You can feel the change in the air." For the first time, praise **outnumbers** complaints on customer survey sheets. (291 words) (2002 年 12 月第 4 篇)

【段落译文】

近年来,随着人们富裕程度的提高和阅历的增加,以色列的消费者的消费需求也越来越高。出国旅游成为一种时尚;仅今年夏天就将有十分之一的以色列人出国旅行。由于在其他国家享受了高水准的服务,以色列人希望回国后也能得到同样的待遇。美国公司已开始大量进驻以色列。肯德基、麦当劳、必胜客等连锁店正在制定新的客户服务标准,实施严格的员工培训,时刻监控一线服务员工对客户是否友好。甚至连服务生在客人离店时说的"祝你愉快"这样的美国习惯也在以色列全国流行开来。一家咨询公司的主管 Itsik Cohen 说,"没有人在早晨醒来时说:'让我们做得更好'。如果没有竞争,这一切就不会发生。"

私有化,或私有化的威胁,也是导致这些变化的一个缘由。以前不把顾客放在眼中的垄断者现在也开始害怕被市场营销学教授 Michael Perry 称之为的"消费者的报复"。当政府放开竞争后,一家名叫 Bezaq 的电话公司,尽管提出了富有竞争力的价格,但它的国际分公司还是丧失了 40% 的市场份额。Perry 说:"顾客们想为他们多年来所受的低劣服务进行报复。"电力公司的垄断日子可能即将结束,它突然不再让用户再为维修服务等上半天时间;现在,只要半小时公司就能派人来。原来服务质量极差准备拍卖的 EI AI 航空公司,已重新培训雇员,强调服务质量。在一次广告促销活动中,以广告语"你能在空中感到变化"向公众展示雇员再培训后的结果。在顾客调查单上,表扬第一次多于投诉。

【难词解释】

passion 激情,热情

privatization 私有化

monopoly 垄断,垄断者

graceless 粗野的,态度恶劣的

boast 吹嘘,夸耀

constant 经常的,不断的

motivation 动机,动力

schedule 把……列入计划,安排

retrain 再培训,再教育

outnumber 数目超过,比……多

【写译语块】

1. one in 10 citizens 十分之一的公民,百分之十的公民
2. be exposed to higher standards of service 享受了高水准的服务
3. begin arriving in large numbers 开始大量进入
4. be free to take their customers for granted 不把顾客当回事
5. appointments are scheduled to the half-hour 预约维修都被安排在半小时内

【难句分析】

1. (第一段第一句)In recent years, Israeli consumers have grown more deman-

ding as they've become wealthier and more worldly-wise. 这是一个主从复合句, as 引导的是一个原因状语从句, 表明主句中 consumers have grown more demanding 的原因, 需求增加的原因一是人们越来越富裕, 二是人们的视野开阔了。

2. (第一段第四句)Chains such as KFC, McDonald's and Pizza Hut are setting a new standard of customer service, using strict employee training and **constant** monitoring to ensure the friendliness of frontline staff. 该句的谓语是由三个部分构成, 即 setting a new standard, using strict employee training 和 constant monitoring, 不定式短语 to ensure the friendliness of frontline staff 作目的状语, 修饰说明前面三个行动的目的。

3. (第二段第一句)Monopolies that until recently have been free to take their customers for granted now fear what Michael Perry, a marketing professor, calls "the revengeful consumer." 该句虽然主体上是一个 "主＋谓＋宾" 结构的简单句, 但主语受到一个由连接代词 that 引导定语从句的修饰, 连接代词 that 在定语从句中作主语, 宾语是一个由连接代词 what 引导的从句, 宾语从句的主语还带有一个同谓语。

【原题再现】

451. It may be inferred from the passage that _____.

    A) customer service in Israel is now improving

    B) wealthy Israeli customers are hard to please

    C) the tourist industry has brought chain stores to Israel

    D) Israeli customers prefer foreign products to domestic ones

452. In the author's view, higher service standards are impossible in Israel _____.

    A) if customer complaints go unnoticed by the management

    B) unless foreign companies are introduced in greater numbers

    C) if there's no competition among companies

    D) without strict routine training of employees

453. If someone in Israel today needs a repairman in case of a power failure, _____.

    A) they can have it fixed in no time

    B) it's no longer necessary to make an appointment

    C) the appointment takes only half a day to make

    D) they only have to wait half an hour at most

454. The example of EI AI Airlines shows that _____.

A) revengeful customers are a threat to the monopoly of enterprises

B) an ad campaign is a way out for enterprises in financial difficulty

C) a good slogan has great potential for improving service

D) staff retraining is essential for better service

455. Why did Bezaq's international branch lose 40% of its market share?

A) Because the rates it offered were not competitive enough.

B) Because customers were dissatisfied with its past service.

C) Because the service offered by its competitors was far better.

D) Because it no longer received any support from the government.

【单词详解】

【重点单词】**schedule** / ˈskedʒuəl, ˈʃedjuːəl/ *n.*

[基本词义] 时刻表,日程安排表;清单,明细表

[用法导航] ahead of schedule 提前 // on schedule 按时间表,及时,准时 // behind schedule 落后于计划或进度;迟于预定时间 // tight schedule 排得紧紧的时间表;难以遵守的时间表 // have a full schedule 预定计划排得很满 // a spare parts schedule 零件清单 // The task will be finished ahead of schedule if nothing prevents. 如果没有什么阻碍的话,这项任务将提前完成。

[对比记忆] (1) **arrange** / əˈreɪndʒ / *vt.* 安排,准备;整理,布置 *vi.* 作安排,筹划

(2) **budget** / ˈbʌdʒit / *vi.* (for)编预算,作安排 *vt.* 规划,安排

(3) **format** / ˈfɔːmæt / *n.* 设计,安排;格式,样式,版式

(4) **layout** / ˈleɪˌaut / *n.* 布局,安排,设计

[真题衔接] The task will be finished ahead of _____ if nothing prevents.

A) format   B) blank   C) standard   D) schedule

【重点单词】**boast** / bəust / *vi.* & *vt.*

[基本词义] (of, about)自夸,夸耀;夸口,吹嘘;以拥有……而自豪

[用法导航] a boastful disposition 自负的性格 // The boy boasted that his bicycle was of the best quality of all the bicycles in the school. 这男孩夸口说他的自行车是学校中质量最好的。// It has never been the boast of a modest person that he alone could accomplish such a hard task. 一个谦虚的人从来不会夸口说只有他才能够完成这样一件困难的任务。

[词性转换] **boastful** / bəustful / *adj.* 自吹自擂的,自夸的,自负的

[对比记忆] (1) **coast** / kəust / *n.* 海岸,海滨

218

(2) **roast** / rəust / *v.* 烤,炙,烘 *n.* 烤肉 *adj.* 烤过的,烘过的

(3) **toast** / təust / *n.* 烤面包;祝酒,祝酒词 *vt.* 烘;为……干杯

[真题衔接] It was his proud _____ that he had never missed a day's work because of illness.

A) boast   B) display   C) praise   D) confidence

【句子翻译】

456. In economic crisis, _____(这家工厂十分之四的工人)were laid off.

457. _____(享受了高水准的服务),all athletes from all over the world spent a wonderful time during the Olympic Games in Beijing.

458. Soon after the earthquake happen, emergency help _____(开始大量进入).

459. _____(我想你应该知道那件事情)that you knew the fact, I didn't tell you at that time.

460. _____(你要与汤卜逊先生会面)of ABC Company at eleven this morning.

Passage Forty-seven

It is hard to **track** the blue whale, the ocean's largest creature, which has almost been killed off by commercial whaling and is now listed as an **endangered** species. *Attaching radio devices to it is difficult*, and visual sightings are too **unreliable** to give real insight into its behavior.

So biologists were delighted early this year when *with the help of the Navy* they were able to track a particular blue whale for 43 days **monitoring** its sounds. This was possible because of the Navy's formerly top-secret system of underwater listening devices **spanning** the oceans.

Tracking whales is but one example of an exciting new world just opening to civilian scientists after the cold war as the Navy starts to share and partly *uncover its global network of underwater listening system* built over the decades to track the ships of potential enemies.

Earth scientists announced at a news conference recently that they had used the system for closely monitoring a deep-sea volcanic **eruption**(爆发)for the first time and that they plan similar studies.

Other scientists have *proposed to use the network for tracking ocean currents* and measuring changes in ocean and global temperatures.

The speed of sound in water is **roughly** one mile a second — slower than through land but faster than through air. What is most important, different layers of ocean water can act as channels for sounds, **focusing** them *in the same way a stethoscope* (听诊器) *does* when it carries faint noises from a patient's chest to a doctor's ear. This focusing is the main reason that even relatively weak sounds in the ocean, especially **low-frequency** ones, can often travel thousands of miles. (283 words) （2002 年 6 月第 1 篇）

【段落译文】

跟踪蓝鲸是很困难的,这种海洋中最庞大的动物因商业捕鲸几乎快被杀光了,现在被列为濒临灭绝的物种。要在它身上安装无线电跟踪器是很难的,而光靠肉眼观察又太不可靠,很难了解它们的行为。

今年年初,在海军的帮助下,生物科学家跟踪了一只蓝鲸 43 天,监听了它的声音,他们高兴极了。由于使用了海军以前的最高机密——遍布海洋的水下听音系统,使监听成为可能。

跟踪蓝鲸是冷战结束后,海军开始分享并部分地解密在过去几十年建立起来的追踪潜在敌舰的全球水下监听网络系统,从而向民用科学家开放的新的激动人心的世界的一个例子。

地球学家最近在一次新闻发布会上宣布,他们应用这套系统第一次严密地监听了深海火山爆发的情况,并计划继续进行类似的研究。

其他科学家也已建议,使用该监听网络来跟踪洋流、监测洋流和全球温度的变化。

声音在水里的传播速度大约每秒 1 英里——比在地下慢一点,但比在空气中快一点。更重要的是,海水的不同层次可以作为声音传播的渠道,这种汇集声音的原理与听诊器把微弱的声音从病人胸腔传到医生耳朵原理类似。这种汇集,正是大海里相对微弱的声音,特别是那些低频的声音,常常能传到数千英里之外的原因。

【难词解释】

track 追踪,跟踪	**endanger** (使)遭到危险,(使)濒临灭绝
unreliable 不可靠,靠不住的	**monitor** 监视,监控,跟踪
span 遍布;跨越	**uncover** 揭开,解密
eruption 爆发	**roughly** 大约,粗略
focus 汇集,集中	**low-frequency** 低频的

【写译语块】

1. attaching radio devices to it is difficult 安装无线电跟踪器是困难的
2. with the help of the Navy 在海军的帮助下
3. uncover its global network of underwater listening system 解密全球水下监听网络系统
4. propose to use the network for tracking ocean currents 建议使用该监听网络来跟踪洋流
5. in the same way a stethoscope does 其原理与听诊器的原理类似

【难句分析】

1. （第一段第二句）Attaching radio devices to it is difficult, and visual sightings are too unreliable to give real insight into its behavior. 本句由两个并列单句组成，前一句由动词-ing 短语作主语，其谓语用单数形式；后一句的主语是复数意义"肉眼观察"，所以其动词不能用单数，而必须用复数；attaching sth. to sth. else 在本句中的意思是"将某物安装到另一物上"。

2. （第五段）在 Other scientists have proposed to use the network for tracking ocean currents and measuring changes in ocean and global temperatures 中，有两个由介词 for 引导的动词-ing 短语，即 for tracking ocean currents 和 measuring changes 作状语表示 to use the network 的目的。

3. （第六段第二句）在 What is most important, different layers of ocean water can act as channels for sounds, focusing them in the same way a stethoscope does when it carries faint noises from a patient's chest to a doctor's ear 中，What is most important 是一个固定表达结构，表示递进关系；act as 意为"用作"；动词-ing 短语 focusing them in the same way 作补充说明状语；介词短语 in the same way 意为"以相同的方式"。

【原题再现】

461. The passage is chiefly about _____.

    A) the civilian use of a military detection system

    B) the exposure of a U. S. Navy top-secret weapon

    C) an effort to protect an endangered marine species

    D) a new way to look into the behavior of blue whales

462. The underwater listening system was originally designed _____.

A) to replace the global radio communications network

B) to study the movement of ocean currents

C) to monitor deep-sea volcanic eruptions

D) to trace and locate enemy vessels

463. The deep-sea listening system makes use of _____.

A) the capability of sound to travel at high speed

B) the sophisticated technology of focusing sounds under water

C) low-frequency sounds traveling across different layers of water

D) the unique property of layers of ocean water in transmitting sound

464. It can be inferred from the passage that _____.

A) blue whales are no longer endangered with the use of the new listening system

B) military technology has great potential in civilian use

C) new radio devices should be developed for tracking the endangered blue whales

D) opinions differ as to whether civilian scientists should be allowed to use military technology

465. Which of the following is true about the U. S. Navy underwater listening network?

A) It has been replaced by a more advanced system.

B) It is now partly accessible to civilian scientists.

C) It became useless to the military after the cold war.

D) It is indispensable in protecting endangered species.

【单词详解】

【重点单词】 **uncover** / ʌnˈkʌvə / *vt.*

[基本词义] 揭露,暴露;揭开……的盖子

[用法导航] uncover the box 打开盒盖 // uncover the hidden riches 找到埋藏的财宝 // uncover new evidence 揭示新的证据 // He uncovered the dish and showed us the food. 他揭开盘子的盖儿给我们看吃的东西。 // The police uncovered a plan to steal some money. 警察揭露了一个盗款的计划。

[对比记忆] (1) **bare** / bɛə / *vt.* 露出,暴露

(2) **expose** / iksˈpəuz / *vt.* 暴露,显露;(to) 曝光;揭露,袒露

(3) **reveal** / riˈviːl / *vt.* 揭露,泄露;展现,显示

(4) **disclose** / disˈkləuz / vt. 揭露,泄露,透露

[真题衔接] The investigation _____ evidence of a large-scale illegal trade in wild birds.

A) uncovered　　B) exposed　　C) exhibited　　D) demonstrated

【重点单词】**focus** / ˈfəukəs / v.

[基本词义] (on)(使)聚集,(使)集中,聚焦

[用法导航] focus one's mind on work 集中精力于工作 // be a focus of attention 成为注意力的中心 // focus all their attention on finding a solution to the problem 集中全部注意力寻找解决问题的办法 // a campaign that focused on economic issues 一次集中解决经济问题的运动

[词性转换] focus / ˈfəukəs / n. 焦点,焦距,聚焦;(注意、活动等的)中心

[对比记忆] (1) **adjust** / əˈdʒʌst / vt. 校正,调整;调节,改变⋯⋯以适应 vi. (to)适应

(2) **concentrate** / ˈkɔnsentreit / vi. 全神贯注,全力以赴;集中,聚集 vt. 集中,聚集;浓缩 n. 浓缩物,浓缩液

(3) **spotlight** / ˈspɔtlait / n. (舞台的)聚光灯;公众注意的中心 vt. 使公众注意,使突出醒目;聚光照明

[真题衔接] Because of his strange clothes, he immediately became the _____ of attention when he entered the office.

A)attraction　　B)feature　　C)focus　　D)spark

【句子翻译】

466. I stood by the lathe, _____(看它是如何操作的).

467. _____(在国际国内志愿者的帮助下)the victims in earthquake overcame all kinds of difficulties to rebuild their homes.

468. _____(禁止赌博)in our country.

469. Although PCs have many different functions, they all essentially _____(以同样的方式工作的).

470. The Ancient Greeks were the first _____(发现多重世界秘密的人), at least four thousand years ago.

Passage Forty-eight

Most **episodes** of absent-mindedness — *forgetting where you left something or wondering why you just entered a room*—are caused by a simple lack of atten-

223

tion, says Schacter. ***"You're supposed to remember something***, but you haven't **encoded** it deeply."

Encoding, Schacter explains, is a special way of paying attention to an event that ***has a major impact on recalling it later***. Failure to encode properly can create **annoying** situations. If you put your mobile phone in a pocket, for example, and don't pay attention to what you did because ***you're involved in a conversation***, you'll probably forget that the phone is in the jacket now **hanging** in your wardrobe（衣柜）. "Your memory itself isn't failing you," says Schacter. "Rather, you didn't give your memory system the information it needed."

Lack of interest can also lead to absent-mindedness. "A man who can recite sports **statistics** from 30 years ago," says Zelinski, "may not remember to drop a letter in the mailbox." Women have slightly better memories than men, possibly because they pay more attention to their **environment**, and memory relies on just that.

Visual **cues** can help prevent absent-mindedness, says Schacter. "But ***be sure the cue is clear and available***," he **cautions**. If you want to remember to take a medication（药物）with lunch, put the pill bottle on the kitchen table — don't leave it in the medicine chest and write yourself a note that you keep in a pocket.

Another common episode of absent-mindedness: walking into a room and wondering why you're there. Most likely, you were thinking about something else. "Everyone does this from time to time," says Zelinski. The best thing to do is to return to where you were before entering the room, and you'll likely remember. (295 words) （2002 年 6 月第 2 篇）

【段落译文】

　　大多数走神的情况——忘记了你把东西放在哪儿了，或你走进一个房间，却不知道为什么进去——这些情况都是由于缺乏注意力造成的。沙科特说："你应该记住某事，但就是没有对它深入地编码。"

　　沙科特解释说，编码是注意某件事物的特殊方法，它对于后来的回忆有重大的影响。未能够恰当地编码会造成麻烦。比如，如果你把手机放进口袋里，但你对所做的这件事情并没有留意，而只注意与别人谈话去了，你就可能会忘记手机放在挂在衣柜中的上衣口袋里。沙科特说："你的记忆力并没有辜负你，而是你没有给你的记忆系统它所需的信息。"

　　缺乏兴趣也同样导致走神。"一个人能背诵 30 年前的体育运动统计数字，"泽林斯基说,"但可能忘记去邮箱投信。"女人比男人的记忆力稍好些,可能是因为她们对周围环境更关注,而记忆力恰恰依赖于这点。

视觉提示可能有助于防止走神,"但这种提示必须是清楚而容易得到的,"沙科特告诫道。如果你想记得午饭时服药,就应该把药瓶放在餐桌上——而不是把它放在药箱里,只写一张便条并把便条放在口袋里。

另一种普遍的走神情况是人们走进一间屋子却不知道为什么去那里,这很可能是你在想别的什么事情。"每个人时不时地都会遇到这种情况,"泽林斯基说。最好的解决办法是回到进屋前所在的地方,很可能你就会记起来。

【难词解释】

episodes 事件,发生	**encode** 编码,译码
impact (on)影响	**annoying** 恼人的,讨厌的
involve (in)潜心于,涉及	**hang** 悬挂
statistics 统计资料	**environment** 环境,外界
cue 提示,暗示,线索	**caution** 告诫,警告

【写译语块】

1. forgetting where you left something or wondering why you just entered a room
   忘记东西放在哪儿或不知道为什么进这个房间
2. be supposed to remember something 应该记得某事
3. have a major impact on recalling it later 对后来的回忆有重大的影响
4. you're involved in a conversation 只注意与别人谈话去了
5. be sure the cue is clear and available 这种提示必须是清楚而容易得到的

【难句分析】

1. (第一段第一句)Most episodes of absent-mindedness — forgetting where you left something or wondering why you just entered a room — are caused by a simple lack of attention. 该句破折号中的两个动词-ing 分句作状语,补充说明主语发生走神的具体情况。
2. (第一段第二句)You're supposed to remember something, but you haven't encoded it deeply. 句中短语 be supposed to do sth. 意为"应该做(而没有做)",是一种特殊的虚拟语气表达形式。
3. (第二段第二句)Failure to encode properly can create **annoying** situations. 名词短语 failure to do sth. 含义为"未能够做某事",在句中作主语,相当于一个动词

不定式或动词-ing 的否定式作主语，即 Not to encode properly ... 或 Failing to encode properly ...

4. (第三段第三句)Women have slightly better memories than men, possibly because they pay more attention to their environment, and memory relies on just that. 该句的从句为原因状语从句，而从句中含两个并列句，即 they pay more attention to their environment 和 memory relies on just that,前者表明女人更关注周围环境,后者强调关注周围环境正是记忆所需要的,从而说明女人的记忆力略比男人稍好些的原因。

【原题再现】

471. Why does the author think that encoding properly is very important?

A) It expands our memory capacity considerably.

B) It helps us understand our memory system better.

C) It slows down the process of losing our memory.

D) It enables us to recall something from our memory.

472. One possible reason why women have better memories than men is that _____.

A) they are more interested in what's happening around them

B) they have an unusual power of focusing their attention

C) they are more reliant on the environment

D) they have a wider range of interests

473. A note in the pocket can hardly serve as a reminder because _____.

A) it might get mixed up with other things

B) it's not clear enough for you to read

C) it will easily get lost

D) it's out of your sight

474. What do we learn from the last paragraph?

A) Repetition helps improve our memory.

B) Memory depends to a certain extent on the environment.

C) If we focus our attention on one thing, we might forget another.

D) If we keep forgetting things, we'd better return to where we were.

475. What is the passage mainly about?

A) The causes of absent-mindedness.

B) A way of encoding and recalling.

C) The process of gradual memory loss.

D) The impact of the environment on memory.

【单词详解】

【重点单词】**impact** / ˈimpækt / *n.* & *v.*

[基本词义] 影响，作用；冲击，碰撞

[用法导航] collapse under the full impact of the blow 受到重击而倒下 // impact of modern science upon society as a whole 现代科学对整个社会的影响 // How will the war impact on such a poet? 战争对这样一个诗人会产生什么影响？ Poverty has a bad impact on people's health. 贫困严重地影响了人们的健康。// The war has impacted the area with military and defense workers. 战争使那个地区挤满了军队和防御工程人员。

[对比记忆] (1) **contact** / ˈkɔntækt / *n.* 接触，联系，交往

(2) **compact** / kɔmˈpækt / *adj.* 紧凑的，小巧的；紧密的，坚实的

(3) **contract** / ˈkɔntrækt / *n.* 合同，契约

(4) **interact** / ˌintərˈækt / *vi.* 相互作用，相互影响

[真题衔接] When the car hit the wall, the _____ broke the windscreen.

A) collision   B) crush   C) impact   D) damage

【句子翻译】

476. （她被大多数人认为是）_____ the most influence member in the organization.

477. An informer supplied the police with _____（涉及这次犯罪的人员名单）.

478. Their aim was to create films _____（能对社会产生积极影响的电影）.

479. Our products are superior in quality _____（比市场上其他品牌）.

480. （如果你未能爱与原谅）_____, you will live your karma to the bitter end.

Passage Forty-nine

In the 1960s, medical researchers Thomas Holmes and Richard Rahe developed a checklist of stressful events. They appreciated the tricky point that any major change can be stressful. Negative events like "serious illness of a family member" *were high on the list*, but *so were some positive life-changing events* like marriage. When you take the Holmes-Rahe test you must remember that the score does not reflect how you deal with stress—it only shows how much you have to deal with. And we now know that the way you handle these events dramatically affects your chances of staying healthy.

By the early 1970s, hundreds of similar studies had followed Holmes and Rahe. And millions of Americans who work and live under **stress** worried over the reports. Somehow, *the research got boiled down to a memorable message*. Women's magazines ran headlines like "Stress causes illness!" If you want to stay physically and mentally healthy, the articles said, avoid stressful events.

But such **simplistic** advice is impossible to follow. Even if stressful events are dangerous, many—like the death of a loved one—are impossible to avoid. Moreover, any warning to avoid all stressful events is a **prescription** (处方) for staying away from **opportunities** as well as trouble. Since any change can be stressful, a person who *wanted to be completely free of stress* would never marry, have a child, take a new job or move.

The notion that all stress makes you sick also ignores a lot of what we know about people. It assumes we're all **vulnerable** (脆弱的) and passive in the face of **adversity** (逆境). But what about human **initiative** and creativity? Many come through periods of stress with more physical and mental **vigor** than they had before. We also know that a long time without change or challenge can lead to **boredom**, and physical and mental **strain**. (320 words) (2002 年 6 月第 3 篇)

【段落译文】

20 世纪 60 年代,医学研究人员托马斯·霍尔姆斯和理查德·雷赫共同研制出一种精神压力事件与健康相关联的核对表。他们明白这一棘手的要点:任何重大变化都会给人造成精神压力。像家庭成员患了重病之类的负面事件位于前列,而像结婚这类正面的生活变化事件也同样位于前列。在接受参加霍尔姆斯·雷赫测试时必须记住:得分并不反映受测者如何对待压力,而只是表示受测者必须应付多少压力。如今,我们已知道处理这些压力事件的方法显著地影响人们保持健康的可能性。

截止到 70 年代早期,数百项类似的研究追随霍尔姆斯和雷赫的研究,数百万在压力下工作、生活的美国人对那些研究报告倍感忧虑。不知什么原因,这些研究被归结为一句令人难忘的信息:"压力会致病",并作为头条新闻刊登在《妇女》杂志上。该文说,要想保持身心健康,必须避免高压力事件。

但这种过分简单的建议难以遵循。即使压力事件是非常危险的,许多——诸如亲人的逝世等——是难以避免的。何况,告诫避免所有压力事件是远离麻烦的

228

良方,同时也失去了许多机会。因为任何变化都可能是有压力的,一个想完全摆脱压力的人就只能永不结婚、永不生子,永不接受新的工作,永不搬家。

　　所有压力都会使人生病的观念同样忽略了很多人类的弱点。它假设在逆境面前,人人都是脆弱和被动的。但人的主动性和创造性怎样了呢? 很多人经历了高压力时期后,身心比以前更具活力了。我们也知道:长时间没有变化或挑战会导致厌倦和身心疲惫。

【难词解释】

stress 压力,紧张   **simplistic** 过分简单化的

prescription 处方   **opportunities** 机遇,机会

vulnerable 脆弱的   **adversity** 逆境

initiative 主动性   **vigor** 活力,精力

boredom 厌倦,令人烦的事物   **strain** 负担,疲惫

【写译语块】

1. be high on the list 名列前茅,名列榜首

2. so were some positive life-changing events 某些正面的生活变化事件

3. by the early 1970s 到 20 世纪 70 年代早期

4. the research got boiled down to a memorable message 这些研究被归结为一句令人难忘的信息

5. want to be completely free of stress 想完全摆脱压力

【难句分析】

1. (第一段第三句)Negative events like "serious illness of a family member" were high on the list, but so were some positive life-changing events like marriage. 该句中的第二个句子是由 so 引起的倒装句,因为在肯定句中,用 so 代替上一句的谓语,表示不同的主语"也……"时,句子要用倒装语序。

2. (第一段第四句)When you take the Holmes-Rahe test you must remember that the score does not reflect how you deal with stress — it only shows how much you have to deal with. 该句是一个多重复合句,when 引导一个时间状语从句,主句是 you must remember . . . ;主句的宾语又是两个宾语从句,即 the score does not reflect how you deal with stress 和 it only shows how much you have to deal with,而两个宾语从句中又分别包含一个宾语从句,即 how you deal with stress 和 how much you have to deal with。

3. (第二段第一句)By the early 1970s, hundreds of similar studies had followed Holmes and Rahe. 由 by 加时间构成的短语,意为"截止(⋯⋯时间),到(⋯⋯时间)为止",主句谓语动词往往要用完成时态,如果该时间为过去时间,则谓语动词要用过去完成时态,例如:在 The millions of calculations involved, had they been done by hand, would have lost all practical value by the time they were finished(这数百万次计算如果用手工计算,到完成时这些计算已没有任何实际价值了)中,如果该时间为将来时间,则谓语动词要用将来完成时态,例如:By the time of 2015, there will have been added to the earth about 6,500,000,000 people(到 2015 年,地球上的人数将增加到 65 亿)。

4. (第二段第二句)在 Somehow, the research got boiled down to a memorable message 中,短语 boiled down to 含义为"归结为,归纳起来",get boiled down to 为被动结构。

【原题再现】

481. The result of Holmes-Rahe's medical research tells us _____.

   A) what should be done to avoid stress

   B) what kind of event would cause stress

   C) how to cope with sudden changes in life

   D) the way you handle major events may cause stress

482. The studies on stress in the early 1970's led to _____.

   A) popular avoidance of stressful jobs

   B) widespread concern over its harmful effects

   C) an intensive research into stress-related illnesses

   D) great panic over the mental disorder it could cause

483. The score of the Holmes-Rahe test shows _____.

   A) how much pressure you are under

   B) how stressful a major event can be

   C) how positive events can change your life

   D) how you can deal with life-changing events

484. Why is "such simplistic advice" (Sentence 1, Para. 3), impossible to follow?

   A) You could be missing opportunities as well.

   B) No one can stay on the same job for long.

   C) No prescription is effective in relieving stress.

   D) People have to get married someday.

485. According to the passage people who have experienced ups and downs may become _____.

A) physically and mentally strained

B) nervous when faced with difficulties

C) more capable of coping with adversity

D) indifferent toward what happens to them

【单词详解】

【重点单词】**stress** / stres / *n.* & *vt.*

[基本词义] *n.* 压力，紧张；强调，重要性；应力；重音 *vt.* 强调，着重，重读

[用法导航] lay / place / put stress on 把重点放在……上；在……上用力 // under the stress of poverty 在贫困的压力下 // Worry over his job and his wife's health put him under a great stress. 对自己工作及妻子健康问题的忧虑使他陷于过分的紧张中。 // She is under stress because she has too much work to do. 她的压力很大，因为她的工作太多，做不完。

[词性转换] **stressful** / 'stresful / *adj.* 紧张的，压力大的

[对比记忆] (1) **emphasis** / 'emfəsis / *n.* 强调，重点

(2) **tension** / 'tenʃən / *n.* 紧张，紧张状态；拉紧，绷紧；张力，拉力

(3) **pressure** / 'preʃə / *n.* 压(力)，压强；强制，压迫

(4) **anxiety** / æŋ'zaiəti / *n.* 焦急，挂虑；渴望，热望

[真题衔接] Financial hardship places severe _____ on married couples, but it does not usually cause divorce by itself.

A) stress   B) crisis   C) horror   D) raid

【重点单词】**strain** / strein / *n.*

[基本词义] 拉紧；极度紧张；扭伤，拉伤；(pl.)旋律；品质；气质，个性特点

[用法导航] suffer from mental, nervous strain 精神、神经极度紧张 // the strain of managing both a family and a career 既要持家又要照顾好工作的巨大负担 // hear the strain of the church organ 听到教堂风琴演奏的音乐 // strain to reach the finish line 努力到达终点 // strain one's ear to hear a conversation 聚精会神地听别人交谈 // strain a muscle, one's heart 肌肉、心肌劳损 // The rope broke under the strain. 绳子拉断了。

[词性转换] **strain** / strein / *vt.* 扭伤，拉伤；使紧张；拉紧，绷紧 *vi.* 尽力，努力

[对比记忆] (1) **restrain** / ris'trein / *vt.* 阻止，控制；抑制，遏制

(2) **constrain** / kən'strein / *vt.* 限制，约束；克制，抑制

(3) **tension** / ˈtenʃən / *n.* 紧张，紧张状态；拉紧，绷紧；张力，拉力

[真题衔接] She married a man of different religion, and that ＿＿＿＿＿ her relationship with her parents.

A) transformed   B) strained   C) violated   D) distressed

【句子翻译】

486. ＿＿＿＿＿＿（截止到本月底），we surely will have found a satisfactory solution to the problem.

487. John had been working hard and ＿＿＿＿＿＿（他的弟弟也是如此）.

488. Learning English ＿＿＿＿＿＿（能总结为三个简单的因素）：persistence, proper ways and good teachers.

489. He said that the driver must have had an accident; otherwise ＿＿＿＿＿＿（到那时他应该到达了）.

490. Tom is diligent and in the final exam ＿＿＿＿＿＿（他第三次名列榜首）.

Passage Fifty

The fitness movement that began *in the late* 1960*s and early* 1970*s* centered around **aerobic** exercise（有氧操）. Millions of individuals *became engaged in a variety of aerobic activities*, and literally thousands of health **spas** developed around the country to **capitalize**（获利）on this **emerging** interest in fitness, particularly aerobic dancing for females. A number of fitness spas existed prior to this aerobic fitness movement, even a national chain with spas in most major cities. However, their *focus was not on aerobics*, *but rather on weight-training programs* designed to develop **muscular** mass, strength, and **endurance** in their primarily male **enthusiasts**. These fitness spas did not seem to benefit financially from the aerobic fitness movement to better health, since *medical opinion suggested that* weight-training programs offered few, if any, health benefits. In recent years, however, weight training has again become increasingly **popular** for males and for females. Many current programs focus not only on developing muscular strength and endurance but on aerobic fitness as well.

Historically, most physical-fitness tests have usually included measures of muscular strength and endurance, not for health-related reasons, but primarily because such fitness **components** have been related to performance in athletics. However, in recent years, evidence has shown that training programs designed primarily to improve muscular strength and endurance might also offer some health benefits as well. The American College of Sports Medicine now ***recommends that weight training be part of a total fitness program*** for healthy Americans. Increased participation in such training is one of the specific physical activity and fitness objectives of Healthy People 2000, National Health Promotion and Disease Prevention Objectives. (273 words)　（2002 年 6 月第 4 篇）

【段落译文】

　　有氧气操是始于 20 世纪 60 年代末、70 年代初的健身运动的核心。数以百万计的人热衷于各种各样的有氧活动。事实上,数以千计的健身房在全国建立起来并利用人们的健身活动从中获利,因为这种新兴的健身活动,尤其是为女士的有氧舞蹈,倍受人们的喜爱。在这种有氧健身运动出现之前,就有很多健身中心了,甚至在大都市出现了全国健身中心连锁店。但是他们的注意力不在有氧运动,而主要在为男性体育爱好者锻炼肌肉、力量和耐力而设立的增重运动上。这些健身中心似乎没有从有氧健身中获利,因为医学界认为增重运动很少增强健康,即使有也是微乎其微。但近年来,增重训练又变得越来越受男士们和女士们的欢迎。现在的训练计划不仅把重点放在肌肉力量和耐力的培养上,而且也放在有氧运动上。

　　从历史的观点来看,大多数健康检查通常包括肌肉力量和耐力的测量,主要是因为这种健康成分与运动员的成绩有关,而不是与健康有关的原因。然而,近年来,有证据表明,那种设计主要是为了增强肌肉力量和耐力的培训可能对健康也有益处。所以,美国运动医学学会提倡举重训练应是健康的美国人总体健身计划的一部分。让越来越多的人参加这种举重锻炼是具体的体育活动和 2000 年健康人的健身目标之一:促进全民健康和预防疾病。

【难词解释】

aerobic 需氧的;增氧健身法的

capitalize 获利

muscular 肌肉(发达)的,强健的

enthusiasts 狂热者,爱好者

components 成分,部件

spas (有体育锻炼和沐浴设施的)游乐场

emerging 新兴的

endurance 耐力,忍耐

popular 受欢迎的,喜爱的

recommend 推荐,建议

【写译语块】

1. in the late 1960s and early 1970s 在 20 世纪 60 年代末、70 年代初

2. (be) engaged in a variety of aerobic activities 热衷于各种各样的有氧活动

3. focus was not on aerobics, but rather on weight-training programs 注意力不在有氧运动,而是在举重运动上

4. medical opinion suggested that 医学界认为

5. recommend that weight training be part of a total fitness program 提倡举重训练应是总体健身计划的一部分

【难句分析】

1. (第一段第二句)Millions of individuals became engaged in a variety of aerobic activities, and literally thousands of health spas developed around the country to capitalize on this emerging interest in fitness, particularly aerobic dancing for females. 该句是一个简单的并列句,结构不复杂,但修饰成分比较多,应该特别给予注意;短语 became engaged in 的含义为"忙于,热衷于",a variety of 的含义为"各种各样的",capitalize on 含义为"利用……获利";副词 particularly 引起的副词短语作状语,作补充说明,起强调的意义,含有"尤其从女士的健身操中获利"之意。

2. (第一段第四句)在 These fitness spas did not seem to benefit financially from the aerobic fitness movement to better health, since medical opinion suggested that weight-training programs offered few, if any, health benefits 中, since 引导一个原因状语从句,对主句所阐述的"健身中心似乎没有从有氧健身中获利"的原因进行说明;动词 suggest 的含义为"认为",所引导的宾语从句不需用"(should＋)动词原形"虚拟语气结构;if any 是一个省略结构,原句是 if it offered any health benefits。

3. (第二段第三句)在 The American College of Sports Medicine now recommends that weight training be part of a total fitness program for healthy Americans 中,动词 recommend 意为"推荐,建议",所引导的宾语从句通常要求用"(should＋动词原形"的虚拟结构,暗含"应该是……但目前还不是……"之意,类似的动词还有 request, advise, command, consent, decide, demand, desire, insist, maintain, move, order, propose, recommend, require, suggest, urge, vote, ask 等,比如:We desire that the tour leader inform us immediately of any change in plans(我们希望导游负责人及时告知我们计划的变更情况)。

4. (第二段第四句)在 Increased participation in such training is one of the specific physical activity and fitness objectives of Healthy People 2000, National Health Promotion and Disease Prevention Objectives 中,短语 one of the n. 含义为"……之一",短语中的名词必须用复数形式,但该句中的 one of the objec-

tives of Healthy People 2000(2000 年健康人的目标之一)结构被其修饰语 spe-cific physical activity and fitness 分隔开了。

【原题再现】

491. The word "spas" (Sentence 2, Para. 1) most probably refers to _____.
     A) sports activities
     B) recreation centers
     C) athletic training programs
     D) places for physical exercise

492. Early fitness spas were intended mainly for _____.
     A) the promotion of aerobic exercise
     B) the improvement of women's figures
     C) endurance and muscular development
     D) better performance in aerobic dancing

493. What was the attitude of doctors towards weight training in health improvement?
     A) Negative.
     B) Cautious.
     C) Positive.
     D) Indifferent.

494. People were given physical fitness tests in order to find out _____.
     A) what kind of fitness center was suitable for them
     B) whether they were fit for aerobic exercise
     C) what their health condition was like
     D) how well they could do in athletics

495. Recent studies have suggested that weight training _____.
     A) has become an essential part of people's life
     B) will attract more people in the days to come
     C) contributes to health improvement as well
     D) may well affect the health of the trainees

【单词详解】

【重点单词】endurance / inˈdjurəns / n.

[基本词义] 忍耐(力),持久(力),耐久(性)

[用法导航] beyond / past endurance 忍不住,不可耐,忍无可忍 // come to the end of one's endurance 已不能再忍受,忍无可忍 // test a runner's endurance 检测一个跑步运动员的耐力 // Sailing the Atlantic single-handed requires great endurance. 一个人驾驶帆船驶过大西洋需要极大的耐力。//

Through hard work and endurance, we will complete this project. 通过努力工作和坚持，我们将会完成这项方案。

[词性转换] **endure** / in'djuə / *vt.* 忍受，容忍 *vi.* 忍受，容忍，耐住；持久，持续

[对比记忆] **patience** / 'peiʃəns / *n.* 忍耐，耐心

[真题衔接] Sailing the Atlantic single-handed required great _____.

    A) foundation   B) qualification   C) incentive   D) endurance

【重点单词】 **recommend** / rekə'mend / *vt.*

[基本词义] 推荐，举荐；劝告，建议；使成为可取，使受欢迎

[用法导航] recommend sb. for the job 推荐某人做那项工作 // recommend extreme caution 奉劝多加小心 // a plan with nothing to recommend it 毫无可取之处的计划 // a plan with much to recommend it 有多种可取之处的计划 // I recommend you meeting him first. 我建议你先见他。

[词性转换] **recommendation** / ˌrekəmen'deiʃən / *n.* 推荐，推荐信；劝告；优点，长处

[对比记忆] (1) **advocate** / 'ædvəkeit / *vt.* 拥护，提倡，主张

    (2) **oppose** / ə'pəuz / *vt.* 反对，反抗

    (3) **commend** / kə'mend / *vt.* 表扬，称赞；推荐

[真题衔接] The headmistress agreed to _____ the teacher's proposals to the school governess.

    A) communicate B) transfer   C) render   D) recommend

【句子翻译】

496. The speaker gave us a sketch of _____(19世纪90年代的生活概况).

497. He is a clerk in a bank, at the same time, he _____(一直在从事小说的写作).

498. It is recommended that _____(才开始这项工作)until all the preparations have been made.

499. It is advisable that you should _____(最好现在开始专心学习)as you have wasted so much time.

500. Statistics suggest that the population of this country _____(十年内将翻一番).

Passage Fifty-one

Some **pessimistic** experts feel that the automobile *is bound to fall into disuse.*

They see a day *in the not-too-distant future* when all autos will be abandoned and allowed to rust. Other authorities, however, think the auto is here to stay. They hold that the car will remain a leading means of urban travel in the foreseeable future.

The motorcar will undoubtedly change significantly over the next 30 years. It should become smaller, safer, and more **economical**, and should not be powered by the gasoline engine. The car of the future should be far more *pollution-free* than present types.

Regardless of its power source, the auto in the future will still be the main problem in urban traffic **congestion**. One proposed solution to this problem is the automated highway system.

When the auto enters the highway system, a **retractable** arm will drop from the auto and *make contact with* a rail, which *is similar to* those powering subway trains electrically. *Once attached to the rail*, the car will become electrically powered from the system, and control of the vehicle will pass to a central computer. The computer will then **monitor** all of the car's movements.

The driver will use a telephone to dial instructions about his destination into the system. The computer will calculate the best route, and reserve space for the car all the way to the correct exit from the highway. The driver will then be free to relax and wait for the **buzzer** that will warn him of his coming exit. It is estimated that an automated highway will be able to handle 10,000 vehicles per hour, *compared with* the 1,500 to 2,000 vehicles that can be carried by a present-day highway. (271 words) （2001 年 12 月第 1 篇）

【段落译文】

　　一些悲观的专家感到汽车注定要被废弃。他们看到不久的将来所有的汽车都会被抛弃,任其生锈。然而,别的权威们认为汽车还会存在。他们认为在可预见的未来,汽车仍将是城市交通的主要手段。

　　在以后的 30 年间汽车毫无疑问会有重大变化。它应该变得更小、更安全和更经济,而且不应当由汽油发动机驱动。未来的汽车应当比现在的汽车更无污染。

　　无论用什么能源,将来的汽车都将依然是城市交通拥挤的主要问题。对这个问题提出的一个解决办法就是自动公路系统。

　　当汽车进入公路系统,一支伸缩臂从车上落下与铁轨接触,这种铁轨同给地下列车供电的铁轨相似。一旦与铁轨连接,汽车就由系统供电,汽车的操纵交给中心计算机,然后计算机将监控汽车的一切状况。

驾驶员将用电话将目的地的指令拨入监控系统。计算机将计算出最佳线路并且为汽车预留通道,使它一路畅通直达正确的公路出口。然后司机可以自由休息,只等蜂鸣器提醒他到了出口。估计自动公路每小时能够运送一万辆车,而现在的公路每小时只能运送 1500 辆~2000 辆。

【难词释义】

pessimistic 悲观(主义)的　　　　　　　**economical** 节约的,省俭的,经济的

congestion 拥挤　　　　　　　　　　　　**retractable** 可伸缩的

monitor 监测,检测　　　　　　　　　　　**buzzer** 蜂鸣器

【写译语块】

1. be bound to fall into disuse 注定被废弃

2. in the not-too-distant future 不远的将来

3. pollution-free 没有污染的

4. regardless of its power source 无论用什么能源

5. make contact with a rail 接触铁轨

6. be similar to 与……相似

7. once attached to the rail 一旦接触铁轨

8. compared with 与……相比

【难句分析】

1. (第四段第二句)在 Once attached to the rail, the car will become electrically powered from the system, and control of the vehicle will pass to a central computer 中,从句使用了"连词+过去分词结构",使用此类结构的条件是从句主语与主句主语一致,从句为被动语态。再如:Wait until (you are) called(等到有人叫你)。

2. (第五段最后一句)It is estimated that an automated highway will be able to handle 10,000 vehicles per hour, *compared with* the 1,500 to 2,000 vehicles that can be carried by a present-day highway. 该句为主语从句,句首的 it 为形式主语,真正的主语是后面的 that 分句。

【原题再现】

501. One significant improvement in the future car will probably be _____.

238

A) its power source B) its driving system

C) its monitoring system D) its seating capacity

502. What is the author's main concern?

A) How to render automobiles pollution-free.

B) How to make smaller and safer automobiles.

C) How to solve the problem of traffic jams.

D) How to develop an automated subway system.

503. What provides autos with electric power in an automated highway system?

A) A rail. B) An engine.

C) A retractable arm. D) A computer controller.

504. In an automated highway system, all the driver needs to do is _____.

A) keep in the right lane

B) wait to arrive at his destination

C) keep in constant touch with the computer center

D) inform the system of his destination by phone

505. What is the author's attitude toward the future of autos?

A) Enthusiastic. B) Pessimistic.

C) Optimistic. D) Cautious.

【单词详解】

【重点单词】**bound** / baund / *adj.*

[基本词义] 一定的,必然的;受约束的,有义务的;(for, to)准备到……去的,开往
（或驶往）……的

[用法导航] It was an absurd arrangement, and bound to lead to catastrophe. 这
是一种荒唐的安排,注定会导致灾难。// Appreciation of works of art is
bound to be dominated by a particular kind of interest. 对于艺术作品的欣
赏必然受到一种特殊的兴趣爱好的支配。// On the liner bound for Amsterdam people are always filled with anticipation. 在驶向阿姆斯特丹的客
轮上,人们心里都满怀期待。

[对比记忆]（1）**abound** / ə'baund / *vi.* 大量存在;(in, with)充满,富于

（2）**pound** / paund / *n.* 磅;英镑 *v.* (连续)猛击,(猛烈)捣打,捣碎

[真题衔接] Children are _____ to have some accidents as they grow up.
（CET6-9001）

A) obvious B) indispensable C) bound D) doubtless

【重点单词】**power** / ˈpauə / *n. & vt.*

[基本词义] *n.* 权力;精力;动力;强国 *vt.* 给……提供动力,使开动

[用法导航] She agreed to buy the car, but stipulated racing tyres and a turbo-powered engine. 她同意买这车,但规定要装赛车车轮和涡轮动力引擎。// The tractor is powered by a diesel engine. 这台牵引机是用柴油机发动的。// An air ship powered by energy from the sun has been suggested. 还有人建议用太阳能作动力来驱动飞艇。

[词性转换] **powerful** / ˈpauəful / *adj.* 强大的,有力的,有权的;强壮的,强健的

[对比记忆] (1) **tower** / ˈtauə / *n.* 塔,高楼 *vi.* (above, over)高于,优于

(2) **energy** / ˈenədʒi / *n.* 活力,干劲,精力;能,能量,能源

(3) **strength** / streŋθ / *n.* 力,力气;实力,力量;强度,浓度

【重点单词】**attach** / əˈtætʃ / *vt.*

[基本词义] 系,贴,连接;使依恋,使喜爱;认为有(重要性、责任等);使附属

[用法导航] attach the horse to a tree 将马拴在树上 // Do you attach any importance to what he said? 你认为他说的话重要吗? // We should attach primary importance to the development of economy. 我们要把发展经济的工作放在第一位。// The hospital is attached to that university. 这医院附属于那所大学。

[对比记忆] (1) **glue** / gluː / *n.* 胶,胶水 *vt.* 粘合,粘贴

(2) **label** / ˈleibl / *n.* 标签,标记;称号 *vt.* 贴标签于;把……称为

(3) **affiliate** / əˈfilieit / *vt.* 使隶属(或附属)于

[真题衔接] As far as the rank of concerned an associate profess is _____ to a professor though they are almost equally knowledgeable. (CET6-9601)

A) attached   B) subsidiary   C) previous   D) inferior

【句子翻译】

506. Competition is seen as an open and fair race where success goes to the swiftest person _____(不管他的社会阶级背景).

507. Her mind was too simple to separate things from professions, and she _____(对人的名号看得分外认真).

508. _____(这出戏注定失败); the plot excites little interest or curiosity.

509. Living in a town can't _____(在许多方面比不上在乡村生活).

510. Similarly, we feel comfortable with _____(身体素质与我们相似的人).

Passage Fifty-two

Foxes and farmers have never ***got on well***. These small dog-like animals have long been ***accused of*** killing farm animals. They ***are*** officially ***classified as*** harmful and farmers try to ***keep their numbers down*** by shooting or poisoning them.

Farmers can also ***call on the services of their local hunt*** to control the fox population. Hunting consists of pursuing a fox across the countryside, with a group of specially trained dogs, followed by men and women riding horses. When the dogs eventually catch the fox they kill it or a hunter shoots it.

People who take part in hunting ***think of it as a sport***; they wear a special uniform of red coats and white trousers, and ***follow strict codes of behavior***. But owning a horse and hunting regularly is expensive, so most hunters are wealthy.

It is estimated that up to 100,000 people watch or take part in fox hunting. But over the last couple of decades the number of people ***opposed to fox hunting***, because they think it is **brutal**, has risen sharply. Nowadays it is rare for a hunt to pass off without some kind of **confrontation** between hunters and hunt **saboteurs**. Sometimes these incidents ***lead to violence***, but mostly saboteurs ***interfere with the hunt*** by misleading riders and disturbing the **trail** of the fox's smell, which the dogs follow.

Noisy confrontations between hunters and saboteurs have become so common that they are almost as much a part of hunting as the pursuit of foxes itself. But this year supporters of fox hunting face a much bigger threat to their sport. A Labor Party Member of the Parliament, Mike Foster, is trying to get Parliament to approve a new law which will make the hunting of wild animals with dogs illegal. If the law is passed, wild animals like foxes will be protected under the ban in Britain. (321 words) （2001 年 12 月第 2 篇）

【段落译文】

狐狸和农场主从来就不能和睦相处。这些小的像狗的动物长期因咬死农场动物而受到谴责。狐狸被正式划为有害动物,农场主通过枪死和毒杀减少它们的数量。

农场主还可以要求当地人帮助追猎以控制狐狸的数量。追猎就是用一群经专门训练的狗在乡村追杀狐狸,后面跟着骑马的男人和女人。当狗终于抓住狐狸的时候,狗咬死它或者猎人枪杀它。

参加追猎的人把它看成是一项运动，他们穿着红上衣白裤子的特别制服，严格遵守一些规则行动。但拥有一匹马和定期追猎的费用很昂贵，所以大多数猎手都是有钱人。

据估计有高达十万人观看或者参与追猎狐狸。但是最近几十年反对猎杀狐狸的人数急剧上升，因为他们认为这样做很残酷。现在几乎没有哪一次狩猎不因狩猎者和阻拦者之间发生某种冲突而告终。有时这些事件导致暴力，但大多数阻拦者都是通过误导骑马的或打乱猎犬跟踪的狐狸嗅迹来干预狩猎。

狩猎者和阻拦者之间发生的喧嚣冲突很寻常，几乎成为整个狩猎过程中与追捕狐狸本身同等重要的一部分。但是今年猎狐支持者面临着更大威胁。议会工党员迈克·福斯特力图让议会批准一项使用狗来猎取野生动物为非法的新法律。如果这项法律被批准通过，像狐狸这样的野生动物将在英国禁止令下得到保护。

【难词释义】

brutal 残酷的　　　　　　　　　　**confrontation** 冲突

saboteurs 阻拦者　　　　　　　　　**trail** 痕迹，足迹，踪迹

【写译语块】

1. get on well 相处融洽
2. be accused of killing farm animals 因咬死农场动物而受到谴责
3. be classified as 被归为……
4. keep their numbers down 控制它们的数量
5. call on the services of their local hunt 寻求当地猎人的帮助
6. think of it as a sport 把它看成一项运动
7. follow strict codes of behavior 严格遵守行为规则
8. be opposed to fox hunting 反对猎杀狐狸
9. lead to violence 导致暴力冲突
10. interfere with the hunt 干预狩猎

【难句分析】

1. （第四段第二句）在 But over the last couple of decades the number of people opposed to fox hunting, because they think it is brutal, has risen sharply 中，because 引出的原因状语被放在句子中间，形成分割结构，即将主句主语 the number of people opposed to fox hunting 与主句谓语动词 has risen 分开，opposed to fox hunting 用作定语，修饰先行名词 people，可实际上是由从句 who

are opposed to fox hunting 改写而来。

2. （第五段第一句）在 Noisy confrontations between hunters and saboteurs have become so common that they are almost as much a part of hunting as the pursuit of foxes itself 中使用了 as ... as ... 引出的同等比较结构。

【原题再现】

511. Rich people in Britain have been hunting foxes _____.

    A) for recreation   B) in the interests of the farmers

    C) to limit the fox population   D) to show off their wealth

512. What is special about fox hunting in Britain?

    A) It involves the use of a deadly poison.

    B) It is a costly event which rarely occurs.

    C) The hunters have set rules to follow.

    D) The hunters have to go through strict training.

513. Fox hunting opponents often interfere in the game _____.

    A) by resorting to violence   B) by confusing the fox hunters

    C) by taking legal action   D) by demonstrating on the scene

514. A new law may be passed by the Britain Parliament to _____

    A) prohibit farmers from hunting foxes

    B) forbid hunting foxes with dogs

    C) stop hunting wild animals in the countryside

    D) prevent large-scale fox hunting

515. It can be inferred from the passage that _____

    A) killing foxes with poison is illegal

    B) limiting the fox population is unnecessary

    C) hunting foxes with dogs is considered cruel and violent

    D) fox-hunting often leads to confrontation between the poor and the rich

【单词详解】

【重点单词】**classify** / ˈklæsifai / *vt.*

[基本词义] 把……分类,把……分级

[用法导航] The biologist classified the big plant as a flower, not a tree. 生物学家把那种大的植物分类为花草,而非树木。// The books in the library are classified according to subjects. 图书馆的书是根据学科分类的。// Would you classify her novels as serious literature or as more entertainments? 你认为她的小说属于文学类呢,还是属于通俗读物类?

[词性转换] **classification** / ˌklæsifiˈkeiʃən / *n.* 分类,分级;类别,级别

[对比记忆] **sort** / sɔːt / *vt.* 分类,整理

[真题衔接] Men in the post office _____ mail according to places where it is to go.

    A) classify   B) deliver   C) transport   D) arrange

【重点单词】 **interfere** / ˌintəˈfiə / *vi.*

[基本词义] (with, in)干涉,介入;妨碍,干扰

[用法导航] Any nation that interferes in the internal affairs of another nation should be universally condemned. 任何一个干涉他国内政的国家都应该普遍受到谴责。// Don't interfere with him. He's preparing for the final exams. 他在为期末考试作准备,不要打扰他。// Complete absorption in sport interfered with his studies. 对体育活动的极度迷恋妨碍了他的学业。

[词性转换] **interference** / ˌintəˈfiərəns / *n.* 干涉,介入;阻碍,干扰

[对比记忆] (1) **intervene** / ˌintəˈviːn / *vi.* 干涉,干预;干扰,阻挠

    (2) **interrupt** / ˌintəˈrʌpt / *vt.* 打断,打扰;中止,阻碍

[真题衔接] Mary said that her mother _____ in her adult life and treated her like a child.

    A) troubled   B) disturbed   C) interfered   D) annoyed

【句子翻译】

516. The atmosphere is as much a part of the earth _____(就像地球的土壤和湖泊、河流和海洋的水那样).

517. _____(他起初反对这个计划), but we managed to argue him round.

518. My brother the Duke of Clarence is the elder brother, and has certainly the right to marry if he chooses, and I _____(无论如何不干涉他).

519. Be conscientious, any mistake _____(会导致整个试验的失败).

520. You know, if you really want to be someone, you _____(需要学会和人们相处融洽).

Passage Fifty-three

For an increasing number of students at American universities, Old is suddenly in. The reason is obvious: the graying of America means jobs. *Coupled with* the aging of the **baby-boom** generation, a longer life span means that the nation's elderly population is bound to expand significantly over the next 50 years. By 2050, 25 percent of all Americans will be older than 65, up from 14 percent in 1995. The change poses *profound questions* for government and society, of course. But it also creates *career opportunities in medicine* and health professions, and in law and business as well. "In addition to the doctors, we're going to need more sociologists, biologists, urban planners and specialized lawyers," says Professor Edward Schneider of the University of Southern California's (USC) School of **Gerontology**.

Lawyers can *specialize in* "elder law," which covers everything from trusts and estates to nursing home abuse and age **discrimination**. Businessmen see *huge opportunities in the elder market* because the baby boomers, 74 million strong, are likely to be the wealthiest group of retirees in human history. "Any student who combines an expert knowledge in gerontology with, say, an MBA or law degree will have a license to print money," one professor says.

Margarite Santors is a 21-year-old senior at USC. She began college as a biology major but found she was "really *bored with* bacteria", so she took a class in gerontology and discovered that she liked it. She says, "I did volunteer work in retirement homes and it was very satisfying." (264 words)　（2001 年 12 月第 3 篇）

【段落译文】

对越来越多的美国大学生来说,老年学突然时髦起来。理由很明显:美国的人口老龄化意味一些就业机会。随着生育高峰一代的老龄化,人的寿命延长就意味着全国老年人口在今后 50 年内必然有相当大的增长。到 2050 年,65 岁以上的美国人将从 1995 年的 14％增长到 25％。当然,这种变化给政府和社会提出一些深刻的问题。但是这也给医药卫生界以及法律和商业界创造了就业机会。南加利弗尼亚大学老年学学院的爱德华·施奈德说:"除了大夫,我们将迫切需要有更多的社会学家、生物学家、城市规划人员和专业律师"。

律师可以成为"老年人法"专家,"老年人法"包括从财产委托、房地产到敬老院虐待和年龄歧视。商人在老年人市场看到巨大的商机,因为生育高峰期人数高达七千四百万的产儿很可能将成为人类历史上最富有的退休群体。一位教授说:"任何学生只要有老年学的专门知识,再有一个学位,例如工商管理学硕士或法律学位,就如同有印制钞票的许可证一般"。

玛格丽特·桑托斯是南加利弗尼亚大学的一名 21 岁的四年级学生。她上大学时是个生物学学生，但是她发现了"实在厌烦细菌"。所以她上了一堂老年学课程，发现很喜欢这门课程。她说："我在退休老人福利院做志愿者，这使我非常满意"。

【难词释义】

baby-boom 生育高峰　　　　　　　　　　**gerontology** 老年学
discrimination 歧视

【写译语块】

1. be coupled with 伴随，与……结对
2. profound questions 深刻的问题
3. career opportunities in medicine 医学方面的就业机会
4. specialize in 主修，主攻
5. huge opportunities in the elder market 老年市场方面的巨大商机
6. be bored with 对……感到厌烦

【难句分析】

1. （第一段第二句）在 Coupled with the aging of the baby-boom generation, a longer life span means that the nation's elderly population is bound to expand significantly over the next 50 years 中，词组 coupled with 的本意是"与……结对"，此处理解为"伴随"，aging 是动词 age（老化）的动名词修饰，life span 的意思是"寿命"，be bound to 的意思是"注定，一定"。

2. （第二段最后）一句在 Any student who combines an expert knowledge in gerontology with, say, an MBA or law degree will have a license to print money 中，say 表示列举，表示此意时，经常出现在句中，形成分割结构。再如：You may learn to play the violin in, say, three years. （你可以，比如说，在三年内学会拉小提琴）。

【原题再现】

521. "… Old is suddenly in" (Sentence 1, Para. 1) most probably means "_____".

　　A) Gerontology has suddenly become popular

　　B) America has suddenly become a nation of old people

C) More elderly professors are found on American campuses

D) American college have realized the need of enrolling older students

522. With the aging of America, lawyers can benefit _____.

A) from the adoption of the "elder law"

B) by enriching their professional knowledge

C) from rendering special services to the elderly

D) by winning the trust of the elderly to promote their own interests

523. Why can businessmen make money in the emerging elder market?

A) Retirees are more generous in spending money.

B) They can employ more gerontologists.

C) There are more elderly people working than before.

D) The elderly possess an enormous purchasing power.

524. Who can make big money in the new century according to the passage?

A) Retirees who are business-minded.

B) The volunteer workers in retirement homes.

C) College graduates with an MBA or law degree.

D) Professionals with a good knowledge of gerontology.

525. It can be seen from the passage that the expansion of America's elderly population _____.

A) will create new fields of study in universities

B) will impose an unbearable burden on society

C) will provide good job opportunities in many areas

D) may lead to nursing home abuse and age discrimination

【单词详解】

【重点单词】**expand** / iksˈpænd / *v.*

［基本词义］扩大,扩张,扩展;膨胀

［用法导航］The gas will expand with the temperature increasing. 气体随着温度增加而膨胀。// As a result of their rise in temperature almost any substances expands. 由于温度升高,几乎任何物体都膨胀了。// His modest business finally expanded into a supermarket empire. 他原先不大的生意扩展成了超级市场集团企业。// Irons expands when it is heated. 铁加热时就膨胀。

［词性转换］(1)**expansion** / iksˈpænʃən / *n.* 扩大,扩张,扩展;膨胀

(2)**expansive** / iks'pænsiv / *adj.* 扩张的；辽阔的，广阔的

[对比记忆] (1) **expend** / iks'pend / *vt.* 花费，消费，消耗

(2) **extend** / iks'tend / *vt.* 延伸，延长；扩展，扩大；提供，给予，发出

(3) **magnify** / 'mægnifai / *vt.* 放大，扩大；夸大，夸张

(4) **swell** / swel / *vi.* 肿胀，膨胀，鼓起；增强，增多，扩大

(5) **enlarge** / in'lɑːdʒ / *v.* 扩大，扩展，扩充；放大

[真题衔接] The board of the company has decided to _____ its operations to include all aspects of the clothing business. (CET4-0406)

A) multiply　　　B) lengthen　　　C) expand　　　D) stretch

【重点单词】**profound** / prə'faund / *adj.*

[基本词义] 深度的，深切的，深远的；知识渊博的，见解深刻的；深奥的

[用法导航] We had a profound lesson in ideological education yesterday. 昨天我们上了一堂深刻的思想教育课。 // The old man had a profound faith in the power of truth. 那位老人深信真理的力量。 // A philosopher's profound insights into life inspire his readers. 一位哲人对生命的深邃见解启迪了他的读者们。

[对比记忆] (1) **deep** / diːd / *adj.* 深的，厚的；深切的，强烈的；深刻的，深奥的

(2) **versatile** / 'vəːsətail / *adj.* 多才多艺的，有多种技能的；有多种用途的

[真题衔接] Young people's social environment has a _____ effect on their academic progress. (CET6-9306)

A) gross　　　B) solid　　　C) complete　　　D) profound

【句子翻译】

526. After qualifying, Thomas followed his parents' advice and _____（专门从事合同法业务）.

527. I _____（在农村待得厌倦了）. Let's go off to the bright lights and see a film or a show.

528. Increase the temperature of the gas _____（气体将会膨胀）.

529. This is interesting because the immigrant _____（有深远的影响）the character of our native newspapers.

530. _____（乐观者在每一场灾难中都看到机遇）and a pessimist sees a calamity in every opportunity.

Passage Fifty-four

The decline in moral standards — which has long concerned social analysis

— has at last *captured the attention of* average Americans. And Jean Bethke Elshtain, for one, is glad.

The fact that ordinary citizens are now starting to think seriously about the nation's *moral climate*, says this **ethics** professor at the University of Chicago, is reason to hope that new ideas will come forward to improve it.

But the challenge is not to be underestimated. Materialism and individualism in American society are the biggest **obstacles**, "The thought that I'm in it for me' has *become deeply rooted in* the national consciousness," Ms. Elshtain says.

Some of this can *be attributed to* the **disintegration** of traditional communities, in which neighbors looked out for one another, she says. With today's greater mobility and with so many couples working, those **bonds** have been weakened, replaced by a greater emphasis on self.

In a 1996 poll of Americans, loss of morality topped the list of the biggest problems facing the U. S. And Elshtain says the public is correct to sense that: Data show that Americans are struggling with problems unheard of in the 1950s, such as classroom violence and a high rate of births to unmarried mothers.

The desire for a higher moral standard is not a **lament** for some nonexistent "golden age" Elshtain says, nor is it a **wishful** longing for a time that denied opportunities to women and minorities. Most people, in fact, favor the **lessening** of **prejudice**.

Moral decline will not be **reversed** until people find ways to **counter** the materialism in society, she says, "Slowly, you recognize that the things that matter are those that can't be bought. " （2001 年 12 月第 4 篇）

【段落译文】

社会分析家关注很久的道德水准下降问题终于引起了普通美国人的注意。作为一名社会分析家,简·比思克·艾尔斯顿很高兴。

普通美国公民现在已经开始严肃思考国民道德风气问题,这使我们有理由希望会产生新思想以改进这种状况,芝加哥大学伦理教授说。

但是不要低估这种挑战。美国社会的功利主义者是两个最大的障碍。艾尔斯顿女士说:"'我干这事是为自己的'思想深深植根于民族意识之中"。

她说:其中某些方面应归咎于邻里之间的互相关照的传统社区的解体。由于当今流动性更大,很多夫妻都工作,这种联系已经被削弱,取而代之的是更加强调自我。

1996 年的一项美国民意测验中,道德沦丧名列美国所面临的最大问题榜首。艾尔斯顿说,公众认识到这点是正确的:资料表明美国人正在与 50 年代从未听到过的问题作斗争,如:教室暴力、未婚母亲生育率。

艾尔斯顿说,提高道德水准的愿望不是对某个并不存在的"黄金时代"的挽歌,也不是对一个曾拒绝给妇女和少数民族以机会的时代一厢情愿的愿望。实际上,大多数人赞成减少歧视。

她说,直到人们克服社会上功利主义现象时,道德沦丧才能扭转。"慢慢地你会认识到:要紧的东西是那些买不到的"。

【难词释义】

ethics 伦理学	**obstacle** 障碍(物),妨碍
disintegration 解体	**bond** 联结,联系
lament 挽歌	**wishful** 一厢情愿的
lessen 减少	**prejudice** 偏见
reverse 颠倒,翻过来	**counter** 对抗,反驳

【写译语块】

1. the decline in moral standard 道德标准的下降
2. capture the attention of 引起……的关注
3. moral climate 道德风气,道德环境
4. become deeply rooted in 深深植根于……
5. be attributed to the disintegration of traditional communities 归于传统社区的解体
6. the desire for a higher moral standard 提高道德水准的愿望

【难句分析】

1. (第六段第一句)在 The desire for a higher moral standard is not a lament for some nonexistent "golden age" Elshtain says, nor is it a wishful longing for a time that denied opportunities to women and minorities 中,nor 引出倒装结构,由于前后两个分句没有重复部分,nor 分句没有使用省略结构。再如:All the children were apparently miserable, nor were the nurses satisfied with the conditions in the kindergarten. (显而易见孩子们非常不幸,阿姨们对幼儿园的状况也不满意)。

2. (第七段第一句)Moral decline will not be reversed until people find ways to

counter the materialism in society, she says, "Slowly, you recognize that the things that matter are those that can't be bought."该句中，recognize 后面的宾语从句里包含两个定语从句，that matter 是一级定语从句，that can't be bought 是定语从句中的定语从句，属于二级定语从句。

【原题再现】

531. Professor Elshtain is pleased to see that Americans _____.

    A) have adapted to a new set of moral standards

    B) are longing for the return of the good old days

    C) have realized the importance of material things

    D) are awaking to the lowering of their moral standards

532. The moral decline of American society is caused mainly by _____.

    A) its growing wealth

    B) the self-centeredness of individuals

    C) underestimating the impact of social changes

    D) the prejudice against women and minorities

533. Which of the following characterizes the traditional communities?

    A) Concern for one's neighbors.   B) Great mobility.

    C) Emphasis on individual effort.   D) Ever-weakening social bonds

534. In the 1950s, classroom violence _____.

    A) was something unheard of

    B) was by no means a rare occurrence

    C) attracted a lot of public attention

    D) began to appear in analysis's data

535. According to Elshtain, the current moral decline may be reversed _____.

    A) if people can return to the "golden age"

    B) when women and men enjoy equal rights

    C) when people rid themselves of prejudice

    D) if less emphasis is laid on material things

【单词详解】

【重点单词】**attribute** / əˈtribjuːt / v. / æˈtribjuːt / n.

［基本词义］v. (to)把……归因于，把（过错、责任等）归于 n. 属性，特性

［用法导航］He attributes his success to hard work and a bit of luck. 他认为他的

成功是由于勤奋加上一点运气而得来的。// David attributed his company's success to the unity of all the staff and their persevering hard work. 大卫说他们公司之所以获得成功是由于全体员工的团结和坚持不懈努力工作的结果。

[词性转换] **attribution** / ˌætriˈbjuːʃən / *n.* 归因，属性

[对比记忆] (1) **contribute** / kənˈtribjuːt / *v.* 捐款，做出贡献；(to)有助于，促成；投稿

(2) **distribute** / disˈtribjuːt，ˈdisˈtribjt / *vt.* 分发，分送，分配；使分布，散发

(3) **ascribe** / əsˈkraib / *vt.* (to)把……归因于；把……归属于

(4) **owe** / əu / *vt.* 欠；(to)应该把……归功于；感激，感恩

[真题衔接] The car accident was _____ to the driver's violation of the traffic regulations. (CET6-9301)

A) assigned   B) contributed   C) attributed   D) transferred

【重点单词】**emphasis** / ˈemfəsis / *n.*

[基本词义] 强调，重点

[用法导航] I think we should put as much emphasis on preventing disease as we do on curing it. 我认为我们应该像重视疾病治疗一样重视疾病的预防。

[词性转换] (1)**emphasize** / ˈemfəsaiz / *vt.* 强调，着重，加强……的语气

(2)**emphatic** / imˈfætik / *adj.* 强调的，着重的；无可置疑的，明显的

[对比记忆] (1) **highlight** / ˈhailait / *vt.* 强调，突出，使显著

(2) **stress** / stres / *n.* 压力，紧张；强调，重要性 *vt.* 强调，着重，重读

(3) **underline** / ˌʌndəˈlain / *vt.* 在……下面画线；强调，使突出

[真题衔接] In recent years much more emphasis has been put _____ developing the students productive skills. (CET4-0106)

A) onto   B) in   C) over   D) on

【句子翻译】

536. After several months' study, the doctors _____ (把这种病的起因归结为一种未知的病毒).

537. Any parents should _____ (非常重视)their children to keep the balance between play and study.

538. The actual record _____ (显示了物种的递减过程)that occurs over several thousand years.

539. She emphasized in her speech that for all women work _____ (与获得独立

的愿望联系起来).

540. You need never worry about calling a business office for information, _____（不必担心各行各业在午餐时休息）.

Passage Fifty-five

In 1993, New York State ordered stores to charge a **deposit** on **beverage** containers. Within a year, consumers had returned millions of **aluminum cans** and glass and plastic bottles. Plenty of companies were eager to *accept the aluminum and glass as raw materials for new products*, but because few could *figure out what to do with the plastic*, much of it wound up buried in **landfills**. The problem was not limited to New York. Unfortunately, there were too few uses for second-hand plastic.

Today, *one out of five* plastic soda bottles is **recycled** in the United States. The reason for the change is that now there are dozens of companies across the country buying **discarded** plastic soda bottles and turning them into fence posts, paint brushes, etc.

As the New York experience shows, *recycling involves more than simply separating valuable materials from the rest of the rubbish*. A discard remains a discard until somebody figures out how to give it a second life—and until economic arrangements exist to give that second life value. Without adequate markets to absorb materials collected for recycling, **throwaways** actually depress prices for used materials.

Shrinking landfill space and rising costs for burying and burning rubbish are forcing local governments to look more closely at recycling. In many areas, the East Coast especially, recycling is already the least expensive waste-management **option**. For every ton of waste recycled, a city avoids paying for its **disposal**, which, in parts of New York, *amounts to savings of more than $100 per ton*. Recycling also stimulates the local economy by creating jobs and **trims** the pollution control and energy costs of industries that make recycled products by giving them a more **refined** raw material. (302 words) (2001 年 1 月第 1 篇)

【段落译文】

1933 年,纽约州规定各商店就所销售的饮料瓶收取押金。一年内,消费者退回了上百万只铝制易拉罐、玻璃瓶、塑料瓶。很多公司都抢着回收这些可以当作原材料生产新产品的铝和玻璃,可怎么处理塑料却无人知晓,所以塑料只是被一股脑地埋在垃圾填埋场里。该问题不仅出现在纽约。遗憾的是,二手塑料的用途实在太少了。

今天,在美国,已有五分之一的塑料汽水瓶得以回收利用。这一改变的原因是什么呢?原来有不少跨国公司在收购废弃的塑料汽水瓶,从而把它们加工成栅栏、画笔之类的东西。

纽约的经验说明,回收利用不仅仅是把垃圾和有用的材料分开来这样一件简单的事。某种废品只有人们想出怎样赋予它第二次生命,即用经济的手段使之具有重新利用的价值,才不能算作废品。倘若为了回收利用而收集的材料找不到相应的市场,废弃物就只是用过的东西,分文不值。

垃圾填埋场的空间正在减少,而填埋和焚烧垃圾的成本却不断增加,这些都迫使地方政府更密切地关注"回收利用"问题。在很多地方,特别是东海岸,回收利用是实惠的废物处理方案。每回收一吨垃圾,一个城市可以不用支付处理垃圾所需的某些费用。在纽约的某些地方,每处理一吨垃圾就可以节约 100 美元处理费。回收利用同时也刺激地方经济的发展,创造就业机会,减少某些企业的污染问题和能源成本问题,因为这些企业可以利用回收品提炼生产所需的原材料。

【难词释义】

deposit 押金

aluminum cans 铝罐

recycle 回收利用

throwaways 废弃物

disposal（垃圾）处理

refined 精制的

beverage 饮料

landfills 垃圾填埋场

discarded 废弃的

option 选择

trim 削减,控制

【写译语块】

1. charge a deposit on beverage containers 向饮料罐（瓶）征收押金

2. accept the aluminum and glass as raw materials for new products 把这些铝和玻璃当成新产品的原材料

3. figure out what to do with the plastic 想出处理塑料的办法

4. one out of five 五分之一

5. recycling involves more than simply separating valuable materials from the rest of the rubbish 回收利用不仅仅是把有用的材料和垃圾分开

6. amount to savings of more than ＄100 per ton 每吨可节约 100 多美元

【难句分析】

1. （第一段第二句）在 Plenty of companies were eager to accept the aluminum and glass as raw materials for new products, but because few could figure out what to do with the plastic, much of it wound up buried in landfills 中，词组 accept sth as... 的意思是"把……当作……接受下来"，词组 figure out 的意思是"想出，算出"，do with 与 what 连用时，一般出现在否定句中，表示"不知道怎么办，不知道如何处理"；much of it wound up buried in landfills 中，it 代表前面的 plastic，wind up 表示"结束"，而 buried in landfills 与 wound up 构成双谓语动词结构，说明 much of it"结束"时的状态：被埋进垃圾填埋场。

2. （第三段第一句）在 As the New York experience shows, recycling involves more than simply separating valuable materials from the rest of the rubbish 中，"as ＋名词词组＋动词"结构表示"正如……"；involve 在这里的意思是"包含，意味着"，用作此义时，它后面一般接用动名词；more than 在此句中的意思是"不仅仅是，不只是"。

3. （第四段第三句）在 For every ton of waste recycled, a city avoids paying for its disposal, which, in parts of New York, amounts to savings of more than $100 per ton 中，recycled 用作后位修饰语，修饰名词 waste；in parts of New York 将非限制性定语从句的引导词 which（在从句中作主语）与从句的谓语动词 amounts to 分开了。

4. （第四段第四句）在 Recycling also stimulates the local economy by creating jobs and trims the pollution control and energy costs of industries that make recycled products by giving them a more refined raw material 中，stimulates 和 trims 是并列谓语动词，其中，动词 trim 后面又有两个名词词组（the pollution control 和 energy costs of industries）并列作它的宾语。

【原题再现】

541. What regulation was issued by New York State concerning beverage containers?

    A) Beverage companies should be responsible for collecting and reusing discarded plastic soda bottles.

    B) Throwaways should be collected by the state for recycling.

    C) A fee should be charged on used containers for recycling.

    D) Consumers had to pay for beverage containers and could get their money back on returning them.

542. The returned plastic bottles in New York used to _____.

A) end up somewhere underground   B) be turned into raw materials

C) have a second-life value   D) be separated from other rubbish

543. The key problem in dealing with returned plastic beverage containers is _____.

A) to sell them at a profitable price

B) how to turn them into useful things

C) how to reduce their recycling costs

D) to lower the prices for used materials

544. Recycling has become the first choice for the disposal of rubbish because _____.

A) local governments find it easy to manage

B) recycling has great appeal for the jobless

C) recycling causes little pollution

D) other methods are more expensive

545. It can be concluded from the passage that _____.

A) rubbish is a potential remedy for the shortage of raw materials

B) local governments in the U. S. can expect big profits from recycling

C) recycling is to be recommended both economically and environmentally

D) landfills will still be widely used for waste disposal

【单词详解】

【重点单词】**involve**/ in'vɔlv / *vt.*

[基本词义] 包含,含有;使卷入,使参与;牵连

[用法导航] the job which involves travel 一份需要出差的工作 // involve the by-standers in his dispute with the police 把旁观者牵扯进他与警察的争执中 // involve sb. in expense, a lot of trouble 使某人破费、招惹许多麻烦 // That's no concern of mine. I'm not involved. 那与我无关,我未卷入。

[词性转换] **involvement** / in'vɔlvmənt / *n.* 卷入,缠绕;复杂的情况;困难;财政困难

[对比记忆] (1) **resolve** / ri'zɔlv / *vt.* 解决;决定;(into)分解 *vi.* 决定

(2) **dissolve** / di'zɔlv / *vi.* 溶解;减弱 *vt.* 使溶解,使融化;解散,结束

(3) **evolve** / i'vɔlv / *v.* (使)演变,(使)进化,(使)发展

(4) **revolve** / ri'vɔlv / *vi.* 旋转

[真题衔接] Building that railway was very difficult and involved _____ ten tunnels. (CET6-9206)

A) dig   B) having dug   C) to have dug   D) digging

【重点单词】**stimulate** / 'stimjuleit / *vt.*

[基本词义] 刺激,激励

[用法导航] stimulate sb. to further efforts 激励某人作更大的努力 // Light stimulates the optic nerve. 光刺激视神经。// She was stimulated into new efforts. 她受到鼓励做出新努力。// The exhibition stimulated interest in the artist's work. 这次展览引起人们对这位艺术家作品的兴趣。// The government will do everything in its power to stimulate economic growth. 政府将竭尽全力去刺激经济发展。

[词性转换] **stimulation** / ˌstimju'leiʃən / *n.* 激励,鼓舞,刺激

[对比记忆] (1) **excite** / ik'sait / *vt.* 使激动,使兴奋;引起,激起

(2) **spur** / spə: / *vt.* 激动,鞭策,促进

(3) **boost** / bu:st / *vt.* 提高,使增涨;推动,激励;替……作广告,宣扬

(4) **encourage** / in'kʌridʒ / *vt.* 鼓励,激励,怂恿;促进,助长,激发

(5) **motivate** / 'məutiveit / *vt.* 作为……的动机,激励,激发

[真题衔接] John Dewey believed that education should be a preparation for life, that a person learns by doing, and that teaching must _____ the curiosity and creativity of children. (CET4-9806)

A) seek   B) stimulate   C) shape   D) secure

【句子翻译】

546. They _____(收你 20 美元)just to get in the nightclub, then you have to pay for drinks.

547. She _____(如此投入于这部戏)that she cried in the final act.

548. _____(十分之一的人)said they preferred their old brand of margarine.

549. The book was an attempt to _____(激起对全球变暖问题的讨论).

550. Keeping silent in this case _____(等于支持发言者).

参考答案

Passage One

【原题再现】1～5　DACCA

【句子翻译】

6. When asked about her career

7. Every time you press a key

8. withstand the ups and downs of the economic cycle

9. be equal to at least 10% of the floor area of each room

10. subject to any damages which may be due

Passage Two

【原题再现】11～15　BACCB

【句子翻译】

16. This coat was supposed to keep rain out

17. Although many opposed his plan

18. High interest rates and protectionism in potential export markets

19. ours, in contrast, has declined

20. turn you into your heart's desire

Passage Three

【原题再现】21～25　CBDCA

【句子翻译】

26. giving him personal attention on a regular basis

27. all my letters went unanswered

28. kept me fascinated for twenty-four hours

29. For better or worse

30. focus on the good qualities of your spouse

Passage Four

【原题再现】31～35　ABDAC

【句子翻译】

36. shouldn't rely on sheer enthusiasm

37. keep pace with the rising level of economic activity

38. a foreign country which I am familiar with

39. a steady decline in numbers

40. to promote wider use of private medical care

Passage Five

【原题再现】41~45   ADDAB

【句子翻译】

46. Thanks to (或 Owing to) a series of new inventions

47. stopped to rest on a big rock

48. be aware of

49. aiming at helping the poor children to be educated

50. used to students' being late for

Passage Six

【原题再现】51~55   BCBAC

【句子翻译】

56. rely on herself at an early age

57. the increase in demand resulted in the rise in prices

58. has aroused a heated discussion all over the country

59. nothing is more attractive to me than reading

60. As she grows older

Passage Seven

【原题再现】61~65   CBADB

【句子翻译】

66. According to the scientific research

67. reacts three times as fast as that substance

68. Compared to western countries

69. might have survived

70. rather than spend a lot of time on the way every day

Passage Eight

【原题再现】71~75   BDBAC

【句子翻译】

76. Instead of going swimming

77. do more harm than good to one's health

78. solely responsible for the traffic accident

79. complained of the poor service to the man who is in charge of the hospital

80. mainly due to stress and tension in their work

Passage Nine

【原题再现】81～85　DCABB

【句子翻译】

86. regardless of other people's feelings.

87. was condemned to a wheelchair

88. you may never hit the target

89. the less likely it is that any one of them will offer to help

90. is projected to reach a 25-year high in the next half year

Passage Ten

【原题再现】91～95　ACBDD

【句子翻译】

96. make it easy for them to pick up a foreign language

97. (Whether you) Like it or not

98. Only when we start our study in college

99. having left her post without permission

100. where your son can't get his hands on it

Passage Eleven

【原题再现】101～105　ACDCB

【句子翻译】

106. by any measure

107. There has been a boom

108. on the basis of his performance

109. there is evidence

110. from the unique female perspective

Passage Twelve

【原题再现】111～115　DBCAB

【句子翻译】

116. failed to live up to their coach's expectations of them
117. it's just not as easy as it looks
118. There is no shortage of
119. without even realizing it
120. occupies herself in

Passage Thirteen

【原题再现】121～125　DBCBA

【句子翻译】

126. than the ability to transform adversity into an enjoyable challenge
127. in raw form
128. kept mother on the fly all day
129. end up ruining oneself
130. make Britain the country with the worst record on pollution

Passage Fourteen

【原题再现】131～135　BACDC

【句子翻译】

136. Shocked at what he had heard
137. While your opinions are worth considering
138. in the least
139. speak in his behalf
140. what some politicians and scholars see

Passage Fifteen

【原题再现】141～145　CBDAB

【句子翻译】

146. in terms of changing our many unhealthy behaviors
147. rather than "opponent"
148. Regardless of your age
149. As a result
150. whereas refined sugar is not

Passage Sixteen

【原题再现】151～155　CADBC

【句子翻译】

156. focus on immediate interests only
157. In a purely biological sense
158. are concerning themselves with environmental problems
159. distinguish between tax avoidance and tax evasion
160. make a point of introducing new members to the chairman

Passage Seventeen
【原题再现】161～165 DCABC
【句子翻译】

166. Not given careful and thorough consideration
167. a range of stimulating entertainment available to them
168. we should work out a practical plan.
169. is far from satisfactory
170. to hold North Korea to account

Passage Eighteen
【原题再现】171～175 DBCCD
【句子翻译】

176. in terms of how long it took to complete
177. under the attacks of a predator
178. To a certain extent/degree
179. justify the title of one of the era's most influential books
180. is awaiting a decision

Passage Nineteen
【原题再现】181～185 DDABC
【句子翻译】

186. adapt to change
187. identified as
188. It can't be denied that
189. compete with each other
190. accounts for 35% of the company's revenue

Passage Twenty
【原题再现】191～195 ACBAD

【句子翻译】

196. ease the tensions

197. thoroughly approved of it

198. school sports fund

199. offered to drive me to the station

200. forgive you the $3

Passage Twenty-one

【原题再现】201～205　ABCBC

【句子翻译】

206. boost brain power through exercise

207. cope with her toothache

208. It pays in the long run

209. sustain relationships with women

210. sit through nearly two hours of speeches

Passage Twenty-Two

【原题再现】211～215　DBCBD

【句子翻译】

216. see the gift as a sort of bribe

217. resorted to standing outside her window

218. commit more money to protect the environment

219. aware of Smith's ability

220. rendered her completely unable to go on working

Passage Twenty-three

【原题再现】221～225　DABCA

【句子翻译】

226. doesn't smell fresh

227. think independently

228. had to cut back on entertainment expenses

229. has benefited me a lot

230. bargain with the boss

Passage Twenty-four

【原题再现】231～235　BBACB

【句子翻译】

236. sets a good example

237. what you said make sense

238. lead to a large increase in the number of students

239. rather than how much he owns

240. a chemical reaction is occurring

Passage Twenty-five

【原题再现】 241～245　CABCA

【句子翻译】

246. have a long way to go

247. on average

248. how we focus on a task

249. In order to meet the needs of agriculture

250. Though the details of seamanship might confuse the reader

Passage Twenty-six

【原题再现】 251～255　BDDAC

【句子翻译】

256. attracted many people's attention

257. The key to the solution to the problem

258. have attributed the cause of the illness to an unknown virus

259. balance the moisture of the skin

260. to cut off the flow of oil to the country

Passage Twenty-seven

【原题再现】 261～265　ADCBA

【句子翻译】

266. It's difficult to tell the two brothers apart

267. The similarity between the two reports

268. keep in contact

269. similar to that of the mass on a spring

270. prevent them from benefiting from modern medicine

Passage Twenty-eight

【原题再现】271～275　CBDCD

【句子翻译】

276. In contrast to his brother

277. turns to her family for comfort

278. is admitted to

279. Emphasis should be put on

280. is introduced

Passage Twenty-nine

【原题再现】281～285　DBDAC

【句子翻译】

286. needed total concentration

287. impact of the President's speech

288. the result of years of bad management

289. enable him to find the house

290. but he's met his match in her

Passage Thirty

【原题再现】291～295　BBBCD

【句子翻译】

296. He is easily discouraged

297. they would rather live in a house

298. vital to my argument

299. to confirm that he was alone

300. have made a few minor adjustments

Passage Thirty-one

【原题再现】301～305　CABDB

【句子翻译】

306. Despite all our efforts

307. Politicians should not engage in business affairs

308. are associated with picnics

309. derives from man's perceptions of the world about him

310. was promoted to be a manager

Passage Thirty-two

【原题再现】311~315　ACADD

【句子翻译】

316. to instruct their elders

317. his claim for money

318. You should think twice about

319. reveal his secret

320. a fatal flaw

Passage Thirty-three

【原题再现】321~325　BCBDD

【句子翻译】

326. was probing into several financial scandals

327. assume responsibility for it

328. added up to no more than one year

329. devoted himself entirely to

330. be based on trust

Passage Thirty-four

【原题再现】331~335　ADBAB

【句子翻译】

336. is filled with the odor of roses

337. brushed aside

338. has approved the building plan

339. emerged from behind the clouds

340. his claim for money

Passage Thirty-five

【原题再现】341~345　DBCCA

【句子翻译】

346. were more or less wounded

347. was struck by his kindness

348. are being exposed to radiation

349. brought on his fever

350. was able to cope

Passage Thirty-six

【原题再现】351～355　DBADC

【句子翻译】

356. chance of winning the game

357. hold true for everyone, everywhere

358. is in line for the scholarship

359. were equal to one pound

360. The lawyer demonstrated

Passage Thirty-seven

【原题再现】361～365　DACAD

【句子翻译】

366. Stick to your post

367. give way to their demands

368. assumed a new form

369. eliminate poverty

370. are catching up with us

Passage Thirty-eight

【原题再现】371～375　CADBC

【句子翻译】

376. located his new store

377. anything but a success

378. reinforce his argument with facts

379. protect the fruit from frost

380. In the event of his death

Passage Thirty-nine

【原题再现】381～385　CBBAA

【句子翻译】

386. will always spend Christmas with my family

387. doesn't make a good doctor

388. to affect the growth of flowering plants

389. comparable to that of his

390. Despite the bad weather

Passage Forty

【原题再现】391~395　BDDCA

【句子翻译】

396. be based on facts

397. refer to a conflict or disagreement

398. driven by electricity

399. in opposition to our friends

400. lay off workers

Passage Forty-one

【原题再现】401~405　DACAD

【句子翻译】

406. fall into the hands of the enemy

407. can be reversed

408. On seeing the plane coming towards me

409. an average of 6.9 years

410. That plane crash occurred

Passage Forty-two

【原题再现】411~415　BACAD

【句子翻译】

416. the same is true of the service

417. remained in her office

418. on my behalf

419. make clear the instructions

420. has maintained their friendship

Passage Forty-three

【原题再现】421~425　ACBBA

【句子翻译】

426. have a weakness for sports and movie stars

427. share a number of characteristics

428. does something worth talking about

429. goes beyond the borders of countries

430. At some point

Passage Forty-four

【原题再现】431～435　ABDBD

【句子翻译】

436. Theory is based on practice

437. is to work for education

438. Only to do that we can

439. in the long run you will succeed.

440. While I admit that the problems are difficult

Passage Forty-five

【原题再现】441～445　DCCBA

【句子翻译】

446. no longer have the option

447. you lose confidence in yourself

448. Thanks to this period

449. want to succeed in the world

450. the rare animals found only in China

Passage Forty-six

【原题再现】451～455　ACDDB

【句子翻译】

456. four in ten workers in this factory

457. Exposed to higher standards of service

458. began arriving in large numbers

459. I took it for granted

460. You are scheduled to meet Mr. Thompson

Passage Forty-seven

【原题再现】461～465　CAADC

【句子翻译】

466. watching how it is operated
467. With the help of the volunteers from abroad and at home
468. Gambling is forbidden
469. work in the same way
470. to uncover the secret of the many worlds

Passage Forty-eight

【原题再现】471~475　BDCBB

【句子翻译】

476. She was supposed to be
477. the names of those involved in the crime
478. which have a positive impact on society
479. to any other brand available on the market
480. If you fail to love and forgive

Passage Forty-nine

【原题再现】481~485　BACDA

【句子翻译】

486. By the end of this month
487. so had his brother
488. can boil down to three simple ingredients
489. he would have arrived by then
490. he is high on the list for the third time

Passage Fifty

【原题再现】491~495　CBCAD

【句子翻译】

496. life in the 1890s
497. has been being engaged in the writing of novels
498. the work not be started
499. begin to focus on your study
500. will be doubled in ten years

Passage Fifty-one

【原题再现】501~505　ACADC

【句子翻译】

506. regardless of his or her social class background

507. did attach importance to a name

508. The play is bound to fail

509. compare with living in the country in many respects

510. people with physical qualities similar to ours

Passage Fifty-two

【原题再现】511～515　ACBBD

【句子翻译】

516. as are its soils and the waters of its lakes, rivers and oceans

517. At first he opposed to the scheme

518. would not interfere with him on any account

519. can lead to the failure of the whole experiment

520. need to learn to get on well with people

Passage Fifty-three

【原题再现】521～525　ACDAC

【句子翻译】

526. decided to specialize in contract law

527. am bored with staying in the country

528. and the gas will tend to expand

529. has had a profound influence on

530. An optimist sees an opportunity in every calamity

Passage Fifty-four

【原题再现】531～535　DBAAD

【句子翻译】

536. have attributed the cause of the illness to an unknown virus

537. place considerable emphasis on

538. shows a gradual decline in species

539. is connected with the desire for independence

540. nor will you find businesses closed at lunch time

Passage Fifty-five

【原题再现】541～545　DABDC

【句子翻译】

546. charged you 20 dollars
547. was so involved in the play
548. One in ten
549. stimulate discussion of the problem of global warming
550. amounts to supporting the speaker